South Wind Home

Gerald Lewellen

PublishAmerica
Baltimore

© 2006 by Gerald Lewellen.
All rights reserved. No part of this book may be reproduced, stored in a retrieval system or transmitted in any form or by any means without the prior written permission of the publishers, except by a reviewer who may quote brief passages in a review to be printed in a newspaper, magazine or journal.

First printing

All characters appearing in this work are fictitious. Any resemblance to real persons, living or dead, is purely coincidental.

ISBN: 1-4241-1202-8
PUBLISHED BY PUBLISHAMERICA, LLLP
www.publishamerica.com
Baltimore

Printed in the United States of America

Dedicated to my parents:

Lloyd W. Lewellen
(1917-1995)
Dorothy P. Lewellen

What gift shall I bring?
On wing of snow white dove.
It's the greatest gift of all,
'tis my undying love.

Acknowledgments

A phone conversation many years ago from a dear friend and fellow sailor prompted me to take pen in hand and embark upon a journey that would encompass the better part of ten years. Your gentle words of wisdom have guided me through both good times—and bad. Mike Yurkovich Jr., this one's for you buddy!

I would be remiss if I did not publicly thank Brad Gamble for freely offering his time when he had other things to do. You are indeed a fountain of new ideas that I constantly drink from.

To Kenneth Cansler, my high school English teacher, I owe you a debt of gratitude I can never repay. You have made a lasting impression upon my life—thank you!

To each of you, and many others whom I have failed to mention, thank you one and all; any success this work enjoys is partly yours. I would be lost without your kind words of encouragement and criticism.

A special thank you to my wife and life partner, Linda, for enduring the long hours as an "Author's Widow." I love you more than you'll ever know.

Last, but certainly not least, the editors and staff of PublishAmerica for having faith in me. It has been a distinct pleasure. Your skills have turned a rough manuscript into a tale that flows like an ebb tide.

Gerald Lewellen
Bolivar, Missouri

Foreword

    The H.M.S. *Rose*, a fourth rate of fifty guns, sailed before a steady south wind. Well-built and ballasted with thirty feet below the water line, nicely making foam, under all plain sail, the ship met each wave with a hunger for more speed. Two-and-one-half-months out of port and drifting toward the equator at eight knots, she rode a thundering sea fed by the energy of the southwest trades. Below decks in his cabin above the wardroom, Captain James Howlette was attempting to make the best of a somewhat-less-than-desirable situation. The voyage was beginning to take a toll. Hours spent in tedious boredom scanning the horizon from first light until last for French shipping seemed endless; orders for daily drills in ordnance and seamanship accomplished nothing more than draining the energy of the crew. They were alone in a vast world of blue; blue ocean…blue sky. Nothing had been sighted.
    Captain Howlette had not been especially overjoyed from the outset of the mission. Gathering intelligence on French activities in the south latitudes was not something he was very fond of. The heavy, oppressive heat that permeated the entire ship made matters worse. Most of the idle crew was now sleeping on deck in an attempt to escape the sweltering heat below. James sat quietly at the small desk in his stuffy cabin. Beads of sweat slowly formed tiny rivers that began to trickle down the side of his face. Taking a deep breath, he exhaled in a vain attempt to calm himself, and reflected back to the day he had received his orders and letter of command to the *Rose* from the Admiralty. Watching the small ship's lantern hanging from the bulkhead sway to and fro, casting shadows that kept time with the roll of the deck below his feet, he dragged a soggy handkerchief from a vest pocket and mopped the sweat from his face as he recalled the letter to mind.

To his Majesty's Captain James Howlette.

*You are hereby ordered and directed to proceed on a southerly course for the south tropic latitudes, thereby to observe any and all French shipping and the activities thereof. At **NO** time are you to use force of arms unless necessary in the defense of the ship against hostile boarding parties. You are to remain out of sight as much as you deem prudent to the mission. All information will be subsequently relayed to me at the earliest possible date upon completion of these orders six months hence. The H.M.S. Rose is at your disposal, and you are hereby ordered to take command on the morrow, making all due haste to said southern destination. I shall expect a complete, detailed, written report on my desk upon your return post haste. My sincere wishes are extended to you for the best of luck, a fair wind, and God speed...*

Admiral Sir J.C.L. Morris, KB.

He had reluctantly accepted the command. Any fleeting thoughts of refusing an order from the Admiralty were quickly dismissed when faced with a bleak existence on half pay and no hope of ever achieving the rank of post captain; a goal he would gladly sacrifice body and soul for. With orders that plainly stated "No force of arms," any hope of prize money and the fame it would bring were clearly tossed out the window. For some unknown reason the French had plagued British shipping for the past year. Admiral Morris was quite outraged over the matter. Rumor had it that the good king himself was watching the affair closely and had taken Morris to task over the latest capture of the *Sexton* and one hundred eighty good British sailors pressed into service for the French. Yes…the atmosphere around admiralty headquarters was tense. A solution to what appeared to be an unfortunate run of good luck for the French had to be found. Changes in departure schedules and strategy proved unsuccessful. The tragic loss of life and ships continued. England could not let the mystery remain unsolved. He sat at the desk in his cabin, sweat pouring down his face, realizing that the mission, in some respects, might prove to be one of great importance. He just might discover a clue as to why the French were always on station when a British war ship departed, although, on this particular day, he had his doubts. The winds were becoming fitful, unable to decide from which direction they wanted to blow; a sure sign that a gale was in store.

Captain James Howlette's life was about to take a dramatic turn. A series of events would unfold, forcing him to make one of the most difficult decisions of his professional career.

CHAPTER ONE

James sat at a small desk in his cramped quarters leafing through a stack of scribbled notes made during the past twenty-four hours, attempting to piece together a report to the Admiralty. The main top watch had spotted a French man-of-war escorted by two frigates, hull down. He was following them, making every effort to match their speed, always keeping his prey off the port bow, just over the horizon. The weather was turning fowl. A howling southeast wind continued to gain strength as night approached. He squinted at a chart across the cabin barely illuminated by the feeble glow of the cabin lantern; trying to dead reckon an approximate course. The wind roared like a thousand demons unleashed from the gates of hell.

"This will never do…she'll have to come about," he mumbled under his breath.

Picking up the notes and placing them back on the shelf above his bed he carefully made his way to the door and down the passageway, bracing against the bulkheads for support as the deck lurched under him. A blast of wind and salt spray fairly took him off his feet as he threw open the door leading to the quarterdeck. Hanging on to the railings he gained the deck, and with difficulty, stumbled to the wheel watch. The man had tied himself down to keep from being washed overboard.

"How goes it?" he shouted in the ear of the man standing next to him.

The expression on the face of the sodden figure never changed but continued to stare intently at the top royals that threatened to be blown to rags at any minute.

"I say…how goes it?" Howlette screamed in his ear.

"She'll not take ta strain much longer, Cap'n; the royals'll have to come in, 'n ta sooner ta better."

"Quite right…I shall see if I can find the bosun and pass the order," he shouted.

Making his way down the quarterdeck ladder to the waist of the ship he saw a figure looming ahead, staggering about as though he were drunk and fighting his way forward to the main mast. Howlette struggled toward the outline of the man as salt spume and rain pelted his face like burning embers. Eventually they came together just aft of the main mast and James grabbed him by the sleeve with both hands and shouted above the screeching wind.

"Clue up those top royals…have your best men at it at once, if you please."

"Aye, sir…I was just making my way to ta forward hatch to call up ta watch now, Cap'n. It'll take some fancy footwork, but clued up they'll be," he bellowed above the howl of wind and thunder.

"Clue up fore and aft as lively as you can and bring her about. We'll run before the wind until the gale blows out. Drag in every rag of canvas and furl 'em up as tight as you can or she'll dismast herself before the light of day."

A huge wave struck the bowhead threatening to broach the ship as both men desperately clung to each other. "I'll be in my cabin…carry on," he shouted as he fixed a coil of rope around his waist and made the other end fast to a deck ringbolt as a precaution to being washed over board.

Pulling himself hand over hand along the tariff rail he slowly stumbled and slid toward the door that led to the passageway and his quarters below. It took him all of fifteen minutes to gain the door that had been only sixty feet away. With trembling hands he held onto the latch as he gasped for air to fill aching lungs. Blowing salt spray and rainwater came in such torrents that breathing was all but impossible.

Minutes dragged by until he regained a measure of strength and freed himself of the rope around his waist. Taking a deep breath he threw open the door and flung himself through in one swift move, slamming it closed behind him along with fifty gallons of sea water. Returning to the cabin he quickly changed to dry clothing and collapsed behind his desk.

"We're in for it now," he thought. "With any luck the gale will blow the Frenchie along with us…where ever that might be." He reached above the desk, retrieved several maps, unrolled them and placed a paperweight at the corners leafing through each until he found the one he was looking for. A few quick calculations gave him a rough idea of where the ship would be in three or four days if the storm didn't tear her apart before then. "There's plenty of sea room to the northwest—a relief," he thought. All the men were up working watch and watch. It would remain that way until the danger had passed.

The storm continued to rage through the night, howling and screeching in rigging and sheets like a tortured soul. Waves battered the hull with such force that it sounded like cannon fire. Timbers groaned and creaked, protesting the punishment they were receiving as several feet of foaming sea water cascaded over the ship to rush through the scuppers, only to be replaced by another wave. After an eternity of darkness, a weak dawn broke through black swirling clouds as the sun fought its way over the horizon. The storm was at its crest. The sea had turned an angry gray color with streaks of green laced through each towering wave. Gale winds blew long wisps of curling, twisting mist from the tops of each wave that crashed over the bulwark of the ship as she plunged ahead in a race for survival.

One day dragged into another as the storm made every attempt to destroy the *Rose*. The ship was holding her own and with crews manning the pumps every four hours, she was staying ahead of the rising water in the bilge. Patches of clear sky were beginning to appear at three bells on the first watch, when suddenly the howling wind abruptly stopped. Howlette sat bolt upright in his bunk at the eerie quiet. The only sound that could be heard was the crash of wave after wave across the decks. Jumping out of bed he raced down the passageway, through the door, and up the quarterdeck ladder as fast as he could.

"Down with the helm, I say...put the helm over at once! We're in the eye of a typhoon. She'll come aback within the hour. Clap on the main sails...look lively, my lads! Give her some steerage way to bring her about as quickly as she'll come."

The wind had died to a gentle breeze and despite the spread of white canvas over the yards the ship struggled in her stays making the turn. The sky directly above was completely cloudless. They sat motionless in the center of a gigantic whirlpool of swirling, angry black clouds. The ocean had calmed, salt spray no longer flew over the ship, and the rain stopped as if a faucet had been turned off. A gentle breeze was beginning to veer to the opposite direction as the ship slowly came around. Canvas popped like rifle shots as they filled with wind from first one direction, then another. Howlette paced the quarterdeck from one side to the other, watching the approaching cloudbank, the list of the ship, and the set of the sail. With the wind picking up again from the opposite direction he ordered all sail furled. She was just coming about when he heard the distant roar.

Within minutes a white wall of water descended upon the laboring vessel with such force that the starboard rails went five feet under water. An unrelenting wind assailed the ship and literally blew her through the rest of the turn. With a groan she slowly righted herself and plunged headlong into a trough of water that towered above the main mast. Somehow she rode it out and emerged on top of a following forty-foot wave as if she belonged there. Howlette was astounded.

"Damned fine little filly, this one, he thought as he pulled himself up, clinging to a railing. Despite the danger they were in, he couldn't help the slow smile that creased his lips. Blood pounded at his temples. Some of the crew members were cheering high above on the yards and waving hats with wild abandon, despite aching fatigue and raw bloody hands. As he rose a hand in salute the royal yard arm suddenly snapped. Spinning wildly and following the motion of the ship, it came full around and hit one of the men stationed on the lower topgallant yard in the head. Disappearing in a cloud of pink mist he was torn from the yardarm and tossed overboard like a rag doll. It happened so suddenly that Howlette wasn't sure he'd seen it. Men scrambled up the ropes to cut away the broken spar before it could do further damage and minutes later it fell harmlessly to the sea. The surprise was so sudden and complete that he stood, transfixed, staring at the empty space where the man had been.

"Dear God!" he exclaimed.

Life at sea was indeed cruel and short lived at times. He had been through many bloody battles and witnessed the gore of men torn apart by grape shot and flying splinters. It was bad enough when one was prepared for it, but quite another when taken by surprise.

"Take the man's name and pass it on to me as soon as you find out...I'll enter him dead in the ships log," he shouted in the ear of the officer standing next to him on the quarterdeck.

The following day the gale began to subside and forty-eight hours later the watch was relieved and allowed to go below. The galley fires were lit and for the first time in a week the aroma of hot food filled the air. They had survived the storm without much damage and spirits were high despite the loss of young Talmidge. His sea bag and belongings would be sold off to the crew later in the week. Daybreak found him intently studying maps and making notes; calculating the drift caused by the storm and comparing the noon sightings, trying to get some idea of where they were. Hopes of sighting the French ships were the furthest thing from his mind at the moment. With rule and dividers he finally came to the conclusion they were somewhere around 39 degrees of north latitude. Several more noon sightings would have to be taken before an accurate plotting could be made with confidence.

The hot, humid temperatures had returned and the ship fairly steamed as the tropical sun baked the moisture from the sodden deck and timbers. They resumed daily lookouts for the French ships with little hope of ever locating them again. Gradually making their heading south by south west they continued on, day after day. James thought the French ships might still be in the vicinity and he planned to stay west of his original course just in case he was right. They crept steadily along keeping the rising sun just off the port bow. He knew from years of experience in navigation that only a fool would look into the rising sun through a telescope. It was, in some cases, days before normal sight returned. Occasionally permanent damage resulted, leaving the crewmember blind in one eye. Using this tactic he knew that the ship would remain undetected if he kept the morning sun off the port side. It was a challenge to his nautical skills that he was determined to win. His goal was simply to out sail the French bastard and play this little game out to its end.

Re-rolling the maps and placing them back on the shelf, he retrieved the report he'd started several weeks ago and dipped a pen in the ink well, then closely examined the tip. Thoughts of a favorable review with the Admiralty and permanent commission to post captain quickly left him as a drop of sweat fell from his forehead to land on the foolscap report smearing the ink.

"Damn these tropics!" he bellowed, throwing the quill down on the ruined report splattering ink on the desk and him.

The thought of having to start over was more that he could cope with at the moment. Pushing away from the desk, he stood much too quickly, forgetting to stoop under the low overhead deck beam. His head connected with the rough-hewn timber and caromed off the starboard side of the beam leaving a tuft of hair and skin wafting in the stale air of the cabin. His hand instantly flew to the knot of throbbing, bruised flesh. Hissing through clenched teeth he lowered his hand to find fresh blood on two fingertips. The sound of shuffling feet on the wooden deck alerted him to the fact that his cabin boy was just outside the door.

"Is ta captain all right, sar?" he squeaked in a high-pitched voice filled with concern.

"Yes!" he shouted. "I'm fine...and I'll thank you not to watch over me like a mother hen!"

"Yes, sar!" the boy croaked.

"While you're here, boy, fetch me a dram of rum. My nerves are in a foul humor. Now off with you...and damned quick!"

"Aye, sar!" the boy echoed as he spun around and crashed forward in search of the ship's purser.

James groaned, shaking his head slowly to clear it, and stepped to the door. A breath of fresh air was in order and the sooner the better. The stifling heat below decks was so great he was panting as he made the short trip down the passageway to the quarterdeck ladder. Turning to the right he began the ascent. As his head cleared the deck he stopped momentarily on the ladder, his attention drawn to a lone slop bucket sitting behind the wheel watch. Regaining his composure in an instant he continued up the ladder and stood on the quarterdeck. Several moments of heavy silence passed before he addressed the man standing at the wheel.

"Mister Nelson, would you be so kind as to explain to me why yon slop bucket remains on the quarterdeck at this late hour?"

Nelson blanched at the critical look being given to him by the captain. Inhaling sharply, he came to attention and launched into an explanation.

"Of course, Cap'n, sar...wouldn't want the good Cap'n upset at what's got a reason for being here. You see, Cap'n, sar...'twas my rightful turn o' duty at the wheel, 'n me with a dose o' the flux it is. Well...I couldn't very well abandon my wheel to go or' the scuppers every little bit so's I got me that there slop bucket you be a lookin' at. Now I just has to heave when the urge strikes me. Don't have to leave me post, cause that's a floggin' offense, sar. We all know that, sar...we surely do indeed!"

"Aaaahummmm!" James cleared his throat, clasped his hands behind his back and silently paced the quarterdeck.

He stopped suddenly as his gaze fell upon the after cabin hatch cover standing open that provided fresh air to his quarters below. He spun on a heel, and putting a finger along side his nose said.

"Mister Nelson, if I were you...I'd pay special attention to my aim at yon bucket. I shall not mention what would happen if you were to over shoot the bloody thing and pour a broadside into my quarters below! I shudder to think of being the only officer in the British fleet to die from the foul and evil contents of the helmsman's stomach! I would entertain thoughts of watching you dance from the yardarm if such a misfortune should ever occur!"

"Aye, sar...aye, sar, Cap'n, sar. I get yer drift full and by, sar. I'll take extra care to aim just so before I touch the slow match to 'er, sar...there be no stray grape shot a'headin' down that hatchway, no, sar!" Nelson was terrified.

With the captain standing behind him, he felt his gut cramp with an urgency he was all too familiar with. He was visibly shaking as his condition worsened by the minute. James turned to face the port side of the ship. A look of intense concentration brought a frown to his face as he watched the western horizon. Looking to windward impatiently he took a few short steps forward to stand by the helmsman and said.

"Drop off a point to port if you please, Mr. Nelson. Hold her steady as she goes."

"Aye, aye, sar...steady as she goes."

The ship rolled to port as he looked up and shouted...

"Mast! Where away, if you please."

Time seemed to stand still as the ship continued to fall off as every eye strained to catch a glimpse of anything unusual on the horizon. James began to wonder if his calculations were incorrect and they had lost their prize for good and all. He paced the quarterdeck to relieve the unrelenting tension building in his chest like a keg of powder ready to explode. Eternity seemed to pass as silence overpowered the sound of the thundering sea. Then...suddenly, a thin voice drifted down from the crow's nest high above.

"Four points off ta starboard bow, hull down, all sail up 'n' running hard, Cap'n."

James stopped pacing and whirled about to face the western horizon. Although unable to see anything but distant whitecaps, he continued to stare at the point where sky and sea merged. It must be a mission of great importance to be running with top royals out, a dangerous business indeed in these heavy seas.

"Bosun!" he said curtly. "Hands to set sail. I shan't have the bloody devils outrunning us. A point closer to the wind, if you please, Mister Nelson. If I see one of those sheets flutter, it's bread and water for you. Is that quite clear?"

"Aye sar...quite clear," replied the sweating Nelson.

The ship came alive as crewmen swarmed the decks, running up ratlines and out onto the yardarms as the bosun bellowed orders in a voice that literally shook the deck. Satisfied that all was in good order, he said.

"Carry on...as you were!"

He immediately left the quarterdeck, descended the ladder, and returned to his cabin closing the door behind him. He hastily retrieved the roll of charts again from the small shelf above the desk unrolling them and placing paperweights at each corner while muttering to himself. "An absolute stroke of luck! I *must* be sure of our position if I'm to discover their little plan." Sweat began to bead on his forehead as he studied the charts intently.

"Master Charles!" He shouted suddenly, "Where's that dram of rum? God rot your flaming soul. Must I beg for strong drink or fetch it myself?"

A few moments later a quiet knock at the door announced the arrival of the cabin boy.

"Yes…yes…enter." The door opened to reveal Charles with cup in hand. "Pardon me sar, for ta slow wit that I am, but I couldn't locate ta purser right off," he barked.

"And where do you think the purser might have gone…pray tell, on shore leave when we've been eighty days out of port?" Howlette roared. His nerves now had the better of him.

"The rum, boy…the RUM…hand it over!"

Master Charles came to attention and shoved the cup forward so quickly that the amber liquid sloshed over the rim and onto the deck at his feet.

"Imbecile!" James bellowed as he snatched the cup from the trembling hand.

Sitting it down on the corner of the desk and taking a deep breath to calm himself, said in clipped tones.

"While you're here…I've another errand for you. If it pleases the ships surgeon, have him report to me at his earliest convenience. I've a matter to discuss with him. Now off with you at once before I lose myself and give you a sound thrashing!"

"Aye, aye, sar!" Charles yelped and raced down the short passageway leaving the door open in his haste to be gone from what he thought was the very devil himself.

James raised the cup to his lips and took a sip of the fiery liquid and returned it to its place. With elbows on the desk he leaned forward, sighing deeply and put his hands to his head as he relished the warm glow of the rum coursing through his veins.

"Damned fine bit of luck finding the French so soon after the storm. Fate must indeed be with us. It's a miracle we survived the typhoon." He thought as a headache began to throb in his temples.

Minutes later a knock at the door caused him to jump at the interruption of his thoughts, causing his headache to beat a tattoo inside his skull.

"Pardon...sir, you sent for me?"

James leaned back in his chair. "Yes...yes, please come in...have a seat, my good man. I've a matter to discuss with you."

The surgeon entered and sat down in the small chair facing the desk. James gazed at the overhead for an instant, noticing the bit of hair and skin still firmly attached to the beam.

"Are you aware of Nelson's condition?" he asked.

"Aahh, yes...I'm aware of it. He seems to be especially weak to the affects of the ague. I've taken the liberty of dispensing a blue pill and saline drought, which should rid him of the foul humors shortly."

James sighed, relief flooding through him and easing the throbbing in his head. "Thank you, my good man, for being so observant. You are indeed a blessing to me...more than you know. I'd offer you a dram, good surgeon, but I've only this small cup. A thousand pardons for the oversight. It fairly skipped my mind," he said apologetically.

"No offense taken," Beale said in a relaxed tone.

James always appreciated Beale's ability to calm him down in any situation. He could not recall a time when the surgeon was ever upset, always a pillar of strength. He envied him more than he knew. James always had to force himself to control nerves that were just under his skin ready to explode at the slightest provocation. How Beale did it was a complete mystery to him.

Beale quietly cleared his throat bringing him back to reality.

"I say, Beale...this business with the French." He hesitated, trying to sort out his thoughts. "I'd like to hear your view of the situation, if you please."

With a look of dismay and confusion the surgeon placed a hand to his chin and began rubbing it slowly, deep in thought.

"Well!" he snapped, nerves as tight as a sheet in a fresh gale.

The surgeon, startled by the sudden outburst, looked intently at the captain trying to read some hidden thought in his face. Frowning, he said. "I'm quite unaware of any situation, Captain."

Drumming his fingers on the desk, Howlette continued impatiently. "Well...do you have an opinion?"

"An—an opinion?—Beale said looking more confused than ever.

"Yes...yes—of course, man! Your thoughts on why the Frenchie carries such a reckless amount of sail."

"She's full of gold."

"Yes, yes there's *some* amount of gold...I *know* that!"

"No, Captain, she's FULL of gold...to pay for powder and ball purchased from the Spanish to re-supply the French war effort. Don't you see?" Beale leaned forward to emphasize his point by tapping a finger on the desk. "That's the reason for the escort frigates! You can bet they'll beat a hasty return just as fast, once they've victualed and taken on cargo."

"You're quite certain about the gold?" James began to beam at the thought of fabulous wealth.

"What are you thinking, Captain? You *are* aware of our orders." Beale cautioned.

"Yes...of course," he said with an air of indifference and a wave of hand as if to dismiss the matter. "But, I *must* admit...in all candor, that a thought entered my mind—when you spoke of the gold."

James pushed away from the desk to close the door for more privacy. Hesitating, hand still on the latch, collecting his thoughts, he continued.

"I must confess...if your assumption is correct, might we look for an opportunity to take the ship."

"Have you any idea of what you've just proposed? With all due respect, sir...have you lost your mind!" Beale exclaimed, fairly leaping from his seat. "What you've just stated is nothing less than disobeying direct orders. Should you fail in the attempt, the entire crew will be hanged...or at best...thrown in prison for the rest of their lives! You *must* have some consideration for the men, sir!"

"It's just a thought. Our orders state we're to gather intelligence. Sooo...we'll follow them to their destination. The man-of-war always drops anchor in deep water. The frigates sail further in the harbor, leaving her under the protection of the shore batteries. We'll wait off-shore and observe...nothing more. Should fate decide to smile down on us we'll drift up on her, lights out, and snatch her away in the dead of night...right under their fancy, powdered noses; a prize crew to sail her out to open waters and home to fame and fortune for us all. Not only do we have the gold...we've gained a ship for his lordship. I'm sure you realize what that would do for my commission to post captain. Eh...my good man?"

Beale was astounded.

As much as he tried to deny it, here was the means to be rich for a good long while. He smiled and rubbed his hands together at the thought of untold wealth. He saw Beale's expression soften and moved closer.

"If we come away from this in one piece—I'll personally see you set up in grand style. Of course, we may lose all in the attempt, but is there not risk in any great venture?"

A look of doubt clouded the surgeon's face. "Losing all is one thing…losing one's life seems to me to be rather final, don't you agree?"

"Quite right. We'll plan out each detail to a fault."

"I should hope so, Captain," Beale said in hushed tones as his eyes darted nervously at the cabin door, then back to him. "For if we choose to contradict direct orders from the Admiralty…and fail in the attempt, it's the hangman's noose for one and all!"

Silence engulfed the small, humid room, as sweat poured down their faces. Each of them deep in thought as to how the deed should best be accomplished. James at last broke the silence by taking a deep breath.

"Very well…I'll keep in touch. We'll step back and watch the affair closely. If anything changes we can always forget the conversation ever took place…agreed? I'm betting the Frenchies will lead us right into a little trap we'll spring on them, given half the chance. Master Charles!" he said turning toward the door.

"Sar!" the boy sang out instantly.

"Fetch a round of rum for us…smartly now, lad!"

James had no sooner finished when the door flew open to reveal the cabin boy with a bottle of rum in hand, and an extra cup. His jaw dropped.

"What's the meaning of this?"

"Well, Cap'n, sar…I thought to meself, you and Mr. Beale is a gettn' a tad dry with all that talkin' 'n plannin'. So's I taken me on ta task o' waitin' out here with dram in hand, just in case ye' be needin' a sip…so's ta speak." Charles beamed proudly.

"Damned if you're not right about that, my young lad!" James clapped the boy on the back, giving him a fatherly smile. "You'll make midshipman yet! Bring on that bottle; we'll have a toast."

Charles set bottle and cup down then turned to leave.

"By-the-by, my boy…you didn't happen to hear a word of our conversation, did you?"

"No, sar, not a single word, sar."

"That's a good boy…see that it stays that way. Do you understand?" he cautioned, shaking a finger at him. "Pass the word for the Bosun, and I'll see him at once."

"Aye, aye, sar." Charles said and took off at a dead run down the passageway.

They raised a cup to the king, and downed a fiery shot of the captain's finest Jamaican rum. Within minutes a knock signaled the arrival of the chief bosun and James bade him enter.

He was a burly giant of a man, occupying the space of the small cabin with muscle and sinew. Black hair in shining lovelocks fell over forehead, ears, and cascaded down his back. A nose, broken years past, sat askance on a face lined with scars. Dressed in duck trousers, a tar covered blouse and barefoot. His hazel eyes darted through sunburned eyelids as he took note of the bottle, then back to the captain. "Reportin' as ordered, sar!" coming to attention and knuckling his brow.

"As you were. Take a seat; the surgeon was just about to leave. I've a bit of business to discuss with you."

The bosun heaved himself into the chair, exhausted after sixteen hours of hard labor. "At yer service, sar," he said exhaling a cloud of fetid breath that smelled of yesterday's salt beef, saurkraut, and stale grog; eyes never leaving the bottle. James caught the look and handed him a cup saying.

"I'll break ship's rule…just this once…have a dram with my compliments."

The bosun eagerly poured a brimming cup full and tossed it off in one fluid motion.

"I've an idea. What say you to taking the Frenchie if the opportunity should arise? Mr. Beale seems to think she's full of gold…enough to make us all rich men if we're fortunate and God willing."

His eyes narrowed, a wicked grin creased a leathery face burned from years of salt spray and tropical sun as he let go a thunderous belch and replied. "I'd follow ya to ta gates o' hell, Captain, sar…to take that ship from them French dogs! ta gold's just a bonus."

James pursed his lips, and raised an eyebrow, appraising the man intently before saying. "As you know, the man-of-war will anchor in deep water under the shore batteries, leaving her vulnerable. I may very well put your seamanship to the test in the near future, for I've half a mind to take her at night if the opportunity should present itself. Are you up to bringing the ship alongside her without a sound?"

"Aye, sir…it can be done…but I've got me a better idea."

"And what might that be?" James questioned cautiously.

"Drop off a boardin' crew a couple o' leagues out. We pull in, board her, cut ta watches' throats, throw belaying pins on ta hatch covers to lock 'em down tight, 'n she's ours before they be a knowin' what's hit 'em." He slapped a fist into his palm to drive home his point.

"We'll be gone come first light. They won't even know which way she's went.... ha! ha!...just disappeared."

"Seems you've given this matter considerable thought...am I not correct?"

"Quite right you are,. Cap'n. We might not get close ta a stealin' her away. Depends on the harbor, how she lays to, who's alongside...ye' git ma' drift, Cap'n?"

"Indeed..." James said as he leaned back in his chair pressing a finger to his lips in thought.

"Very well, let's hound them; mark their position...etc...etc...They must have *something* of great value on board. That would explain why the frigates have escorted her all the way."

James realized he was thinking out loud, the bosun hanging on every word. "Well...what say you, bosun?"

The man was smiling at the thought of a good fight. He loved it more than using the cheap whores that lined the docks waiting for the jolly boats to tie up.

"After she's well secured, ta land breeze will carry us out afore dawn."

"Very good; that will be all, gentlemen; carry on," James said coldly, leaning over the desk.

"Yes, sar!" The bosun said, leaping from the chair, narrowly missing the same beam he'd had connected with a few hours ago.

The door closed quietly. James drummed his fingers on the desk, his pulse racing. Several stiff shots of rum had eased the throbbing between his temples. He glanced down at the ruined report, studied it intently, and laughing out loud, crumpled the sheet and tossed it across the room. "If my little plan succeeds, the Admiralty will hear of it long before my report is posted in *The Times*," he mumbled under his breath.

He wondered how proud Molly would be. He'd be the toast of the town! People stopping on the street to shake his hand, and praise him at every turn, inviting him to fancy dress balls in honor of his brave feats. Tables loaded with fresh roast beef and mutton cooked to a turn...the fine wines...the...the. Thoughts of it all fairly set his mouth to watering. It had been so very long since he'd set tooth to anything but rancid corned beef, saurkraut, and ship's biscuit.

Poor diet and lack of sleep had not taken much of a toll on him. Life at sea had chiseled his features. Captain James Howlette still struck a fine pose in many a young woman's eye. He was tall, a tad over six feet, with dark flowing hair that lay gently over his shoulders, thin at the waist, broad shouldered and well muscled. He had a noble face with deep blue eyes and a mischievous grin that often turned the heads of wenches at every port.

He preferred to be alone. Keeping to himself being content with silence. It helped soothe his nerves. His passion—dining at the finer hotels and restaurants. A flair for the finest that life had to offer had been his down fall for many years. He'd been wealthy—and broke so many times he'd lost count. Try as he might, he simply could not put any money away in savings. Although several years past he'd been wise enough to purchase a small estate just outside London with prize monies taken from the capture of the *Endeavor*, and had put Molly up in a lavish style that was already cramping his purse. He knew, someday, he'd eventually marry her, but being away at sea had tempered his judgment on the subject, and he'd never found the courage to talk to her about it, let alone propose. He could face a French broadside with more grace and courage than those shimmering blue eyes of hers!

The cabin heat was becoming more than he could bear and the rum was making matters worse; sweat cascaded down his face in torrents. Arising, more carefully this time, he returned to the deck. The ship listed sharply with all the canvas shook out, and drawing every breath of wind possible. A look over the side showed her bow nicely making wave. The helm watch had been changed and Nelson was, no doubt, below in the head taking care of urgent business. He made a turn of the decks. All eyes upon him, as usual. With hands behind his back making mental notes of the least thing out of order he strolled the port side railing. The crew seemed to be very busy on the starboard side. He knew they would, in turn, be busy portside when his tour of the starboard side commenced. Sailors avoided their captain at all times unless directly addressed by him. That was the way it was—and the way it should be.

"Helmsman, has anyone tossed the log of late?" He said as he turned around to the starboard side.

"Yes, sar!" was the reply. "Eight knots, full and by she is, sar."

"Let's have a care not to out run them. Ease off a point, if you please, and run the log at seven knots…no more. We'll plot our course tomorrow, and see if we've matched her speed."

"Aye, aye, sar, " was the immediate reply.

James stopped at the bow; grasped a rope and smiled at the taunt drumming pulse he felt. She's alive and bearing her burden well. The ballast and trim was indeed as good as he could make it. The flying salt spray that drenched his face was a welcome relief from the unbearable heat below. He envied the crewmen sleeping on deck at night while he roasted below. Rank, at times, *did not* have its privileges!

His stomach reminded him that evening was fast approaching and he'd not taken a meal today. The cook's fire below decks smelled of stale pork and the usual saurkraut, just like so many days before. Thoughts of roast beef drifted back to him again and with a sigh, he turned and looked once more about the decks before going below in search of the purser.

"A moment of your time, Mister Daniels, if you please." James said.

The purser looked up from his tally sheets, stood, came to attention and said. "At your service, sir."

"I suppose it's pointless to ask a question…but might there be anything on board that is not of corned beef?" he said bluntly.

A smile raised the corner of Daniel's mouth. He turned around to look at a wooden crate chained to a bulkhead. Thumbing through a ring of keys; he selected one, inspecting it closely; stooped and unlocked it, throwing open the lid. Setting the ring of keys aside, he brought forth a cloth-covered bundle.

"And what might that be?" he asked, a look of surprise on his face.

"I took the liberty of bringing aboard a side of smoked venison, and…if they've not went to the bad, several firm heads of cabbage for you, sir." Daniels said, beaming inwardly to himself.

James's mouth dropped open as he clapped his hands together, rubbing them back and forth saying. "By Jove! Daniels…you rascal! This day has come to a fine end after all! My compliments to the cook, and have him prepare a small repast for the three of us…the surgeon, you, and myself! My cabin at eighth bells sharp. What say you?"

"Well…I…I…Thank you, Captain—I had no intention of sharing." Daniels said quite astonished.

"Think nothing of it, my man. Anyone thoughtful enough to lay away such fare for his captain, deserves a good meal from it, wouldn't you agree?"

"I suppose…if you say so," was Daniel's meek reply.

"Fair enough then…eight bells it is!" he said cheerfully.

The time had flown by. With roast venison, boiled cabbage and small beer to wash it all down with; followed by several generous rounds of rum made it an evening fit for the king himself. James had called his first officer to sit in for a few fast paced hands of wist. As the rum took its effect the games grew livelier and their laughter could be heard through out the ship far into the night. He now lay contentedly in his hammock; hands resting behind his head, savoring the moment. The roll of the ship soon put him to sleep and dreams of how he'd spend the French gold danced through his head.

Dawn broke with him on deck as the ship came about on a southern tack. The masts of two ships eventually showed themselves on the horizon just slightly ahead of them.

"Excellent! Come about if you will, helmsman. Hands to the braces! Put her over; if you please, lads…look lively now."

Crewmen scrambled up ratlines to shake out more canvas and adjust the sheets as the bosun shouted and shoved his way forward to check the trim. James was greatly relieved at sighting the ships so soon "If they continue on their present course, they'll make land fall at Gandia." he whispered to himself. "It's well guarded with shore cannon, and a garrison of solders, but a night attack will have them at a disadvantage. With a little luck, we'll take her without a shot fired. One of the frigates must be lost…or fallen behind. It all depends on where the man-of-war drops anchor, and what other shipping lies in the harbor."

Weeks passed as the cat-and-mouse game played itself out. If the French knew they were being followed; they showed no sign of it. Possibly, they thought themselves safe from attack by a single British fourth rate, or maybe they had not seen them in the glaring sun of early morning. James was pleased as punch, and one evening he had the crew assembled on the afterdeck.

"Lads," he began after silence fell over the throng of sailors. "I'm sure, by now, that you are all aware of our intentions concerning yon ship. It seems every man jack of you has gotten word of it somehow." He shot a steely glance toward the bosun and then the cabin boy.

"You are equally aware of our orders that state we are to follow, learn of their intentions, and report any and all findings to the Admiralty. As of late—a new plan has been brought to mind…that of seizing the ship and the cargo of gold she surely *must* be carrying! I'm sure you're all aware of it by now." Another glance confirmed his suspicions; the bosun was intently staring at the top yards.

A thunderous cheer arose from the crew and it was several minutes before he could continue. "You must also be made aware that if our plan fails we will be in direct disobedience of orders, and as such labeled traitors in the eyes of the crown and hanged one and all. During the past fortnight I've worked out a plan…that might succeed. If the Frenchie anchors in deep water, at the mouth of the harbor...and such other ships as may be there are anchored far enough away as to give us a chance at taking her...then take her we will! What say you to that, me hearties?" he said bringing his fist down on the quarterdeck railing.

The crew cheered and danced about the decks as hats flew in the air. Some few minutes later he continued, "Very well. It's a tricky deed we plan, but God willing, we'll return to jolly old England as rich as barons if luck is on our side. Are you with me, lads?" he shouted.

Cheers rang out until he raised a hand to silence the crew.

"In a few days, if I'm correct, we'll make landfall at Gandia. In the meantime I'll expect our bosun to conduct cannon practice and boarding drills twice daily until you get it right. There will be an extra ration of grog to those who excel. That is all...as you were."

Another cheer followed. The prospect of a good fight and gold lining their pockets was the best news they'd heard since the voyage started.

In the days that followed, James called the surgeon and bosun to his quarters and after they were seated he began.

"Our only problem...as I see it...is the distance our boarding crews have to pull to get there. They may well be worn out and too weak to put up the fight that will be necessary to secure the ship. Have you any ideas, gentlemen?"

The bosun was the first to offer a solution to the problem. "Beggin' yer pardon, sar...it's no problem atall. We drift ta *Rose* in on ta sea breeze and haul up short o' ta harbor with lights out, put over ta jolly boats...maybe half a league out...pull over real quiet like, and wait till they's just about to change ta watch. They be tired by then and not payin' attention if all's been quiet on their side. We'll keep an eye peeled from here, and if ta prize crew takes ta ship...they's flash a light in our direction. We haul up our sea anchor...hoist sail. Th' *Rose*'ll be safely away, with ta prize following, within ta hour."

Several minutes passed in complete silence as each of them pondered what the bosun had said.

"Very well...it just might work. Let us not take this lightly gentlemen...keep the men at daily drills should we have to fight our way out of the harbor."

As the days dragged by, events unfolded that led him to believe the French ship and her escort would indeed anchor at the Spanish port of Gandia. He felt sure he would have no problem locating the harbor entrance, because of the large looming cliffs on each side that could be seen from miles out to sea. This would provide a reference point for the boarding crews as they crept up on the ship after dusk fell. With only enough lower sail to make steerage way, and the rest furled, it would be hard for the fort lookouts to see bare masts that far out to sea. All appeared to be going according to plan.

"In two days the French shall be taught a lesson they'll not soon forget, or we'll die in the trying." he thought.

The ship dropped anchor at the quiet little port just as he had thought. He had taken a last quick look at them early that morning and dropped over the horizon to verify his bearings and wait until tomorrow for one last confirmation with the glass to see how the ship lay at anchor and check the position of any other ships that might pose a problem to the boarding crews. Until then it was ordered a day of rest for the crew after they had holystoned the decks, swabbed out all cannon and re-charged them for possible action the following night.

The next morning, as the sun came blazing out of the east, James ordered the ship to carefully approach the horizon for a last look before the attempted capture. All eyes were straining to catch a glimpse. At last the crows nest watch shouted.

"Ship ahoy...off ta starboard bow. She's in deep water, sar...but me thinks ta frigate is alongside her, sar."

"The hell you say!" Howlette said, a note of dismay in his voice. "Have a closer look...there must be no mistake about this."

A moment later another distant reply drifted down to the deck. "She's sure 'nough anchored with th' frigate close by. It's too far ta tell how they lay from here, sar. I can barely see 'em, but she's with th' man-of-war...no doubt about it, sar."

James was stunned. His mind reeling, he placed his hands behind his back and strolled the quarterdeck in silence for several minutes. All hands watched, in quiet anticipation, for orders that appeared not to be forthcoming. At last, he stopped, and turning to his bosun said, "Ware ship, bosun, take her out to deep water for the time being. I must have some time to think this matter through. It appears we've bloody well led ourselves on a merry chase. I shall be in my cabin, and I'll thank you kindly not to disturb me!"

He quickly left the quarterdeck, descended the ladder, and went straight to his quarters below. Collapsing in his chair, he sat staring down at his trembling hands, his mind completely blank. He could feel his nerves welling to the surface again, haunting him and clouding his judgment as they had in the past.

"Calm down…calm down." he mumbled. "I *must* risk a closer look…tonight…a closer look…that's all…"

CHAPTER TWO

The evening twilight was laced with shards of purple that somehow carried with it a dark somber mood. Sailing easily, full and by, under double-reefed, lower fore sheets there was little activity on deck. Johnson was surprised at how quiet a night could be. A feeble glow from below shown through the deck gratings, casting an eerie shaft of light across the dark faces of the men gathered just abaft the main mast. An obscure figure leaned forward for more comfort, and said.

"This be yer first boardin' party...eh, young in'? There be blood spilt afore ta nights out, I'm thinking', 'n' if ye ain't careful, nipper...it'll be yourn."

Johnson stood nervously twisting the hem of his blouse; unsure if a reply was necessary. His eyes darted around the group, looking for some reassurance that he was doing the proper thing.

"Put a stopper in it, Cully! Ye can plainly see ta lad's terrified. Ye be a doin' him no good...'n' it'll come back on ye double!"

"Settle down, Wiggins. I was just funning' with ta boy. I meant him no harm." Cully declared matter of factly.

Wiggins cleared his throat and said under his breath. "I've a feeling about me tonight. Bad luck's all around...and there be no call askin' for more o' ta same. If we pull this off we'll be a sailin' her out in broad daylight afore there's enough land breeze to give steerage way."

"Don't ye want ta be rich? Are ye not willin' ta risk a little for it? If we be real quiet while we're a thumpin' heads, them Frenchies that's on shore won't know nothin's wrong! If any o' them decides to row back ta th' ship, we thump 'em on th' head just like th' others. Damn, Wiggie! You an' yer black, demon hoodoos are 'bout ta wear me to a frazzle. We hoist some canvas, real casual like, and pretend we're just out fer a Sunday offing. Th' shore batteries'll not give a hoot as long as all's quiet. Hell, they'll probably be a soberin' up fer all we know!"

"Say what ye will, Cully…ye'll soon see fer yerself." Wiggins stated with authority.

The light breeze freshened as darkness fell. The sea grew restless; waves building in intensity. A waning moon high overhead cast just enough light to make out the ghostly figures of men as they moved about the decks in preparation to ware ship and lower away the jolly boats for the long pull ashore. The helm was put over while the sails were furled and after the initial fuss of clearing away the lines, canvas covers and arranging of block and tackle the officer on deck, finally satisfied, gave the order to lower away the lee boats. Johnson, Cully and twenty-two men descended the rope ladder armed with cutlass and boarding pikes. They piled into the violently swaying boats with Johnson pitching into the stern sheets after accidentally tripping over a dark form huddled in the waste.

"Watch where yer goin', ye damned idgett! I'll be lame afore we even git where we're goin'!"

He mumbled an apology while pushing himself to a sitting position.

"That's enough o' yer comments!" The bosun growled, as his starter whistled through the air connecting with the back of the man sitting next to him. A muffled thud followed by a painful groan was enough to remind Johnson to remain silent. The oars were manned, four to a side, with the bosun at the tiller, followed by the bow lookout, and two men in the stern sheets. James piloted the second craft against the adamant objections of the surgeon and several officers. John Kingston, the senior lieutenant, was appointed acting ship's captain until he returned.

"Bosun…are we secure?" James questioned, his voice echoing above the crash of the waves against the *Rose*.

"Aye, sar, all secure."

"Very well then, give way, me hearties…put your backs into it…cheerily now. We've a fortune waiting for us!" he ordered with lusty exuberance.

The boats lurched forward; oars slapping the water until they found a rhythm and measured their stroke accordingly. The lee side of the ship had a calming effect on the sea, sheltering the boats from wind and wave. Leaving that protection was both thrilling and terrifying at the same time. The change was so sudden and unexpected it was akin to being transported to another world. The bosun leaned on the tiller, panting and grunting, fighting to turn the bow. Johnson frantically grasp at anything he could, trying desperately to stay calm and keep from being thrown overboard, his knuckles turning white in the attempt. Wave upon wave crashed over the stern as they ran before the wind. Within minutes the entire crew was soaked to the skin. Flying sprays drenched them, pelting the back of their necks with cold salt water.

Entering the breakwater an hour later, they could just make out the harbor entrance and the silhouettes of the two ships. The frigate was anchored dangerously close and posed a serious problem. Howlette ordered the boats to come about and tie up for a short discussion.

"How far apart do you make them to be?"

"My guess be more 'r less a hundred yards, Cap'n. They be within earshot fer sure. There ain't no way we can take 'er without bein' heard. I'm pret' near sure th' frigate has a broadside toward er', and 'll not dither about openin' up th' twenty pounders if'n we's so much as raise a dish rag o' canvas. My advice, Cap'n, sar—we give 'er up fer lost 'n pull back ta th' *Rose* 'n' weigh anchor afore it's too late," the bosun stated, spitting a black stream of tobacco juice over the side to emphasize his point.

Howlette instantly replied, "Yes...I do believe you're right. From where we sit it would appear we've little chance indeed...take your boat just forward of the catheads; if all's quiet we'll make an attempt to secure the companionways and hatch covers forward of the main mast. I'll take care of the aft hatches and quarterdeck. Quietly men...let's have a closer look before we decide."

"As ye wish, sar." The bosun was beginning to think Wiggins might know something the rest of them didn't. Experience told him the odds were stacked heavily in favor of the French. If, by some stroke of luck, they overpowered the crew and secured the ship; the frigate was close enough to blow them out of the water. It was not a pleasant thought. The waters were much calmer inside the sheltered cove as they pulled silently toward their prey. Now only a few leagues away, they could just make out the weak orange light coming from the quarterdeck and after cabin.

The bosun steered along the port side gently while several men held the boat off as it crept forward. They stopped, for several minutes, and listened for any noise that might give a clue to the number of crewman on board. Minutes passed, and finally James motioned for the bow lookout to tie off on a ring bolt to steady them as they prepared to climb the short distance to the anchor ties. He secured the second boat forward of the tiller. Minutes later a man was sent up the side to tie off a boarding line to haul up a rope ladder for the rest of the boarding party. Satisfied that all was in order he gave the word and they started the long climb up the side of the ship. Fifteen minutes passed while the crew of the first boat huddled at the foremast waiting for the last of the stragglers. The decks were quiet. If the night watch was about, they had failed to see them. With a wave of his arm the bosun signaled the group to split up and move forward to the hatch covers while Johnson, Cully and Wiggins crept silently in the direction of the two companionway doors just ahead of the foremast. Kneeling beside one of the doors; Cully slipped a short length of line through the latch and tied it off securely. Johnson knelt with his back to the bulkhead watching the dark shapes of men glide about the deck, then disappear as they prepared to lock down the hatches. The moonlight faded as a bank of low thin clouds drifted overhead. Johnson was turning to follow Cully to the second door when, unexpectedly, the bosun's voice roared; splitting the calm atmosphere like a thunderclap, "It's a trap! Th' hatch covers is gone…abandon ship!"

Johnson was struck dumb. Where could the hatch covers go? They were hinged to the deck. Before he could make sense of the warning an earsplitting scream turned his blood to ice. A cutlass had weaved its way through the bosun's stomach, collapsing a lung and slicing his heart to ribbons. Blood and bile gushed out along with several feet of intestine. He died before he hit the deck. The surprise was swift and complete. Men swarmed out of the open hatches like a hoard of angry bees. Johnson heard a dull thud. He turned and looked down just in time to see Wiggins's head bounce on the deck at his feet; eyes fluttering and mouth gaping silently. He screamed in sheer terror at the sight; staggered back, turned and retched; heaving the hot bitter contents of his last meal down the front of his blouse. Instantly Cully grabbed him by the collar, shoved him forward against the bulwark and shouted in his ear.

"Jump boy—save yerself afore it be too late!"

Fighting erupted everywhere. Johnson was too terrified to move and stood frozen to the spot, mesmerized by the hellish scene before him. Eighteen men were no match for the dozens of heavily armed French marines pouring onto the deck. Shouts, grunts and screams of agony shattered the night as men fought for their lives. Pistol shots rang out above the clang of steel as the tide of battle surged on.

Captain Howlette was climbing the quarterdeck ladder when he heard the warning cry and turned to see the bosun collapse in a heap of gore. With cutlass in hand, he leaped up the remaining steps to the quarterdeck and slashed the wheel watch across the chest. Flesh and bone parted in a gush of blood that splattered across his face. Looking frantically around he realized he was alone and bounded down the ladder to join the intense fighting taking place in the waist of the ship. It was close, dirty, grueling work. They were packed so tightly together it was hard to recognize an enemy. Elbows jabbed into sweat covered bodies from all directions. His men had been herded into a tight circle which made a tricky fight of it. The bitter taste of copper filled his mouth as an arm was severed inches in front of his face, showering him with blood and blinding his eyes momentarily. Any hopes of taking the ship vanished with the first pistol shot. He saw, above the horde of shouting attackers, squares of dim yellow light in the distance as gun ports opened on the frigate and boats were put over the side. They'd fell prey to a cleverly prepared trap…lured to their doom. Now he knew why the convoy had paid no attention to being hounded for weeks on end. The French had evidently anticipated an attack and had positioned the frigate close by. If the signal was given to fire a broadside of grape shot into them; the effects would be devastating.

The savage hand to hand combat surged forward, then back like a minuet from Hell. Blood soaked the deck, making it hard to stand. Howlette faintly heard water splashing above the din of chaos surrounding him. Johnson heard it too and tore his eyes away from the carnage taking place before him. It saved his life. A bullet struck the bulkhead exactly where his head had been seconds before, showering him with splinters, cutting his face and neck bringing him back to reality. Looking frantically around for some means of escape, he blindly stumbled to the railing, completely oblivious to the danger surrounding him. His bowels suddenly cramped—then turned to water as a hot gush of foul-smelling liquid filled his trousers. He leaped over the side, arms and legs flailing wildly, and crashed into the water knocking the wind from his lungs. Surfacing some distance away, coughing and gagging on the cold salt water, he swam back to the ship; feeling his way along the side trying to locate the boats in the darkness. He panicked when he couldn't find them; then realized he'd jumped off the starboard side. Swimming frantically around the bow he crashed into the last remaining boat as it was casting off. Someone hauled him in and he fell headlong to the bottom gasping for air in great gulps as violent spasms racked his body. He was one of seven survivors to escape.

Someone yelled, "Throw down your weapons—or die!"

The scene drifted through Howlette's exhausted mind like a surreal nightmare that he couldn't awake from. He realized, in an instant, that the fight was lost and looked around hysterically for some reassurance, but found none. Something snapped inside him. It was akin to unleashing a caged animal. He lost all fear of death and raged onward, lashing out at anything that moved. He made a wild lunge with his cutlass; thrusting the cold steel completely through an unfortunate marine with such force that the hilt made a wet slapping sound as it violently struck his stomach splattering blood everywhere. He raised his foot and kicked the man off the blade then charged forward slashing crazily left and right as the enemy separated to let him pass. For a few hapless moments the remaining crew rallied around him to give one last futile attempt at saving themselves, but it was too late; they were badly outnumbered and the only prudent decision to be made was surrender. The few members of the boarding party that remained standing threw down their weapons as he fell to the deck under a throng of blood soaked marines screaming like a demented madman set free from an asylum.

It was over almost as fast as it had begun. The only sound that could be heard above the overpowering silence was the exhausted gasping of air to satisfy the burning lungs of bloodied warriors. A door opened from a companionway that led to the captain's cabin below the quarterdeck casting a slanting beam of light across the group. What appeared to be the captain of the ship clad in full dress uniform with hands clasped behind his back casually strode toward the group of tattered men. A look of complete boredom lined his face as though a battle of this sort happened every day. He appraised each of the prisoners as though he were picking out a plump piglet for slaughter.

"Nettoyer Ce désordre—tout de suite! Throw these filthy dead maggots over the side, and be quick about it! Have the surgeon on deck at once to attend to the wounded then secure the ship. The prisoners will form up in a line to be stripped and chained to the mast until morning. Those who bleed to death before dawn will be the lucky ones!"

He pulled a white lace handkerchief from a vest pocket to cover his nose as a look of disgust distorted his features, and then continued. "Garde!—T'avoir votre disposition! I shall deal with these grubby beggars after I've enjoyed a good night's sleep and a hot breakfast on the morrow. That is all!"

Johnson hadn't the slightest idea of how long he lay in the stern sheets drifting in and out of conscience as the waves rolled the boat from side to side.

"What's that gawd-awful smell?"

He sat up rubbing his red gritty eyes, and then threw an arm over the side to balance his swaying body.

"I do believe th' youngin' be-shit his pants!" Cully commented sarcastically.

Some half-hearted chuckles acknowledged the remark, but fatigue kept any further observations from being uttered. He leaned over the railing and vomited violently and collapsed in a wet heap as yellow bile bubbled and dripped from his chin.

"Git up off yer dead arse, youngin', and give a hand with this here oar, or we'll never make it!" Cully shouted back at him, then turned and lashed out with a swift kick that overset him again, causing the boat to rock cruelly.

He pulled himself to a seat, fumbling about for an oar; leaned over and retched again and then began rowing. Hours later they sighted the *Rose* looming ahead in eerie world of swirling fog and half twilight. A half hour later they pulled along side and hailed the deck. A rope ladder was thrown over the side and five exhausted men climbed aboard. A bosuns chair was rigged to bring up Johnson and another badly wounded man.

Lieutenant Kingston came on deck as the last man was swung over the railing.

"It was a slaughter—Cap'n, sar...they's a waitin' fer us. Frigate was stationed close along...sar with her broadside on us. Them hatch covers was took off 'n covered with canvas so's ta make it all look natural like. As soon as we's touched them canvas covers they's threw 'em off and...well sar, th' bosun was th' first man down. T'was awful, it was, sar. Them marines took us right quick like—blood and guts was everywhere so thick we's a fallin' down in 'um. We's surrounded in a heartbeat, Cap'n, sar...we's trapped— pure 'n simple. What ye see here afore ye is all's left. Cap'n Howlette...well he's either dead or took prisoner...don't know fer sure. All I knowed is I heared th' bosun call out ta abandon ship...'n I obeyed orders right quick like. As ye can see...I damn near lost me arm afore I made it over!" Cully said, between deep breaths, as the description of the battle tumbled out in chopped sentences.

"Sixteen casualties? You *must* be mistaken! Where's the second boat? Did you not see the other boat...somewhere?"

"If 'n it's out there, we'll know by daybreak. My guess, Cap'n, sar, is she's gone under. It was a blood bath...worst I ever did see...Gawd-amighty, sar, they gave us twelve yards o' pure hell, they did!"

Kingston shook his head in disbelief.

"Report to the surgeon, all of you, and have him attend to your wounds. My compliments to the purser, and have him issue dry blankets for these men at once," he said to the midshipman standing by the railing.

They slept until late afternoon and would have slept longer if it were not for young Johnson screaming and wildly flailing his arms about, desperately trying to fend off the blood soaked demons haunting his sleep. A resounding slap across the face soon brought him back to his senses. Additional watches were posted through out the morning hours in hopes of sighting the second boat but it was never seen again. They stayed on station the entire day, wearing ship, hoping to sight the missing boat but as the sun set in an aura of golden orange, Lieutenant Kingston reluctantly ordered the *Rose* over the horizon for the night fearing retaliation from the French. The men were unusually quiet and somber at the evening mess. The unceasing laughter and banter that passed back and forth between the watches as they ate salt pork and ships biscuit was conspicuously absent; a pall of silence pervaded the gun deck as a wake, of sorts, was observed for their missing comrades. The following day the *Rose* returned on station and remained in sight of the harbor. The ships remained in their original positions as if nothing had taken place. Risking a closer look, they sailed to the mouth of the harbor but all the lookout could see from the mainmast was the usual small boat traffic as they re-supplied the ships anchored about the harbor. Kingston was visibly shaken and struggling with a decision he knew he would have to make within twenty-four hours. James had given orders for an alternate course to be set within seventy-two hours if the mission failed, but the young lieutenant never dreamed he would be the officer to carry it out. The weight of responsibility was almost more than he could cope with…and what would happen to them when, and if, they returned to England was something he dare not think about.

Reluctantly, after waiting twelve hours longer than ordered, as the morning sun peaked above the horizon Kingston ordered the sails trimmed and the helm put over bringing the *Rose* before a light east by southeast breeze and within the hour the harbor could no longer be seen. The following day they altered course, heading due south for the island of Formentera some one hundred fifty leagues away. If any survivors escaped, and were lucky enough to steal a sea worthy craft, there was an outside chance they could rendezvous. The only problem was the twelve to fourteen days they'd estimated it would take for a small single masted vessel to make the offing and sail to the island. Without a sextant and time piece they would be hard pressed to arrive within leagues of their destination, let alone find them in the maze of islands that all looked the same at a distance. It would fairly be impossible but it was the only chance they had.

The *Rose* sailed leisurely down the coast; there was no need to crack on more sail than was necessary. The longer it took to reach the rendezvous, the less they'd have to wait. The ship seemed to know where she was headed and needed little attention. The crew members were wondering what would happen to them when they arrived back to England. The words of Captain Howlette echoed in their minds.

"We will be in direct disobedience of orders, and as such will be labeled traitors and hanged one and all."

With that thought constantly weighing on their conscience there was little conversation shared around the mess. Kingston remained in Captain Howlette's cabin throughout the day and made an appearance on deck every twenty four hours to take the noon sightings. When he toured the decks to check the trim of the ship it was done quietly and he was usually satisfied with what he saw. The log was tossed at the appointed hour and duly noted. The watch turned out and the *Rose* sailed smoothly on a due south by southwest course making about eight knots. One day slowly dragged into another and six days later, after altering course to west by southwest they sighted the chain of islands off the starboard bow early the following morning. The *Rose* slowed to three knots after the sail was shortened and they crept along searching for the coral inlet they would call home for the next three months. Ninety days later they would weigh anchor and return to England. Until then they would wait in hopes that some of the prisoners could escape and find their way to the sheltered coral harbor on the southern tip of the island.

Late that afternoon the ship crept past the sharp coral growths. The lead was tossed repeatedly to make sure there was thirty feet of depth. The coral shoaled up rapidly and with new growth constantly changing position from year to year it was a delicate procedure to maneuver her through the small entrance and keep her from being stranded on a reef. Several hours later, to the great relief of the crew, the *Rose* dropped anchor in a serene natural harbor bordered with white sandy beaches on two sides and tropical fruit trees on the other. A stream emptied into the harbor from the north that was just wide enough to accommodate a small boat. Some of the men rowed ashore and set up makeshift tents from spare canvas, gathered firewood, and went in search of fresh meat and fruit. A routine soon evolved that seemed to suit everyone. Lieutenant Kingston assigned a daily watch schedule and two men kept a sharp lookout at the mouth of the tiny harbor for any sign of a small craft.

The island provided an abundance of fresh tropical fruit and fish. Several of the more resourceful sailors soon discovered large schools of fish gathered around the coral reefs and devised ways of trapping them. Along with shellfish lining the shores of the inlet and turtle eggs buried in the warm sands they enjoyed table fare fit for the good King himself.

Eight men huddled together around the mast head of the French war ship. Cold, exhausted and hungry there was nothing left but to lay on the wooden deck planks and shiver, waiting for the sun to rise on what might very well be the last day of their lives. One man bled to death shortly after being chained to a ring bolt and two others died sometime in the night. The first gray hint of dawn revealed five men in the most despicable condition one could imagine. Dried blood matted their hair, they had numerous cuts and bruises and infection was setting in as fever shook them from head to toe. One man was delirious and thrashing about while two men attempted to restrain him. Howlette awoke in the gray dawn, after a few fitful hours of restless sleep, and appraised their situation through bloodshot eyes. Unarmed and completely naked; they had taken everything, including the shoes off their feet. Two armed marines stood guard over them even though they were heavily chained to the mainmast. Iron shackles bound their feet so tightly that a step of twelve to fourteen inches was all they could take without falling down. The sun was creeping over the horizon, casting rays of slanting golden light across the deck when two marines came forward and brutally kicked them to their feet. Minutes later the sail maker brought enough dirty squares of canvas with holes cut in the center to slip over their heads. The guards removed the chains long enough to allow them to slip the ponchos on and then laced it through their shackles allowing them to stand, but they were too weak and decided to sit on the deck to await their fate. An hour passed before the French captain came on deck to address them.

"Garde à vous!" The marine guards forced them to stand at attention before the captain. The injured men were helped to their feet and the motley group of sailors formed a line that apparently satisfied the officer. He strolled by each man, appraising them carefully. After a few minutes he stepped back and placed his hands behind him. Looking over their heads, he keenly studied the skyline as his eyes swept the horizon from east to west. One of the injured men moaned from the intense pain of a badly lacerated thigh.

"Réduire au silence!" he shouted. A guard stepped forward and cruelly struck the man across the face, sending him to the deck in a crumpled heap.

"Leave him where he lies! I have little tolerance for weakness—and cowards that steal in the night." He stepped closer and asked, "Who among you is the leader of this miserable band of miscreants?"

The huddled group of men glanced among themselves, then gave the captain a brooding stare of pure hatred.

"So—you wish to play ze little game with me—oui?" He chuckled behind a wicked grin. "Captain Rondeau likes to play le jeu—oui?"

He took a saber from the closest marine, appraised the steel, testing its edge with a thumb then, faster than a striking asp, plunged the cold steel through the foot of the nearest men in front of him pinning it to the deck. He instantly fell, screaming dreadfully at the top of his lungs, frantically trying to free himself, but the shackles that bound his hands were too short. He lay writhing in pain, thrashing about from side to side as blood gushed forth in great torrents. Captain Howlette lunged, attempting to strangle the captain.

Rondeau feinted to one side saying, "So it is you—is it not? You are the instigator!"

He laughed, stepped closer, and savagely struck him across the face with the back of his hand sending him to his knees. He looked up, shook his head to clear his vision, then stood on shaking legs glaring at the man before him. He took a deep breath and spit a mouthful of blood in his face. The French captain balled his fists, struggling to control himself then said, barely above a whisper,

"It will be a pleasure to place the noose around your neck! I shall ask the magistrate, personally, for the honor of taking your life!"

The man, whose foot was still pinned to the deck, wailed out in pain begging for someone to help him. Rondeau glanced down at him, raised an eyebrow, removed the saber from his foot and calmly ran it through his chest. He died, gasping for breath, as his lungs filled with pink foaming blood.

"I will see to it that you are imprisoned for a *long* time before the hangman comes. When I'm finished, you will beg for the cold hand of death, and I shall be only too happy to oblige. Call away the captain's gig! I shall escort the prisoners ashore myself. The magistrate and I are close friends, and I've no doubt that he will give you a hearty welcome. I'll clean up a bit…and we'll pay a visit to his majesty."

Howlette trembled with rage as he watched the captain disappear through a companionway door. How could he have been so stupid? The position of the frigate should have raised a warning flag, but his greed had overpowered his better judgment and it might very well cost him his life. He shook his head again and sat down on the deck with the three remaining prisoners.

The captain was summoned shortly after the gig was lowered to the water. They were escorted over the side and chained tightly together while he settled himself in the stern sheets. The crew was ordered to give way and minutes later they pulled away from the ship and headed for the placid shore. The sun shone with a brilliance only the southern latitudes could provide. Sea gulls winged and dived through a clear deep blue sky calling out to them in raucous cries as if to warn them of their impending doom. A short time later the boat struck the stony shore grinding to a halt amongst a crowd of curious onlookers. They were swiftly brought ashore and marched through the dusty streets amid shouted insults and a barrage of stones hurled at them from every direction. Rondeau ordered the guards to halt numerous times allowing the crowd to pelt the prisoners with anything they could find. Eventually they arrived at a shabby adobe building and were shoved through rough hewn doors into what appeared to be the local constabulary. The cool air smelled of stale sweat and rancid garlic, a smell they would soon become accustomed to. The captain entered a door to his left and a few minutes later motioned the guards to bring in the prisoners.

They were told to stand in front of a tall bench that looked more like a hitching rail than court room chambers. Seconds later a fat, greasy, middle-aged Mexican strode into the room from a side door, approached the bench, and sat down. Rondeau took a chair to one side, crossed his legs, fanning himself with a handkerchief he'd produced from a vest pocket. The magistrate appraised the three men for several minutes, poured a stiff shot of tequila, and then set the bottle down.

Raising his glass to them he said, "I've just been informed of your daring adventure. I salute your bravery, amigos. A few insignificant mice have dared to fight the eagle—yes—no? He laughed at his joke, tossed off the drink, belched, coughed and then continued.

"But...I'm afraid I must inform you—the eagle has won. Ha ha! For you see...El Captain is a friend of Rodrigo's—and that is bad for the gringos! I am sorry to say that I must place you under arrest. The good captain tells me you filthy maggots have taken the lives of many, and I cannot allow such a thing to take place on Spanish soil. When the autumn arrives, and the days, they cool off some, I will order the fiesta, and we will watch you dance at the end of a strong rope. Ha ha. I will be looking forward to the occasion…the good captain informs Rodrigo that he would like to personally send you to Hell…I think he has the good idea—yes—no?"

He roared with laughter, slapping the rough bench with a filthy hand. "If you are good…and cause no trouble for Rodrigo…you will be fed in a few days…until then…adios, amigos!"

CHAPTER THREE

"I shall expect a report on my desk at your earliest convenience," demanded the Right Honorable Lord Cambridge, waving Admiral Morris off with a bony hand. He strained to lift his ponderous bulk from the chair and stood at what would pass for attention, jowls quivering, as he attempted a smart salute.

"As you wish, Your Excellency; the report shall be on your desk within a fortnight."

Without another word he turned and left the room as quickly as his aching knees could carry him. Returning to his office and closing the door, he crossed the room and collapsed in a heap behind the desk. The large over stuffed leather chair groaned as it took the punishment.

He'd been in conference with his Excellency for most of the morning concerning the investigation pertaining to the loss of British ships. He'd patiently listened to the insufferable boor until he was thoroughly exhausted. No one had the slightest idea how the French were obtaining information about British shipping activities, but it was quite obvious a spy was in place and doing an excellent job of intelligence gathering. All attempts to uncover the person, or persons, had failed. Morris had watched Cambridge become hopelessly feeble minded over the years and had begrudgingly tolerated it in hopes that some tragedy might befall him. His appointment to the office was waiting, but it appeared the decrepit old beggar was going to live forever!

Morris had only two immediate goals in mind for the future. The first was to discover a way to pursue the young Miss Molly Bidwell; the other, to discover some means to relieve the venerable Cambridge of his command,

and the sooner the better. He'd become increasingly aware of Miss Bidwell over the year, often lustily drinking in her beauty at the banquets they'd attended. The thought of her cascading blonde hair, brown eyes, pearl-white teeth, hour-glass figure, and those milky white breasts pouring out of her evening gown was always tucked away in the back of his mind. He was obsessed with her and God only knew how he wanted her.

With the deployment of the *Rose*, she'd began to write letters to him weekly asking about the welfare of the ship and crew and especially that of Captain Howlette. He was insanely jealous of him. The young upstart had climbed the chain of command much too quickly to suit him and he was under constant pressure from Cambridge to submit the paperwork necessary to promote the man to post captain despite his many attempts to put him in a bad light. He was so desperate to put off the promotion that he now resorted to conjuring up a few falsehoods against him.

His aide knocked on the office door bringing him out of his reverie.

"Enter," he said in a bored, matter-of-fact voice. The aide ushered himself in and came to the desk, bowed curtly, and said.

"Miss Bidwell to see you, sir. Should I ask her to return later? Your audience with his Excellency has surely worn you down…and you've not supped at all today."

Only a week had passed since Molly had obtained an audience with him to inquire about the *Rose* and any news of her dear captain. For some reason she'd stopped writing and was seeing him in person…quite strange. Morris casually raised his eyes from a disheveled assortment of papers scattered over the top of a spacious mahogany desk. His pulse began to race at the thought of another meeting with her. Trying desperately to calm down…and failing miserably he said,

"Yes, it has indeed been a rather trying affair, and the lack of a hearty meal has taken a great toll on my strength. I know she's greatly concerned about the safety of the *Rose*, and rightly so, I suppose. Please show her in at once and I'll try to put her mind at ease."

"As you wish, sir," he said, coming to attention and saluting. Turning on his heel, he prepared to leave the room.

"A moment, if you please, before you go. I've a letter to be posted. It's of the utmost importance and I'm afraid you *must* leave at once. Please deliver it…as you've done before. I'll just seal it and then off you go. Oh, by the way, it's a long ride, as you well know, so please, return to your quarters after the task. You have my permission to take the remainder of the day off," he said.

"But what of your repast, sir? I've not yet made arrangements for your evening meal!" The aide said.

"Of course, of course, my good man. You are indeed attentive to a fault, but I shall take care of the matter, rest assured, after I've met with the young lady," Morris said as he signed the document with a flourish and sanded the wet ink. He proceeded to fold the letter, melting sealing wax over a candle flame and affixing his personal seal. After addressing it he handed the letter over to the aide, trying to conceal his shaking hand. His excitement was rising to a fever pitch at the thought of watching those lovely breasts rise and fall with each delicate breath she took.

"Now, off with you, lad. I shall need your services on the morrow...bright and early...as usual."

"Very well, sir." The aide left the room, softly closing the door behind him.

Morris clasped his trembling hands tightly together and placed them atop the desk. His heart pounded with such force he wondered if Molly would hear it. A frown crossed his face, knitting his brows. What were her intentions? Why was she seeing him in person? Surely their meeting last week had been enough to reassure her doubts about the safety of the *Rose*. Suddenly he realized that all was not as it should be. A vague feeling of foreboding swept over him, and departed just as quickly, leaving his mind confused and his thoughts scattered. He had only a bare notion of how to proceed.

A soft knock at the door announced the arrival of Molly.

"Please, come in, Miss Bidwell," he said as cordially as he could. The door opened as Molly entered with a swish of petty coats and lace. She crossed the spacious office and politely seated herself in a chair directly across from him.

"Please forgive my constant intrusion upon your valuable time, Admiral Morris. You must surely think I've nothing better to do than fret over dear James. I've a premonition that he'll come to some harm. Call it a woman's intuition if you will, but I've not been able to put my mind to rest, and I've not slept a wink for days," she said quickly, raising a trembling finger to touch the small hollow at the base of her throat, then trace its way slowly down to rest between the ample cleavage that his eye's were glued upon.

"Please...please, Miss Bidwell," he stammered. "Think nothing of it. It is I who should be apologizing to you for sending Captain Howlette off at a moment's notice with no time for a proper good-bye. I know you wanted to see him off, but you were at Briarwood, and it was such a long ride. Time was of the essence. I'm sure you are quite well aware of how the military operates in time of war."

"Yes, I know, but I did so want to wish him well," she cooed, her finger now toying with the lace at the bodice of her dress. Morris was beginning to sweat despite a frosty October morning that had brought a crisp breeze with it. Taking a deep breath he forced himself to look Molly in the face, saying, "Please, Molly, may I call you Molly? Let's put an end to these formalities. Call me John. We've known each other for quite some time, and I feel we're surely friends by now, are we not?"

"Well, yes, I suppose you're right, Admiral...uh...John," she said softly. Her eyes suddenly became firmly fixed on his. An eternity seemed to pass in silence as they stared at each other. A battle waged as each tried to fathom the other's thoughts. Morris was the first to speak, his voice unexpectedly loud.

"Let me assure you, Molly, I've taken *every* precaution to see your James safely returned home. As I said at our last meeting his orders plainly state that he is *only* to observe. I've specifically stated no force of arms is to be used unless necessary for the defense of the ship. There's no need to worry for his safety, my dear. Foul weather is a much greater threat than the French."

"I suppose you're right...John. Thank you so very much for your patience and understanding. I'm afraid I've allowed myself to fret over this until I'm simply a wreck," she said, her voice breaking.

"There, there, Moll, take hold of yourself. Constant worry will bring a harm to your health, and we can have none of that, now can we?" He hesitated, and then hurriedly said, "A thought has just occurred to me. I've not taken a meal today, and if you would agree, I would be most honored if you would be my guest at dinner. Some good food and light conversation would do you good; I'm sure of it. I'll have a carriage summoned and we'll be off in a few minutes. What do you say, Moll?" he asked as innocently as he could muster.

"Oh, my, John, I think not!" She said, aghast, placing a hand to her cheek. "What would people think if we were seen dining together. Tongues will wag all over London with the worst of rumors, and none of it true!"

"Psshawww!" he said with a wave of his hand. "Think nothing of it, my dear. I'm a man of some importance in the city, and as such I'm constantly in the public eye, my every move known to one and all. Dining with the fiancée of Captain Howlette will be viewed as strictly social, nothing more, a mere gesture of kindness. You are aware, of course, that my wife and I are seldom seen in public together due to my being called away so often on matters of great urgency. A pity it is, but a price I must pay. You understand, don't you?"

"I understand...John, but I feel that no good can come of this," she said somewhat agitated. "You are quite sure of this being proper?"

"Of course! Now not another word on the matter. If you'll excuse me I'll have a carriage come 'round and then we'll be off." Morris arose stiffly from the over-stuffed chair and smiled down at Molly for a few seconds then left the room. The office was deathly quiet as Molly dropped her hand to her lap and smiled.

Arriving at the hotel, Morris offered his arm as Molly stepped down from the carriage. Smiling demurely she took it and gave it a delicate squeeze as they proceeded up the walk and into the foyer. A waiter dressed in white, starched shirt, black bow tie, with matching vest and trousers escorted them to the dining room. Morris felt a soft breast brush against his arm as he helped her to her chair. The little wench, in a very subtle way, appeared to be quite bold, he thought to himself. He was pleasantly surprised.

After they had seated themselves at a nice, private corner table away from the noise and prying eyes of other guests; each ordered from the menu then sipped a cordial while the meal was being prepared. The silence soon became awkward as his mind raced for something to say. Finally he cleared his throat and forged ahead.

"Forgive my intrusion into your private thoughts, Moll, but I've heard, and mind you, there's not a grain of truth to it, but some say you're suffering financial woes at Briarwood Estates," he said, trying his best to sound concerned.

"I'm afraid there's more truth to it than I should care to admit," she said, looking down at the glass twirling between her delicate fingers. "As of late it has become increasingly difficult to keep the creditors at bay. I've no skills at all, and rely completely on James for my livelihood. His pay, at times, is barely sufficient to make ends meet. He was on half pay for the better part of two years before the commission to the *Rose* came forth."

"My goodness! I had no idea you were *that* desperate, Moll. It's such a pity there are so many officers and so few commissions to assign. Only the most promising are called to active duty, and then only quite rarely. Perhaps there's a way I can be of service to you during this most difficult ordeal. How may I be of assistance?" he asked sincerely, silently beaming to himself at this fortuitous turn in the conversation.

"Oh please, John, I could *never* ask for your assistance! James would be mortified were he to ever find out. He'll return in a few short months, God willing, and I'm sure he can straighten everything out then. I simply *must* make ends meet until then. I'm really not doing so badly," she said with a sigh.

The conversation was interrupted as the waiter set steaming plates of food before them and refilled their glasses. "May I be of further service, sir?"

"No, thank you," Morris said waving him away. Directing his attention to Molly he said, "Let's put the conversation on a lighter note while we enjoy our meal. I'll give some thought to what we've just talked about…perhaps I can be of assistance…in some small way. Here's to a safe voyage for our Captain Howlette," he said, raising his glass in a toast to Molly.

She smiled, touched his glass, and drank deeply before saying, "Yes, let's change the subject. I've been in a blue funk of late worrying about it."

Molly unfolded the napkin at her plate, placing it in her lap. She looked at the food before her, appraising it for some reason. Morris thought this a bit unusual but said nothing. Finally Molly looked up; a faint smile fluttered at the corners of her mouth and was gone as quickly as it came. She picked up knife and fork and began her meal in silence and they continued in this manner for several minutes. Finally after touching the napkin to the corners of her mouth, she said,

"I was just thinking about what you said earlier at the office. You must spend many long hours at your desk. You're responsibilities, at times, must be overwhelming."

"You're quite right, my dear. It can be taxing to both body and soul," he said around a mouthful of food.

"Perchance, do you control the cargo manifests of the local merchants? I've watched, from the docks many times, as the ships are off-loaded, and I've always been amazed at the variety of goods. It's all quite fascinating to me."

He answered, "My position dictates that I be involved in all aspects of shipping activities, including the cargo. The merchants, both buyers and sellers, must submit, in writing, mind you, a formal solicitation. The paperwork must be on my desk several months in advance. There is limited available space in the cargo holds, and it must be allocated to the foot. At times, it can become very tedious, and one must show a great deal of patience. Suffering the wrath of an angry merchant who's just been told there's no room for his goods can become trying, to say the least."

"I suppose military cargo must always come first," she said, "and those poor merchants must have to wait forever to have their goods loaded, while each day of delay is eating away at their profits, my goodness!"

"Indeed it does, my dear. In times of war some cargo will never see its destination. Even in the best of times there are always endless delays and problems to be solved. One must always keep the weather in mind. A sudden storm at sea can send a ship to the bottom in a heart beat, taking a tremendous toll in profit, and lives, and there's nothing we can do about it. It's the cost of doing business. Everyone realizes the risk involved," he said, wiping grease from his chin.

"You seem very interested. I find that unusual for a young lady; especially one so beautiful. Generally speaking, officers' wives and fiancées show little interest in the day-to-day affairs of the military. You're the first one I've met who shows a genuine concern; most unusual, I must say."

An intense, questioning look crossed his face as he tried to fathom her thoughts. Molly laughed nervously and said, "James and I have often talked at great length on the subject. I've spent many late nights listening to his stories of the sea, how ships are sailed and all the wonderful sights he's seen. I must apologize for prying into your affairs."

"No offence taken," he said pleasantly. The waiter came to clear the table and Morris ordered another round of cordials. They talked late into the evening until he suggested they call it a night. Molly agreed it had been a long day and confessed she was very tired after the long ride to London from Briarwood. Morris summoned the waiter, gave him a generous tip, and asked for a carriage to be brought around for them.

Their ride back to Admiralty Headquarters was spent in hushed silence; each lost in their thoughts. Morris could not dispel the notion that something was not right. A feeling of uneasiness crept over him again and again.

"A lovely evening, is it not, John?" He jumped at the sound of her voice. "So peaceful and serene; one would hardly think a war was being waged," she said as she watched the moonlit scenery dash by the window.

"Yes, it is very tranquil, isn't it? The crisp October air makes it seem like the calm, placid city I knew as a child. God willing, this business of war will soon be over, and we can, one and all, return to those carefree days we've longed for all these years," he said in a hushed, muted voice.

Something was wrong, peculiar, odd. He felt a vague empty void pass quickly through his mind, leaving him cold, chilled to his very soul. It was a darkness he could almost touch. Try as he might, he could not put it out of his thoughts. At last they arrived at Headquarters. Morris climbed down, paid the coachman and offered his arm to Molly.

She looked at him and smiled faintly saying, "It's truly been a lovely evening, but I'm afraid I must be off at once; it's a long ride home and I'm so very tired."

"Nonsense! I'll not hear of it. You're much too exhausted to suffer such a trip at this hour. Highwaymen are lurking at every turn. You'll stay the night and leave on the morrow," he said sternly

"If you wish, John, I *must* insist on a private room. I shall settle for nothing less!"

"Of course—of course, now not another word."

He offered his arm and she accepted, placing hers gently through his as they walked the cobblestone sidewalk leading to the massive doors that housed the Admiralty Headquarters. Once inside they ascended a flight of stairs to the second floor turned to the right and walked down a long hallway with plush red carpet. Stopping at one of the many doors Morris turned to Molly and said,

"Please take this room for the night. You'll be completely safe. The door locks from within, and there are no other guests or means of access to the room. Guards are always posted in the building 'round the clock. Before I say goodnight, may I offer you this?" he said, reaching into a vest pocket and withdrawing a small leather pouch. "Take it. Call it a loan if you will, but please take it with my blessing."

"Oh, but I must protest most *strongly!*" she said, raising a hand to her cheek.

"Use the money until you're in a position to pay me back. It's only a gesture of kindness…nothing more!"

He reached for her hand, placed the purse in it, and folding her fingers over the soft leather held her hand in his for a brief moment. Smiling down at her he said softly, "Now off to bed, and a good night's rest for you. I'll not see you off in the morn', for I shall be at my office early attending to business. Sleep well."

Molly looked up into his eyes and said, "My goodness, John. You are so kind and generous! I shall pay back every cent, I promise."

She stood on tiptoe and placed a light kiss on his plump cheek.

"That was quite unnecessary, but far be it from me to turn down a kiss from a lovely young lady!" He stuttered, face turning red, his breathing becoming labored.

"I'm sorry, John; I hope you don't think it improper of me. I sometimes act before I've considered the consequences. I trust I've not offended you," she said timidly.

"Of course not, Moll; besides, it's only a small amount. Should you need further assistance in the future don't hesitate to ask," he said, patting her on the hand. "Now have a restful sleep. Good night," he whispered, with one last quick glance at her cleavage; he smiled and strode down the long hallway.

Molly stood at the door and watched him leave, waiting until she could no longer hear his footsteps. Smiling to herself she dropped the small leather bag inside her purse and entered the room. Locking the door behind her; she surveyed the room closely. A solid cherry dresser with mirror, matching dry sink, and pillared, four-post bed with several beautiful throw rugs on a polished hardwood floor, windows trimmed with lace curtains, a night stand with an exquisite oil lamp, and of course, the chamber pot close under the bed: everything one could want…and then some. She crossed the room to stand before the dresser. Looking at her reflection she appraised every small detail of her form. She removed the pins in her hair and let it fall gently down her back. Disrobing, she turned slowly, first left…then right, looking intently for the slightest flaw. Satisfied with what she saw, she slipped on a thin nightgown from a travel bag she'd brought with her. Sitting down in front of the dresser she began combing out her hair with long slow strokes until it glowed and shimmered in the lamp light.

"So, John *is* married. I was under the impression the lady was only an escort." Cambridge had failed to inform her of that fact. "An oversight, but an important one!" she mumbled to herself. "The task at hand may be easier than I was led to believe. The man's made an ass of himself staring at my breasts all evening. I wonder if he would recognize my face in a crowd; he certainly never looked at it!" She laughed softly at the thought. "He fancies himself to be a shrewd man, but I shall prove him wrong. He's eating from the palm of my hand, offering money for what he believes he'll get in return. What a pompous ass, and a fat one at that!" Molly couldn't help but laugh out loud. "Powerful men always think they can control everything and everyone. Power, money and women consume their minds every waking moment. What fools!"

She arose from the dresser, went to the bed, turned down the covers, sat down, and took a deep breath. It had been a long day and she was exhausted. She was extremely uncomfortable with the entire affair and the stress that came with it left her nerves frayed. Turning down the lamp on the night stand; she lay back and tucked the covers tightly about her neck. She lay in this fashion for a length of time, just staring at the ruffled canopy above her head. "Yes, yes much easier than I'd thought, but I must proceed with great caution.

An old wolf may lose his teeth, but never his nature." She turned to lie on her side and gazed at the flickering lamp flame. Later—much later—she drifted off to sleep without knowing it.

Morris hummed a merry tune as he walked back to his office. The evening had turned out much better than he'd ever hoped for. "An audacious wench, and beautiful, too: a winning combination," he thought to himself. I must approach her carefully. She's quick witted and cunning to a fault. Poor James, if he only knew how he was being used. His hard earned money wasted—thrown away, by what he believes is his true love. Morris laughed out loud. She's using the poor devil like a whores bed sheet, and he none the wiser! A few coins doled out to her could certainly do no harm. I'll just sit back and see where this little scheme of hers leads to. A gold guinea says I'll have bedded the scurrilous little bitch before dear James returns home. The nerve of her! I know what she wants, and she'll pay a *dear* price for it before this is said and done.

Morris entered his office and locked the door behind him. Crossing the room he lit a lamp on the desk and sat down with a disgruntled snort and cleared away an assortment of letters, memos and disheveled paperwork with a swipe of a hand. Removing a gold necklace with key attached to it; he turned to a lower drawer and unlocked it. Opening the drawer he searched through the folders and removed one fixed with red ribbon and wax seal. Holding the folder to the light of the lamp he proceeded to check the seal carefully and finding it undisturbed, opened it and placed the contents on the desk. Thumbing the papers he found the most recent letter and re-read it again, eyes gleaming as he hurriedly scanned the page, mumbling a word here and there to himself. "On or about 10 August 1805...cargo of...aahh, let me see...yes, yes, there it is...I'd forgotten...your humble servant." Satisfied that all was in order he carefully replaced all the papers in the packet and brought the ribbon around it. Melting sealing wax over a candle, he used his special seal, one on which he'd filed two small nicks into the round border. No one else knew of this seal, and he intended to keep it this way.

With the packet safely tucked away in the locked drawer he leaned back in the large leather chair and stared at the glimmering lamp light. Pressing his fingertips together and bringing them to rest under his chin, he sat in the lonely room. The only sound to be heard was the ticking of the mantle clock and his heavy breathing. The letter he'd posted earlier in the day was now delivered and his aide must have returned, and with a bit of luck, in one piece. Highwaymen were as thick as fleas and meeting a violent death on the road was always a constant fear. Morris never rested until the man had returned. Exhaling slowly, he came to the realization that further thought on the subject was out of the question. He could think of nothing but those firm breasts peeking from her dress. His pulse was throbbing again as he lifted himself from the chair and blew out the lamp. Locking the door behind him he walked the length of the corridor to his sleeping quarters; passing by his aide's door he took note of the dim light that filtered through the crack underneath, and breathed a sigh of relief.

He entered his sleeping quarters and locked the door. Turning around, he took in every small detail, making sure nothing was out of place. Satisfied that all was in order, he crossed the room and sat heavily on the bed. It took all the strength he could muster just to remove his boots. The events of the day...his audience with Cambridge...the constant passionate thoughts of Molly, had left him spent and exhausted. Not bothering to remove his cloths he lay back on the bed in a heap and was soon sound asleep.

"The letter was delivered as instructed?" Morris questioned the aide early the following morning.

"Yes, sir. Delivered to the hand of the courier," he said.

"Then I take it you had no trouble on the road?" he asked, turning away from the window overlooking the street below.

"No, sir. All went well. It was a pleasant ride, although quite long and tiring with the round trip, you understand."

"Yes, yes, I know very well. Glad to see you safe and sound," he said, matter-of-factly. "I'll have my usual tea and muffin, if you please."

"I've brought the morning mail. I'll just leave it on the desk before I go."

"Thank you," Morris muttered.

Molly slept late the next morning enjoying the comfort of the warm covers pulled tight around her neck. The cool October temperatures hinted at the freezing cold months that lay ahead. The leaves had all but fallen leaving only the pines to show their dark green glory against the gray sodden sky that hovered just above the tops of the taller trees. Sunlight tried desperately to peek through the heavy overcast but succeeded only in raising a heavy, cold fog that drifted in wisps along the ground. Finally she decided she could no longer squander the morning hours and throwing the covers back, went to the sink; poured water in the basin and washed her face. She took much longer than usual dressing, combing her hair and powdering her face. She was very disturbed about the conversation between her and Morris the previous evening. Several of his comments had left her confused and unsure about what he'd implied. I must win his trust and somehow learn his intentions. I should talk to Cambridge...but I need some definite proof before then. If I told him what I heard last night; he'd roar with laughter, she thought. Molly stood before the dresser mirror, and satisfied with her appearance, went to the bed and retrieved her handbag. After final look around the room to make sure she'd forgot nothing, she closed the door behind her.

She walked down the hall, descended the stairs, through the large brass bound doors to the cobblestone street finding her carriage and driver waiting. Strange—she thought. The carriage must have been summoned early. She stepped onto the street, and the driver met her, taking her bag. "Have you waited long, Harold?" she asked.

"Only a short time, madam, less than an hour," was his reply. "I was called out early so you wouldn't have to wait. Will madam be having breakfast this fine October morning?" he asked.

"I think not. I'll be returning to Briarwood at once."

"As my lady wishes," he said, turning to place her bag inside the carriage. As the driver took her hand to assist her, she looked up to the window of Morris's office and saw him watching her. When their eyes met he stepped from sight, leaving her to stare at the dark, empty window, causing her to hesitate. "Is my lady all right?" the driver questioned, looking at her with some anxiety. "Yes, of course. I'm afraid you caught me day dreaming," she said stepping in and sitting down.

They were away in minutes and out of the city within the half hour. Molly sat staring at the passing scenery, not really seeing it, her mind far too occupied. Hours later the carriage rounded a sharp bend in the road and turned into the lane leading to Briarwood Estates. A beautiful sight, she thought. Much more than James could afford. A sprawling two-story mansion with shake roof, four fireplaces, and large reflection pool nestled in a manicured yard surrounded by a circular drive that led up to the massive marble steps of the house. Majestic elm trees were scattered throughout, lending a quiet dignity to it all. Trimmed hedge bushes accented the house. A lovely garden located behind the house overlooked a duck pond with gazebo. The entire estate covered over two hundred acres of rolling hills. The driver reined in the horse, hopped down from the seat, opened the carriage door and helped her out. Retrieving her bag he escorted her up the steps and through the large double doors of the house. Entering a large reception area with a high vaulted ceiling he stopped and said, "Will there be anything else?"

"I think not, Harold. Thank you for a very pleasant trip," she said with a smile.

"My pleasure, madam." He bowed slightly and touched the brim of his riding cap.

The driver left, closing the doors behind him, leaving her alone in the foyer. Turning to a red rope trimmed with gold finial, she rang for her housemaid, Mary, and asked her to prepare a light repast, saying, "I'm quite weak from lack of nutritious food," fanning herself despite the cool temperature of the house. "It's so good to have madam home again. A pleasant trip was it?" Mary asked. "I'm almost faint from hunger. Please call me as soon as you have refreshment for me. I shall be in my room freshening up and changing clothes."

"Yes, madam," Mary said, and hurried off to the kitchen located in the rear of the house.

Molly climbed the stairs to the short hallway leading to her bedroom and closed the door behind her. She removed her frock and traveling clothes and poured fresh water in the basin of the dry sink. Carefully washing the dust and grime of the long ride from her face she selected a comfortable robe from the closet and slipped it over her head. She sat in front of the dresser and drew a deep breath letting it out slowly. The constant trips to the city were taking a great deal of time, and her strength along with it. She sat quietly in front of the dresser mirror just looking at her reflection. She was simply too tired to think, her mind a blank. A light knock at the door startled her as Mary entered and announced that her meal was ready. She slowly stood as Mary came forward to help her place a shawl over her shoulders. They went downstairs to the dining room where Mary seated her in a favorite chair, unfolded a linen napkin and placed it in her lap. She returned moments later with steaming platters of food that made her mouth water. It smelled delicious. Mary also brought the mail that had accumulated over the past few days and placed it beside the silverware before leaving. As Molly casually leafed through the letters her hand stopped abruptly as her eyes fell on the one before her. Her lips silently formed the words as she read. "From his Excellency, Lord Cambridge." Suddenly…she no longer had an appetite.

Morris sat at his desk casually thumbing through the morning mail. A look of disgust creased his plump, round cheeks as the corners of his mouth lifted in a tight lipped grimace. There before him was *another* letter sealed with the French coat of arms. He was receiving far too many such letters. Opening it he read it carefully, then refolded the letter and placed it in his vest pocket. "Damn the greedy beggars...can't leave well enough alone," he said under his breath. "I must make arrangements at once to stop them from being posted to my office. I'll hire someone to deliver them to me from another address. *They've not honored our agreement!* I'm getting far too many...and it must stop immediately!" he muttered, his anger rising to a fever pitch. "If the bastards are entertaining thoughts of blackmail, I'll have their heads on a pike," he hissed through clenched teeth. He sat at the desk drumming his fingers on the polished surface, mumbling to himself. His aide, Lieutenant Harry Cromwell, returned with tea and muffin, placed the tray on the desk, turned and left the office closing the door quietly behind him.

He ate in silence. The only sound to be heard was the tick of the mantle clock across the room and the wet smacking of his mouth as he set tooth to the muffin. The hour was still early and already his day had gone sour. He realized he must complete the report to Cambridge. Trying to pamper the damned lunatic with page after page of gibberish was starting to tax his imagination. He had long since run out of ideas and had now resorted to long nights at his desk racked in mental torture trying desperately to think of something—anything to please the old coot. Cambridge and his endless paperwork would be the death of him! He tossed off the cup of tea in a single gulp and patted the corners of his mouth dry with a napkin and threw it down on the empty plate. The report would simply have to wait—there were more important matters to be attended to. He needed a day away from his desk. He summoned his aide, tersely informing him. "Cancel my appointments for the remainder of the day. I have some personal business that simply cannot be put off another day. I shall be in the city and will not be returning until late this evening. Don't bother holding a meal for me," Morris said curtly.

"As you wish, sir. I shall arrange for a carriage at once," said the aide.

He went quickly to his room and packed a carpet bag with some street clothes, put a few gold coins in his purse, and tucked a small pistol in the bag just in case he encountered any trouble. Satisfied that he had everything, he went down the hallway to the stairs and out on to the sidewalk. Minutes passed and just as he was growing impatient the carriage came around the block at a brisk pace. Pulling up to a stop, the driver climbed down and opened the door. "Thank you," Morris muttered. The carriage swayed wildly as he put his foot on the step, his considerable weight threatening to topple the entire affair before he finally heaved himself in to collapse heavily in the seat.

The driver closed the door and asked in a Cockney accent, "Where to, m'lord?"

"Twenty-seven Concord Street," was his brief reply.

"Are ye quite sure, m'lord?" the driver said astonished. "That be a rough part o' the district, 'n not fer the likes o' ye, sar."

"Quite sure, you ninny! Now off with you...and none of your whimpering...do you hear?" he snapped back at the man.

The carriage lurched over the rough cobblestone streets as Morris quickly changed from his uniform into the dirty street clothes he'd brought with him in the carpet bag. A final check satisfied him that his manner of dress would not draw attention. He checked the loads in the pistol and placed it under his belt out of sight. Concord Street was a seedy part of town littered with taverns, drunks, thieves, whores—it was the absolute worst that mankind offered up. The carriage bounded over streets in disrepair, the scenery growing worse along with the filth, until nothing but shacks and shanties falling apart at the seams could be seen. Waste, muck and sewage filled the gutters with a squalid odor to match. Finally the coach reined up and lurched to a stop, the driver jumping down to hurriedly open the door.

"Beggin' yer pardon, sar...but th' quicker 'm 'way from here,.th' better off I'll be, I'm a thinking' he said, very agitated, stealing a quick look over his shoulder.

"Yes...I quite understand," Morris said, placing a coin in the trembling hand of the driver. "Mind you return to this exact spot at 3:00 P.M. sharp or I'll have my man search you out and soundly thrash you to within an inch of your life...do you understand?"

"But sar...'tis a great risk to me health jus' bein' here at any hour!" the driver said, his eyes darting nervously from side to side.

"Three o'clock this afternoon, I said, and not another word out of you!" Morris roared grabbing up the man's shirt and shaking him violently about.

"Yes, sar, yes, sar...I be here!" the driver pleaded. Morris released his hold and the man scrambled up to the seat, slapped reins to the horse and disappeared in from sight. He picked up the carpet bag and walked down the dirty street glancing into greasy windows. Eventually he found a grimy tavern that looked promising. Stepping through the soiled doors, he went to the bar and sat down.

"A dram of your finest...if you have it," he said. The bartender reached under the counter and produced a bottle of whiskey and a shot glass, then fixed Morris with a steely gaze.

"I've a bit of business to conduct, and I'm in need of a reliable man who knows how to keep his mouth shut," Morris said returning the stare.

The bartender eyed him for a length of time as he polished a glass then said, "And ye be a payin' customer."

"Handsomely—to the right man," was his reply.

"A gentleman sits at a table directly behind ye' to th' right facin' th' door. Talk yer business with 'm," the bartender said as he cut his eyes over Morris's shoulder. He sipped the cheap whiskey for a few minutes then picked up the bottle and crossed the smoky room to stand in front of the man seated at the table. The man looked up, his eyes filled with such bitter evil that Morris's heart froze in his chest.

He said nothing—only stared until finally Morris said, "A word with you…if you please." The man shifted his eyes to indicate the empty chair across the table from him and nodded his head. Morris took the seat, set the bottle down and rubbed his chin appraising him. Finally he said. "I'm in need of a man to do some errands for me. One who can keep his mouth shut and forget everything he sees. Might you be such a person?"

After a long, cold silence the man spoke in a deep voice that rattled in his chest. "My price be a dear one—can ye pay it?"

"Yes."

"Then speak," the man said through an aura of stale cigar smoke. Morris cleared his throat after taking a sip from his glass and forged ahead.

"I'm in need of a courier to intercept my mail from the post and deliver it to me without being seen."

The man laughed quietly. "You're joking—and I don't like to be toyed with!" The smile instantly left his face.

"This is no joking matter!" Morris said. "If you do as I say, and all goes well, there may be another bit of business for you in the future…if I'm satisfied with your work."

"Very well," he said. "What do you have in mind?"

"I shall go to the post and set up a box for my mail. You are to check the box daily and bring whatever there may be to me at once…without being seen, mind you! If I have a letter to post, you will take it to the addressee in person. Should you ever have thoughts of blackmailing me you will pay for it with your life! I'm a man of power. If you doubt it for one minute—you'll wake up dead. Do I make myself clear on the matter?"

The shadowy figure stared at him for a long time studying the expression on Morris's face, finally saying. "Done."

Morris leaned close, then said. "You'll start next week…on Monday. Call at the third window from the left, ground floor behind Admiralty Headquarters. Tap the window three times…gently! You will receive your instructions then. We do business from the window, and *only* the window! When I leave here, there will be a purse on the chair with your pay. I shall continue to pay you each month thereafter. You'll find me generous to a fault. Do a good job and I'll make you quite wealthy."

Morris tossed off the rest of his drink with a flourish, got up slowly, straightened his clothes, turned and left the tavern without another word. He walked back along the path he'd taken earlier and hailed a carriage which he took to the local post office where he made arrangements to rent a box paying for it with coin, refusing a receipt. He left at once and dined at a sleazy hotel some distance from the post office. He ate alone and out of sight behind a curtained wall reserved for business meetings. After his meal he returned to Twenty-Seven Concord street and found the carriage and driver waiting for him.

"You're late!" the driver said. "I might well o' been stabbed on th' spot! Where ye been…what's kept ye?"

"None of your damned business!" Morris said as he climbed in and shut the door with a resounding crash. "Now off with you—the hour grows late." The driver took the hint and vaulted to the seat touching whip to the steed. With a sudden lurch they were off at such a reckless pace that Morris had to hang on for dear life to stay seated.

As the sun set during the long trip back he changed into his uniform and placed the pistol in the carpet bag. When they arrived, he paid the driver and quickly went inside and to his quarters. Tossing the bag on the bed he went to his office to catch up on any business left for him during the time he was away and attempt to make a few notes for the report due in a few days. He sat down at the desk, and going through the days mail, noticed a parcel that made his pulse quicken. Tossing the rest aside he hurriedly opened it with a small dagger. With trembling hands he tore into the package. His glassy eyes filled with greed as he chuckled softly to himself watching the bundle of pound notes tumble to the desk. He picked up the notes and thumbed through them over and over.

CHAPTER FOUR

An early morning autumn sun cast slanting rays of soft warm light that fell across the dining room table where Molly sat holding the letter in her hand. A look of apprehension distorted her features as she reluctantly picked up the knife lying at the side of her plate and broke the seal. She carefully unfolded it and placed the letter on the table in front of her. Clasping her hands together and placing them in her lap, she leaned forward slightly. Her lips silently formed each word as she slowly read its contents.

His Excellency, Lord Cambridge
Admiralty Headquarters, London

This is to inform you that I have taken the liberty of extending your letter of credit against the Crown indefinitely. Our investigation has broadened to include all officers of flag rank, and their aides. We will continue to enlarge our search for the saboteurs involved in disclosing secret information to our enemy. Since our last meeting I have enlisted the services of several agents, each assigned to a particular flag officer.

I shall make arrangements for a formal banquet honoring the birthday of our good King in late November. You, along with a number of hand-picked agents, are to use this opportunity as a staging ground to launch your own personal strategy. Use the occasion to implement your plan and obtain any information that seems suspicious.

Admiral John Morris is your contact, and will remain so until

further notice. Additional instructions will be forwarded to you at a later date. I need not remind you of the importance of the mission before you. If we are successful, I've no doubt the Crown and England, will reward you handsomely.
   Destroy this letter upon reading its contents.

Lord Cambridge

   She carefully refolded the letter and placed it beside the stack of mail on the table. She brought both hands up and ran fingers through golden locks of blonde hair before resting her elbows on the table to cradle her head as she stared down at the empty plate. Life had become so complicated. Her mind drifted back over the events of the past year and her first encounter with Cambridge. It all seemed so innocent. She and James were attending one of Cambridge's many banquets and she had stepped onto the balcony for a breath of fresh air. A short while later she found herself in the company of the host, Lord Cambridge. They had passed the time with idle chitchat when he abruptly turned to her and very hastily outlined his plan. She had been shocked by his suggestion that she spy on someone and thought it preposterous. She remembered laughing out loud. Cambridge didn't laugh and subtly suggested she reconsider her position on the matter. There was a hint, buried in the conversation that Captain Howlette might expect to spend the remainder of his career on half pay.
   She told him, in the strictest of terms, that she had no experience in such matters. He had said, "That's the beauty of it…who would suspect you?"
   She would become the first of many such "informants." As the months passed he had ordered her to become even more involved in covert activities, constantly assuring her that no harm would come to her as she spiraled deeper and deeper into the plot. Loathing and apprehension were her constant companions. If James should ever discover her involvement in this, more than a few people would regret it. Now it appeared she would have to get Morris alone…somehow. How she would approach the matter was beyond her. First, she must make arrangements with a tailor in the city for the fitting of an elegant evening gown, one that showed her assets to their best advantage. The banquet was less than three weeks away. There was not a moment to lose and she must have some sort of plan in place by then.
   Mary entered the dining room to see if her breakfast was satisfactory. Noticing the empty plate she said. "Is madam all right? You've not touched

the food. Have I not prepared it correctly?"

With her head still resting in her hands Molly replied. "Yes, thank you, I'm fine. I'm just so very tired from the long ride, and I was just going through the mail."

"Madam looks troubled. Was there a bit o' bad news...is someone ill...perhaps a death?"

"No...all is fine. Some news is always good...some bad. Today's was...unexpected I suppose," she said as she picked up a platter of fresh scrambled eggs spooning some to her plate.

"Pour a fresh cup of coffee for me, will you dear? I'm in need of something to cure my doldrums, and those blueberry muffins baking in the kitchen smell divine...bring some in...piping hot, mind you. I'm sure I'll feel much better after I've dined. Yesterday was a long day...a very long day."

"I feel, beggin' your pardon, madam, you're making more trips to the city than's good for your health. A long rest to regain your strength is what you be a'needin'. The good captain will return soon, 'n you must find a way to stop a'frettin' over him. He'll come to no harm; ye *must* believe it!"

"Yes Mary...my dear sweet Mary. I wish it were just James I had to worry about. If you only knew." Her words drifted off in silence. "If you only knew."

A gentle tap at the window brought Admiral Morris out of a sound sleep. He rolled over, groaned, and pushed himself to a sitting position on the edge of the bed. Brushing the stray hair back from his face he sat for a few minutes rubbing the sleep from his eyes and clearing the cobwebs from his mind. The taps came from the window again, this time a little louder.

"All right...all right," he said under his breath. He stood, stretched, straightened his nightclothes and shuffled to the window. Raising it slowly he said. "What have you?" Not a word was returned to him in reply; only a hand appeared out of the dark night with a letter. Morris took it, closed the window and crossed the room to sit at the dresser. Turning up the lamp he held the letter to the light and peered closely at the seal. Satisfied that it had not been tampered with, he broke open the letter and read. His eyes narrowed unexpectedly.

"My God!" he uttered in disgust. Taking a deep breath, he threw the letter on the dresser. His eyes crept slowly up to stare at his reflection in the mirror. A look of repulsion pinched his face. Decades of life at sea had aged him far beyond his years. He was overweight, white haired, his complexion laced with tiny spidery blood veins. He couldn't tell where his chin ended and his neck began. It was all a huge roll of blubbery fat that fell over the collar of his nightshirt. He drew a ragged breath; he was not pleased with what he saw. He had struggled for years; in fact most of his life, hoping to save enough money to some day retire and enjoy what remaining time he had left. Then…a stroke of luck! He'd been unexpectedly appointed Admiral of the Blue and assigned to British Headquarters in London. It was a dream come true, and for many years all went well until one day a French diplomat called requesting an audience. He could recall the day, and the conversation, as if it had happened yesterday. If only he'd thrown the man out of the office, none of this would have happened! He had known then, as well as now, that he could not refuse the offer. His weakness for women and money had been his downfall. It had ruined his life and now his future hung in the balance. Taking another ragged breath, he slowly exhaled and shook his head from side to side. The diplomat had entered the office, sat down in front of his desk, and without uttering a single word; opened a carpetbag filled with British pound notes dumping them in a heap on his desk. *It was a fortune in cash!* He could recollect the very instant it had happened, he was speechless and all he could do was stare, open mouthed, as the money spilled over the desk before him. Before he had a chance to collect his thoughts and recover his composure the diplomat quickly outlined his demands and he had agreed without a second thought.

Months turned into years and the money kept coming. It was above suspicion at the start. Leaking a bit of information here and there—nothing of great importance—cargo manifests seemed to be all they were interested in. As the years passed he found himself being drawn deeper and deeper into their plot. The past year had found him furnishing, not only cargo manifests, but armament lists, dates of departure, course and destination orders along with crew rosters. He was becoming hard pressed to find enough information to keep them at bay. They were, in the letter before him, now threatening to disclose him unless a detailed list of future departure schedules was forwarded along with any current pending orders.

"Dear God!" he muttered. If he supplied everything they asked for it would mean weekly correspondence. He had no choice. The weight of grim reality settled over him crushing the life force from his very soul. Complicating matters further, he'd hired a perfect stranger whom he knew nothing about into this tangled web of deceit. He was caught in a trap and he'd be lucky to escape. The French were generous with their money. He was wealthy beyond his wildest dreams, but tonight money was of little value as the cold, cruel hand of abject fear gripped his throat. He found himself panting, gasping for breath, as if he'd run a foot race; His only hope…to come out alive.

He should have known this would happen. Pride goeth before a fall. He assumed that a high ranking French diplomat would not stoop to something as loath as blackmail. A sly grimace crossed Morris's face.

"I shall just have to outwit the French bastards at their own game." He chuckled at the thought. The stranger he'd hired for his dirty work would not be a problem. If the man ever gave a hint of anything more than delivering letters…he'd find himself VERY dead! That would shut his mouth permanently. Morris began to relax. The man had no idea where the letters were coming from. If one appeared in the box he simply delivered it. If there was a letter to be forwarded he took it back to the post office. How simple could it be! The man probably didn't care as long as he was paid on time.

Molly, on the other hand, was a different matter altogether. He recalled the evening at the hotel and how uncomfortable he'd felt. She was prying into his affairs, using her anxiety for Captain Howlette as a means to meddle in areas that should be of no interest to her. She'd been in his office each week, making idle excuses, using her concern as a cover. For reasons known only to her, she had dropped out of sight. It had been almost a fortnight since he'd seen her. There was the slim possibility that she was just curious and making an attempt to draw him into conversation, but he couldn't shake the thought that she was up to something.

He stood away from the dresser, went to the night stand by the bed and retrieved a ring of keys. Returning to the dresser he selected one and opened a drawer then tossed the letter inside. Locking the drawer he crossed the room, tossed the keys on the stand and sat down heavily on the bed. He'd forgotten to turn down the lamp, but it didn't matter, his career was over—all because of *one man* and a carpetbag full of money. He knew, deep inside, that Miss Bidwell was aware of what was taking place…or was his guilty conscience just getting the better of him. A look of resignation knitted his eyebrows in a frown as he fell back on the bed, rolled away from the light, and stared at the blank wall.

A loud, insistent knock brought him from a deep troubled sleep. Turning over he vaguely heard a muffled voice beyond the door say.

"Forgive the intrusion, sir. It's after eight o'clock in the A.M. and I felt I should call about your welfare, sir," his aide, Harry Cromwell, said in a nervous voice.

Morris turned over, coughed, cleared his throat and mumbled. "I'm quite all right…thank you. Sleep could not find me last night…must have drifted off in the wee hours. I shall be in the office within the hour."

He pushed himself up swinging his legs over the edge of the bed and sat there for a few minutes until his head cleared. Yawning, he stretched and stood beside the bed. After pouring fresh water in the basin of the dry sink he washed and shaved. Dressed in a clean uniform he returned to stand in front of the dresser mirror. His lips formed a thin line. He was ashamed of what he saw. The uniform barely fit over his ever-increasing waistline. A face so puffy and bloated he could hardly find his chin. The dashing good looks of his youth were gone and he hardly recognized the reflection in the mirror. An old, white-haired, overweight man looked back at him. Years of suffering with the poor diet offered while on the high seas had been his undoing. The fresh, delicious food at the local hotels was something he could never refuse—nor get enough of. It had been many years since he'd eaten hardtack biscuit and salt pork, but he could vividly remember the black weevils crawling from the biscuit and the corned beef—so rancid he swallowed it in chunks just to get it down.

He turned from the mirror, dressed and left his room going straight to the office. Harry met him at the door with the morning mail. He noticed *another* invitation from Cambridge. The man seemed possessed with hosting banquets.

Lord Admiral Cambridge sat at his desk leafing through the latest intelligence reports submitted to him yesterday. He was not happy with what he read. His intuition told him that the informant was inside the Headquarters building or had access to confidential files located in the basement. The incoming mail might be intercepted, but that thought had entered his mind many times and he'd immediately dismissed the idea. All the seals remained intact. Strict orders stated that all incoming mail be delivered unopened to the officer it was addressed to. The seals could not be re-attached to the letter without being noticed and he always checked each seal carefully before opening his correspondence. It was mysterious. All of the files in the basement were locked in drawers and the entrance to those files was locked also. Two identical keys had to be inserted in the locks simultaneously to gain entry—and he knew who had the keys. Both were loyal men he'd known for over three decades, still information was pouring from the building. The person responsible could be one of a dozen or more officers. He trusted all of them with the possible exception of Admiral Morris. He had grown very tired of being patronized by him and always came away with the impression that Morris thought he was superior to him in one-way or another. His attitude was one of arrogance, and his mannerisms always put an edge on their conversations. To put it bluntly, he was never at ease and always on guard as to what information to divulge and what not to. All of his officers were dedicated and offered, quite willingly, to do whatever he'd asked of them, and he'd oftentimes asked the impossible. He couldn't fault Morris because their personalities clashed and it was certainly no reason to suspect him of any wrongdoing. Yet, something didn't fit...call it a hunch; he'd harbored the impression that Morris was up to no good. He had exhausted every means at his disposal trying to discover something...anything to substantiate his thought that Morris was somehow involved, but he'd found nothing, not even the slightest clue. He was now looking elsewhere.

Cambridge leaned back in his chair to gaze at the ceiling. He placed finger and thumb to his chin inhaled slowly and pursed his lips in thought. He must have a talk with Harry Cromwell; it was a risk he'd have to take. Drawing another person into the inquiry didn't sit well with him. It meant the possibility that someone would eventually spill the entire investigation to the public. Molly had been a disappointment. She wasn't interested and he knew, full well, that she was a very reluctant party to this. He had boldly asked her to become more involved with Morris in hopes he'd warm to her and give himself away. So far...nothing.

"Mister Baldwin, fetch Lieutenant Cromwell. I should like a talk with the young gentleman." Cambridge said casually.

"Yes, sir!" A shuffle of feet could be heard in the office down the hall as Baldwin hurried off.

He was uncertain about how to broach the subject with the aide. The man would immediately come to the conclusion that Morris was suspect, but he dealt with Morris on a daily basis and might know something. A knock at the door brought him from his thoughts.

"Enter."

Young Harry Cromwell strode briskly into the room, stood at attention and saluted smartly. "At your service, sir!"

"Yes, yes, at ease. Have a seat; I've a matter to discuss with you."

The man promptly sat down on the very edge of the chair; his back as straight as an arrow and placed a hand on each knee. Cambridge gave the young fellow a critical look, measuring him, appraising the result of what he was about to say, trying to decide the best way to open the conversation. Finally, he cleared his throat, swallowed and said.

"Let me be perfectly clear on this matter! What I'm about to say to you is to be held in the strictest confidence. It is indeed a matter of national security, and the fate of England may very well hang in the balance. Any breach of my trust shall be viewed by this office as an act of treason, and as such, your death will be swift and sure! Do I make myself clear?"

He paused briefly to let the statement have its full impact before leaning over the desk to push a Bible in front of the stunned man.

"Place your right hand upon the Holy Word and swear, as God is your witness, that what you hear and do from this day forward will be known only to me!"

The statement visibly shook Harry. The blood drained from his face as he sat in utter disbelief. A trembling hand came to rest on the Bible as he hesitated, unsure if any response was necessary, before saying, "I swear…God as my witness."

"Very well then. It has come to my attention that for some time now, secret information is being passed to our enemy, the French, apparently from this very building. I have taken on the task of finding those responsible and seeing them hanged!" He shouted with great convection as his bony hand slapped the desk with a resounding clap that sounded like a pistol shot. Harry jumped, leaned back in the chair, and grabbed the arms for support, his head reeling.

"I've absolutely no doubt that information is escaping from this very building in some form or another. I intend to ferret out the black devil, whomever it may be, and personally hang the blackguard myself! My question to you is this. Are you aware of anything unusual concerning your superior, Admiral Morris? Have you observed any deviation from normal activity in his office…or for that matter, in the building?" Now take your time, man…think on it. Can you recall anything out of the ordinary…even the smallest detail?"

Harry brought a hand up to rub his chin, eyelids narrowing as he searched his mind thoroughly before saying. "I can think of nothing that has roused my curiosity." He continued staring at the wall behind Cambridge. "But…I must say…one particular thought does come to mind."

Cambridge placed his hands on the desk, leaned forward and said. "And what might that be?" His keen, cunning glance struck Harry by surprise, putting him off his guard for a few seconds.

"A few days ago Admiral Morris sealed a letter with a crest he carried in his vest pocket attached to a watch chain. It seems odd that he chose not to use the official crest sitting on the desk."

"And what of the letter? Can you describe it?" Cambridge drummed a rapid staccato on the desk with his fingers, waiting impatiently for Harry's answer.

"It...was...official business, as I recollect, sir. I believe it was addressed properly. I'm sure it's nothing, my lord; it's the only thing that comes to mind."

"Any unusual correspondence arriving addressed to his office?" he pressed on, hoping to jog his memory.

"No...no, none that is out of the ordinary. I can think of nothing that would point a finger of doubt at Mister Morris."

"Very well. Carry on with your daily routine as if this conversation never took place. If you notice *anything* suspicious, report it to me *at once!*" he said, pointing an arthritic finger at Harry.

"Yes, sir...if I might add, sir, Miss Bidwell has frequently been in audience with Admiral Morris. It appears she is most concerned about the safety of Captain Howlette. Rumor has it that they were seen dining together a few days ago. I'm sure you are well aware of her beauty, and I fear, with Admiral Morris's idolatry of the passions, Captain Howlette may take a dim view of the situation."

Cambridge settled back in his chair crossed his arms and gently rocked to and fro. A troubled, pensive expression lined his frail features. "Now that you've mentioned it, there's another bit of news that may shock you even further. I hesitate to say this...but Miss Bidwell has been in my employment for the better part of the year, along with several special agents. All are involved in the investigation that you are now a part of. She and you are two of many such persons."

"I had absolutely no idea, my lord!" Harry crumpled in the chair as though he'd been struck a blow from some invisible foe.

"Captain Howlette is unaware of my arrangement with Miss Bidwell...and I intend to keep it that way. I'm making preparations for a banquet in honor of our good king's birthday. The entire affair is a ruse, an attempt to let our agents single out their contacts and obtain any information they can...nothing more. You will see that Admiral Morris attends the banquet *alone*. Miss Bidwell will be attending. In the meantime I will inform her about the crest he's carrying on his person. She may be able to shed some light on it. I have narrowed my search to Admirals of flag rank. They are assigned to duty in this building. It is my plan to test the loyalty of each of them in the months to come. You will receive instructions, at a later date, as to what I shall require of you."

"Yes, sir!"

"Very well, then. Keep in mind what has transpired behind these walls and your sacred oath. You're dismissed. Carry on!" He said waving him from the office with a bony hand.

Harry stood, saluted, and said, "Yes, sir!"

Harry returned to his room, entered, closed the door and collapsed behind the desk. His hands were shaking badly. The meeting had lasted only ten minutes, but the impact of those ten minutes had shattered him. His heart pounded in his chest. Clinching his fists, eyes tightly closed in an attempt to control his rapid breathing. He heard Admiral Morris shuffling some paperwork in the next room and prayed he would not call him until he could pull himself together. Reaching for a handkerchief in his vest pocket he quickly mopped at the sweat pouring down his forehead. Thoughts were running through his mind so fast that none of it made sense. He swallowed several times and cleared his throat wondering if Cambridge would really hang him. It was a dangerous business.

Days turned into weeks and gradually Harry found himself attending to his daily affairs as if nothing had happened. He became more at ease and had made a few mental notes of things that even he thought were foolish. Despite close observation nothing raised a flag of doubt, all appeared to be proper. He was beginning to think Cambridge had singled Morris out in an attempt to force him into retirement and was drumming up anything he could to use against him. He'd known for some time that the two didn't get along. Morris could be difficult to deal with and Harry wondered if Cambridge was attempting to create some sort of falsehood to justify his actions once he threw Morris out. The longer Harry thought about the situation, the more he came to realize there were no "spies." He and Miss Bidwell were being used for nothing more than to cull a bad sheep from the flock. Cambridge was a shrewd old seagull. It was a personality conflict, nothing more. Morris was on the verge of being tossed out with the bath water if he made one false move.

Harry felt more comfortable after coming to that conclusion. He was back to his old self, paying little attention to Morris's affairs. Indeed—there was no call for it. Morris came and went as usual; generally informing him of his whereabouts should Cambridge or some dignitary stop by and inquire of his services. The mail came on time. Memos and directives were sent through proper channels and arrived at their destinations without incident. The report Morris had agonized over for the better part of a week had been re-written and submitted. The poor fellow had spent many long nights at his desk researching intelligence reports. He felt sorry for him. Harry was now quite sure there was no spy. The reports were probably being thrown in the trash without even being read. The whole thing was a hoax; a sham...and he decided he would have nothing to do with it. He was an officer of the British Navy and aide to an Admiral of flag rank. A sense of pride welled up within him. He would not allow himself to become a part of this...regardless of what Cambridge thought. He was an officer and a gentleman.

He would not compromise his self-respect!

CHAPTER FIVE

Molly stood in front of the full-length mirror appraising herself carefully. Turning first one way then the other, her hands resting lightly on her hips. She adjusted the front of the dress smoothing the sides and raising a bodice that barely contained her. Yes…this was the gown she'd wear to the banquet next week. If the bodice were any smaller…or tighter she would spill out of it!, she thought as a wicked smile crossed her face. A beautiful red satin evening gown with layer upon layer of lace that shimmered and floated like puffy clouds on a light summer breeze. She pictured, in her minds eye, the looks she'd receive at the banquet. All those sophisticated ladies raising fans to cover their open mouths when they saw her enter the room. The gown was rather modest, but she knew her ample figure made it appear more revealing than it actually was. She took a deep breath and watched her cleavage rise and swell, threatening to burst free of the tight confines holding her in check. After an hour of trying on countless gowns, this was the one. If only she could choose a means of dealing with Admiral Morris as easily, her worries would be over—at least for a short while. She had come to the realization, almost from the start, that she must maintain complete control of any situation that confronted her. Lord Cambridge had stated his desire to obtain a copy of the stamp Morris carried on his watch chain in a letter posted to her a few days ago. She had, for insurance, placed a stick of sealing wax in her purse along with a small candle just in case an opportunity presented itself.

She had dropped by the local pharmacy, before her appointment with the tailor, asking the clerk for a sleeping powder, telling the elderly man that her lover had been away at sea for several months and she was sick with worry and having difficulty sleeping. The old man's face softened with a smile and a wink, recalling his own blind passions of youth. He quietly went to work measuring out a number of ingredients and blended them together with mortar and pestle. Retrieving a small glass bottle he carefully poured in the white powder, tapping the bottle gently on the counter top to settle the contents. He spent several minutes rummaging through a drawer full of assorted corks until he found one that seemed to suit him. Holding it up, he inspected it, and finding it satisfactory, placed it in the neck of the bottle giving it a firm tap. She suffered through a tedious lecture on its usage; paid the man, smiled demurely, and left him with his fantasies. Her immediate problem was how to get the sleeping powder into a drink and then into Morris. She knew him to be fond of strong drink and hoped he would be feeling the effects of it before the evening was over. She thought he might throw caution to the wind and think nothing of her offering him *another* drink.

She saw herself shudder in the mirror as she thought of what she must do and what liberties she must allow him to take before the medication took affect. She had always welcomed the touch of a man, at times she yearned for it, but the thought of Morris's fat hands groping her fairly turned her stomach. *Why had she ever let Cambridge talk her into this!* She knew...deep down inside, it was her weakness for money and high society.

She had quickly grown accustomed to spending the Admiralty's money. Lord Cambridge never questioned any of the credit vouchers. He'd extended her line of credit indefinitely, and she was beginning to like that *very* much. The money Morris had given her, after their evening together, had stunned her when she poured the contents of the leather purse on her bed after returning to Briarwood. It had been her impression that it was only a few quid, but it was over half a dozen gold guineas. Where he'd acquired so much coin was beyond her. An Admiral's commission was meager at best, and he had given her over a month's pay as if it were nothing! There was some possibility he had put away a good deal of prize money from his earlier days at sea. Young, energetic captains in command of well-trained crews had many opportunities to become wealthy very quickly—if they were lucky.

"Forgive me, madam, should we try something a little more demure perhaps," the young dressmaker said with a frown of concern etching her face as she came to stand behind Molly, appraising her reflection in the mirror.

"Oh, no. Quite the contrary; it's absolutely gorgeous! I shall take this one," Molly said, her mind jolted back to the present by the girl's voice.

"It's rather revealing—considering madam's figure. Are you sure? Perhaps something a bit more modest would be in order. Exposing too much of one's self is often viewed by others as offensive and in poor taste."

"Point well taken, but I've made up my mind. I shall take the dress—you will take a note of credit against the office of the British Admiralty?"

"Yes, of course, madam," she answered with a polite curtsy.

"Then the lovely evening gown shall be mine. I'll be the talk of London before the month is over."

"Indeed you shall, madam," said the young lady as she lowered her head and blushed. "I shall put it up in a nice box as soon as madam changes. Will there be anything else for my lady today?"

"Yes—I believe a pair of white gloves would be the finishing touch, don't you agree. Do you have something above the elbow, perhaps?"

"What a lovely idea! I'll fetch a pair at once." The dressmaker hurried away to the storeroom at the back of the shop.

Molly made a mental note to tell Cambridge about the money Morris had given her as she changed into her street clothes. It was probably of little consequence, but she'd leave it to him to sort out.

"A good morning to you, sir. I see you have an invitation from his Excellency, Lord Cambridge, requesting your presence at a formal banquet honoring the king's birthday. If I may be so bold as to say, sir—I have it on good authority that Miss Bidwell will be attending as well. Rumor has it that she'll be wearing a *very* revealing red satin evening gown. A young dressmaker seems to have dropped a word, and well…you can be assured it's true." His aide said with a wry grin on his face.

"Very well…my compliments to his Excellency and tell him I shall be most honored to attend." Morris said, trying to conceal his excitement.

"If I may suggest, sir, that you arrive alone, Lord Cambridge may use the opportunity to meet with the staff officers in private chambers. Admiral Nelson's aide passed the word late yesterday. It seems matters of foreign affairs concerning the involvement of the Spanish fleet will be discussed at some length. Your lovely wife may not take kindly to waiting long hours for the meeting to dismiss. It would be a boring evening for her with nothing to do but chat it up with the ladies. Lovely music and no partner make for an awkward situation to be sure."

"Yes, yes, you do have a point. I shall take your advice. Helen would indeed be bored to tears, and I should not hear the end of it for months to come." Morris said. "Thank you, my good man. Your advice has always been on point. What a pity—such a fine affair spoiled with a conference. But…I must say his Excellency has the welfare of Britain in his hands at every turn and must make use of any opportunity to conduct business. We have a war to win, and no sacrifice is too great for jolly England!" He said raising a fist in the air, shaking it, to emphasize his point.

Morris turned, entered his office and closed the door behind him. He stood for a while with his hand on the door latch as a wicked smile slowly creased his face. "A revealing gown." He chuckled to himself as visions of Molly's heaving breasts ran through his mind. He drew a deep breath, the grin suddenly gone, as he realized what he was about to do. He was powerless to control his lust for her. One moment he told himself he'd do whatever it took to seduce Miss Bidwell, the next a cold shadow of impending doom closed around him turning his stomach to ice. Molly would ruin his marriage and possibly his life. He knew he couldn't resist her charms. Her blonde hair, red lips…a laugh that fairly set his soul on fire; those sultry eyes shimmering with unbridled passion. He shrugged his shoulders. She was a delightfully sweet little tart sent to him by the devil himself to lure him to his doom. Miss Molly Bidwell—the black widow spider would devour him one piece at a time while he watched his own blood drip from her chin! He closed his eyes and clenched his fists in trembling rage.

"Gawd! What's happened to me?" His voice cracked as a sob caught in his throat. Staggering to his desk he collapsed heavily in the chair. He brought his hands up to cover his face and placed his elbows on the desk to steady himself. He sat, unmoving, for a length of time, then reached down to open a drawer at his side. His hand found and gripped the butt of a pistol and brought it up to lie on the desk in front of him. He stared at the weapon, fascinated, unable to comprehend the thought of what he would eventually do.

Lord Cambridge stood at the head of the reception line in the foyer of his mansion shifting his weight from one foot to the other. He had been there for most of an hour and his knees were starting to protest. Admiral John Morris had been one of the first to arrive and was now seated in the reception area chatting with the other guests. The remaining staff officers had drifted in one at a time, politely late, with their wives. The only exception was Miss Bidwell. He retrieved his watch from a vest pocket and checked it again for the third or fourth time wondering where she could be. The meal was scheduled to begin at eight o'clock sharp, and the festive mood would suffer if they were made to wait much longer. With a frown he turned and invited the remaining group of guests in the foyer to join him. "Ladies and Gentlemen, let us not waste another moment of time. Please join me, if you will, in the dining room." He led the procession through the reception area where the remaining guests followed his lead.

It was a feast. Several exclamations were murmured by a small number of guests when they beheld the sight before them. Roast leg of lamb, boiled roast beef surrounded with carrots, potatoes, onions and basil. The last of the fall vegetables had been harvested from the gardens and along with steaming green beans and ears of golden sweet corn piled high on platters were large bowls of fresh lettuce and spinach topped with diced green onions. Carafes of sparkling red wine sat within easy reach. A glazed roasted piglet centerpiece with an apple in its mouth graced the massive dining table. Dozens of candles sent flickering light over the food to lend a romantic air to the entire room. Cambridge stood, after the guests were seated, and brought his wine glass up tapping it lightly with a spoon. Silence fell over the crowded room as he cleared his throat and said. "Ladies and Gentlemen…it is my great pleasure to welcome you here tonight. As you enjoy the fine fare before you, let us keep in mind that it is in honor of our good king. Long live the king!"

"Here, here!" a few cheered amid a round of hearty applause as glasses were raised in a toast. After a few moments he continued.

"Before our fine food grows cold I would also take this opportunity to personally thank all the officers and staff for the many long and tedious hours spent at desks preparing reports and conducting daily affairs of business. England and the crown are much indebted to you. I take great pride in serving my country with each and every one of you, for you have all done very well! Let us pray that, God willing, the war will come to a swift conclusion, and the French will be taught a lesson they'll not soon forget!" Cambridge raised his glass again amidst a roar of cheers and applause.

Steaming platters of food were passed around the table by servants and handmaids. Glasses were filled time and again as everyone enjoyed one of the finest meals they'd had in many months. Light conversation and much laughter filled the room amid the clatter of knife and fork laid to fine china. Three main courses were served up with the final course being a lightly poached white fish in cream sauce and white wine. Desert followed with fresh apple pie, cherry tarts, sweet breads, and blueberry muffins and spiced hot cordials to wash it down with. After the meal Cambridge invited the men to enjoy cigars and a tot of rum in his chambers while the ladies visited in the adjoining room. Later, after everyone had a chance to digest the meal, a dance would be held in the hall.

Cambridge, seated in his favorite chair, lit a cigar, blowing a huge cloud of smoke that engulfed him. His gaze drifted across the room to where Morris sat with pipe and rum in hand. He could tell, at a glance, that he was well on his way…ten sheets to the wind, as they say. His eyebrows knitted wondering what could have happened to Miss Bidwell. He made a mental note to reprimand her, but on the other hand, she may have taken ill. He checked his timepiece. A quarter to ten and the dance was scheduled to begin in thirty minutes. It was an opportunity lost. What a shame…all this for nothing. Such is life…one did not always succeed every time. Bringing his mind back to the business at hand, he cleared his throat loudly to draw attention and waited for the officers to end their conversations. With everyone's attention focused on him he began by saying, "I trust all are enjoying the evening. I'd like to take a few moments of your time to discuss the activities of the Spanish. I'm afraid I must tell you that it appears they are playing an ever-increasing role in the war. Intelligence reports are indicating to us that Spain is receiving gold from the French war effort at an alarming rate, and it can only mean a much greater price paid by England in lost ships and lives. We must discover a means of breaking their supply lines, especially that of Spanish powder and ball. The French cannot fire a shot without powder, and reports indicate they are desperately low. We cannot stop the Spanish from *producing* charcoal and saltpeter, so we must halt *delivery* of such goods at their ports. Our only hope lies in discovering these ports and establishing a blockade. It is my intention to issue orders for said blockades to begin within the next thirty days. Our ships will depart, and with fair winds, be on station come spring of 1806."

Cambridge watched Morris from the corner of his eye. He was listening intently along with the entire room of officers. He could read nothing in his features. His pipe had gone out, and the glass of rum sat on the table before him completely forgotten.

He continued, saying, "But…I've decided we've all had enough of this war, and so we shall enjoy this evening and put those thoughts behind us for a few hours. Let us, therefore, relish this fine rum and rekindle our cigars, for within the hour I will expect all of you to waltz your cares away. Gentlemen—here's to your health and the success of our efforts. May French blood run in the streets and their black souls rot in Hell!" He raised his glass high amid shouts of encouragement from the men gathered in the room. He wondered if Morris had even noticed that Miss Bidwell was not there. He acted as if he didn't care, talking, joking and laughing with his fellow officers. As the evening wore on, Morris stood and strolled about the room, engaging other officers in conversation, Cambridge watching all the while.

The time approached for the waltz to begin and, one by one, the officers began to drift out of the room to find their wives or finance's and make their way to the main hall. Eventually Cambridge stood and invited the remaining officers to join him. The music had already begun and several partners were swaying to the delicate strains of an elegant waltz. Morris was seated next to one of the officer's wives and engaging her in conversation. Cambridge entered the hall and said with a wave of his hand. "Let us not be bashful—please, dance one and all, for we know not what the morrow brings!"

The musicians began in earnest playing a majestic waltz as gentlemen offered arms to wives and lovers. Soon the floor was crowded with couples flowing around the floor. Wine flowed generously as they quenched their thirst and returned to the dance. Morris made a few turns around the floor but chose to remain seated watching the younger couples. Sometimes he raised a hand to keep time with the music. A young lady, in the arms of her partner, turned and appeared to stumble as if losing her balance. She stopped; her left hand covered her open mouth as she gasped. Her stare soon brought the other dancers to a halt as their eyes followed her lead. Within seconds the room was silent as every head turned to behold a young woman standing in the arched entryway as a servant announced, "Miss Molly Bidwell of Briarwood Estates."

The awkward silence continued as fans rose to cool blushing faces. A low murmur began as several ladies whispered amongst themselves. Morris fairly leaped from his seat, his mouth working like a fish out of water. He looked as if he might collapse at any moment, the color completely drained from his face.

"A thousand pardons for my late intrusion, my carriage threw a wheel after striking a stone, and we were rather hard pressed to make repairs." Molly said as she flowed into the room in a cascade of red satin and lace. Her shimmering blonde hair piled high with sequins and pearls glistening from every curl. Her white gloves seemed to glow in the flickering candlelight as she crossed the room to stand in front of Cambridge.

"My dear—how very lovely you look this evening! This occasion is now complete, for you were the only guest not attending. I was afraid some harm had come to you on the road," he said. As he turned around, his eyes swept over the crowded room. A broad smile creased his wrinkled face as he addressed the gathering. "Let us rejoice…Miss Bidwell has arrived safely. A merry waltz if you please, gentlemen, for I shall have the honor of the first dance with this beautiful young lady."

He took her hand as she bowed her head and said. "Thank you, my lord, I should be most honored." The music resumed with vitality as the couples began the dance, led by Cambridge and Molly.

Morris stood, transfixed, as though turned to stone on the spot. Completely unaware of his surroundings; his leaden feet felt as if they were nailed to the floor; ears deaf to the music; eyes seeing only Molly floating across the floor. He held a glass in front of him like a bum on the street corner begging for a coin. He stood in this fashion until the music ended. A young officer beside him jabbed an elbow in Morris's side and said, "Have a care, Admiral sir, or you'll catch a fly in that open hatch and go down with all hands!"

Morris jumped as if he'd been struck with the tip of a cutlass. "Yes, yes…right you are, Captain. Damn me if I've ever seen anything more lovely! Excuse me if you will, for I must have a breath of fresh air to clear my head." He downed the remainder of his drink and promptly poured another from the decanter on the table. He went straight to the double doors and out onto the balcony. Closing the doors behind him he turned and went to one of the many stone benches and sat down. His pulse pounded as his breathing grew shallow and rapid. He stared down at the trembling glass in his hand and tossed off the rum with one gulp in a meager attempt to calm himself…it didn't work. "My Gawd!" He muttered. "I've just witnessed Venus on the half shell!" He looked up; staring through the glass doors again to make sure he wasn't dreaming. There she stood chatting with Cambridge. Suddenly she turned to look directly at him. Her eyes bore completely through the glass rending his soul in a thousand pieces. "This can't be happening!" he said, aghast. "No one can possibly see me on this dark balcony! Not only can the sweet little witch read my mind…she can see in the dark as well!"

A black shadow of despair unexpectedly swept over him like a tidal wave. It was the same familiar feeling he'd experienced a few weeks ago. He was helpless: drawn to her like an insect to a spider web. His passion for her far outweighed his common sense. He forced himself to look away and out over the moonlit landscape to the reflecting pool. Grass sparkled as the first drops of dew turned to light frost. He started to take another drink from his glass; realized it was empty and tossed it into the bushes. He stood, and moved to the stone steps that led down to the gazebo by the pool.

He found himself walking along the bank of the pool and could not recall how he'd gotten there. Stopping abruptly, he looked around and went back to the gazebo and sat down.

He had no idea how long he sat there as the faint music drifted down to him for what seemed a lifetime.

CHAPTER SIX

The disquieting sound of softly approaching footsteps unnerved him. Someone was coming. It must be young lovers stealing away from the party to have a moment alone. Morris made an attempt to leave quietly and not disturb them. A soft voice drifted through the gray moonlit darkness. "John...is it you?"

He stopped, turned and looked for the person who called his name. The voice sounded indistinct, too far away to recognize. He stammered, "Yes, it is I, John Morris. Please come forward; to whom am I speaking?"

"Why, John, it's Molly; surely you must know my voice by now! I've come in search of you. Are you all right? You've left the banquet early, and I thought you had taken ill."

"Yes, I'm fine, Molly. I stepped out for a breath of fresh air, and time seems to have slipped away."

"May I join you? It's such a lovely evening, although a bit cool for this time of the year."

"For a few moments: please take a seat if you like. Should you become chilled we must return at once, for it will do you harm."

"We'll return in a few minutes, but the moonlight on the pool is so beautiful and peaceful. The ducks make such lovely little waves on the water. I simply must sit and watch them. Come...join me, if you will. Sit with me and we'll enjoy the evening together," she said, sitting down and patting the stone bench beside her.

"Well...if you insist."

"I insist! Sit with me. We'll take pleasure in this quiet time alone...together."

"I must have fallen asleep," he thought. "This is all a dream; it's too good to be true." They sat in silence, gazing over the scenery before them. The frost slowly turned the blades of grass to sparkling diamonds of moonlight as the night settled gently over them. Morris was at a loss for words, unsure as how to proceed; his heart pounding away in his chest as he felt her soft thigh press firmly against his leg.

"Oh, John," she sighed. "I've been so worried about James, and I so long for someone to talk to. I'm so lonely. I don't know what's come over me. I've *never* felt this way before."

His blood seemed to have pooled in his chest as he wrung his tingling hands trying to bring warmth and a measure of feeling back to them. He could think of nothing else to say but, "There, there my dear, all will be fine...you'll see."

"Yes, I suppose you're right. I'm just so very lonely. The trouble with the carriage wheel made me feel so helpless and out of control. There I was...a single woman on a dark road at night. Why—anything could have happened!" she leaned toward him placing her head against his shoulder, as a sob caught her voice.

"My goodness, Molly, if anything should happen to you I would *never* rest until the scoundrel was arrested and hanged! You have my word as an officer and a gentleman. Captain Howlette would expect—no, *demand* that I look after your safety and well being while he is away at sea," he said sternly, giving his fat knee a resounding blow with his right hand to emphasize the point.

"You've been such a comfort to me, John. I don't know what I would have done without your constant support and encouragement. I must admit I'm not very good company tonight, and I'm afraid I owe you an apology for spoiling your evening."

"There's no need for an apology, my dear, and you've certainly not spoiled the evening. If I may be so bold as to say, you're the crowning touch."

He gathered all the courage he could, took a deep breath, and forged ahead. "I hope you'll not take what I have to say the wrong way—but would you care to join me later for some light conversation in my private quarters?"

"I'm not sure that's proper, John. You're a married man," she said, toying with him like a cat with a mouse. He was making this much easier than she had anticipated. She leaned away from his shoulder and attempted to stand.

Morris immediately placed an arm around her shoulder forcing her to sit as he urgently said, "I've only the best of intentions in mind, Miss Bidwell. During these past few weeks I've grown quite fond of our conversations and have enjoyed them immensely. Won't you please accept my invitation? A few short hours can do no harm."

She turned and addressed him with a decisive tone to her voice that took him aback, surprising him with its formality. It sounded as though she were giving him a direct order. He sat in silence, hanging on her every word, nervously fidgeting as though he were about to be chastised for his indiscretion.

"I'll go back to the banquet and mingle with the guests. Within the hour I will make my apologies and leave early. Return to your quarters. I'll meet you there in a short while. I'll leave word with my driver that I shall be returning to Briarwood two hours later than planned. I shall *not* spend the night with you under any circumstances, is that clearly understood?"

"Yes—yes, anything you say!" his voice sounding like that of a boy making an excuse to the school master. He removed his arm and stood quickly, turned and without looking back, disappeared into the night.

A look of disgust swept over her face as she watched him leave. Bile rose in her mouth making her swallow several times. She quietly retraced her steps along the path leading to the stairs and onto the balcony. She paused there for a moment, looked around to make sure she had not been seen, opened the glass doors and made a gracious entrance smiling demurely at the guests that took notice of her. Going straight to the side bar she poured a fresh drink. Taking a sip, she swished the fiery fluid around her mouth to rid the foul taste that lingered there. Turning, she noticed Cambridge studying her from across the room. She gave a quick nod of her head in his direction—nothing more. He acted as if he saw nothing, but she knew his look had spoken volumes.

She made small talk with several guests before making her exit saying the trouble they had incurred on the road had exhausted her to the extreme and she was most anxious to return to Briarwood. Making her apologies she left shortly thereafter and hired a private carriage to Admiralty Headquarters. Along the way she checked her purse to make sure she had not misplaced the small stick of sealing wax and vial of sleeping powders. She was anxious for the evening to be over and the trip seemed endless. She wanted nothing better to do than return to Briarwood and put this nightmare behind her but she had become too deeply involved in the scheme to back out now. As the moonlit countryside sped past a recurring thought returned to haunt her. One she had given much consideration. A smile brightened her worried brow as she recalled it. The temptation to falsify charges against Cambridge's account was never far from her mind and with the money Morris was giving her she could accumulate a small fortune within a year or so. As soon as everything was in place she would simply disappear. She had always thought the Swiss Alps would appeal to her.

"Arriving at Admiralty Headquarters, m'lady," the driver said as the carriage began to slow. At this late hour the streets were deserted; the horses' hooves echoed loudly on the cobble stone street. The night seemed to close in around them as the carriage rolled to a stop. Gathering up her purse she took the drivers hand as he opened the door and assisted her from the coach. Paying the fair and offering a generous tip for his trouble, she walked quickly down the sidewalk, up the stairs and through the massive doors without knocking. The guard standing at the door paid little attention as a slight smile raised a corner of his mouth, his eyes following her around the corner. The knowing look on his face convinced her that activity of this sort was viewed as nothing unusual. High-ranking officers bought their pleasure and she was sure the house guards saw a never-ending parade of debauchery every night.

Once out of sight she hurriedly walked down the hall to Morris's quarters on the ground floor. Stopping just outside his door she looked down the hall in both directions and knocked softly. A shuffling sound, followed by swift footsteps, as the door opened suddenly to reveal Morris with drink in hand.

"Come in—come in, my dear. Look lively now," he said urgently. His complexion was already showing the effects of the alcohol he'd consumed during the evening. She stepped in and slipped to the left, her back to the wall, just as the door closed behind her. Clutching her purse before her as a barrier against any advances he might have in mind. He made a feeble attempt at pinning her against the wall, but she had anticipated this and rapidly stepped to the side and out of his reach.

"That's *not* what we're here for, John," she said sternly, shaking a finger in his face. He stepped back, mumbled something, possibly an apology; Molly could not make out the words, smiled brazenly and gave him a wink. She thought he would drop the glass he held in his trembling hand.

"Not so fast, John. You *must* pace yourself. Pour another drink for us while I freshen up," she said, watching his every move closely.

Morris found his faltering voice and said, "Yes, of course, my dear—forgive me. I'm afraid the heat of strong drink has clouded my judgment. I must confess I've never seen a woman as beautiful as you. I've sailed the seven seas and enjoyed the treasures of many a lovely lass, but you are the most perfect creature…" his voice trailed off into silence as he turned, stepped across the room and sat down in a chair beside a small table. He placed his left arm on the table raised his glass and tossed off the contents in one swallow.

She went straight to the table, retrieved his glass and took it to the dry sink by the night stand where the half empty bottle of rum stood. "You've another glass for me?"

"There, on the right hand corner of the sink, my dear—above, on the top shelf," he said, directing her with a finger that he waved in her direction.

"Oh yes, here they are. I'll pour a small tot for myself while I remove some of the dust from my face."

She refilled his glass, along with hers and returned his to the table where he sat, went back to the dry sink, poured water into the basin, patted her face with a damp cloth, then toweled it dry. She noticed him watching intently from across the room, sipping from his glass. Sitting down, she removed the pins from her hair letting it fall down her back in a tumble of golden curls, then brushed it out with long slow strokes. A few minutes later she picked up her glass, then crossed the room to sit across the table from Morris. "A toast to an enjoyable evening." They touched glasses. Molly took the smallest of sips from her drink as she watched him toss the entire contents off in one fluid motion. He set the glass down on the table with a resounding thump, belched, wiping off his mouth on a shirt sleeve.

"My—my, John, I fear you may take too much drink. I must insist that you have only *one* more. I'll fetch another for you," she said returning to the sink to pour another round for him. "Oh my—clumsy me, I've made a fine mess and spilled it," she cooed, pushing his glass back. She turned and brought the bottle to her lips, licked the small opening, and then set it down again. Morris was in a trance, watching spellbound, as his mouth hung open gasping for air. She leaned back found her purse and opened it while she pretended to brush off the remaining drops of rum from her bosom. Eventually locating the small vial she worried the cork from it and poured the entire contents in the glass behind her. She distracted him further by leaning back, and then swept the empty vial and cork into her purse as she pretended to concentrate on removing a stain from the front of her gown.

The rum made his ears ring while he watched speechless at the scene unfolding before his eyes. Molly, finally satisfied that the imaginary stain had been removed, picked up the glass and brought it back to sit it in front of

Morris. He made an attempt to grasp the glass, realized his hand was shaking too badly; reconsidered, then leaned back in his chair, looking at the ceiling trying to clear his mind of what he had just witnessed.

"Are you feeling well, John? You're acting rather strange."

"Yes. I'm...I'm...feeling fine."

"It's so very thoughtful of you to invite me here tonight. There's no one to talk with at Briarwood—just the maid and grounds keeper, and they're usually away doing daily chores and the like. It's so boring—and lonely, and I have no means of keeping up with news of the war. Tell me, is everything going well? Are we ever going to see an end to it all? I've heard tell the French are beginning to take the upper hand. Does that mean James is in imminent danger of losing his ship...or his life?"

Morris continued to stare at the ceiling as he replied, "I'm delighted at having your company this evening. I, too, am without someone to talk to. The war has taken away most of my private life. There's been little time for those precious moments one enjoys as a married man. The quiet dinners alone with the wife have been nonexistent for longer than I care to remember. I must apologize, again for...well...what happened just a few moments ago. You *must* understand...your beauty...and I've...well, been without companionship for such a long time."

"Apology accepted, John. I quite understand, for I, too, have been without James for several months. We must be brave and make the necessary sacrifices no matter how great we may think them to be."

"You're quite right, my dear. I must admit I feel greatly relieved...may I ask a personal question of you?"

"Yes, you may. I'll try to give you an honest answer."

"James...and...well, are you betrothed? Does he intend to ask your hand in marriage?"

Molly laughed gently and replied, "James and I have been close friends for many years, and at times we've thought of marriage, but I'm afraid that will never take place. He truly loves me, or at least I think he does, but his first love is the sea. When he's at Briarwood his thoughts are never far from it, and occasionally I see him gazing out over the hills yearning to return to his ship and be off on another voyage. No...we'll never marry."

Morris visibly relaxed and took a long draught from his glass. Sitting it down again he continued, "Of course you must realize I cannot discuss the daily affairs of the war. I will confess...the French appear to be gaining the upper hand. We are making every attempt at disrupting their supply lines. If we succeed we will have gained a foothold. Our main objective is stopping the flow of gunpowder and ball. Intelligence reports indicate that most of these supplies are coming through Spanish ports. Finding them has been an exasperating task and not easily solved. Not to change the subject…I was wondering if I may be so bold as to invite you to dinner again at some later date? My wife suffers so with the gout and at times is completely bedridden for weeks. The time I spend with her drains the energy completely from her physic, and I'm afraid it leaves her susceptible to the fevers more often than not. I'm sure she wouldn't mind if I spent an evening, now and then, with the lovely *friend* of Captain Howlette. What do you say, my dear? It can do no harm."

His elbow slipped off the edge of the table. He leaned back in the chair; eyes blinking several times trying to clear his vision. "What's…I…my head, I'm not…" Placing his hands on the arms of the chair he tried to stand but slipped and collapsed back into the chair. He looked at Molly, with glassy eyes, completely confused. His head drooped as his eyelids became heavy and then closed.

Molly sat motionless in her chair waiting for the drug to take full effect. Minutes later his heavy, rhythmic breathing told her he was sound asleep. She rose immediately and went to the dry sink and picked up her purse returning to the table where Morris sat. Making a careful search of his pockets and finding nothing of interest, she detached the watch chain from his vest pocket and removed it along with the seal. Pulling the chair closer she sat down across from him and rummaged through her purse until she found a small slip of paper and the stick of sealing wax. Drawing the lamp close she removed the glass chimney and held the flame to the wax melting a small puddle onto the paper. She carefully picked up the seal and pressed it into soft wax, blowing on it until it was cool to the touch. Studying the impression intently for an instant before putting it in her purse; she saw nothing wrong with it. She shrugged her shoulders leaned over and placed the watch and chain back in his vest pocket attaching the chain through a button hole closing the clasp.

With a look of disgust she stood and went to the wash basin, sat down, and twisted her hair up in a bun pinning it quickly in place. Returning to the table she swept the stick of wax into her purse and with one last look around the room went to the door. Glancing over her shoulder to make sure Morris was sleeping soundly she gripped the door knob.

"Swine!" she hissed, a sneer curling her lip. Closing the door behind her, quietly, she hurriedly left the building.

Wanting nothing more than to escape, to get as far away from Morris as quickly as she could, she returned to the ball and hurriedly instructed her personal driver to make haste to Briarwood in the early hours of the morning. Completely exhausted, she slept most of the day, arising in the late afternoon. She ordered a hot bath brought to her room and soaked until the water began to cool, scrubbing herself until her skin was rosy pink, trying to wash away the soil from the previous night.

Time seemed to fly as she busied herself around the house. She often took long walks on the grounds enjoying the last of the brilliant fall colors. Early one day the geese that had been a part of the scenery for the better part of the summer decided it was time to fly south for the winter and had startled her as they arose in a great flapping cloud of white wings. Stopping to watch them as they joined up with another flock high overhead she lifted her dress turning around and around, laughing as she fanned her petticoats higher and higher attempting to fly away with them. At last the noise of wings and calls faded; the flock disappeared from view. She strained her ears as one last call drifted down, beckoning her to follow. Standing motionless, her arms hanging limp, still clinging to the hem of her dress; she sighed, wiping the tears from her eyes and continued her walk alone.

Riding silently along in the swaying carriage Molly clutched her purse tightly in her lap. The day she dreaded had, at long last, arrived. It was just after 9:00 P.M., and she was anxious to be off the road; it was not safe to travel alone at such a late hour. She tried to think of some way to tell Lord Cambridge that she wanted out of this nightmare and secretly hoped that after tonight he would dismiss her after he got his hands on the copy of the wax impression she carried in her purse.

"Please come in, Miss Bidwell, and have a seat. I'm sure you recognize Lieutenant Harry Cromwell, Admiral Morris's aide, so I'll not take the time to introduce you." Cambridge said, rather matter-of-factly, as he motioned her to a chair in his private study.

Molly took a moment to study Lieutenant Cromwell and for the first time realized just how handsome he was. His dashing good looks and polite innocent smile reminded her of a young mischievous school boy.

"You will recall that I've requested a copy of Admiral Morris's private seal—the one he carries on his person. Were you successful…have you obtained the copy?"

"Yes," she said, reaching into her purse, drawing forth the slip of paper with the wax seal attached, placing it on the desk in front of Cambridge.

"Ah....Excellent! Please gather 'round, for we were fortunate in obtaining another impression Lieutenant Cromwell has taken from the official seal on Admiral Morris's desk."

They each took a turn looking keenly at the two seals, comparing them closely for the slightest imperfection. Finally Cambridge was the first to speak. "I can find nothing unusual. What say the two of you?"

"I found nothing out of the ordinary the evening I made the copy. Both impressions appear identical."

"If I may be so bold as to ask, m'lord, to make an impression of the seal on your desk, sir. Let us then compare the three of them."

"Very well, although I see no need of it."

They examined the seals carefully again and found nothing.

"Well—the bloody things are all identical. I haven't the foggiest idea of what he's doing with the seal on his watch chain. I'm beginning to think we are on the wrong trail to be sure," Cambridge said tapping his bony fingers on the desk.

Harry continued to inspect each of the seals closely as they sat in hushed silence. Molly sat with hands in her lap. She had not the slightest interest in any of these proceedings and only wanted to be away. She decided not to reveal the comments Morris had made while they dined at the hotel some weeks ago. The gift of money was no one's business. She was on the verge of making her excuses and take leave of all this nonsense when Harry suddenly spoke.

"See here—there *is* a difference! Take a look at these two small nicks, m'lord. Could this be what we've been searching for?"

Cambridge leaned forward in his chair, bending over the desk to closely study the marks Harry was pointing out. Turning them around several times, he finally spoke. "What could it be? It appears to have been put there on purpose, but then again it could have been caused by abuse of some kind—or normal wear. They appear to be perfect, too uniform to be caused by accident: precisely the same depth and spacing. Exactly placed at the bottom of the seal. Morris must have placed them there for a purpose…but why? This is indeed a puzzle," he said, slowly shaking his head.

Molly desperately wanted to be away; anywhere…it didn't matter, just away. "I must be insane. How could I have gotten myself into this horrid mess! They'll pay a dear price. I'll make sure of it!" she thought to herself, while Cambridge and Lieutenant Cromwell continued to study and compare the two seals. Her plan was set in stone from that moment on. Cambridge and Morris would rue the day they ever met her. Morris would be in rags begging on the street when she was through with him.

"Swine!" she whispered under her breath.

"Did I hear you say something, Miss Bidwell?" Cambridge asked glancing at her with a questioning look.

"Oh…it's nothing m'lord," she stuttered, somewhat unnerved that she'd said it loud enough for someone to hear.

Harry was next to speak. "Something has just crossed my mind. I've just now realized that I've not been called upon to post any letters with Admiral Morris' personal seal for several weeks."

"What do you mean by that? It seems to have no bearing on the matter, whatsoever."

"I've been called upon to post letters on a weekly basis. Mind you—all were sealed prior to being received by me. I've witnessed the use of his personal seal on only two occasions and *both* were addressed to the *same* courier. I've just this minute realized the letters have suddenly stopped."

"Huummm…we *must* intercept one of the letters, but if they've stopped it must not be anything important. Was anything unusual about them? Did the name stand out in your mind?"

"No, they appeared to be a matter of daily official correspondence, and the courier I delivered them to is in our employ."

"Well…that leaves me no choice but to find a way to search Morris's files without him knowing," Cambridge said as he casually glanced at Molly.

"NO!" she said with authority, "Not again! I'll not be a part of any scheme you have in mind, and I shall not sleep with the man for all the keys…or gold in England! I have allowed myself to be used much more than I've ever thought possible. NO! Find another way or I shall inform James of the bloody affair you've put me through—I swear—I'll do it!"

"Yes, yes, Miss Bidwell, I quite understand your position on the matter. If we can—with your assistance of course, uncover Morris's activities, and if by some slim chance, he proves to be our spy, England and the Crown will reward you handsomely. Do you understand what that could mean? You'll be put up in the grandest of styles for the remainder of your life. You could name the price of your pension from the king himself…and no small one at that!"

"Well…" Molly hesitated. She realized she may have spoken too soon and was having second thoughts.

"Miss Bidwell, I've had your honor in mind since the evening I confronted you on the balcony of my estate. I apologize. I've been out of turn asking you to put yourself in a situation that's certainly not proper for a lady. Keep in mind, if England should lose the war we'll pay for it for generations to come. The lifestyle we have enjoyed will be gone forever—never to return. If I survive to stand trial I will surely be hanged, shot, or placed in prison to rot, and you may rest assured, my dear, that no good will come to you. God only knows what will happen! We *must* sacrifice ourselves! I've given you an opportunity few will ever have. Fame and fortune will be ours if we succeed."

Lieutenant Harry Cromwell was stunned at the statement he'd just heard. He stared, unable to comprehend the full impact of it, at the mantle clock over the fireplace across the room. *Self respect be damned*, he thought. *It's all true! This is indeed a grave matter and not something from Cambridge's imagination.*

The naked truth of the situation struck Molly as if she'd been slapped across the face. She knew now, for the first time, that she could *never* walk away. She was committed, body and soul, for good or evil—whatever the outcome.

She'd either be rich...or dead!

CHAPTER SEVEN

The hotel dining room was quiet now, after the mid day rush had passed. Molly sat alone at a corner table twirling the long stem of a wine glass between her fingers, watching pedestrians stroll by the window enjoying the warm sunshine. Now half past two in the afternoon the hotel waiters were beginning to cast sidelong glances in her direction wondering how long she intended to stay; they were anxious to clear the tables and prepare for the dinner crowd that would soon start arriving. She was wrestling with the problem of getting a copy of Morris's keys and was completely unaware of her surroundings. Today, just like yesterday and the day before, she hadn't the slightest notion of how it could be accomplished. She kept seeing that dreadful set of keys over and over in her mind. She could have copied them at the same time she made an impression of the seal if she'd only known! She'd have to think of a new approach, but the more she thought about it the more she realized, for all practical purposes, it was impossible.

It was an exceptionally warm day. The entire month had been sunny and mild for some reason known only to Mother Nature. Rain and fog had replaced the usual winter snows and freezing temperatures. Seven days after the banquet she had received a letter from Morris begging her forgiveness and asking for another chance to make amends. He suggested the two of them enjoy the unusually warm weather with a picnic on the downs. He also stated in the letter that he'd slept for the better part of forty-eight hours and had not awakened until late Sunday night. Molly came to the conclusion that the sleeping powder could very well have killed him. She had forgotten, until reading the letter, that he had consumed the entire vial. A smile crossed her face for a fleeting moment. It was a shame it hadn't killed him. Her part in the affair would end and she could carry on with her life. The most exquisite torture still lay ahead. She intended to extract a dear price from him before another year passed.

The waiters were busy preparing tables; spreading fresh linen and arranging clean silverware for the coming evening meal. A handsome young man approached her asking, "May I refresh m'lady's drink?"

"No, I think not. I shall be leaving shortly; I've another appointment to attend to this evening." Rising from her seat and brushing her dress with a napkin, she gathered her purse from the chair; tipped the waiter generously, and went to the front desk to pay her bill. Passing quietly through the dining room and into the lobby of the hotel, she paused to take in the grandeur before her. It was one of the finest hotels London had to offer. The attention to detail and splendor of the surroundings, at times, overwhelmed her, making her feel like royalty. I could grow accustomed to this treatment very quickly, she thought, as she passed through the lobby and on to the street where she hailed a carriage.

The driver stepped down, taking her elbow to assist her into the cab, then asked."Where to, m'lady?"

"Admiralty Headquarters if you please. I'm afraid I'm in a bit of a hurry. I would appreciate it if we could move along quickly."

The driver touched his hat, climbed to the seat, picked up the reins and touched the whip to his steed. Molly gazed out the window of the carriage as it sped over the cobblestone street and watched the couples stroll along the avenues enjoying the warm late afternoon sunshine. Slanting rays of sunlight flickered through the majestic elm trees lining the street, casting playful shadows that danced and ran around the interior of the carriage. The brisk air racing across her face made her skin tingle. Taking a deep breath she closed her eyes, enjoying the invigorating sensation. The carriage continued winding its way along the streets as the sunlight slowly faded, turning from bright yellow to a crimson orange, signaling the close of another warm, lazy day. An hour passed as they sped through the city. The evening light gradually gave way to twilight as a golden yellow moon rose from the east to proclaim its dominance over the night. The carriage slowed, and then stopped in front of the massive building she'd grown so accustomed to seeing. The driver jumped down from his seat, opened the door and politely offered his hand. Molly accepted and stepped onto the street giving him a generous tip for his trouble. She turned and discreetly climbed the polished marble steps leading to the front entrance. The guard on duty recognized her as she passed in front of him. He smiled and winked, remembering the visit she'd made a few short days ago. The look on his face left no doubt that he also remembered the revealing red dress. With a look of disgust, she flipped her hair, raised her chin, covered her neck with a fan, stiffened her back and hurriedly walked past him. Passing through the foyer, she turned left and walked the length of the long hallway to Morris's office. Admiral Morris's aide, Harry looked up when he heard the approaching footsteps and courteously said, "Good evening, Miss Bidwell."

"Yes, it is a good evening. Quite lovely, if I may say so."

"May I be of some assistance?" he asked. A brief note of tension laced his voice as his eyes bored into hers trying to discover some dark secret buried deep within her. She stood in front of his desk and returned his stare for some time as volumes of thoughts drifted between them. They both knew what she was there for. As if by magic, a silent pact was formed between the two of them; in an instant fate had bonded them. Years later, both would recall this day and the precise hour it happened, remembering the experience as though it were only yesterday. Neither of them spoke. Words were not necessary. Harry lowered his eyes and awkwardly shuffled through the papers on his desk for lack of something better to do and said without looking up. "A moment, if you will...I shall inform Admiral Morris of your arrival." He stood, nervously pulling down his vest with both hands, and passed down the short hall to the door. He straightened his coat and thrust his chest forward, pulled his chin back and knocked three times.

"Enter."

He immediately opened the door, stepped in, closed it, and crossed the room to stand in front of Morris's desk. Coming to attention, he said, "Miss Molly Bidwell has arrived. May I show her in?"

"Well—what a pleasant surprise! Yes, of course! Please show her in at once. The cargo manifests can wait a bit longer."

"As you wish, sir." Harry turned and left the office without another word. Closing the door behind him he looked across the short distance that separated them and simply gave a nod of his head. A diminutive smile briefly touched the corners of her mouth and was gone as quickly.

"Thank you," she said coming close to him. She stopped unexpectedly and placed her hand lightly on his arm saying, "Don't worry—I'll be fine." Harry made an attempt to reply but couldn't find the words. She opened the door, but before she entered the office; glanced over her shoulder to find

Harry's eyes upon her. She smiled softly, closing the door behind her.

"Moll—my sweet. How lovely it is to see you again. Please—have a seat. I'll pour you a drink," he said fumbling with the decanter and glasses. "Let me extend another apology to you for the way I behaved last week. I remember your admonition quite well. Strong drink, I'm afraid, seems to have gotten the better of me. I can only imagine how very upset and disappointed you were. Let's just put the entire matter behind us; good things always come to those who wait." He filled another glass and passed it to Molly. He raised his in a salute to her and without waiting for a response, took a healthy snort of sherry, downing it in a single swallow. Molly took a small sip and smiled faintly.

"Damn me...ah, pardon my French...but damn me if I can figure it all out. I've been on more than a few roarin' drunks in my younger days, but for the life of me, I can *never* remember taking two days to sleep it off! I thought I had several more sheets to put to the wind so to speak...can't recall a thing after that. Perchance...can you clear the matter up for me?" He sat down in a large, over-stuffed chair, then leaned back with a puzzled look on his face.

"Oh...John, it's all so perfectly clear! You must realize you're not as young as you used to be. Mother Nature occasionally makes fools of us now and again, perhaps the sight of these were more than you could take," she said throwing her shoulders back causing her ample breasts to rise.

Morris roared with laughter as he slapped the desk with a fat hand knocking a stack of papers to the floor.

"By Gawd, Moll—I do believe you're right! The very thought fairly sits my head to reeling." He pulled a handkerchief from his vest pocket and proceeded to mop the tears of laughter and sweat from his brow. Minutes later he recovered his composure, saying. "Tomorrow promises to be *another* beautiful day. What say we leave our cares behind and have that picnic on the downs?"

"Why...thank you, John. I would be most pleased to join you; after all— we seldom get this kind of weather, and we must enjoy every moment while we can."

Excellent—excellent! I shall send for a carriage to be delivered at eleven o'clock sharp. You are staying the night in the city—are you not?"

"Yes, I'm at the Hotel Saville."

"May I have the pleasure of dining with you there this evening?" he asked.

"I must disappoint you, John, for as you can plainly see, I've arrived late and have already supped. Now don't look so sad...remember...all good things come to those who wait."

"Well—I suppose you're right, my dear, but I fear I cannot wait much longer. What a pity—I must dine alone...again. But please, stay the night here in the headquarters building. There are *many* vacant rooms, and for your piece of mind you may choose a room on the second floor. Why spend money when you don't have to? Rooms are furnished at no charge to guests...and you are *my* guest."

"I must admit...you have a point, John. I'm rather hard put for lack of funds, and staying here for the weekend will certainly save what precious little I have left. Thank you for your consideration. You always seem to have my best interests in mind. I shall call for a hot bath. I want to be as fresh as a spring tulip come tomorrow morning."

Morris gripped the edge of his desk so hard his knuckles turned white. Sweat poured from his forehead in torrents while he stared, open mouthed, at her gently heaving chest. "Jesus!" he mumbled.

"Tomorrow at eleven, then. I'll not take a moment more of your time; you've work to do," she said, making her way to the door.

"Ah...yes...well...I'm afraid work is the furthest thing from my mind, but I suppose I must press on with these manifests," he said surveying the floor, and then reached down to search aimlessly through the jumbled papers. Clutching assorted sheets in one hand and mopping sweat with the other he said, "I swear Moll, you've cast a spell over me. I'm insane with the very thought of you!"

"You *must* have patience, John," she whispered, letting her hand slide down to rest lightly on her stomach. Morris was speechless. The color drained from his face so rapidly he looked as though he might faint at any moment as she smiled at him.

Closing the door softly behind her she stood with her back to it. Her eyes met Harry's a short distance away. She'd hardly noticed, until now, just how handsome he really was. His shining black hair, blue eyes and broad shoulders foretold of great strength; yet his demeanor appeared to be quiet and gentle. A strange feeling crept over her as he sat looking at her. She realized, deep inside, that somehow they were meant for each other.

"Are you all right, Miss Bidwell?" he questioned anxiously. A pensive look of apprehension briefly knitted his eyebrows as he continued to watch her closely.

"Please...call me Molly," she whispered, raising a finger to her lips, signaling him to remain quiet. "After all...we're working together, and I shall settle for nothing less than first names...Harry."

They continued to look keenly, each silently appraising the other. A magical aura filled the room. The air was electrified with a feeling one gets just before a thunderstorm; charged with an essence one can feel yet not see.

Harry's eyes relaxed as a slow smile softened his face. "Thank you...Molly. It is indeed a pleasure to know you. Captain Howlette must be a proud and happy man to have you by his side."

The sensual sound of his whispering voice made her flush with emotion, confusing her. She was at a loss for words as she walked by his desk. Gently she reached out to lightly brush over his folded hands; then looking over her shoulder she said tenderly, "We shall meet again...soon." She hurriedly left the office before he could reply.

Her heart fluttered like a butterfly on the wing. A flush of heat crept slowly up her neck as beads of sweat formed tiny droplets at the hollow of her throat. His shimmering blue eyes continued to haunt her with each step. She swore the very scent of him followed her down the hall.

She turned and climbed the steps to the second floor going straight to the room she'd used before. The door stood open. Taking the key and entering the room she closed the door and locked it. Tossing her purse on the dresser she crossed the room to lie down on the bed. It had been a long day and the anxiety of dealing with Morris always left her emotionally drained. Sometime later she awoke and realized she'd fallen asleep without knowing it. She sat up, stretched, and began taking off her dress. Standing, she lightly stepped out of it and placed it over the foot of the bed. Pulling the pins from her hair she walked to the dresser, sat down and began brushing it, then poured water in the basin to wash her face and hands patting them dry with a towel; placing the towel over the back of the chair. Something caught her attention as she passed by the window across from the bed. She stopped to see what it was. Someone was cautiously approaching the window of Morris's quarters. She leaned forward and watched intently as the shadowy figure stopped and tapped at the window. A minute or two passed; the window opened and a small parcel passed into a waiting hand. As the shadowy figure started to leave she realized she was standing in plain sight and quickly stepped aside. The shadow paused for a few seconds, turned and melted into the night. Molly stood with her back to the wall, glancing over her shoulder watching the intruder disappear into the night. Suddenly she remembered what Harry said a few days ago. "The letters have suddenly stopped." Had she, by accident, discovered why they'd stopped? Her heart raced at the profound thought of what had just happened. Could it be a blind stroke of luck? She made a mental note to tell Harry. Something suspicious was taking place right under everyone's nose! Admirals simply *did not* conduct business from their bedroom windows in the middle of the night. First the seal on his watch chain…and now the devious little scene she had witnessed. A malicious eyebrow raised as a smile fluttered across her face. Her plans had just taken a turn for the better. Humming to herself, she went straight to bed and turned down the lamp. Pulling the covers tightly around her chin she fell fast asleep; her bath completely forgotten.

She slept late the following morning; ringing for breakfast around 10:00 A.M. and asked the maid to prepare a bath. A knock signaled the arrival of the bath just as she finished her tea and muffin. Shortly after the maid left with the breakfast tray she filled the tub, carefully testing the temperature, removed her gown and gingerly stepped into the water. She gradually eased into the tub sliding down until only her head was above the soapy bubbles. Completely relaxed, she floated in a wistful reverie enjoying the caress of hot water on her body. She rubbed the rough wash cloth over her again and again feeling the dust of the long carriage ride melt away to leave her fresh and clean. She closed her eyes letting her mind drift and float in the misty cloud of steam surrounding the tub. Harry's face appeared unexpectedly. He was trying to tell her something. She could see his lips forming the words over and over. What was he saying? The words looked familiar…she seemed to know what they were but just couldn't put them together. Gasping, she sat up, holding on to the sides of the tub. Frowning, she lay back again. For another half hour she soaked until the water grew cold, trying to make sense of the strange premonition. Finally, she decided to put the whole thing behind her. She had just finished toweling herself dry when a soft knock echoed at the door.

"Excuse me, m'lady, the carriage has just this minute arrived. If you're decent, may I enter and help you dress?" a young voice asked from beyond the door.

She rose from the tub and wrapped a towel around her saying. "Yes, of course…please come in. I could certainly use some help, for I fear I must have dosed off—I seem to recall a rather strange dream."

The young maid entered and crossed the room to stand by the bath. Molly removed the towel and placed her foot on the side of the tub to dry it. Hearing a gasp, she turned to see the maid with a hand covering her mouth staring. "Oh—excuse me m'lady…but…forgive me for saying this…you are *very* beautiful indeed! Such a small waist…and those hips—my word!" she stammered. "As you are well aware, few of us are so blessed!"

Turning slowly in front of the maid Molly smiled and said. "I suppose you're right. I've always had a problem finding clothes to fit in a proper manner," as she pointed to her ample bust line.

"I should say so, m'lady!" the young maid said with a chuckle. "As you can plainly see—I've *never* had that problem!"

With the maid's help she hurriedly dressed and was just finishing with the last of the buttons when she heard Morris's voice just outside the door. "Forgive me, Moll—but our carriage awaits, and we should be off. Are you properly dressed?"

"A moment longer, John," she said picking up her purse and hurrying toward the door, leaving the maid to clean the room.

Morris offered his arm to her as they went down the hallway and out onto the street. It was a beautiful day. Puffy clouds floated through a deep blue sky as bright sunlight peeked from behind them. Their carriage waited by the curb and Morris helped her in, then sat down heavily in the seat beside her, slapped reins to the horse, and they were on their way. A brisk ride through the city soon brought them out into the open country side. It was unusual to see barren trees and brown grass in contrast with such warm temperatures and sunshine. Several deer and a flock of wild turkeys took notice as a red fox peeked from behind a tree to watch them as they sped along. An hour later found them traveling down a secluded country lane. Molly was very concerned. It was evident that he'd chosen a private location somewhere ahead and intended to get her as far away from civilization as possible. If he forced himself upon her she would be unable to fend off his attack or call for help. To save herself from harm, she would have to submit to his advances. He'd been strangely quiet, probably thinking about what he intended to do once they arrived. A cold chill of fear crept up her spine at the thought. She jumped as she felt his hand pat her on the knee. "Not too much further, my pet. Just over the rise—where those trees are in the distance," he said. The hand remained on her knee as she felt his fingers dig into her flesh.

"I've taken the liberty of not bringing dessert—do you mind? I believe it's sitting beside me!" He said as his hand slowly began to creep up her thigh.

She forced a seductive smile, trying to remain calm as she stuttered.,"Nnnnnot in the carriage, John! Please…we have all afternoon." She placed her hand over his to stop its advance as they continued to ride along in silence. A wicked smile creased his face as she cast a sidelong glance in his direction. She had to stall for time; as much time as it took to think of a way to handle the situation that confronted her.

They crested a small hill at a fast trot and descended into a peaceful meadow dotted with trees. A lazy stream trickled over glistening, round stones as it wandered along to some unknown river far away. They reined up and helped her down then unhitched the mare to let her graze on the lush early winter grass that lined the meadow. Molly walked to the tree-lined stream, eyes searching the vast, open countryside. It was a desolate, vast, empty space. She noticed the clouds building in the far southwest. The breeze had picked up somewhat since noon. Morris approached with the picnic basket and blankets. The heavy basket was almost too much for him. When he arrived, he was red faced and completely out of breath.

"My goodness, John...here—let me help you. I'll spread out the blanket. You look as if you might faint," she said fanning out the blanket and letting it settle to the ground.

"Thank you, Moll. I seem to recall someone telling me I'm not as young as I used to be," he chuckled between gasps for air.

Molly knelt and threw open the basket lid saying. "There...there, sit down and rest while I unpack our lunch."

Looking inside, she was astonished at the quantity of food. Several pieces of fried chicken surrounded with slices of cold ham with kale stuffing, a large container of potatoes, fresh baked bread, soft cheese, with green onion and carrot spears. On the side were small containers of butter and jam along with a bottle of wine and another of rum. Sorting through everything she noticed a brown bag of something she'd never seen before. Reaching inside she brought out a crisp slice of thin potato. Holding it up for a closer inspection she said. "What could this be?"

"It's a sliced potato fried up in hot pork fat m'dear, then lightly salted. Try one—I'm sure you'll enjoy it."

She sampled one and found it delightful: crisp and crunchy with just a hint of rich taste. "Wonderful!" She exclaimed around a mouthful of potato chips. "You simply *must* tell me how they're made, and I'll tell Mary to prepare them for me as soon as I return to Briarwood. They're delicious!"

"If memory serves me correctly—my chef discovered the trick quite by accident. A slice of potato slipped from the cutting board into a pan of hot fat. He fried up a few more and I've insisted on them ever since."

John had a strange look on his face. "Are you feeling ill, John?" she questioned. "You seem to be rather pale...and you always sweat so much."

"As of late, I've been having these spells—indigestion, I suppose, and my breath grows shorter with each passing year. I'll have just a small portion of food, if you please. I'm afraid I may have overdone myself with yon basket. I'm sure I'll be all right in a short while. Whatever it is usually passes once I've rested for a few minutes," he said holding a trembling hand to his chest.

"Here's a tot of rum for you. It helps relax the stomach."

"Thank you." He took the glass and tossed it. "Aaahhhh…" he said with great relish. "That should do the trick."

Molly unpacked the basket and prepared two plates of food and poured a glass of wine. She noticed he was feeling much better when she offered him a plate. He sat up, leaned back against a tree and began to attack a chicken leg with a purpose. Quickly cleaning his plate he passed it to her saying, "Another round, if you please, my pet. I seemed to have made a complete recovery." He reached for the bottle of wine and poured a full glass then tossed off half of it, refilled it again, then set the bottle down beside him.

"Some of that stuffed ham, along with the chicken…yes…that's it! Now pass the soft cheese…oh, yes and the bread along with it."

Molly turned her eyes away. He was a glutton, pure and simple, and watching him eat was almost more than she could endure. She had become increasingly aware of the clouds building in the far west. The warm breeze was slowly dying as an eerie calm began to descend, the air heavy with moisture. Concentrating first on a slice of ham, then her, Morris was completely unaware of the menacing clouds. She noticed him looking at her and smiled as a puff of wind lifted her dress. His eyes went immediately to her thigh, so she decided not to cover herself.

"Please, John…slow down a bit. You must save plenty of room for dessert," she cooed as a dress strap slipped off her shoulder.

"Don't fret, my lovely. I've a sweet tooth that's *never* been satisfied," he said around a mouth of food. "Now for a bit of bread and butter…and jam for the finishing touch. Come—sit here beside me. We'll rest a short while and digest our meal. I've a delightful afternoon planned for just the two of us. He patted the blanket beside him and she had no choice but to move closer. Finishing off the last crumbs of bread and jam he put his arm around her waist, forcing her against him. She leaned over, looking up at the sky, as the clouds began to turn an evil yellowish-green color. An unexpected gust of fitful wind caught her skirt again and brought it up to cover her face as Morris sat up quickly to rub a grain of dust from his eye. A large cold drop of rain landed heavily on her bare leg causing her to flinch.

"What? I say…we're in for a bit of a blow!" he said squinting at the darkening sky. The wind gained strength as more rain began to fall. They scrambled to pick up the food trying to hold down a blanket that threatened to take leave at a moment's notice. A roaring wind preceded a white wall of water approaching in the distance. A brilliant flash of lightening stabbed the afternoon sky followed by a resounding clap of thunder. Morris looked up just in time to see the mare in full flight. "Whoa there!" he shouted as the mare fled, tail held high. He struggled to his feet and started after her as fast as his fat legs would carry him. "Avast that damned running, will you! Come 'round, if you please!" He whistled loudly and the mare's ears perked up. Slowing down to a trot; she turned around to look in his direction, snorted, then stopped about a quarter mile away.

Molly rolled with laughter as she watched the comical sight. She held her sides catching her breath just as the torrent of rain struck. She could hardly see between the sheets of water that separated them. Pulling the blanket over her head in a feeble attempt to protect herself from being drenched she backed against the tree to wait for Morris. A half hour later he returned with the mare, hitched up, loaded the sodden blankets and food in the carriage. Both were soaked to the skin; cold and shaking—there was nothing left but suffering. The clouds rolled and boiled as a frigid wind blew from the north making the ride almost unbearable.

Hours later they arrived at the Headquarters building. Molly was so cold she could barely move as Morris escorted her to her room. Deep concern lined his face as he asked, "Are you going to be all right? You're shaking like a leaf."

"Call for a hot bath at once, John. I'm afraid I've taken a chill. I'll soon know if the fevers have set in!" She said through chattering teeth.

CHAPTER EIGHT

Immediately Molly entered the room, closed the door and hurriedly pulled off her wet clothes. Stripping to the skin she went straight to bed, tucking the covers over her head. Curling her knees up and placing her arms around them, she lay in this fashion until the maid arrived. Peeking from beneath the comforter, Molly watched her prepare a bath and a few minutes later she came over to the bed, asking. "May I assist m'lady? Your bath is ready."

"Yes...you most certainly can!"

Another maid entered the room just as she threw back the covers and made a dash for the steaming tub.

"See—I told ye so!"

"Right ye are—Bonnie. I don't believe it, but I've seen it with me own eyes—'n it's the truth fer sure," exclaimed the second maid.

Molly appraised the gawking faces while she settled into the steaming water; a heavy silence engulfed the room. Although she desperately tried, she couldn't help the hearty laugh that came from deep in her; the maids joined in, laughing and slapping their thighs, the tension broken.

"Perchance—did someone lose money on the wager? A pity if you did, for I cannot help the way I look," she said. They all roared with laughter. After drying their eyes and catching their breath, one of them said jovially, "I've not the coin to bet, but I would surely 'a lost this 'un. A more beautiful body I've yet ta see."

She soaked for a long time. As the water cooled it was replaced with more hot water brought from the kitchen downstairs. Bonnie brought a steaming hot towel to wrap around her head and neck. Molly lay back, feeling the warmth penetrate and chase the chill from her bones. A soft knock at the door, "How are you feeling, Moll?" It was Morris. "May I be of further assistance? I've ordered hot soup from the kitchen—and a pot of tea. Would you care for anything else…anything at all?"

"No, John. I shall know if I've caught the fever soon enough."

"I should *never* forgive myself if you do, my dear. I'll check on you in the morning; get some rest, and have the maids heat some bricks in hot towels to place at your feet tonight." He coughed several times, cleared his throat, then left, his footsteps echoing down the hallway. The soup and tea arrived shortly, and she sipped a bowl while in the tub, then washed it down with a bracing cup of tea and a muffin. Feeling much better she raised a hand and a maid promptly helped her stand, covered her with a towel, and began rubbing briskly.

"Thank you both for being so attentive. I believe I'm quite able to take care of myself now." She went straight to bed and watched the maids remove the bath and wet towels.

"Ring if ye should have the need, m'lady. One o' us will be awake all night, a'cleanin' what needs it and makin' the breakfast fer the morrow. I'll make sure them hot bricks is brought up right away so's ta snuggle yer toes to."

"A good night's sleep and I'll be fine—I'm sure." Molly lay in bed thinking about the events of last night. What could Morris be doing?

What correspondence was so secret that it had to be passed through a window at midnight! She remembered Harry saying that secret documents were *always* assigned to military couriers during normal business hours. What type of document was so important that not even Admiralty couriers could deliver it? She wondered if the shadowy figure saw her at the window. Probably—she was standing in plain sight. Did the stranger care if he was seen? Yes—no…it was difficult to say for certain. Out of the blue, an idea popped into her head. She would pretend to be sick and stay in her room for several days recuperating. Each night she would sit by the window, out of sight, to see if the stranger returned. Morris could be doing nothing more than paying for the services of a prostitute. It was possible the stranger was a pimp collecting his fees. Her thoughts were interrupted by a maid bringing hot bricks wrapped in towels to place at her feet. The soothing warmth soon put her fast asleep.

Early the next morning Morris came up to check on her. She didn't let him enter the room saying that she was not well and feared a fever was setting in. She could tell, by the tone of his voice that he was beside himself with worry. Her breakfast was brought in shortly thereafter and she enjoyed a quiet meal alone. Days passed and Molly settled into a routine of sleeping during the day and sitting by the window at night with the lamp turned down. Morris continued to check on her several times each day and was beginning to be nuisance. She had established the perfect alibi and intended to make the most of it. The room was dimly lit—just enough light to move about and no more. She sat alone on the hassock by the window peering over the sill. She was beginning to think it was all a waste of time. Four nights had passed and she had seen nothing; this was the fifth night and she was running out of time. She couldn't pretend to be sick for weeks—Morris would become suspicious. Visions of Harry crept into her mind as she stared blankly out the window to the ground below. She saw his face drift in and out of her mind, his whispering voice and those shimmering blue eyes. She bit her lower lip gently and drew a deep breath letting it out slowly. She knew nothing about him, yet something told her differently. It was as if she'd known him all her life, but how could it be? They'd hardly talked. What strange attraction could possibly draw her to him? His image constantly flashed into her mind, distracting her thoughts, making her feel giddy inside.

 Her body tensed as she gripped the edge of the window sill. Something or someone moved just outside Morris's window. Maybe it was just a stray cat. There were plenty of them in the alleys at night. Watching intently, eyes just above the edge of the window waiting for the slightest sign of something out of the ordinary; she was beginning to think her eyes were playing tricks…when…there…yes—just outside the window a shadowy figure appeared. The sound of three faint taps drifted up to her. Moments later the window raised and another parcel passed into Morris's waiting hand. He then passed a similar parcel to the stranger. She was watching the scene unfold just as it happened days ago. The shadow paused, looking directly at her window. Her breath caught in her throat as she fought to remain deathly still, her heart racing. As quickly as it appeared the shadow melted into the night. She immediately came to the realization that the stranger had seen her at the window before and was watching the *same window* again! Sitting with her back to the wall breathing in ragged gasps she pondered the question of what to do. She found herself, an hour later, still sitting on the floor afraid to move in fear that the stranger was still watching and waiting for her to reappear at the window. If she planned to survive and carry out her extortion against

Morris, she had to make absolutely sure that someone else knew what was going on. She knew that she would have to make Morris realize that killing her would accomplish nothing and her untimely death would expose him and whatever little scheme he was up to. Only one possible thought came to mind and she quickly stood, crossed the room and put on her robe. Opening the door, looking both ways to make sure the hall was empty; she quietly went downstairs to Harry's quarters. Taking a deep breath to calm down she lightly knocked at his door. Waiting a few seconds she knocked again, a little harder, and heard the muffled sound of footsteps. The door opened to reveal Harry clutching at his robe with one hand and rubbing his eyes with the other. His mouth dropped when he recognized her.

"What the deuce! Miss Bidwell—Molly—what's the matter? I was under the impression you were quite ill. This is *most* improper…what on earth!" He stuttered, completely taken aback by the sight of her standing before him.

"Sssshhhh—may I come in?" she whispered, holding a finger to her lips.

"Well…well…I suppose, but we're not properly dressed…and…"

She quickly pushed him aside, entered the room, and promptly closed the door behind her.

"If Captain Howlette should hear of this…I'll be…"

"*Enough* of James! We have to talk…*now!* Come—sit with me, for we must not be heard." She took his hand and led him to the bed and sat down motioning him to do the same. He reluctantly sat down beside her mumbling, "I don't believe this is happening! What in God's name is the matter?"

"Be quiet! I've something to tell you—now listen to me!" She said, sternly shaking a finger in front of his face to get his attention. He sat, looking intently into her eyes, waiting for her to speak. She continued. "Saturday night of last week, as I was preparing for bed, I saw a strange man tap at Morris's window and pass a letter—or small package of some sort to him. There were no words spoken—at least none that I could hear. It happened so quickly I was hard pressed to remember exactly what took place. Tonight—it happened *again!* The same tapping—another parcel…or letter passed through the same window. This time he gave the man something in return, it looked like a letter. These past few days I've pretended to be ill with a fever. I've waited at the window each night for the man to return, and fifteen minutes ago—he appeared! I'm here to ask a favor of you. You must come to my room and sit with me. I want you to be a witness to this. Late tonight, after everyone has retired, scratch at my door with your finger…I'll know it's you. You can return to your room before dawn to catch enough sleep so as not to draw attention to yourself. I'll pretend to be recovering from the fever until we *both* see him again. *Something* is taking place right under our noses, Harry. This is not normal...he's up to something."

Harry sat in stunned silence. "Cambridge may be right after all. The very man I've served under all these years could well be a spy! My Gawd...it can't be true. Perhaps it's something innocent. Could it be he's paying for the services of a woman and doesn't want it known publicly?"

"Yes, Harry...it could be something entirely different. It's too soon to know at this point. We must get our hands on one of those letters. Put some thought on it, Harry. I *must* know what's going on here...I *have* to know!"

"Now don't take it so seriously, Molly; we'll find a way. You're taking the entire matter much too personally. After all, it's Cambridge's responsibility to take action against Morris. We're only here to gather information—nothing more."

"Don't patronize me, Harry! You don't understand. We've only known each other for a short time, but trust me on this. It is imperative that I know what's in those letters!"

"Very well, Molly...very well. If it will ease your mind, I'll sit with you. I agree with you. It doesn't seem proper—passing something through a window in the middle of the night. I'm sure Admiral Morris would be quite embarrassed if he were found out. I still find it hard to believe he may be passing secret documents out the window! There seems to be nothing unusual about his daily activities...but...but maybe it's all taking place at night with no one the wiser. This is all so confusing. I can't make sense of it all."

"Tomorrow night, Harry...I'll be waiting for you," she said rising and walking to the door.

"Yes, yes, of course. I'll be there," he said, slowly shaking his head from side to side in dismay.

"Please, Harry—be patient with me on this. I shall explain it all to you soon enough. I have our best interests in mind. It's just you and me, and we must look after each other," she said softly. "Remember what I said a few days ago; don't worry!"

Harry looked up at her from across the small room and said, "All right...but be careful...for me."

They watched vigilantly from the window of Molly's room for several nights, working out a schedule that allowed each to catch a few hours of sleep. A routine soon fell into place that was comfortable for them. Harry usually returned to his quarters around 4:00A.M. Molly learned a great deal about

Harry while they passed the long hours at the window with conversation about their past. He'd worked his way up through the ranks to captain. After receiving his commission and commanding more than a dozen ships he soon realized he couldn't control the crew. The ships company soon discovered that he was too kind hearted and unable to lead with authority. When the crew became unruly he was transferred to another command and allowed to start again. His reputation always preceded him and he was eventually re-assigned to staff headquarters as an aide. It was a crushing blow for his career. Over the years he'd begun to see it as a blessing for he still remained on active duty and had learned to make the best of his situation. For the most part, he was satisfied with his lot in life. As an only child he felt quite comfortable living alone, had never married, was rarely seen in the city and preferred dining by himself. He took great pride in being thrifty and saved most of his monthly allotment in the hopes of retiring early.

Molly found him very easy to talk to. His gentle actions and quite voice had a calming effect on her and his sense of humor, at times, made her hold her sides with laughter. They'd been together for only a few short nights but she knew, that should they ever part, her heart would leave with him.

Molly's mother passed away when she was very young, just seven years of age. Her father couldn't cope with the responsibility of raising a young child and had sent her to foster parents a year later. He had stopped by, from time to time, to see about her well-being but the visits grew farther apart and soon after he remarried they stopped altogether. Years passed and she had lost track of him completely. Her foster parents had doted on her; spoiling her with the finest clothing and toys that money could buy. She was now a beautiful mature woman in the prime of her life. Blonde hair fell over her shoulders in a cascade of bouncing curls. She had a creamy white complexion and an hour glass figure. Despite her best efforts at modesty she always turned the head of every man that saw her. Rather tall for her age of twenty-six, she stood five feet six inches on long slender legs. Harry was only about five of six inches taller; she guessed him at about five feet eleven inches. Dark shining black hair, blue eyed, with fine features. Broad shoulders and flat stomach with a trim waist and strong legs, he was a gentleman in every sense of the word. He had never made an advance toward her during their many late night watches together. Somehow she was disappointed at this but appreciated the fact that he could control himself in an intimate situation. She was wondering how she could break the ice without seeming too forward. Sitting with her back against the wall, she turned her head and quietly studied his features while he watched the window below. Her eyes drifted from his face to watch his slow steady breathing. A feeling of joy constricted her throat as she thought of the rare treasure before her. Swallowing hard, she said. "Thank you, Harry."

He looked at her and smiled, then returned his gaze back to the window. She reached out, and on impulse, laced her fingers through his and gave them a light squeeze. He studied their hands for a few seconds, and then looked at her face; a slight frown knitted his eyebrows as his thumb began to gently rub the side of her hand.

"Harry, James and I are friends. We've known each other for many years but...we're just friends. I wanted you to know that."

"I had no idea! I've was under the assumption that you were betrothed and would marry him."

"No...I'm afraid not, for you see, dear James is married to the sea. I've known for some time that sailing was his first love. I *do* care about him...but I don't love him. Do you understand?"

"Yes...I do," he said pursing his lips, melancholy sweeping through him like a tidal wave of destruction. It was some time before he could continue. "I, too, loved the sea...but it was not to be."

"In a way...I'm glad. I would not have met you were the circumstances different."

A bewildered look came over him. "What do you mean?"

"How can I say this without seeming immodest? It is so very difficult for me...you see..."

"You'll not offend me," he said turning toward her. "Take your time—it's all right." He clasped her hand in his, studying her expression. "What can it be?"

"As strange as it may seem—I've grown fond of you. It all started a few weeks ago. Forgive me, Harry. I'm so uncomfortable with this...trying to explain myself...I'm so nervous. I've *never* felt this way before."

Harry said nothing. He sat very still just holding her hand and studying her intently. Completely defenseless, Molly trembled uncontrollably. She could feel his eyes boring through her flesh, searching for the soul she had long since given up for lost.

"It's time for me to go. I'll return tomorrow night and we'll talk. I thought...well...you and...I didn't know. Now things will be different."

"Oh,.Harry...she sobbed, as a tear ran slowly down her cheek.

"Until tomorrow." He stood, turned and was suddenly gone.

Crushing silence descended upon her. She had no idea how long she sat on the floor rubbing her hands together, biting her lip and staring at the door. What did he think of her? Had she said too much? She had only intended to tell him that she and James were friends, but it had all tumbled out. For an instant, regret overpowered her, threatening to force the very air from her lungs. Rising from the floor she crossed the room and sat down on the bed. Tears spilled from her eyes as she lay back and fell asleep; completely exhausted.

She awoke the following morning to face a day she thought would never end. The conversation they'd had last night was constantly on her mind. She paced the floor for hours on end, attempting to eat when she had no appetite only made matters worse. Morris checked on her twice during the day and she jumped each time he knocked at the door. Evening finally came and she stood by the door for hours waiting for the faint scratch that would signal Harry's return. At last, she heard soft footsteps approaching and held her breath with anticipation. *A scratch!* She threw open the door, immediately causing Harry to step back in surprise. Reaching out, she took his hand and pulled him into the room closing the door behind her.

"I'm sorry, Harry. I'm *so* sorry," she pleaded. "I've made a complete fool of myself. You must surely think me a trollop...a scarlet woman...but...I..."

"Ssshhhh..." he said placing a finger on her lips to silence her. "You only spoke what was in your heart."

"Yes...but I was so bold...so outspoken...It was not proper for me to say such things. We hardly know each other."

"Take hold of yourself, Molly...you've not offended me. I've seen the look on your face after you've met with Admiral Morris, and it's spoken volumes about your character," he said reaching down to hold her hand.

"I just don't want to lose you. Promise me, Harry, please," she begged.

"I promise."

And so they stood, their hands clasped tightly together, feeling the tide of tender affection—of deep admiration course through them. Years later they would fondly recall the moment they had became one; drawing upon each other in times of distress. From that precious moment on, they were forever calm and unshaken by the storms of life. Complete, as it were—their love tied by a golden chain that could never be broken.

"Look at you! You're crying again. We have work to do—such as it is," he said gently as a smile raised the corners of his mouth.

They laughed. Molly felt the tension drain from her. "Yes—you're right.

I'd almost forgotten. I've been so upset," she said wiping the tears away. "I'll just wash up a bit."

Harry pulled the hassock up to the window then sat down to make a quick check of Morris's ground floor window. He turned to watch Molly wash her face then comb out her hair. She was the most beautiful woman he'd ever seen. He felt as though he'd known her all his life. It was so comfortable—so complete—so peaceful just to be near her. She crossed the room to stand in front of him. He patted the seat saying, "Come...sit here with me."

She sat beside him and felt his arms circle her waist. Leaning back against his chest she gave a sigh of contentment. They sat through the long hours of the night clinging tightly to each other, sometimes swaying gently to and fro as he hummed a waltz in her ear. With the lamp turned low; the warmth of his body soon put her fast asleep.

She felt his muscles tense as he suddenly leaned forward. Rubbing the sleep from her eyes she vaguely heard him whisper, "Ssshhh...look!" Molly blinked her eyes several times and squinted over the window sill.

"Yes...that *must* be him. He's here again. See, I told you," she hissed. "You're an eye witness to this, and that's all I need."

They watched as the dark figure tapped at the window. Within minutes, two letters were exchanged, and the man left hurriedly.

"That's *exactly* what I saw a few nights ago," she whispered. "What do you think they're doing?"

"I haven't the foggiest idea!" he exclaimed. "They can't be passing secret documents—the trick appears much too simple."

"But who would suspect it?" she asked. "Something is being passed out the back window—why not an official document? It's so simple. Who would ever dream such a thing could take place right under their noses?"

"We must inform Cambridge of this at once."

"NO...not yet. We need to discover exactly what's going on, and intercepting one of those letters is the *only* way. Harry—can you arrange for someone to overpower whoever is receiving the parcel and bring it to us? It will have to take place away from headquarters so as not to draw attention to us."

"Well—I suppose I can. It will take some time—maybe a few days—possibly a week, but I think it can be arranged."

"Good...then all I have to do is wait."

"Very well then. I see no further need of watching Admiral Morris's window. I shall inform you when we get a letter."

"When will I see you? She asked urgently. "Can we not meet tomorrow night—just for a little while?"

"I think not. It's a great risk just being here, and a small wonder I've not been found out. The less we're seen together—the better. I'll see you…when you've recovered," he said with a sly wink of his eye.

Molly pretended to remain weak from the effects of her fever and told Morris she was making a slow recovery. A few days more and she'd be strong enough to return to Briarwood. Morris was overjoyed with the news and ordered fresh snow crab and lobster for her lunch. As one day turned into another, Molly became bored. Penned up in her small room with nothing to do, she read every book on the shelf above the bed. She had not seen nor heard from Harry and decided nothing further could be accomplished until they obtained a letter and without it she could not put her plans into action. Later that afternoon she gathered her few belongings together and prepared to leave the next day. The temptation to watch the window each night was almost more than she could bear but the risk of being seen was too great. The run of good luck was more than she deserved and common sense told her not to take too many chances.

Early the following morning Molly rang for the servants to carry her bags down to the street. Before she informed Morris she was leaving, she stopped by Harry's room to tell him, "I'm returning to Briarwood. I can't stay here any longer or Admiral Morris will become suspicious. I can do nothing more. You *must* inform me immediately when we have one of the letters."

"Of course—but I still don't understand why you are so concerned about it. This is really none of our affair. We'll have to be patient and see what develops."

With Molly gone, he was just closing the door when he heard Morris shuffling down the hallway. Breathing a sigh of relief, he collapsed on the bed. It was a waiting game now.

Morris opened the door when Molly knocked and invited her in. "How nice it is to see you've made a complete recovery, my dear," he said enthusiastically. "I've been most concerned about you. A hot meal would do you good…and a breath of fresh air. May I have the pleasure of dining with you this fine morning?"

"I'm afraid not, John. I'm so very weak from the fever and I fear I should faint at the slightest exertion. It has tapped my strength to the limit, and I must return to Briarwood to afford myself a long recovery. You've been so very attentive, and it was such a comforting feeling just knowing you were close by. Would you be so kind as to hail a carriage for me? I simply *must* return to my estate and rest. I only hope the creditors haven't called while I was away. Forgive me, John, but…may I borrow a few coins? There may be unexpected bills to pay. I've kept a record of how much I owe you. Do you mind?"

"Of course not, my dear!" Morris beamed, reaching into his vest pocket to retrieve a handful of gold coins. He placed them in her hand saying, "There you are. Take it with my blessing."

"Thank you. I've had such a difficult time of it lately."

"Yes, I quite understand. Life can be taxing at times, but take heart, it will pass and you'll soon be on top of the world."

"I've an idea you may be right. I feel my luck is about to change, and yours as well," she cooed in a sultry voice as the strap of her dress slipped from her shoulder.

Reaching out, he took a step toward her. "I swear—you are the most beautiful creature to have ever walked the earth!"

"Please, John; I'm far too weak for what you have in mind. I *must* ask you to restrain yourself—until I'm fully recovered," she purred, lacing a finger beneath the strap to toy with it for a moment before slipping it back in place.

Morris was panting, gasping for breath, "Very well—as you wish, my pet. May I sit down? My chest is aching from the want of you—and my breathing has become so difficult of late," he said rapidly. His skin had turned a transparent, sickly white color, as sweat beaded on his forehead. "I've noticed, lately, the spells are coming more frequently. I'm not feeling well at all." He staggered to a chair and said, "I'll just relax for a bit."

Molly watched him intently as he recovered his composure. It was quite obvious he was very ill, suffering from some mysterious ailment. Several minutes passed before he struggled to his feet and said, "I'll hail a carriage for you—but I *must* return to my quarters and lie down. Excuse me." He promptly left the room, leaving the door open. Molly watched as he reeled down the long hallway holding a hand to the wall to steady his trembling legs. He occasionally stopped to draw a deep breath and hold his chest. A look of agony lined his face as though he'd been run through with a saber.

"I hope the bastard doesn't die—before I can fletch his money," she thought to herself. It must be quite a fortune; judging from the gold coins she jingled in her hand. "When I get my hands on that letter; the game will begin."

She said good-bye to the maids, giving each a hug and thanking them for their services, then stopped in to talk to Harry. "How's he doing?" she asked upon arriving at his desk.

"He seems to be quite ill. I've heard him coughing. It's the season for fevers, and he may be coming down with one. Time will tell."

"Maybe he'll die!" she whispered to him wickedly.

"Molly!" he said aghast. "How can you say such a thing?"

"If he'd drop dead, we could leave this wretched business behind," she said as emotion cracked her voice. Harry sat back in his chair. He knew she spoke the truth. With Morris out of the way the entire affair would be at an end, and he and Molly could live a peaceful life together. He swallowed and stood abruptly trying to clear his head. "Well…you may be right…eh…who knows what fate has in store?"

"Are you all right?" she asked.

"I was just daydreaming—about us, and…"

"What were you thinking?" she questioned anxiously.

"It was nothing, just rambling thoughts."

"Can we go to your quarters…for just a little while? Morris is ill, and no one will miss you. I want to be alone with you…please," she whispered to him.

"Molly—have you forgotten! There's a war on! If I leave my post without informing someone of my whereabouts I could be in serious trouble!"

"But I won't see you for so long…and I…"

"I'm sorry—I can't help it. I must carry on with my duties, and you must return to Briarwood. I'll write. Now off with you…and have a safe journey." He reached out to brush a tear that lingered on her cheek.

"I'll shall miss you terribly!"

"And I you…but it must be this way."

She turned and hurriedly left without looking back. Tears blinded her eyes as she ran down the hallway and out onto the street. Her carriage was waiting and the driver politely helped her inside. Seeing her distress and handkerchief held tightly to her face he said nothing. They hurriedly got underway. The carriage bounced and swayed as it gathered speed.

"Dear God!" she sobbed, as fresh tears flooded her eyes, realizing, for the first time, that she'd loved him from the first day they'd met.

CHAPTER NINE

A giant whirlpool of kaleidoscopic color swirled around Morris as he lay in a cold sweat; thrashing about in bed, desperately fighting the demons pulling at his limbs attempting to draw him into the abyss. A hacking cough had grown continually worse forcing him to bed three days after Molly returned to Briarwood. Several physicians were called in for an opinion but after administering a saline drought and a bleeding, his condition grew worse. Proclaimed him in the hands of God they packed their instruments and left shaking their heads. His prognosis appeared bleak at best and his recovery, if he survived, would take months. Harry posted a letter to Molly explaining the situation and the probable outcome the day after Morris took ill.

Two days later the letter arrived at Briarwood and Molly immediately packed a small valise while the carriage was brought around. Within the hour she was on her way to London. A rare opportunity had presented itself, if she arrived before Morris's fever broke, she would enter his room and make an impression of the key that fit his desk. If a copy could be made quickly, it would allow her to search it, and with any luck, find *something* to substantiate the claims against him. Watching the scenery pass by the carriage window she fitfully drummed her fingers on the wooden ledge. If Morris should die unexpectedly, she would be in poverty. Her lifestyle had grown quite lavish on the open account provided by Cambridge and the offerings of Morris. The meager funds James provided were little more than four pence in an empty larder and had long since ceased to satisfy even her simplest desires. Her insensible greed for money stood in stark contrast between right and wrong. On the one hand she felt compelled to honor England and the king; with the possibility of gaining untold wealth and on the other, blackmailing Morris, while at the same time, emptying the Admiralty coffers of as much money as she could safely put aside. It was a dilemma…but the longer she thought about it the more she realized that she could easily accomplish *both* objectives. Morris would continue to pour coins into her purse as long as she enticed him with her charms and if she were careful about the notes of credit she could amass a small fortune in little more than a year's time.

Evening twilight descended over the countryside as the carriage swayed to a stop before the massive brass bound doors of the Headquarters building. The driver hurriedly retrieved her valise while she searched for a coin to pay for stabling the horse. Dropping a coin into his hand she said, "I shall not need your services on the morrow. Leave word with the stable owner so that I may reach you at a moment's notice, for I may have to depart rather quickly…do you understand?"

"Yes, madam," he said, and then, "I'll take the liberty of sleeping in the stable and taking meals at the Ale house across the street."

"As you wish…I must be assured of your timely arrival…nothing more."

He turned, stepped to the seat and with a flick of the reins set the carriage to motion; the sound of the horse's hooves echoed along the cobblestone street, then faded as he turned the corner and disappeared from sight.

Molly shifted the weight of the valise, turned around, took a deep breath and mounted the steps. The guard lifted an eyebrow and greeted her with a rude stare that she ignored and hurried past him down the hall to Morris's sleeping quarters. Half expecting him to be in the throes of death she gingerly tried the door and to her utter and complete surprise found it unlocked. It swung open with little effort. Stepping lightly into the room she gasped at the overpowering stench of rancid sweat and body odor that permeated the stale humid air. Coughing, she brought a hand to cover her nose and mouth. The smell of sickness and death lay heavily about the small room. Her eyes grew accustomed to the dim light and within a few moments she beheld the ghastly sight of Morris lying in a disheveled, knotted array of twisted bed sheets, thrashing and turning from side to side, moaning and gasping for each ragged breath as if it were his last. Sweat cascaded down his hideous sagging jowls in torrents. He muttered a constant and unceasing gibberish and appeared oblivious to his surroundings.

She had a fleeting thought that she should summon Harry but quickly realized that he was, at best, an unwilling partner in this. It was the same unwillingness to command men at sea, an uncertainty that seemed to plague him constantly. His heart was simply too kind and seeing evil in someone or something was completely beyond his scope. It was a virtue...his kind heart...and that alone was enough. She loved him beyond measure, beyond words, for there was never a more gentle man to walk the earth.

Morris retched and coughed a quantity of evil looking yellowish-green slime that oozed past his trembling lips to drop on the sweat soaked sheets bringing her back to reality. She quickly crossed the room and stood over him, hesitating, building her courage for what she had to do. Turning to the night stand and opening a drawer she thumbed through its contents and found nothing but assorted papers, a quill and tapered bottle of ink...no keys. Crossing the room she sat down at the desk and opened each drawer in turn, carefully surveying, looking for something of interest. The bottom drawer on the right was locked. She had to find the key. A search of his private closet was disappointing. Her interest turned to the garments draped over a chair opposite the bed. It was the clothes he'd worn the day he collapsed. Jumping from the desk she promptly stepped around the bed and had just thrust a hand into a coat pocket when she heard a faint tapping on the window across the room. Panic turned her blood to ice as she gasped, frozen to the very carpet beneath her feet. A few seconds, and then three light taps. Quite abruptly she realized it was the shadowy figure she'd seen at the window some time ago. What to do...three more taps. Without a moments hesitation she crossed the room, then raised the window. A hand appeared from the dark with a letter which she hurriedly snatched and then held to her breast as though it might take flight as she quickly closed the window. Turning, she leaned against the wall to steady herself. Breaths came in heaving gasps as she clutched the letter tightly to her chest.

The mysterious courier chuckled to himself. He'd just placed the letter into the hand of a woman. The admiral was about to fall like so many before him...and by the charms of a common wench. The British High Admiralty functioned on three principles...sex, money and power. Everyone in London knew it...but seemed to take it for granted. He chuckled quietly to himself as he silently trod down the alley and on to a dark street; disappearing into the night. "Hell...he thought...the admiral probably didn't even know the name of the wench that was about to be his downfall!"

Molly took another deep breath, composing herself as best as she could, considered the circumstances, then examined the letter more closely. It appeared to be ordinary in every way. Crossing the room, she turned up the lamp on the night stand to give it a closer inspection. Her eyes narrowed as she held it close to the feeble light…a French seal…and it had the same small nicks she'd noticed on the seal she'd copied from Morris. Strange indeed! She cautiously turned and looked over a shoulder to see if Morris was aware of her presence. His breathing was so shallow that for a moment she thought he'd died. He coughed violently. It shocked her nerves terribly and startled her so badly the lamp on the table swayed and came dangerously close to overturning. She hesitated…heart racing, hands trembling, trying to decide what to do. It was an opportunity…a rare opportunity. Carefully sliding a tremulous finger under the seal she gently forced it open and unfolded the parchment. Her lips silently forming the words as she hurriedly scanned the page held close to the lamp. "Manifest…departure dates sadly misleading…HMS *Peril* scheduled…on station…failure to provide arrival date…blatant and deliberate withholding of requested information…our patience is drawing thin….your last warning…Vice Admiral LeCleef." Lifting her eyes, staring into the flickering light of the oil lamp, she let the letter slip from her fingers, fluttering slowly to the floor. Dumbfounded, she sat down heavily, in total shock, trying to comprehend what she'd just read. It *was* true…Cambridge was right…Morris was passing official information to the French! If the Vice Admiral were to see this letter…Morris would be hanged before the sun rose tomorrow.

 A wicked grin teased a corner of her mouth while she gazed at the tormented form writhing in agony across the room. This was all she needed. She would show the letter to Harry…and her plan would be complete. Morris would rue this day for the rest of his life…if he survived. Chuckling under her breath she picked up the letter, folded it, tucking it deeply in the bodice of her dress and tiptoed to the door. As it swung open she realized she had not found the key to the bottom drawer of the desk, shrugged her shoulders and decided to return later for a through search. It appeared Morris was far short of a miraculous recovery and by the looks of the room the house servants were terrified of contracting the fever and were staying away…at least for the time being. The uniform draped over the chair would probably be there tomorrow and that would be soon enough. She had enough proof nestled in her dress. Closing the door she stepped lightly down the hallway and hurried to Harry's room. The evening was still rather early and hearing him shuffling about she tapped; moments later he ushered her inside.

 Breathlessly she withdrew the letter and clutching it carefully said, "I've just this moment returned from Morris's room…and the most fortuitous stroke of luck has occurred. While I was searching about…a letter arrived."

She held it up and then continued. "It must have been brought by the same person we saw weeks ago from the second floor! I've opened it. Read for yourself. Morris is involved more deeply than you would ever suspect."

She thrust the parchment forward, then continued "You *must* witness this…you have no choice in the matter."

"Morris…involved…he's spying?"

"Yes…I'm telling you the truth. It's all here…at least enough to warrant an investigation."

"I don't believe it!" he muttered, completely struck by the gravity of the situation and what it might imply. He took a second to sort his thoughts, and continued, "Why must you be so insistent? If you are sure he's involved, then turn the evidence over to Lord Cambridge and let the matter rest. Our involvement in this will be at an end…a court-martial will be convened, and due process will run its course."

"Cambridge will see the letter…in due time, but I intend to keep it…at least for a short while. I shall put it in my personal belongings at the bank. Should anything happen to me you are to follow my instructions as to its disposal…do you understand?" she whispered, a cunning look on her face.

Harry was more than a little bewildered by the conversation. Frustration etched his face as he tried vainly to make sense of it all. He shook his head slowly, "I don't believe it! Are you quite sure about this?" Looking deeply into her eyes he studied her intently for some hidden clue, and finding none he forged ahead. "What do you intend to do? Isn't it enough to turn the letter over to Cambridge? I cannot, for the life of me, understand why you would want to keep…" he paused and then, "Surely you're not entertaining thoughts of blackmail!" Complete and total astonishment replaced the vexing look on his face. "Tell me the truth, Molly. This is not a matter for idle jest!"

"*Just read the damned letter!*" she hissed. Realizing what she'd just said she lowered her head. "I apologize…I didn't mean to…but you *must* know the contents of what I hold in my hand. Trust me…it will all come to light. I ask that you be a witness to this…nothing more."

The letter fluttered in a trembling hand before him, and having no choice he reluctantly took it then moved to the desk and better light. Sitting down heavily he carefully opened the parchment and read. Moments later he leaned back in the chair, lips forming a thin line of bitter resentment, and stared at the molding above the window across the silent room. Bringing his hands together he rested his chin upon them; lost in deep and profound thought for what seemed an eternity to her. A heavy, pregnant silence filled the room so completely that Molly found it difficult to breath as she watched him slowly lean forward in the chair shaking his head from side to side. He appeared to be completely destroyed—a mere shell of what he'd been just minutes ago. Unable to face her, he picked up the letter and waved it in her direction; indicating that he wanted her to take it. She stepped forward, took it, crossed to the bed and sat down with her hands in her lap. Remorse flooded through her; knowing that what she proposed to do could very well take her life…if Morris lived.

She jumped at the loud sound of his voice. "This is rather shocking news. I would *never* have thought the man capable of such treachery!" Slamming his fist on the arm chair, his anger building, "I've a good notion to strangle the life from the bastard this very minute! What would possess him to stoop to such disloyalty? The underhandness! The duplicity! Betraying one's country, aiding the enemy: the double-dealing, double-crossing…"

"Money," she said, matter-of-factly, stopping his recitation in mid sentence.

He turned to look over his shoulder.

"Money…we *both* know it. No one is ever above reproach. Everyone…you and I included, will sell our soul to the devil if the price is right. We have only to be confronted at the right time, the right place, and under the right circumstances."

"But…but…how could a man of character stoop so low as to sell the very soil he's standing on? He *must* know the consequences!"

"He is well aware of the consequences. He is too shrewd to be caught…or at least he *thinks* he's too shrewd. It's a deadly game, and the thought of losing his life only fuels the desire to plunge deeper, testing the waters…tempting fate with each heartbeat. It's an addiction, and although he would deny it with his last breath, he'd jump at the chance again if it were offered to him," she said smoothly. She knew the addiction all too well, and the words flowed smoothly off her tongue.

Harry looked across the dim room, studying her…appraising her until she began to feel uncomfortable before saying, "You're about to play the same game…aren't you? You intend to blackmail Morris in much the same manner as he's betraying our beloved England…am I not right?"

"Yes" she said, and then, more boldly. "Does it not serve him right…for what he's done?"

"That's no excuse, Molly…and you know it. You're trying to justify your actions…trying to make something right that's terribly wrong. No good can come from this. If you're discovered you'll be no better than Morris and will face the same end. You'll die for your efforts. Is it worth it?"

"Trust me, Harry. How many times do I have to tell you! Look at it this way. You don't have to confront the man that's delivering the letters. Forget about him! We, you and I, have all the proof that's needed. I'll take care of everything. Morris can't, and won't, touch me for fear of exposing himself."

"I wouldn't be so sure. He's a shrewd man; he'll discover a way to dispose of you without raising suspicion. It's a dangerous game you're playing, and I suggest you think a *very* long time about this before it's too late. No one dies twice…and I don't want anything to happen to you. You hold a special place in my heart."

Molly relaxed. She wanted to tell him the truth but couldn't find the courage. She wanted desperately to tell him of her lavish childhood, the fact that James couldn't afford Briarwood Estates and the lush countryside surrounding it, her insatiable desire for money and the material things she constantly craved, but it was no use. Shrugging her shoulders she merely said, "I have to do this…I know you don't understand. It just *has* to be done."

"Then there's no use arguing. It appears you've made up your mind…but hear me out on this. Once you put your plan into motion there's no turning back. For better or worse you'll cast fate to the wind and only time will tell what the final outcome will be. " He hesitated, wanting to say more. "Molly…I…" and then dismissed the thought with a wave of his hand.

Before she could reply he added, "I'll stand by you. We'll work this out…somehow. I can hardly refuse. I've read the letter."

"Harry…I'm going to make a thorough search of Morris's room. I must find the key to the desk drawer…before he recovers. Will you see that no one enters tomorrow morning? There are more files, somewhere, and I have to locate them."

"That shouldn't be a problem. The physician makes his rounds early. Morris has been unable to take food for two days. The good doctor administers a cold saline drought to bring down the fever and returns late in the evening."

An uneasy hush fell over the room. Finally Harry stood as if to signal an end to the conversation. Molly sat on the bed watching his every move, looking for some measure of reassurance. Finding none, she lowered her head and toyed with the letter as her eyes drifted to the floor. She heard him cross the room to stand before her, offering a hand. Reluctantly she took it.

"It's time for you to go," he said tenderly. Molly rose to meet him as an arm encircled her waist. Leaning forward he kissed her lightly on the cheek. A gentle, calm moment passed between them while they gazed at one another. She watched him draw closer and tilted her head as he kissed her lips delicately.

"I'm sorry. I apologize. I had no right." He stammered and then said, "Please forgive my indiscretion. It was rude of me to assume…"

"I've taken no offence, for I, too, care deeply for you," she whispered. "I'll be off now and see you on the morrow."

Discovering that they were both at a loss for words; she stepped back, turned as if to leave, then said, "Harry…I *have* to say this. If anything happens to me I should never forgive myself if I didn't admit the truth. I love you." Before he could reply she pulled the shawl tight about her shoulders and hurried down the hall.

An early morning chill crept through the window overlooking the courtyard behind the Headquarters building bringing with it moist dew that settled quietly in the room where Molly slept. Shivering, she reached out and pulled the bed sheets closer about her head trying to recover a measure of warmth but failed. Squinting through puffy eye lids she sighed. With sunrise hours away, and after a fitful night, she decided to dress and dine at the Hotel Bellview. A hot breakfast with several cups of coffee would take the chill from her. Descending the stairs to the lobby she left word at the desk to have her driver summoned and took a seat that afforded her an unobstructed view down the hallway to Morris's room. Thirty minutes later a physician arrived with black bag in tow, entered the room, and left shortly thereafter. Another half hour passed quietly as staff and maids made their rounds for the day avoiding his room entirely.

The driver arrived and escorted her to the post chaise, assisted her inside, closed the door and within seconds they were bouncing down the street at a brisk pace. A quarter hour later and they arrived at the Hotel. Instructing the driver to wait outside she entered and was promptly seated in an elegant dining room occupied by several well-dressed couples. A waiter appeared, took her order, leaving a steaming cup of coffee and muffin. The quiet ebb and flow of voices in the room brought her a sense of comfort and well-being, a contented feeling that was sorely missing in her life. Her thoughts drifted from one thing to another but always returned to Morris…and how best to broach the subject…if he survived. The letter *must* be put away for safe keeping. Her deposit box at the bank was the only practical place. She would give Harry an extra key and instruct him to give the letter to Cambridge if anything happened to her. As soon as Morris recovered she would put her plan into action, demanding monthly deposits to her account at the bank to the tune of a thousand quid. A year from now, according to her calculations, she would have enough money set aside to leave the country and live a lavish lifestyle. Along with whatever funds she could amass from Cambridge's open account at the Admiralty she would be independently wealthy. If she grew tired of the game she could always forward a letter to the House of Commons informing the king himself.

Harry kept his emotions so well hidden that she wondered if he held the same feeling toward her, she thought, sipping hot coffee. Almost from the beginning she'd entertained a vague suggestion that someday they would wed; but Harry was timid to the point of being bashful...or was he overly polite? He was certainly not as outspoken as James. They were as different as day and night. James, desperately impatient, tried to hold himself in check but rarely succeeded; while on the other hand Harry appeared to be the fountain of tolerance, always calm, never losing control. The only outburst she'd noticed from him was yesterday, after reading the letter. She hoped eventually he would come to appreciate...and love her, despite the faults she had.

"A good morning, madam. May I serve your morning meal?"

Quite startled at the interruption she cleared her throat saying, "If you please."

A steaming plate of light brown pancakes and fresh pork sausages adorned with a generous dollop of butter and maple syrup appeared before her. The coffee cup was refilled while the young waiter said politely, "Will there be anything else for madam?"

"A copy of the London Times would do nicely...if there's an extra about."

"Certainly, madam. We have several copies for our guests. I shall bring it at once," and with that he left softly, taking the serving tray.

She ate slowly, relishing the piping hot cakes and strong coffee while browsing through the newspaper. Noticing an article on the faltering war effort she wondered if Morris's covert activities were having an impact. It was entirely possible, but to what degree was anyone's guess. Lifting a napkin to the corner of her mouth she decided it was unimportant then hailed the waiter for more coffee. She intended to be far away from England long before the war ground to a halt. The chime of a mantel clock across the way reminded her that two hours had passed and the first rays of morning sunlight were peaking through lace curtains. Leaving a generous tip on the table she rose and paid the bill at the front desk. The driver sat dozing in his seat as she opened the door.

"Admiralty Headquarters at once," she said, tapping the side of the chaise with her knuckles and slamming the door.

"Yes, madam…whoa there…whoa I say!" (He'd jumped when the door slammed, causing the mare some degree of grief and anxiety.) "Whoa, now…steady girl…steady." The young mare snorted loudly, protesting the sudden activity, and then set off at a relaxed trot.

"Can you not go faster? I'm quite sure I'll be late. I've an appointment and can ill afford the consequences if I were a moment past the time," she shouted to the driver.

A slap of the reins brought a noticeable increase in speed, and twenty minutes later she entered the Headquarters building, went straight to Morris's room and entered without knocking. If snoring was any indication of sound sleep she gauged him to be in a world all his own. Closing the door and locking it she crept to the chair where his uniform still hung from the previous night. A careful search of every pocket produced nothing more than an assortment of odd papers and old receipts from several local eateries. The watch chain and seal, that she so desperately sought just weeks ago, now hung from a vest pocket for the world to see. Ironic, she thought, how strange fate can be at times as she placed her hands on her hips. There was a possibility that the key she so desperately sought was tucked away in his office desk but she dismissed the notion immediately. He would never allow it out of sight…it *had* to be in his private chambers…somewhere. With hands still on her hips she strolled slowly around the room looking casually about for a clue. Morris coughed and rolled over, facing her. She froze thinking he might awaken but he resumed snoring. Noticing a glint of sunlight reflecting off a small gold chain around his neck, she approached cautiously for a closer inspection. There was something on the chain, probably a cross, but it was tucked under his arm. Steeling herself she reached out and gently took hold and gave it a slight tug. Morris groaned, swallowed, and mumbled something. A minute later she tried again; this time with more force and watched the chain slowly break free from the greasy, sweaty confines of his armpit. Seconds later she held a small brass key in her palm. Chuckling, she cautiously lifted his head pulling the necklace free from a tangled mat of damp hair then rushed to the desk, sat down, and with trembling hand tried the key in the bottom drawer. To her wide-eyed amazement...the key turned the lock with a metallic click.

She gently pulled the drawer open to reveal an assortment of files in neat order. Leafing slowly through them, she came to a packet of papers in a light brown folder tied up with ribbon and sealed. Removing the packet, she rose and went to the window where the light was much brighter and gave the seal a closer inspection. The two small nicks were just where she'd expected them to be. Morris had sealed it with the stamp on his watch chain. Placing a fingernail under the edge of the seal she pried it up and heard, with satisfaction, a tiny pop as the wax broke free. Within minutes she knew everything.

She sat for a long time on the window ledge as overwhelming sadness consumed her, elated only moments ago and now completely obsessed by the gravity of what she'd read. Shadowy faces of the countless lives sacrificed for the love of money passed before her in sad progression. Hours of toil and sweat by shipwrights now lay moldering at the bottom of the sea. Words could not describe how she felt as the weight of it descended upon her shoulders. Harry was right...she should kill the bastard, here and now, and be done with it! She intended to kill him...oh yes, she would kill him, but much more slowly...and with exquisite pleasure. With fists clenched in silent rage she would watch him slowly shrivel like leaves on an old dying oak tree. Slowly...very slowly.

The last minutes of the hour passed before she rose and replaced the packet where she'd found it. Carefully locking the drawer then placing the key and chain around Morris's neck, she left. It was the last time she would ever enter his room. Standing in the hallway, a few feet distant from the door, she pondered whether it was important enough to tell Harry and decided he should know. He may well have made a valid point...Morris might stumble upon a devious way to remove her permanently. She hoped Harry would have the courage to expose him if anything happened to her.

Minutes later she rounded a corner and stood in front of the desk as Harry looked up from an assortment of papers he was leafing through.

"Good morning, Molly. I trust you had a restful night," he said with a questioning look. "Has everything gone well with you this fine morning?" Leaning forward to give a quick glance down the hallway, he continued. "Have you found anything of importance? The key...did you find it?" She was troubled, he noticed it immediately. Something had happened to her; a solemn manifestation of smoldering hatred seemed to fill the space between them…an evil presence.

"I found the key…it's on a gold chain around his neck. The files are locked away in the bottom right-hand drawer of the desk in his room. There's a packet of particular interest sealed with ribbon, a brown packet with the same seal, the one with two nicks filed at the bottom." Her voice faltered, and then. "It's terrible, Harry…there are letters dating back over two years…it's been going on for a *long* time! I didn't read everything. There were too many: dozens of them. I…" she shook her head saying, "The lives, and all those ships sunk…it's horrible."

Harry sat in complete and utter shock, unable to comprehend what he'd just heard. "You're serious!"

She started to say something but he interrupted with a series of rambling broken sentences.

"Two years! and never a thought of anything out of pocket…never a clue. Two years…. My Gawd!" The color drained from his face, "He'll be hanged…how many letters did you say?"

"Dozens," she replied. "All single pages…the ones I glanced at were all single-page letters from a French attaché…I think. I'm sure they were French from the official letterhead."

"What were the contents? Can you recall it to mind?"

"Demands for departure dates, cargo manifests, armaments, crew rosters, and much more. I'm not well versed in navel jargon; some things I simply couldn't understand, just like the one you read yesterday." She hesitated, and changed the course of the conversation.

"I shall put the letter…our letter…away in my personal safe box at the bank of London. I'll leave a signed, and duly registered letter of instruction with the bank president naming you executor of my estate." She searched through her bag and produced a key, then handed it to him saying, "Here's the extra key to the box. Don't lose it! My key will be at Briarwood Estates in my bedroom in a blue satin bag, top drawer of my vanity," she said swiftly as the words spilled out. Taking a quick breath she leaned forward, placing her hands on the edge of his desk and said, "I'm committed to this, Harry, whatever the outcome."

He lifted a hand, reached out, and placed it over hers saying, "Molly, for God's sake, will you not reconsider? You've gone far beyond the limits of common sense. Have you any notion of what could happen to you? Turn the evidence over to Cambridge. Stay out of it…for my sake…for our future!"

Overcome with emotion her eyes filled with tears as a racking sob constricted her throat. Inhaling a ragged breath past trembling lips took most of her strength, hearing what she had so longed for, "For *our* future."

He stood and swiftly came around the desk sweeping her into his arms, crushing her to him. "Molly, I…"

"Ssshhhhh," she whispered into his ear. "There will be time enough for us." Another sob racked her body causing her to shiver. Their lips met desperately, eagerly, as if never to touch again. Clinging to each other, they stood in silent tribute to an undying love.

"Molly…please…let us be away from here. I have a small savings account put away. It's enough to make a fresh start…the two of us…we can leave…go anywhere you want. Don't do this! I…I couldn't bear the thought of something happening to you…living without you." The words poured from him in a sudden cascade.

"A year…that's all I ask: just one year. We'll have enough to live like royalty in a year."

"It's too long! Something will happen; he'll plan your death before then. He'll not stand to be blackmailed for any length of time."

"The French have used him for over *two* years, Harry. What makes you think I can't do the same thing?

She returned to Briarwood after placing the letter in safe keeping. Days turned into weeks without any correspondence from Harry and she constantly wondered if Morris had died while going about her daily activities. The grounds and quarters of the sprawling mansion took on a new look as winter approached. Angry black clouds scudded slowly across a gray leaden sky from West to North foretelling the approach of colder temperatures. The brilliant color of distant hillsides turned a dull shade of brown as leaves cascaded down in torrents with each gust of wind. Geese had long since flown south in huge "Vs" of raucous honks and flapping wings, a sure sign that winter was not far behind. Beaver constantly plied the calm waters of a small pond dammed with limbs and mud, laying away a larder of green willow twigs for new offspring. Molly made a habit of watching their activities from a gazebo behind the house each afternoon. The sights and sounds of nature gave her a sense of gratification; a peaceful inner calm, and with it, an understanding that good far outweighed evil. She often regretted reading through the packet of letters but realized it was one of the necessary evils one occasionally had to suffer with in life, an evil that stood in the way of a better life for her…and Harry.

Time passed and she came to a decision. A year from now, depending upon how much money she could wring from Morris; she would pay a visit to the House of Commons and leave a short note along with a certain letter. After Morris was tried and summarily hanged she would return to claim the reward for her efforts. "England would pay a handsome price." Cambridge's words constantly echoed in her mind.

Days later, Mary came rushing up the stairs in a fair humor, throwing open the door to Molly's private study, waving a letter and said breathlessly, "A letter has jest this minute come by post…a letter for th' likes o' ye, ma'am. 'Tis a letter from th' Admiralty!"

Molly snatched the parchment from the maid and frantically tore at the seal. It read:

My Dearest Molly,

A note to inform you that Admiral Morris is convalescing at the infirmary. He is making a rather slow and painful recovery while several physicians attend to his every need. They are quite sure his lungs have suffered untold damage, and along with an already weakened heart (they suspicion excessive consumption of spirits and the tobacco leaf) have placed his prognosis somewhat bleak but believe he will eventually fully recover in some months.

His return to active duty is still a question in some doubt and much too early for an opinion. Although weak, he is able to take sustenance with some vigor and bath about the head and shave. His mind appears to be sound, but the body will have to repair itself as only nature can.

Your most humble and devoted servant,

Harry Cromwell…etc…etc.

He *was* alive. "I never thought he would have lived!" she muttered to herself. "What's that ye be a'sayin, ma'am?" questioned the anxious maid.

"Admiral Morris…Mary…he's recuperating at the Military Infirmary. It appears he is going to make a full recovery…in time," she said rather vaguely. Her mind raced, along with her pulse, as she made a mental note of the date.

"I shall mark my calendar…two weeks from today. If you would be so kind as to inform my driver to be available at a moment's notice, Mary, I should be most grateful. I *must* return to London and see to the needs of the dear man. I'm sure he's in need of companionship," she said with a chuckle. "Make absolutely sure the chaise is ready, will you, my dear?"

"Oh, yes, ma'am!" Mary said in a solemn tone. "'Tis only th' right thing ta do fer th' good Admiral…yes, 'tis fer sure! He'll be a feelin' much better after a castin' his eyes on ye."

"I'm sure you're quite right, Mary. I've a surprise that will cheer him in the greatest degree. What joy it will bring just to see the look on his face. I can hardly wait!"

The post chaise rounded a corner and lurched to a stop. Molly stepped to the street facing the Infirmary. Taking a moment, she studied the building in great detail. It appeared a rather somber affair with three floors of small windows and drawn curtains. The entire structure was whitewashed thoroughly from top to bottom (apparently to match the curtains) with not the slightest notion of trim or décor to be seen. A delicate picket fence separated the grounds from passers by (also painstakingly whitewashed) and what appeared to be nurses (in white frocks) attending to those fortunate enough to have the strength to be allowed outside and the stamina to withstand the brisk temperatures offered up by the late fall afternoon. It gave her a disquieting feeling of trepidation that seemed to steal a measure of her resolve and, for a fleeting instant; she entertained the idea of walking away. A shudder coursed through her body at the thought of entering a place filled with the sick and dying. She made a quick promise, a solemn oath, that she would take her life before allowing age to steal her beauty and strength to the point of having someone spoon feed her. Death would be the better choice.

An orderly escorted her to a private room where Morris sat slumped in a chair, fast asleep. A shadow of his former self (he'd lost considerable weight and skin hung in loose folds on his neck and arms) with hollow cheeks attesting to the fact that death had been cheated by the narrowest of margins. The orderly gently shook a shoulder to bring him from slumber saying, "Admiral Morris, a guest to see you: a most beautiful lady to see you, sir."

Morris raised his head slowly, groggy from a profound sleep, gazed about, searching for the location of the distant voice that had interrupted his nap.

"Sir, a young lady has come all the way from Briarwood Estates just to see to your welfare and engage you in a bit of light conversation."

Molly retrieved a chair and sat down, facing him, a few feet distant, and folded her hands atop her purse while Morris gathered himself.

"Moll...how nice it is to see you." He paused to catch his breath, and then continued in a thin, reedy voice she could barely hear. "I've been terribly ill and weak to the extreme. I've gained a measure of strength...but it has been a dreadfully cruel and slow process. I fear it will be months before I completely recover." He closed his eyes for some time. Molly was beginning to think he'd fallen asleep before he resumed. "I'm most painfully sorry for the burden I've placed upon you...the fever...have you suffered?"

"It appears you've suffered most terribly...far more than I," she said while motioning for the orderly to leave the room. "I've a bit of news that I believe will fairly return the spark of life to you."

"What might it be...my dear?" he asked anxiously. "Pray tell...I'm in need of some cheer."

Pulling the chair closer she leaned forward as an evil glint narrowed her eyes. Bringing her hands together she tapped the fingertips together lightly while a slight glimmering smile caused the left corner of her mouth to twitch.

"I called upon your welfare...three days after the fever struck. While I sat at your bedside, comforting you, I heard a sound...a tap...at the window and investigated. Would you believe...a letter was placed into my waiting hand...rather strange? Wouldn't you agree?"

Morris held the arms of the chair with trembling hands, eyes wide; mouth open in complete panic. "A letter...a letter...of all the...who would..."

She interrupted him and continued. "I think you know very well, my dear. While sitting at your bedside I took the liberty of reading it. Most interesting indeed! I have it safely tucked away."

A look of disgust distorted his mouth. "You...you had no right...prying into my personal affairs! I shall have you before a magistrate by the end of the month!"

"I think not. Need I refresh your memory...about the packet? I'm sure you remember the one sealed with ribbon in the file drawer of your desk," she purred. "All those letters...and so much information. My word, it seems the French have been well informed for the better part of two years. Shame on you!" she chastised him, shaking a finger in his face.

"You despicable little wench! You meddling bitch!" he hissed through clenched teeth as drool ran down the corner of his mouth. "It's all a lie, and I'll deny it! Who are you to question an Admiral of Flag rank, an Admiral of the Blue, Knight of the Bath. The Queen will see you hanged for bringing such disgrace upon royalty." A fit of intense wheezing stopped him from saying more.

"The queen will see *you* hanged unless you agree to what I'm about to say!" she shouted in return, pointing a finger inches from his face. "You'll be flogged 'round the fleet and hanged...do you understand? I've proof enough to convict you a hundred times over, and you know it!"

Morris was now wheezing violently, clutching at his chest, as blood rose to color his flabby neck and jowls. "After all I've done for you! You wouldn't..."

She interrupted him saying, "I shall expect a monthly deposit of a thousand quid in my personal account at the Bank of London starting the first of November. At the end of twelve months of timely payments, I will relinquish the letter and leave England quietly. I shall not return, and you will *never* see me again."

"A *thousand quid!*" he said aghast.

"A thousand quid, and not a shilling less: a small price to pay for your miserable soul, wouldn't you agree?"

"But, but I couldn't possibly afford..." a spasm of coughing racked his body.

"A thousand quid, or face the consequences. And should you entertain thoughts of my early demise, I've left instructions with the proper authorities. My, but I do believe your color is returning, and your strength, too!"

"I should be ruined, financially destroyed! It's not possible!"

Cutting him off with an upturned hand she persisted, "I shall expect the first deposit the week of November 7. Should you decide to test my patience I will *personally* deliver a very interesting letter to Admiral Cambridge the following week." She hesitated, bringing emphasis to her point. "I should take great pleasure in watching the noose being placed about your neck!"

She rose from the chair, brushing a stray lock of blonde hair from her eye, and left without looking back.

CHAPTER TEN

The four survivors watched the magistrate leave with the French captain close on his heels. The guards promptly ordered them from the room and onto the street, then marched them to the outskirts of town arriving at a squalid adobe building that would be their home for the summer. The building was located about a quarter mile from the village and sat in a field surrounded by a variety of barnyard animals which included steers, goats, chickens and sheep; all in various degrees of starvation. They marched up to the front of the building and were turned over to what appeared to be a band of filthy renegades, armed to the teeth with all manner of knives, pistols and clubs fashioned from mesquite limbs. The Mexicans surrounded the four prisoners, appraising each man in turn and making comments in broken Spanish and laughing outrageously as they shoved and kicked them. Each carried a unique wooden whip made from some type of willow branch and administered it profusely at the slightest whim, causing a most painful red whelp on the skin that, more times than not, oozed blood and fluid. They quickly learned to avoid contact with the whip. A crowd of curious onlookers, dressed in rags, gathered around to watch the proceedings and poke fun by throwing small stones and dried manure in their faces while they were being prodded by the guards through a small door reinforced with large iron bars. A number of minutes passed before they were able to view their surroundings. A beam of weak light from the opposite end of the building coming through a hole no larger than a clinched fist illuminated the tiny passageway. The cells were without windows of any sort and completely dark; as dark as a moonless night on Halloween. The fetid air was hot, humid and smelled of vomit, urine and stale sweat from too many bodies packed closely together. They were shoved down a long hallway and into a cell occupied by all manner of crawling insects; in less than a month they would relish the juicy roaches as an extraordinary delicacy and would comb the corners of the cell daily for any unfortunate newcomers; at times fighting over the tasty morsels.

It had been twenty four hours since they'd had a meal and they were beginning to feel the effects. The heat of the cell made their fever worse and each man choose a corner in which to lie down and suffer privately as insects, flies and rats roamed over their feet and legs biting any exposed flesh offered to them. Some unfortunate soul in another cell had evidently gone mad and ranted passages of Biblical hellfire and damnation amid a chorus of groans, coughs and flatulence. Occasionally, someone would scream out, threatening the lunatic to cease his never ending dialog of salvation for the sinner; but to no avail. It continued, day and night, stopping only when exhaustion forced him to sleep. Eventually James would grow accustomed to it and pay little attention.

They were too weak to stand before food was brought to them two days later. It consisted of rancid maggot-infested pork floating in a thin, watery soup of beans and peppers. A quart of warm water followed and the tiny door through which it passed was slammed shut leaving the four of them in total darkness to fend for themselves. James insisted the food be shared equally and each man, in turn, fished out a piece of meat taking a sip of the broth and passed the bowl along. The water was drunk later that night before they slept. Only one meal was allotted each day and the diet never changed. A small cube of potato would make an infrequent appearance, but the stale air attested to the fact that beans were the main course. A crusty clay pot served as the toilet and was emptied by an old peon every few days depending on his health and disposition. They soon lost track of time. The meager rations were the only indication that another day had passed. James soon found himself waiting by the tiny door for the next portion of food and anxiously grabbed it from the mysterious hand that offered it. Several weeks passed before he noticed the hand belonged to a woman. The next day he made a particular effort to examine it more closely and discovered, to his complete surprise, that it was quite youthful. The skin was smooth with a healthy light brown tan and long slim fingers that were perfectly formed ending in close trimmed nails. He made no mention of the discovery to his fellow prisoners and pondered the unusual dilemma for hours on end. It was a mystery. Why was a young woman serving food that wasn't fit for dogs? What he'd seen of the local population was enough to convenience him they were almost as desperate as the prisoners. Was it her only means of earning a living? The hand appeared to be well groomed, indicating a sense of pride he'd not seen in his short trip through the village. He decided he'd make an attempt to communicate with her. The next day, when the food arrived, he bent closely to the door and hastily said, "What is your name?" The door slammed shut without a reply. Pondering this for several hours, he decided to try what little Spanish he knew. She had probably never heard English spoken before and had no idea what he was saying. The following day he anxiously awaited her arrival and asked the same question in the native tongue. She hesitated for the slightest moment before closing the door. Each time the food was passed through the door he asked the same question. A number of days passed and he was on the verge of giving up when he thought he heard a faint whisper. It happened so fast he was unsure whether he'd actually heard something or if it was just his imagination playing tricks but, after trying again the next day, he distinctly heard her say, a little louder, "Maria."

He was overjoyed and after finishing his portion of the sour pork, swallowing it in chunks and sipping some of the broth from the bowl, he sat in the corner of the cell rubbing his hands together and giggling like a child anxiously waiting for Saint Nick to arrive. His cell mates crawled over to sit beside him asking after his sanity and he quietly explained that he was trying to establish some communication with the person who was delivering their rations.

"It appears to be a young woman from the looks of her hand," He stated with unbridled enthusiasm. "Her name is Maria. That's all I know."

Each day tired his patience to the limit as he struggled to pry the slightest bit of information from her. He noticed she took a few seconds longer to pass the bowl of food through the door and her hand seemed to hesitate, as if unsure of what to do. His health, along with the three shipmates, was deteriorating rapidly from lack of proper food and infection caused by the filthy living conditions. Their arms and legs were covered with open festering sores that oozed pus and body fluid constantly. He knew they would die shortly unless they received more rations and the only way to accomplish that was to somehow win the trust of the mysterious woman who furnished their meals.

Each day he would beg the woman for more food, explaining rapidly, in limited Spanish, their state of health and the need for fresh air and exercise but she made no reply. He began to think they were doomed and prepared to face death by starvation. He grew noticeably weaker by the day; his teeth began to loosen and his joints became so inflamed and swollen he could hardly stand. Fatigue overpowered him and sleep became his angel of mercy, taking away the constant throbbing pain and giving a few hours of blissful reprieve from the hellish never-ending nightmare of continuous darkness. When sleep came, it was filled with swirling disjointed vignettes of scenes from his childhood intertwined with battles, won and lost, at sea. Sounds of children laughing mingled with the dreadful screams of mortally wounded men. He awoke to the familiar sound of someone gently knocking on a door. Smiling, he turned over on the dirt floor, to greet his dear mother as she entered his bedroom but realized, all of a sudden, that she was not there. A sob caught in his throat as he fell back on the hot floor realizing that his sweet, loving mother had passed away long years ago. Lack of food caused his ears to ring constantly with strange sounds. He heard the soft knock again, quite distinctly, and turned toward the cell door, holding his breath while staring intently in the darkness. This wasn't a dream. He shook his head, attempting to clear away the cobwebs that befuddled his mind. Another knock! This time he was sure it came from the door and crawled slowly toward the sound. Pulling himself forward with his hands calling out in a thin raspy voice, "Please help us, please. I beg of you, in God's name have mercy!"

The tapping continued as he crawled nearer to the door. An eternity seemed to pass before he could reach out and return the signal. He rose up on shaking arms and leaned back next to the door waiting for some response from the person outside. Gold dots swirled behind his eyes; he knew he was about to faint and reached out to steady himself just as the small door opened through which the food was passed and a voice whispered, "It's Maria. Take this!"

His eyes were unaccustomed to the weak orange light that stabbed into the cell and he was momentarily blinded. Instinct took over as his hand searched out and grasped the object before him. The smell of roast beef instantly overpowered him and he greedily tore at the stringy meat in his hands, growling like a hungry lion over a fresh kill.

"Can you hear me?" James stopped abruptly at the unexpected sound of the young woman's voice drifting through the small opening. She spoke perfect English. He leaned forward to squint through the opening, the mouth full of food temporally forgotten for the moment, as he tried to make sense of what had happened. "What?" He questioned tentatively, unsure of exactly what to expect from the mysterious voice.

"Can you hear what I'm saying?" she questioned, a little louder this time.

"Y-y-yes...I can hear—but who are you?" he stuttered, swallowing the cud of beef in a mighty gulp. "What day is it—and the time?"

"It is the tenth day of July and two hours past midnight. Listen to me. I don't have much time. I will bring food to you each night. The jailer is a cousin, and I have told him that it would not be good for him if you were to die before the French captain can have the pleasure of hanging you. He has decided to look the other way while I bring some decent food through the side door. You have been in solitary confinement—and it cannot continue or you will die. He has agreed to move you to another cell with more light and fresh air. I will summon a doctor to tend to your health when you are moved. Until then, try to rest and take comfort in the hope of a brighter day."

The door closed gently and James heard the soft shuffling of foot steps fade in the distance. He chuckled to himself as he crawled over to the other prisoners sleeping on the floor shaking them awake.

"They're going to move us in a few days! I heard the young girl say—they're going to put us in another cell...with some light!" He chuckled, and then laughed outrageously after hearing what he'd just said. One of the men lying on the floor groaned and sat up, his voice sounding eerie as it echoed in the inky blackness.

"Get hold of yer self, Captain. Ye be a'goin' off th' deep end, sar. With all due respect—ye better jist lay down fer a spell till ye be a'gittin' yer senses back."

"No, you damned flaming idiot! I just heard the young woman say that we were moving to another cell within the week," he insisted, reaching out to shake some reasoning into the man.

"Ye be a dreamin', Captain, sar. I heard nary a word spoken this night, and neither did ye. Go back ta sleep!"

Suddenly, he realized he still held the chunk of roast beef in his hand and thrust it forward under the man's nose crying out, "And I suppose *this* is just a dream, too!"

"What have ye, Cap'n? Where did ye find...Jesus! he mumbled, snatching the meat from him. Within minutes the two remaining prisoners were awakened and they greedily devoured the last shreds of beef. Huddling together they listened while the captain explained, in subdued whispers, what was going to take place.

"Luck has smiled down upon us, gentlemen. I seem to recall the three of you mocking my attempts at communication just a few short weeks ago. I've just this minute found out that the night watchman is a cousin of the young woman who brings the daily ration. She has convinced the man that, should we die under his care; the wrath of the French will be upon his shoulders. According to her we will be moved within the week, and a doctor will attend to our health, and our rations will improve. We shall see what the morrow brings."

As promised, the young Spanish girl brought another portion of beef the following night, along with a generous canteen of cool fresh water. James was amazed how rapidly they recovered their strength. Within forty-eight hours they felt much better and slept soundly through the night. He continued to talk with the girl for as long as he could each night.

"Where did you learn to speak such perfect English?" he questioned, as they whispered quietly to each other.

"My father is a very rich man and hired the Jesuits to teach me along with my younger brothers and sisters. I was schooled for many years until they had no more to tell me. They have long since left to teach others, far away."

"If your father is such a rich man, why do you work in these filthy surroundings?"

"I have not been the model daughter my father would like me to be. My life has been one of boredom, and I've entertained myself with stealing small trinkets from the shops in the marketplace. The thrill of thievery has become my downfall and father grows tired of paying for my release. He has chosen to punish my wrongdoing by requiring me to prepare meals for the many prisoners. It is disgusting! My father tells the constable that if I'm caught in the act of stealing again I will go to jail."

"Your father is trying to teach you right from wrong. Can't you see he has your best interest in mind? From what you've just told me it would appear he loves you very much and only wants the best for his children, especially you."

The young girl sighed, and then continued. "I know my parents love me very much, but I lead a lonely life. You see, my family is quite wealthy and we live in a region of poverty. There is no suitor within hundreds of miles whom my father feels comfortable with, and therefore, allows no one to court me. I'm twenty-three years of age and will soon be too old to attract the eye of a handsome man—so I pass the time stealing small objects."

James knitted his brows in the darkness, and then rose up to look through the opening. The light was so bright to his unaccustomed eyes that he could just catch a glimpse of a beautiful pair of dark eyes looking back at him. Curiosity made him wonder about the rest of her features. "Is there not another way to pass the time? Has your mother taught you the finer arts of the home? Can you mend clothing—knit or do needlework of some kind? In my country, every young woman yearns to learn these skills to please her mother and future husband." He instantly regretted the statement, but it was too late to make amends.

"My dear mother has patiently taught the art of homemaking, but what good is it without a husband? You have just proven my point. I'm lonely and without someone to love. There is nothing to occupy my time, and father will not allow any of the local men to court me. He says they are beneath our station."

He reflected on the statement for a few seconds. She was a lonely little rich girl in the prime of her life, and no doubt beautiful, with a very protective, and possibility jealous father, who had placed his only daughter on a pedestal so high that no one could ever touch her regardless of whether they were rich or poor.

"Are you still there?" she questioned urgently, fearing he might not be feeling well

"Yes…I was contemplating what you've just said. I believe I see your point. It is rather unfortunate. But you should not judge your father so harshly. We get one chance at life, and each decision has long-lasting consequences, and should be entered into incautiously. Your father only wants what he feels, in his heart, is right for you."

He could hear the rustle of her skirts as she sought a more comfortable position. A few moments passed before she continued.

"I've often thought I would ask my father for permission to leave home and search out a suitable husband, but I know what his answer will be, even before I ask," she said forlornly.

A brief thought raced through James's mind, but he held it in check for careful consideration. Would it be possible to talk the young girl into helping them escape? Would she be willing to risk her safety—in hopes of leaving the country for the sake of starting a new life? His fate was cast in stone. He would die within months, along with the three unfortunate souls in the cell unless he could devise a plan to escape. Was he asking too much of the naïve young girl to help plan an escape—and take her with them? There was a possibility she could come to some harm, possibly death, if they didn't succeed. If she died, could he live with his conscience knowing he was the cause of her demise? The weight of responsibility caused his shoulders to slump as he drew his face away from the light. He would have to think the entire matter through…plenty of time remained; he *must* be sure. From the tone in her voice he knew she would jump at the chance to start a new life without considering the consequences.

He decided to change the subject. "I'm most curious. Have the French ships re-supplied? Can you tell me if they've sailed?

"It will take several months to make the quantity of powder and cannon balls they have requested. I've heard rumors in the village that this is the largest order ever placed for powder. It will take many weeks to manufacture. It is dangerous work and must be done slowly. There is always the danger of an explosion."

"When do you think they will sail? Two months, three perhaps?" he questioned anxiously, as a plan took form in his mind.

"I'm afraid it will be long after you and your fellow prisoners have left the world of the living," she said nervously with a note of apprehension in her voice.

"Can you tell me how they intend to pay?" he asked out of curiosity.

"The French have *always* paid with gold. It will be in the form of coins or bouillon, and they *only* pay after the order has been delivered. The gold sits in the holds of the ship and will stay there until after the cargo is loaded and counted. They never trust anyone and always ask for an extra measure, like the baker's dozen," she said with a tone of disgust. "The French are arrogant pigs and look down on my people. They seem to think they are more educated and view the Spanish as peons, but they underestimate us. We are the ones who take their gold in return for cheap charcoal and saltpeter. It is the Spanish who will be rich after the war is over! I must go. The hour grows late, and the day watchman will soon come to relieve my cousin. I will return tomorrow night, and we will continue our conversation."

She didn't wait for a reply and hurriedly left the jail. He sat on the floor thinking about what she had said. The future was beginning to appear somewhat brighter than it did a few days ago. The only way out of this predicament was through the girl. He decided to take advantage of her longing to find a husband and use it to lever her into helping them escape. It was a long shot at best, but from where he sat, it was his only option. He would attempt to make her feel more comfortable with idle talk to break the tension. Some casual conversation about England and its comforts just might speed up the process—and he intended to mention the handsome eligible bachelors that abounded in London.

In the nights that followed, James talked at great length about the sights of

London. He could tell Maria was overcome with curiosity from the sound of her voice and her constant interruptions asking for more details. She eagerly plied him with questions about the climate, the fine food and plush hotels lining the streets of London. She'd never traveled from the small squalid village of her birth, and she sat on the dirt floor beside the cell door for hours listening in awe to the descriptions he whispered through the small opening. He spoke of snows blanketing the countryside and the bitter cold that followed. The warm winter hearths and spiced cordials enjoyed by friends and family during the holiday season and the anxious anticipation of early spring, pregnant with the promise of new life for another year. He told of lazy summer days and quiet evenings spent sitting on the porch watching the setting sun paint brilliant, ever- changing colors on a palate of clouds as twilight rushed to overtake the night and about the hushed arrival of fall, suddenly announcing its presence with a splash of brilliant leaves that seemed to change color, as if by magic, only to fade and die as winter reclaimed her supremacy over the land, starting the cycle over again.

With eyes closed and mouth watering, he spoke of fine food and wines offered at the restaurants where he'd dined. The succulent cuts of meat, cooked to a turn, on a bed of steaming vegetables surrounded by crisp salads and freshly baked bread. Maria was astounded by the variety of desserts he described. Chocolate was something she could only imagine—and vanilla must surely be the food of the Gods! Her diet consisted mostly of boiled beef and beans heavily spiced with locally grown chili peppers, garlic and onion; all rolled up in a corn meal and flat bread baked on a cast iron skillet. Sugar was a rare treat brought to them occasionally by traders from far away. Wild honey, when it could be found, was coveted by the lucky family who accidentally stumbled on the hollow bee tree growing along the river banks. Several villagers constructed hives for the bees and placed them by the site after they were robbed in hopes of trapping the remaining swarm. Some were successful and brought the hive back to the village, but collecting the honey destroyed the hive and the bees seldom remained. Vegetables consisted mostly of wild greens collected in the countryside and young green beans plucked from the bushes in the fields before the pods grew too hard to eat. Potatoes grew in abundance in the poor soil surrounding the town and were prepared in every fashion imaginable: baked, boiled, mashed and dried, fermenting them with corn meal and honey produced a rather potent drink that took some getting used to.

Two days later the jailer, accompanied by the local constable, opened the cell door and escorted the ragged group to the opposite end of the building and into better accommodations. James and the three captives staggered forward with hands over their eyes for protection from the bright sunlight that stabbed through the windows lining the long hallway. The sun was setting through a blaze of orange and violet clouds before they could stand the light to any degree. As twilight settled over the land they surveyed their new surroundings for the first time and were overjoyed by what they saw. Their quarters were almost twice as large and the fresh air, such as it was, smelled like sweet nectar to them. The quality of the food improved along with the quantity. Maria brought fresh flat bread rolled around a mixture of ground meat and mashed beans smothered in a hot sauce one Sunday afternoon saying, "It is the Lord's day. You should pray and be thankful He has chosen to give you life."

James looked down at her through the bars that separated them. She was beautiful. Hair as black as ravens feathers outlined a noble face that appeared to be chiseled from amber sandstone. Dark brown eyes glowed from beneath long lashes that fluttered like the wings of a butterfly. A fetching smile highlighted stunning white teeth, ending in a dimple on the left side of her cheek. Somewhat taller than he'd expected; she stood about five feet six inches with dignified grace and a poise that revealed her proud bloodline.

Their long conversations had become a habit and each evening he and Maria would talk for hours through the bars of the cell. On Sunday afternoons, she would pull up a small wooden stool and sit beside him in quiet conversation. Sometimes they sat in silence, content to be close to one another. Weeks passed and James knew he would have to mention the subject of escape eventually, but he was growing fond of the young girl, making the decision more difficult than he'd first thought. His fellow crewmen huddled in the opposite corner of the cell snickering and making comments about the budding affair, cutting their eyes in his direction while raising eyebrows in a knowing fashion.

"We be a'thinkin' ye be gittin' a mite fond o' th' young winch, Cap'n, sar, hee…hee! What da ye think ye gonna do locked up behind these here bars?" a crewman mumbled sarcastically one evening after Maria left the jail.

"Keep your damned comments to yourself, Jacobs! I'm only attempting to build confidence in the young lady. She must be completely comfortable with me before I can ask her assistance in helping plan an escape from this infernal hell. She's our only hope, and our fate lies solely in her willingness to place herself in jeopardy!" he hissed through clenched teeth. "I'm asking a great deal of her, and I must wait for the perfect opportunity to approach the subject!"

"Pardon, sar, I meant no disrespect to ye but it 'pears ta me there's little chance o' us ever walkin' out o' here 'cept to greet the hangman's noose." Jacobs sighed, waving his hand about to emphasize the hopelessness of the situation. After a few minutes he continued, "Thar be too many details ta plan afore we can ever hope ta escape 'n git clean away from here. Th' *Rose*...she be holed up a fur piece from here. Where da ye think we gonna git a boat seaworthy 'nough to make the voyage? 'N what about food ta get us there? Hell, Captain, sar, we's just as good as dead one way or ta other—makes no difference!"

"I just told you to leave your damned opinions to yourself. As long as we draw a breath there's a possibility for escape. I'm convinced the girl will help us. It's just a matter of time. It appears the Spanish will be several months manufacturing gun powder, and as long as the French are anchored and taking on stores we still have a chance."

Maria returned with the evening meal just as the sun was setting. She removed the towel covering the food and waved it above the tray to keep the flies away until she could slide it through the opening below the iron bars. Pulling up a stool she sat down, placed her elbows on her knees and propped her head on her hands watching in silence as the four men ate. James noticed she was unusually quiet but said nothing until he'd finished eating. Turning to face her he asked, "You seem distracted. Is there something the matter?"

"I've been thinking of England, this place you call London, and wondering how many far away places you've seen. Traveling the world must be exciting." She sighed raising her eyes to the grimy ceiling as if trying to catch a glimpse of some exotic land.

"It is something I've *never* grown tired of. Of course there's a certain amount of danger involved. Watching a sailing ship from the shore is a majestic sight—but it's an entirely different matter at sea. It takes years of training and experience, and oftentimes you are at the mercy of the winds and tides. I've been fortunate to have sailed with the best crew anyone could ask for...and by God's grace I shall sail with them again, soon," he stated with pride and dignity as he swept a hand toward the three men seated next to him. "You are looking at three of the finest in the British fleet. There are hundreds more aboard the *Rose*—all fine men to the last!" he cried with emotion, pounding his knee with a fist, and then clapping the nearest man fondly on the shoulder. He blushed at the compliment and gave his captain a bashful grin, then stared at the floor for lack of something better to do.

James could think of no better time than now. The moment had arrived. Mustering all the courage he could summon up, he steeled himself and plunged ahead.

"Maria, I've given a great deal of thought to what I'm about to say. Please, could you move a little closer? I would prefer the other prisoners not hear our conversation."

She scooted the stool as close to the bars as she could, then straightened her skirt and folded her hands in her lap. Looking intently at him with a questioning frown on her face, she nervously brushed at a stray lock of hair, waiting for a reply that appeared not to be forthcoming. The three prisoners gathered around him in eager anticipation, waiting anxiously for the conversation to continue. His eyes anxiously swept each face as if to gain approval for what he was about to do.

"Maria, you are a very beautiful young lady. Your future lies before you. I've oftentimes thought you should have the opportunity to take control of your destiny. You are of noble blood and not for the likes of the common suitors plying your father's door with empty promises. Your destiny is far away from this land and its people. I'm offering you a chance few shall have in a lifetime: a chance to see London!"

Maria stared, wide eyed, unable to believe what she was hearing. "What are you talking about? Can you not see the plain truth before you? You're doomed to the hangman's noose before the autumn leaves fall. Have you lost your mind?"

James scanned the other cells surrounding theirs and noticed most of the prisoners were paying close attention to their conversation. "Maria, do any of these men speak English? As you can see, we have little privacy, and I'm most concerned someone will be able to piece together what we are about to discuss," he said, as a look of apprehension cast a shadow of doubt across his face.

"You may rest assured, we cannot be understood. The men you see are the lowest of the peons and have never heard English spoken," she said, casting a glance over her shoulder, a look of indifference plainly etched in the curve of her tightly drawn lips.

"Very well then, Maria. As you may already know, I've enjoyed our daily conversations immensely. You've given me the strength to endure this unspeakable torture. If it were not for you I, along with my fellow crewmen, would most assuredly have died. If I may be so bold as to make a confession—your intelligence and rare beauty have been an oasis, quenching my parched soul and bringing the refreshing waters of peace and tranquility to fill the void in my heart. It brings me the greatest of pain to ask this question, but there's no other way, for without you I cannot live much longer. Is there not a way to arrange a means of escape from these shores?" he said, and then hurriedly continued before she could reply.

"Can you help me and these poor souls?" He paused to look keenly at the three men beside him. "For the love of God, can you not take mercy upon me and find a way to free us? Are you content to live out your life among people far below your station? Are you bold enough to leave the heritage you so beautifully represent and follow me to foreign shores? There is no other way for either of us. You are imprisoned by culture and I'm imprisoned by the iron bars between us. You are young. Only a few years separate us. Come with me and I shall show you wonders you can only dream of!" He cried passionately as he reached through the rusty iron bars separating them to seek out and hold her trembling hand.

A tear slowly trickled down her cheek. She swallowed several times, drew a deep ragged breath, looked to the heavens and then stared closely at him for a number of minutes. She jumped at the sound of someone coughing loudly in another cell and glanced nervously over her shoulder trying to locate the person who had interrupted her thoughts, then returned to look at him, gripping his hand until her knuckles turned white then released it just as quickly.

"I don't know. I don't know. I must have some time to think," she stammered, glancing around the room.

"Surely there *must* be some way out. Can you suggest to your cousin, that he might join us and have the chance of prospering in a new land? I'm the owner of a rather large estate on the outskirts of London. I would be more than willing to hire his services as grounds keeper and furnish living quarters that would be much more suitable than he could ever imagine. He is the key to our success. Without him all is lost. All that remains is securing a seaworthy boat with a sail, and enough food to last out a voyage of two or three weeks. I have given orders for our ship to sail to a rendezvous point and to remain there for five months before returning to England. There's *still* plenty of time! I noticed *many* small boats in the harbor when we were taken prisoner…you could cache a supply of food somewhere and we could pick it up on the way to the harbor, but first you must convince your cousin," he hastily explained.

"Think what this could mean for us. After the war is over, I have the means to return here, and we can put your father's mind to rest about your well-being. I'm not a poor man. He would be proud of you, and I would be honored to be his son-in-law. The world is at your fingertips. It's the chance of a lifetime!"

He could see by the look on her face that she was beginning to consider the implications of what he was saying. A frown of doubt placed tiny lines at the corners of her eyes as she said, "It's a great chance to take…what will happen if we are caught?"

"I will tell them I grabbed you through the bars and threatened to strangle you if your cousin didn't release us. It will be in the dark of night, and the other prisoners will be unable to witness what happened, and they will believe me and set you free."

"I will send for the doctor to attend to your wounds tomorrow. When he has finished I will ask about your health. There's no use to think about what you've said if you are too weak to survive the voyage…and I cannot sail a boat," she said with assurance. "I will think carefully on the matter. My decision will come within the week. That is all I can say."

The following day the local doctor paid a visit and carefully checked each of them for signs of infection and re-dressed a few open wounds that had not fully healed. Before leaving he ordered the jailer to bring a large bowl of hot water and lye soap. Turning back to James he addressed him with an air of indifference saying, "See that you and the others wash thoroughly with the soap. You are infested with the lice…make good use of the clean water and wash the wounds that have healed first." He turned his back to them and left, choosing not to wait for a reply.

Maria returned with the usual portion of food late in the night and informed him the doctor had pronounced them in good health, considering their surroundings. She appeared to be distracted and had little to say. He thought it better not to pry into her affairs for the time being. Patience was a powerful virtue and he intended to make the most of it. He knew an answer would be forthcoming within a short while and all he had to do was wait.

Days passed in slow progression and Maria seemed to have put the matter out of her mind. She made no mention of the talk they'd had a few nights ago. It was as if the conversation had never existed. James spent many long and sleepless nights pondering the dilemma he was in and wondering what fate held in store if he ever returned to England and trying to figure out how to avoid the hangman's noose should he be lucky enough to escape and survive the perils of the voyage back to the *Rose*. He'd come to the conclusion, many weeks ago, that this was the worse predicament he'd ever been in. If he failed to convince Maria that the benefits far outweighed the risks or if the Spanish filled the order for gun powder before autumn, the French captain would hang the four of them before he weighed anchor. His life and the lives of the three prisoners hung by a silken thread that could snap any day and Maria had made no mention of how they were coming along with the powder. His nerves were getting the best of him and it took all the willpower he could muster to keep himself under control. Their health improved daily and a brisk scrubbing with hot water and soap helped stop the constant itching and oozing sores on their scalps and underarms.

Two days later he was awakened, quiet unexpectedly, by Maria in the wee hours just before dawn. Rubbing the sleep from his eyes, he noticed immediately that she seemed agitated. Glancing over her shoulder she stepped close to the bars and gripped them with trembling hands. "I have convinced my cousin to help with your escape, but he insists we take his three brothers along. If you agree, there will be eight of us, and it will take more food than can be stored in the boat for such a long trip. He refuses to have it any other way. I've pleaded with him to reconsider but he only laughs at me! What am I to do? I must inform him of our intentions soon, for I'm afraid he will not keep our secret much longer! You *must* tell me what to do!" she said, wringing her hands tightly on the bars.

"Tell him we will take his brothers. We have no choice! How soon can you gather rations for about one hundred and sixty meals? That will allow one meal per day for each—and water. It is most important to bring enough water, perhaps two hundred gallons if there's room. Blankets to shade us from the sun…they'll catch rain water to drink, and provide warmth at night," he said swiftly, and then continued. "I'm sure there's a quantity of smoked and dried meats in the marketplace. Buy all you can without raising suspicion…have your cousin and his brothers gather the flat bread you bring to us each day and any vegetables: potatoes, parched corn, apples, anything that will not spoil for three weeks. We *must* maintain our strength during the voyage at all costs! Tell me—how soon can this be accomplished?"

Maria hastily glanced around the hot, humid room to reassure herself before continuing. "I think it will take many days—possibly another week. There is much to be done. I will inform my cousin to start immediately, and ask him to search out a fishing boat with a mast and sail large enough to make the trip. When all is in place, I will come in the night for you and the others."

James was trembling with anticipation as he paced the tiny cell. He stopped suddenly, turned toward her and placed a finger alongside his nose saying, "I would ask only one more favor of you. Before you leave...write a short letter to your mother and father explaining what you have done and ask their blessing for us. Tell them you will be safe and that we will return soon. They will be angry, but I feel it would be proper to inform them regardless of the outcome. I'm an officer and a gentleman, and I shall have it no other way! Continue with your daily routine as much as possible, and try not to draw too much attention. We can ill afford to fail at this late date. Now off with you before the other prisoners awake," he whispered gently. He reached through the bars and tenderly drew her toward him, placing a light kiss on her forehead.

She left quietly without saying another word. He watched her silhouette fade in the twilight. He chuckled to himself. He would tell her, in a day or two, to have her cousins store the rations in the boat before they shoved off. While they were making their way down to the shore he would pretend to have forgotten something and ask her to return for it. In the mean time he would leave without her. He had no intention of taking her with him. Her father would forgive her again, and all would be forgotten in due time. He didn't really care what happened to her as long as he escaped with his life. Laughing quietly under his breath he returned to the corner, stretched out on the dirt floor and was soon fast asleep.

Several days passed before Maria whispered, "There is not enough meat to buy in the marketplace. I'm afraid there will be little for us to eat. I can only purchase a little at a time because the peasants grow suspicious. My cousin is gathering what vegetables he can from the local farmers. He knows some of the Indians that live in the hills north of our village and has brought back a supply of pine nuts and something called pemmican, a mixture of crushed berries, dried venison and fat. The Indians tell him it is made for long hunting trips and keeps the hunger away. We have a boat and are only waiting to buy more supplies."

"Excellent! Have your cousin and his brothers store the water and rations in the boat just before we leave. It will save valuable time if the stores are already in the boat. We *must* be away as quickly as possible if we are to succeed," he said anxiously through the iron bars that separated them.

"I will come for you soon. It will be late in the night..."

He interrupted her saying, "Don't come any later than midnight. If we leave in the morning twilight there is a chance someone will see the boat leave and try to overtake us. We must be gone before the morning sun rises…do you understand?"

"Yyyes…I understand," she stuttered.

"How far are we away from the harbor?" He questioned.

"Less than one half of your miles. It should take less than an hour to reach the shore. I don't know how long it will take to sail from the harbor," she said urgently. "The peasants will be asleep, and if we make no sound it should cause no alarm if someone sees us walking through the streets. I will bring some ponchos for you to put over your heads. You will look like the goat farmers leaving the village to tend to the flocks in the fields. I will try to find more food," she said with a note of hopelessness in her voice. "We will not have enough food for the long trip."

"We will make the best of it. That is all we can do," he said with as much reassurance as he could.

"I will be ready when you come for us," he said looking over his shoulder at the three men gathered close by. "These hearty fellows can make the best of any situation. We'll succeed—or die in the attempt!"

The metallic sound of keys rattling in the lock startled him from a fitful sleep and brought him fully awake. Squinting his eyes, he peered into the humid darkness trying to locate the source of the sound. Swiftly realizing it was coming from their cell door he leaped to his feet and rushed forward to confront Maria's cousin, the night watchman, opening the lock. He turned, and without saying a word, shook the others awake, cautioning them with a finger placed to his lips to remain quiet and follow him. The cell door swung open with an unnerving squeal that seemed unusually loud in the stillness of the night. The night watchman motioned them forward and pointed down the dimly lit hallway to the front of the building. He placed the ring of keys on his belt and without looking back to see if the others were following, strode down the hallway to the office. James and the three men quickly fell into line and tiptoed after the jailer. Entering the dirty room that passed for an office, the night watchman stopped, placed the ring of keys on a nail above the desk, turned and rummaged through a burlap sack, then brought out several ponchos and made motions for them to be put over their heads. He hesitated for a few moments, frowned to himself, picked up a stack of assorted papers and tossed them about the room. He carefully turned over the chair, kicked the spittoon into the corner dashing the foul contents on the adobe wall and onto the floor. Lifting the desk from the floor he kicked one of the legs off and shoved it to the opposite side of the room. Placing his hands on his hips he surveyed the destruction and nodded his head in approval. Waving his hand toward the door, making it quite clear that it was time to leave, he herded them forward and out into the dusty street. Stopping just outside the door he turned to the right and stooped to open a wooden crate. Carefully reaching inside, he brought forth a fat chicken and lovingly stroked its feathers as he entered the office and closed the door softly behind him. James turned to the men gathered around him with a look of utter confusion and shrugged his shoulders, shaking his head while making hand signs that the jailer was obviously insane. Seconds later they could hear a muffled thrashing sound coming from the office that soon faded away to silence. The door opened again and the jailer stepped out carrying the body of the misfortunate chicken minus its head. The night watchman glanced around the blood splattered room and smiled with satisfaction then slung the poor fowl violently through the air several times, slinging the last drops of blood all over the rough hewn boards of the small veranda.

James was impressed. The man had made the office look as though a violent struggle had taken place. Fresh blood splattered the walls, the floor…everything including the jailer. A clever trick indeed. The man laughed, tucked the limp chicken under his arm and started down the dusty street that led to the harbor. Dim moonlight filtered through thin strings of clouds that scudded across the sky as a gentle breeze caressed the sleeping village. Three men appeared from a dark alley and fell into step behind them causing a few tense moments for him before he realized they were the brothers of the jailer. They walked through the sleepy streets completely unnoticed. There was no indication that anything seemed out of place and it appeared the entire village was sound asleep. A dog barked, somewhere off in the distance, and was answered by another as silence overtook the night.

They had walked for the better part of half an hour. James was growing a little concerned that Maria had underestimated the distance and that dawn might overtake them before they could reach the harbor. Maria! Suddenly he realized that she was not with them. He reached out and gripped the arm of the night watchman bringing him to a halt. He turned around and looked cautiously at James, waiting for a response. "Maria?" he asked, turning his hands up to indicate a question. The night watchman shook his head and shrugged his shoulders to show that he didn't know where she was, then turned and continued on. What could have happened to her? Was she waiting for them by the boat, or had her father discovered their plan and was summoning the law to apprehend them? Unexpectedly, James caught the dank smell of water on the gentle breeze, and his pulse quickened. They were almost there! A few minutes longer. It had been much too easy. He realized that something wasn't right…escaping from jail, and taking a stroll down the lane to the harbor, and shoving off without someone noticing was next to impossible! It *must be a setup!* He began to cautiously scan the countryside for something out of place—but could find nothing. The harbor was within sight, and he could just make out the dark lines of the boat swaying softly in the water. There was nothing to be alarmed about—not a soul around!

Moments later they gathered along the shore in front of the boat. The night watchman motioned for them to board, while untying the stiff rope from the piling and tossed the chicken in the bushes. Minutes later they shoved off. The three crewmen picked up the oars and with James manning the fourth, they fell into a smooth, measured rhythm that soon put the boat out into the open waters of the harbor.

"Unbelievable! Gentlemen—we have just gained our freedom…and not a single shot fired!" He chuckled to the other men in front of him.

"Hee…hee…damned if we be the luckiest bastards ye ever heared o', Cap'n, sar! We done went 'n' pulled her off slicker 'n' a greased halyard! If'n I live ta be a hunerd…my granchildern'll never believe this un…no saree, bob!" A voice drifted to him through the damp night air.

The land breeze was making itself known and James soon ordered the sail set and trimmed. The oars were shipped and they relaxed while the quiet waves gently lapped at the sides of the boat. The breeze soon freshened and the little boat plowed through the waters and out into the open sea a few hours later. The four Spanish men were huddled in the waste of the boat looking anxiously at one another and turning various shades of white and green. Before the sun rose in the east, he knew they would be hanging over the side feeding the fish with whatever was left of their last meal. He looked over his shoulder at the receding shores of the harbor in disbelief. They had literally strolled out of the jail as if it were nothing more than a Sunday outing. The crewman was right. If he recounted the story to someone they would laugh and think it the grandest lie that had ever been told. Maria's unknown absence made the entire affair much less complicated…although, he pondered, she was strikingly beautiful. He had to admit…he was taken with her intelligence and character and deep down inside he knew he was fond of her. If the circumstances were different, he would have made every effort to win her affection—but it was not to be and he made a conscience effort to put her image out of his mind and concentrate on the task at hand.

Squinting through the twilight he took note of the sail and pulled on the starboard line to bring about a better trim. Satisfied that it was drawing all the wind it could on this heading he gave the line a turn around a ring bolt and tied it off. Settling himself comfortably in the stern sheets with a sigh he leaned over the tiller and gazed off to the east to watch the sun cast the first shafts of golden light through dark purple clouds drifting just above the horizon. Fate had chosen to be kind—if only for a few fleeting hours. He tried to conjure up an idea of how he could save his reputation. Admiral Morris would have no choice but to uphold the Articles of War…and that would mean death by hanging. He had disobeyed direct orders, causing the untimely deaths of several crewmen and had nothing to show for the effort. A frown crossed his face as he gazed out to sea watching the rollers build in intensity. They were leaving the shelter of the cove and entering open water. Soon he would have to put the helm over and run before the wind, making all the headway he could with the little boat. Time was of the essence and the greatest task lay ahead…locating the island and finding the cove where the *Rose* lay at anchor. The issue of Admiral Morris and the inevitable Court-martial would have to wait.

Dawn suddenly broke over the horizon, as it always does at sea, to find the Mexicans heaving and moaning over the side of the rocking boat. He looked over at the three crewmen from the *Rose*—gave them a knowing grin then unexpectedly threw his head back and laughed heartily. It would be a long voyage. The Mexicans would be of little use to them. He expected them to be sea sick for the better part of a week and by then they should have reached their offing. It was just as well—it was quite evident they weren't sailors. His stomach growled in protest making him aware that it had been over fourteen hours since he'd eaten but he put the thought out of his mind and concentrated on the trim of the sail. Glancing toward the bow of the boat he smiled contentedly at the large pile of canvas covered rations and oak barrels of fresh water. It appeared, at first glance, to be more than enough, judging by its sheer size, to last out the voyage. The wind gained strength and the little boat plunged ahead throwing salt spray and spume over the bow. It was exhilarating…the smell of fresh air was nectar to his senses. Drawing a deep breath, he shouted to the heavens, proclaiming his freedom.

CHAPTER ELEVEN

    Black angry clouds with purple edges set against a ruddy orange sky greeted James as a weak yellow orb of sunlight struggled to break free from the eastern horizon. The wind was calm with light waves lapping across the port bow, much calmer than the day before. It would appear, to someone on shore, that a beautiful early summer day was in the making, but he viewed the eastern skyline with an age old wisdom born from decades at sea. The building clouds, lying quietly in the distance, were a sure sign of foul weather. The summer months were prime for hurricanes and any change along the horizon was always viewed with a great deal of apprehension and foreboding. He knew he was still north of the equator and the prevailing trade winds blew from the west and any weather, good or bad, would always come from that direction. The color of the sky indicated moisture and a lot of it. The clouds were nothing more than vapor building as warm air rode over the top of a mass of cooler air along the surface. It wasn't a good omen.

    Gentle ocean waves hid a distant shore line somewhere over the horizon. It would be a tricky bit of maneuvering considering the wind and the single mast he studied above him. He pondered the odds of making shore before the approaching front overtook them, and then pursed his lips as a tight grimace distorted his features. They were in for a bit of a blow. Glancing forward to his fellow crew members he noticed they were eyeing the clouds with the same careful attention and talking quietly among themselves. He cleared his throat to draw their attention and said, "I do believe we're in for some rough weather before another day passes. By the looks of it, twenty-four hours or there about, would be my guess."

They nodded their heads in unison as Jacobs spoke up, "'Pears ta me, Cap'n, sar, we's oughtta be makin' fer some safe water afore she winds up ta give us Hell!"

"My exact thoughts, Jacobs. Lend a hand to haul the sail as close as she'll take it. It will be a tricky bit of seamanship indeed. We'll have to tack her a few times before we make the offing, but it's our only chance. Without a proper keel under us we'll drift ten feet for every foot we gain to the west, but it's better than what's in store for us if we don't."

They wasted no time pulling the spar about and trimming up the sail to a rakish angle with the wind. James hauled the tiller over to compensate and established a heading as close to the wind's eye as he could manage. Their small boat protested to the additional strain but held her course surprisingly well. The Mexicans, still overcome with seasickness, were lying helplessly between the stays, huddled in a miserable mass of tangled limbs and sodden blankets. James, upon appraising the poor devils, shook his head and wondered what the hell he was going to do with them. His Spanish was limited and instructing them in the finer points of sailing would be impossible. He'd have to resort to patiently demonstrating his desires with hand signs—but from the looks of them he doubted it would do much good. Time would cure their stomachs and in a few days, with any luck, they could make the shore before the approaching storm and recuperate for a day or two.

He scanned the western horizon for the shadowy outline of a distant shore but found none and estimated their position about fifty miles east of land fall. It would take hours of maneuvering to get there. The horizon, at sea, was only ten or twelve miles away. It was possible to be fifteen miles from land and not realize it until it was sighted. The appearance and color of the water told him that they were much farther out. Sea gulls usually plied the waters several leagues from shore, but the approaching storm had driven them to higher ground and the safety of sheltered coves. Sometimes seaweed and algae floated on the surface to give a hint that land was close by, but he'd seen nothing—only gentle rollers of dark blue green coursed by them indicating deep off shore water and a sure sigh they were far out to sea.

The storm grew in intensity with each passing hour. A fine spray of mist parted from the crest of the waves as the wind gained momentum. Clouds descended until they appeared to be within reach, scudding across the gray sky in a swirling mass of tangled wisps. Their small craft was making leeway as the waves relentlessly buffeted the bow pitching the occupants about cruelly. Without warning, a huge wave appeared from nowhere, slamming into the port side with such force it threatened to broach the small boat as it wallowed through its stays trying to right itself. The force of the impact caused two of the Spanish men, which were huddled in the bottom of the boat to roll to the starboard side; as the boat violently pitched back, they were thrown up and over the port side railing; landing brutally across the hard wooden edge. James heard ribs cracking above the howling tempest mixed with screams of pain that were immediately silenced as the two men desperately clawed at the slippery railing before disappearing over the side never to be seen again. The brutal, senseless deaths were the deciding factor in his decision to ware the small boat and run before the wind. As much as he detested it there was no choice to be made. He had to come about and sail back in the very direction he'd came from just two days ago. Crowding the tiller more than was prudent; he intentionally sailed toward the west in hopes of finding decent landfall. Casting a measured eye over his shoulder to gage the direction of the wind he returned his gaze forward to gain a proper bearing when he noticed the water barrels had worked loose from their moorings and were beginning to sway about threatening to break free. "Jacobs, Griswall, look lively there! Have a care to lash those casks down smartly before they cause harm. Batten down that canvas tightly lest the rations become soaked and ruin! Put your backs into it, lads…cheerily now!" he shouted above the howl of the wind.

The two crewmen struggled forward as best they could and began the dangerous task of securing the heavy water barrels. Grunting with the intense labor involved, each worked in unison to pass a line around a barrel while the other snubbed the working line taunt and in this manner they slowly maneuvered their way from port to starboard arranging the stiff canvas over the cargo as they went. They were worrying with the last of the barrels when Griswall exclaimed passionately, "Sweet Jesus, lookee what we have here. I do believe it be th' good Cap'n's sweetie!"

James was concentrating on the set of the sail when he heard Griswall cry out and leaned forward to squint through the swirling spray, trying to discover what the commotion was about. Seconds later he noticed movement beneath the sodden canvas. Maria emerged, with the helping hand of Griswall, to tumble aft; landing amid ships in a heap of tangled hair and petticoats.

Completely stunned at the sight before him, Howlette's mouth gaped open. "What the deuce? Maria, is it really you?" he questioned, his voice rising in a fevered pitch above the gale. "Have you gone completely mad?

Stowing away, for the love of God!" His mind raced for words to reconcile his guilty conscience but none were forthcoming. It was quite obvious she knew he'd intended to leave without her and had outsmarted him at his own game. Deciding that silence was the best course of action, he waited for her to say something before making another blunder.

Maria strained to sit up, clinging to the seat in front of her, and pulled a wet lock of hair back from her face. She fixed a steely gaze upon him, bit the corner of her lower lip, and then arranged her dress. Looking over her shoulder, she noticed Griswall staring at her with a wicked grin as he eyed an exposed thigh. In a blur of motion, she spun around and slapped him across the face with a resounding clap that pitched the poor devil head over heals. He landed in a heap of flailing arms and legs as his head struck a water barrel with a dull thud. "Sonofa.bi…" he began, in pain, rubbing at the knot of proud flesh slowly rising through his matted hair. Sitting up he tenderly probed the red whelp on his cheek while cautiously viewing Maria across the short distance that separated them.

"If you entertain thoughts of touching me, I will cut your throat in the night while you sleep!" She hissed with a sneer of disgust. "And as for you, Captain Howlette, I know about the superstition of women aboard ships that sail the seas. That is why I chose to hide with the cargo," she said turning her attention back to him.

"But, but I…had no intention of…" he stuttered nervously.

She interrupted him, saying, "It is of little consequence. You have two choices. Kill me or take me with you. I don't think you have the courage to throw me overboard in front of my cousins. Your life would come quickly to an end."

He cast an appraising glance over her shoulder at the two Mexicans. They were watching the proceedings with great interest, looking first at Maria, then back to him. "Very well. I'm afraid I must strike the colors and surrender. You've indeed outsmarted me. I doff my hat," he said, making a gesture by touching his forehead with a hand. "I *must* confess I had no intention of taking you, for you see, I thought it better that you remain with your loving parents. What grief they must be suffering at this very moment wondering what has become of you, disappearing in the dead of night without a trace. Your dear mother must surely be at her wit's end. Did you not leave a note? Some explanation, *something?*"

"Enough of your idle talk! You care nothing of my parents. You never did. Your only concern was saving your miserable neck from the hangman's noose, nothing more. It was *my* decision to arrange an escape for both of us. My destiny lies in another country, one of my choosing," she stated with dignity while tapping a finger on the seat before her to emphasize her statement. She frowned and quickly turned around in search of the two men she suddenly realized were missing. "What has happened? I see only two of my countrymen."

"They were lost overboard only a few minutes before you were discovered. Did you not hear their screams?"

"So it was you that…"

He interrupted her, saying, "It was an unfortunate accident…a tidal surge…a huge wave. There was nothing I could do. It came without warning. We're *not* the culprits you seem to think. It will take the labor of all of us to make the voyage to the *Rose*, and now we are short *two* able men. It will make the task even more difficult. Is there someplace to take shelter before the storm overtakes us? He anxiously scanned the distant horizon before continuing, "How far to the western shore? If we sight land—will you be able to identify the coast line?"

Maria hesitated, reconsidering what she had just heard, eyeing him with a cold, measured gaze that bore through to his tormented conscience. "Find land. I will tell you where to take the boat. I have traveled some distance along the coastal roads. There are a few small inlets that will give a measure of protection from the storm," she said, casting a glance westward. She felt his eyes upon her and turned to give him an appraising stare in return.

A smile slowly lifted the corners of his mouth. The thought suddenly occurred to him that he'd met his match—both mentally and physically. He compared her to his beloved Molly and realized the plain truth of the matter in an instant. Maria was, in many ways, akin to a wild animal. Her fiery spirit could never be broken, and the thought left him breathless. He searched his mind for a comparison between the two—Molly was quiet and demure, content to let him make all the decisions, whereas Maria was bold, outspoken and confident. She was—challenging…yes, that described her perfectly…challenging. He realized, while he stared at her, that her features were softening. A wry smile flickered across her lips as an eyebrow arched, waiting for a reply from him. For some strange reason, he nodded his head, accepting the fact that she could never be tamed, and left the matter as it was for the time being. Wind and salt spray soaked her from head to toe as a fleeting ray of angry sunlight broke through the swirling clouds illuminating her glistening face. Curls of black hair stuck to her neck and bosom while drops of water shone like tiny sparkling diamonds caressing her amber skin. James suddenly realized that he was seeing a goddess sent to him under the most unexpected circumstances. They stared at each other, completely oblivious to the peril surrounding them, while the tempest surged on.

He forced himself to tear his eyes from her and concentrate on saving what remained of the crew and rations. The sky turned into molten black lava, boiling and rolling before the tormenting wind—a blazing pyre that threatened to consume everything in its path. He leaned on the tiller and forced more speed from the complaining boat, anxious to make landfall before dusk overtook them. Hours passed in apprehensive silence as crew members took turns relieving each other. It was impossible to rest or catch a few minutes of sleep. Exhaustion eventually numbed them into a dazed dreamy surrealistic world of howling wind and stinging salt spray. The light was fading rapidly and James grew more apprehensive with each passing minute. It was imperative to make landfall before darkness fell or they would parish before dawn. The fishing boat they were in was not designed to withstand gale force winds and was taking water at an alarming rate. He fretfully scanned the dim horizon hoping to sight a change in color that would signify land then looked at the sodden mass of people huddled in the waist of the boat.

"I shall not overstate the importance of keeping a sharp lookout, gentlemen," he shouted over the raging storm. "Sing out if you sight *anything* that would pass for land. We haven't much time, and the light grows dimmer with each passing hour. Jacobs—look lively and take the tiller while I check the mast and yardarm. I can hear it complaining, and we can ill afford to lose them now."

Grasping for handholds, he slowly moved forward, stumbling over the poor souls huddled at his feet and eventually gained the mast. Running his hand over the straining timber he checked carefully around the base to make sure it was properly stepped and not working loose then examined the rigging for signs of chaffing and wear. Much to his amazement, he could find nothing wrong and with a sigh of relief, staggered to the bow of the boat to make a survey of the stores and check their moorings to see if any had worked free. Bending down to gain a closer look at the cordage, groaning and creaking in protest to the undue punishment placed upon it; he was about to reach out and test a particular line when someone cried out in a high, frail voice cracking with emotion, "Cap'n, sar—off the port bow, thair, what da ye make o' it, sar? Is it a bit o' land…er jis' one o' them black devil clouds?"

He stood instantly, placed his hands over his eyes to fend off the relentless deluge of salt water pelting him like a hoard of stinging bees, and peered desperately into the distance. His mouth hung open gasping for air as his pulse quickened while straining to catch a glimpse of the swirling, dark illusion far to the west. It was tantalizing close—but impossible to make out through the blowing mist and spume. "Where away?" He questioned earnestly as the boat tossed violently, threatening to pitch him over the side before he gained a hold on a rigging line.

"Fine off the port bow, sar...west by southwest. She ain't a'movin', sar...I do believe hit be solid land, sar...I sure do!"

Turning to look off the bow to his left and leaning forward, attempting to get a clearer view, he unexpectedly saw a dim shape in the distance. "Land ho!" he cried, and just as suddenly realized they would never make the offing on their present course. "Haul her over, lads...put down the helm...lively now! I fear we'll pass by within a league or two.

For the next hour they fought desperately to gain precious yards, tacking the small boat persistently as the shore line teased them. The water was beginning to shoal up and he could see the white breakwater in the distance, a sure sign of coral reefs. It appeared they were going to make landfall. He began talking to the boat, coaxing and cajoling it forward. "A bit further, ye fine little filly. I'll not let ye disappoint me now. Tack her one last time, lads. Do ye see that stretch of calm water just inside the starboard point, there?" he pointed ahead, indicating what appeared to be a break in the reefs, then turned to beckon Maria forward. Minutes later she stood by his side while he shouted in her ear, "What do you make of it? Do you recognize anything?"

She frowned, concentrating on the dim features and said, "I do not know where this place is. I have not been here before, but we have no choice. You must try to pass through. The Saints be with us!" She crossed herself.

"Look for a wave, lads and try to put the helm down in time to ride her through. It's our only chance," he said earnestly, casting a concerned eye aft to gage the oncoming surf. "Watch for the third wave. Count them. When you see a large one, count the next two. The third one will always be the largest." He staggered back where Jacobs sat straining at the tiller and collapsed beside him shouting, "When I sing out, put her over and brace yourself for a ride. She'll raise up on her beam ends. You've seen it afore, laddie, just like when you were a kid, playin' in the surf, ha ha!"

The boat rode steeply up the fore side of a huge breaker, pausing briefly at the top, wallowing in a frothy blanket of foam and spume tearing from the crest, then gently sagged down the backside, only to start the whole process over again. James sat in great anticipation, watching the waves in the distance, waiting for one that suited him then turned back to gage the breakwater. Minutes later he shouted in Jacob's ear, "Prepare yourself—one more and we'll pay the devil his due!" A stupid grin split the boy's face as if it were all a lark. Bracing his feet on the slippery keel he studied the captain's face intently, waiting with unbridled glee for orders to throw the tiller over. He could feel the boat rise up the giant swell as the strain of the creaking tiller protested in his trembling hands.

"Now, boy! Put her over afore she broaches. Cheerily, lad! She's reaching...damn yer eyes...down with the helm!" Howlette screamed at the top of his lungs, snatching the tiller arm from the boy's grasp, and brusquely shoving him from the stern sheets. He landed under the aft seat boards, sliding forward, flaying away with arms akimbo, and frantically grabbing for something to arrest his plunge toward the bow and over the side. The rakish angle of the deck contributed to his distress. Seconds later he landed, with a thud, against the water barrels tied in the bow and grasped hold of a taunt line with both hands, trembling in abject terror. The boat rose to the crest, gaining speed rapidly, and shot forward at an alarming pace, careening and thrashing about in the throes of wind and water. James leaned back for balance as the tiller suddenly became limp and unresponsive—fate would see them through...there was nothing else he could do. Agonizing seconds passed while the boat fought her way down the rising crest of the roller. The roaring surf grew in intensity as they neared the reef. The wave slowly collapsed under them as the coral took the brunt of its energy and they landed with a sickening crash of cracking timbers and planking just inside the barrier reef. Water trickled through broken seams as caulking gave way. The port side rigging parted with a resounding clap in the dim twilight causing the spar to slant forward at a sickening angle as the sail collapsed and wrapped itself around the mast flapping and flaying about.

A marked decrease in the intensity of waves greeted them inside the shelter of the reef. Wind assailed the stricken craft, tossing it violently toward the rocky outcrop looming ahead in the murky twilight. The sail, now reduced to rags, was hurriedly gathered in and furled as best as could be under the circumstances and stowed forward with the rations. Within minutes a rough, stone covered shore line broke through the flying mist and crashing surf. Jacobs and Griswall, accompanied by Lewis, leaped from the bow and fought their way to the beach pulling a thick line through the pounding surf and scampered up the steep landing while Howlette and the two remaining Mexicans heaved the boat out of the water dragging it to higher ground. A line was secured around a huge boulder and tied off. James went back to the boat to help Maria safely ashore. With all hands gathered around he shouted above the relentless howl of the wind, "Wait here while I search out shelter. We have to retreat to higher ground before the storm surge overtakes the cove. While I'm gone offload the stores. They *must* be stored away from the shore before we are floundered. Be prepared to haul everything from the boat to the highest point we can find, on my orders!"

He turned and dashed off into the fog-shrouded landscape, disappearing within seconds, leaving the throng of shivering retches to fend for themselves.

Maria immediately instructed the two Mexicans in their native tongue pointing toward the boat and gesturing while the crewmen from the *Rose* looked on in a state of total bewilderment. Lewis was the first to speak, "Well, nippers…we best git a move on afore the skipper returns and finds us a sittin' on our arses. 'Pears th' lass has assumed command of these here greasers, 'n' we best be lookin' smart our own selves…hee…hee." He swaggered off a few feet before looking over his shoulder for approval then motioned the others with a sideways nod of his head. Thirty minutes later the rations were piled on the highest part of the beach and covered with a sopping wet canvas weighted down with several large stones to keep it from being blown away by the unrelenting wind. It was grueling work, made all the worse by the deteriorating conditions.

"'Pears ta me there's not near 'nough ta feed th' seven o' us lads…ta my way o' thinking'." Griswall was the first to speak after they had rested and regained a measure of strength.

Lewis nodded saying, "We be a'hurtin' fer sure if this here storm decides ta stay 'round fer awhile. A meal a day would be a right smart 'mount from 'ha looks o' what we dragged up." Jacob's gaze drifted across the gathering darkness to Maria who sat with her head bowed.

"It was all I could find in the short time allotted to me. I was afraid of drawing attention, buying large quantities." She lifted her head and continued, "Is it better to suffer the pangs of hunger or dance at the end of a rope? We'll make the best of it. That is all I can say. Be thankful that you will see another day. God has chosen to spare your miserable lives for some reason."

"Th' noose be a quick way ta die. Starvin' 'll take a bit longer afore ye be a cashin' in yer chit. I'm a'thinkin' it ain't good ta be a havin' a woman along fer tha ride neither. Woman be nothin' but bad luck; always was 'n always will be." Griswall muttered just loud enough to be heard. Cutting his eyes in her direction he continued, "'N' I'll not soon be a forgettin' what ye did ta me." Rubbing the side of his face, he spit a brown stream of tobacco juice and then wiped his chin on the back of his shirt sleeve.

Howlette broke through the dense vegetation and staggered down the rough rock-strewn shore, collapsing on a knee before them. His chest heaved from exhaustion, and it was several moments before he was able to speak. "Bring as much as you can carry. There's a shallow cave, of sorts, about an eighth of a mile from here. It's the best I could find. Night will be upon us soon. It will provide a measure of shelter and keep the rations dry. It will take a few days to repair the damage to the boat—in the meantime we can search out another cave that better suits our needs. Follow me. We have little time to secure ourselves before night falls." He stood, drew a deep breath, and proceeded to gather as much as he could carry in his arms, set off up the shore and then stopped, turned, and said. "Don't just stand there, you flaming idiots, fetch up those stores and fall into line. We've several more portages before darkness overtakes us. All must be safely in the cave while we still have a measure of light. Lively now…there's not a moment to lose!"

They immediately scrambled to their feet with Maria translating his instructions to the Mexicans. Minutes later they formed a line, loaded with all they could carry, and followed him through the thick undergrowth along a narrow game trail. Some minutes later they entered a rough clearing and saw a black outcrop of overhanging lave rock that would be their home for the night. James was the first to enter, pitching his burden into the far corner. The rest followed, falling to the floor, grateful to be out of the howling wind and cold rain. After a short rest he stood and summoned them to action saying, "There's time enough for a good rest once the stores are safe and dry. Cheerily, lads, there's not a moment to lose. Maria, you'll stay behind and see that everything is stored properly. Tell your countrymen to follow my lead and bring all the rations back here as quickly as they can."

She spoke a few short words motioning them toward the opening of their meager shelter. The Mexicans dashed out into the deepening twilight and disappeared without looking back. James and the three crewmen looked at each other in surprise and then ran down the slope after them. While they were gone, Maria sat about arranging the goods and exploring the cave, picking up twigs and leaves along with an assortment of dry branches. The length of the cave appeared to be about forty feet deep. The entrance was ten feet wide with a shelf of overhanging rock forming an opening some eight feet high. She returned, gathered up the dry twigs and branches placing them next to the wall.

Two hours of hard labor and numerous trips finally saw the last of the stores safely in the cave. The canvas and sodden blankets were spread out along the walls to dry. The water barrels were carefully stacked on the opposite side. They decided to leave the barrels where they were if a larger cave was located—they were too heavy to move again. Maria was busy unpacking and checking the rations making sure everything was dry. Anything that showed the least signs of moisture were opened and spread out to prevent spoilage. It was a meager lot of food and quite obviously not enough to last out the voyage. Howlette surveyed the contents. He would have to assign one or two men to scour the area for anything edible. "Maria, is there any palatable fruit close by, along the shore?" he asked, turning toward her in the growing darkness.

"There are a few tropical fruits; papaya and the mangos are the most plentiful this time of the year. Some small coconut and plantains…what you call the tiny bananas. I think they are not ripe yet, and we must find them first. I think it would be the good idea to change the water in the barrels before we continue. It grows stale in the hot weather quickly."

He was beginning to see Maria in a new light. The stark reality of their situation made him realize that he would have to depend on her more than he'd thought. Her knowledge of the local terrain…and common sense would be invaluable. A smile softened his face. Damned if he wasn't growing fond of her self confidence and daunting spirit. He felt intimidated…and as bad as he hated to admit it—frightened of her in a way he couldn't put into words. She was intriguing, dark and mysterious. There was something different about her…something in her past that he couldn't put a finger on. He regretted not meeting her parents; it might have shed some light on the subject. She seemed out of place among the villagers. Could it be the education she'd received from the Jesuits? No…her demeanor hinted of a blood line much higher than the local peons. Her skin color was noticeably lighter; leading him to believe she was the product of a mixed marriage. It was a perplexing dilemma—an enigma. With time, he would figure it all out but there were more pressing matters at the moment—namely survival.

The relaxed ebb and flow of quiet conversation around the closely gathered group brought a contented sense of well being to him. He could barely make out the dark shadows of the men as they eased themselves against the walls for more comfort. Maria was rummaging around in the stores searching for something of interest. He leaned back on an elbow enjoying the warm, soft dry sand. It was a relief to be out of the howling weather. He found it amazing that such a paltry shelter could offer up such comfortable accommodations. Survival consisted of nothing more than a warm place to sleep—and a full stomach; which reminded him that it had been the better part of twenty-four hours since he and the others had taken a meal.

"Maria, I think it's time to celebrate our safe arrival with a bit of food. What the duce are you looking for?" he asked, searching out her form in the afterglow of gathering twilight. He could hear her soft footsteps in the sand as she returned with a few wooden trenchers and tin cups. "I brought my father's pistol and a small flask of powder. Take these cups. There is a small bundle of twigs. I will attempt to make a fire.."

He was astounded. A fire would dry out the blankets and boil some dried meat to make a broth. Rubbing his hands together, he chuckled to himself and stood to search her out in the darkness. She heard him coming and said, "The sticks are by the water barrels...bring them to me. Put them next to the back wall where the fire will give the most light."

Fumbling around in the dark he located the branches. Sifting them from the sand he cautiously laid each twig down about two or three feet away from the wall. Maria quietly came to stand by him saying, "Take the dry wadding and punk I have in my hand and place it next to the smallest of the twigs and grass. I will put a dusting of the powder on the wadding and try to make the spark with the flint."

He followed her instructions, and then took a step back allowing her to kneel in the sand close to the pile of branches. The tiny spark from the pistol seemed pitifully inadequate in the night but she continued, with great patience, until a minuscule orb of red caught hold of the powder and sputtered to life. A bright flash blinded him momentarily as the punk ignited in a petite, dainty yellow flame that was greeted with a rousing cheer from the men. Blowing carefully, she coaxed the flame higher until it leaped hungrily at the pile of branches. She stood quickly and searched through a parcel she had placed close by and extracted a hand full of tallow candles. Holding one to the flame she gave it to James and then lit another; placing it in the sand some distance from the fire.

"Quick, while the fire burns, gather all the wood you can find. The fire will grow hungry in a short while, and we must keep it fed!" A search of the surroundings produced enough to see them through the night. A small pot was hung over the fire and filled with water and smoked beef. After everyone had taken a portion he assigned two-hour watches to the men, instructing them to guard the fire carefully lest it go out in the night. They couldn't afford to waste the gunpowder to start another. Despite their best efforts, the fire eventually went out…it simply took too much time to search for dry wood.

The storm raged for two days before the clouds lifted and the sun began to peek through the heavy overcast. Venturing out on the third day to check on the boat and search for food, they discovered a trickle of water seeping from a crevasse and decided to set one of the water barrels under it to supply their needs until they set sail. A careful inspection of the planking showed a considerable amount of damage that would take the better part of two weeks to repair. The Mexicans had two knives between them—that was the extent of the tools. It would be slow tedious work…but it could be done. Nails fashioned from green wood and driven in with stones would hold the replacement planks after holes were drilled with the tip of a knife. Caulking would have to be made by stripping the leaves of a yucca plant and twisting the tough fiber into a rope while driving it into the cracks with a stone and wooden wedge. Splitting out the planks would take the most time and labor…but they had no choice. Dragging the boat to higher ground and propping it up in a make shift dry dock they set about making the necessary repairs. The knives were never put aside. Each man used a knife while on night watch and when he was relieved the next man whittled on a plank or made wooden nails until daylight. Each piece was fitted to the ribs of the boat and carefully bent into shape while the wood was still green and pliable and then tied into place until it cured. James inspected each plank before he allowed it to be nailed and caulked. Only five planks were damaged but carving a board out of a tree limb was hard cruel work. Freeing a limb from a tree took the better part of a day…that was sixteen hours long.

The search for food turned up little. It was too early in the season and several weeks before any fruit ripened. A few autumn olive bushes produced an abundance of red berries but nothing else could be found to supplement their diet. He ordered one meal a day based on the stores Maria had brought along. Fatigue from lack of food made the work creep slowly along, but after a week two planks were set in place while the third took shape.

The days quickly passed while a new sail was fashioned and the mast and spar were rigged. Two weeks later saw the remaining plank felled from a tree and all that remained was shaping the limb and fitting it to the boat. It would be at least another week before the boat would be sea worthy. A few days after they'd landed Maria discovered a nest of turtle eggs, and it was decided to sacrifice some of the precious gun powder to start another fire and boil the eggs. Smoked ham was put on to simmer in a pot of water. It was to be the best meal they would have for the remainder of the arduous voyage. The food stores were dwindling despite the strict rationing. James was gravely concerned. The storm, along with the unexpected damage to the boat, was something no one could have foreseen. They would have to sail shortly or risk starvation at sea. He estimated another fortnight on the water before they made rendezvous with the *Rose*. The rations would have to last another thirty days, and they simple did not have it.

The hot summer sun was drying out the green planks on the boat, causing them to shrink and pull away from the caulking. The only solution was keeping them constantly wet with sea water. The humidity was so high that the slightest effort brought pouring sweat and extreme shortness of breath. Seeking out the coolness of the cave they voted to work during the evening to avoid the heat. He ordered them to comb the shore line during the day for anything eatable. Their situation was becoming desperate with each passing day. A small number of sand crab and mollusks were found and most were devoured raw. The hot humid temperatures made it impossible to store the shell fish for any length of time, much to his disappointment. There was simply no way to preserve food in this tropical climate; even the salt cured meats were green with mold.

Finally, the last plank was carefully fitted and tied into place. He decided not to wait for it to cure and ordered it nailed and caulked the next day. His apprehension outweighed his better judgment. In two days they would sail.

Dawn broke with a blinding fury unequaled to anything experienced during the past month. Summer was making its presence known with authority as a white hot sun rapidly lifted above the eastern horizon. A lazy fitful land breeze, tainted with the fetid odor of decaying vegetation, wafted gently over the azure blue sea daring them to set sail. The boat had been laboriously moved to the shore and loaded the night before with the last of the meager supplies. Arising early, to make one last check on the integrity of the repairs to the boat, they now stood idly on shore, shuffling about, kicking at the round shiny stones searching for the courage to climb aboard and shove off to face the uncertainty of what lie ahead. Eventually James muttered half heartedly, more to himself than anyone else, "Gentlemen, destiny awaits us, whatever it might be. We stand an equal chance of dying regardless of whether we stay or sail. We *will* find the *Rose* or die in the attempt. That is all I can offer you. The casks are full of fresh water, and we'll have to make the best of the remaining rations."

Silence greeted the statement. The only person speaking was Maria as she translated to the Mexicans. They turned and started to climb into the boat but were brought up short as Jacobs rushed forward and rudely pulled one of them back shouting, "'Tis th' cap'n who's got th' right ta step onta th' ship first! Not th' likes o' you!" Maria stepped between them and quickly explained the proper etiquette to the Mexicans who stared savagely at Jacobs, making gestures that plainly indicated he was about to get his throat cut.

They stepped back when Maria finished and looked in the direction where Howlette stood with hands clasped tightly behind his back. Without a word he stepped lightly in the boat and settled into the stern sheets taking the tiller in hand. Within minutes the boat was shoved into the calm water of the cove; the sail was trimmed to catch the morning breeze as he put the rudder over on a heading toward the open sea. Looking over the boat to make sure everything was secure; he caught Jacobs with a beaming smile on his face; proud of the fact he'd set the Mexicans straight on shipboard life. He chuckled under his breath. Sometimes the innocence of youth was to be admired. Experience tended to temper ones judgment as the years passed. He knew, all too well, what it was like to be young but Jacobs would learn, the hard way, what it was like to grow old.

The wind freshened enough to make steerageway as they leisurely coasted along headed for the small break in the coral reef that had so violently attacked them previously. The wind gained strength as they left the shelter of the coast and waves buffeted the bow as he weaved the craft through the coral and out to open water. Salt spray and foam flew over the starboard quarter for most of an hour before he put the helm down to run before the wind. A cloudless sky provided no relief from the blistering sun hovering overhead. Wet clothing steamed as moisture evaporated and blew away in tiny wisps. White irregular lines of salt crystals dried on their clothing forming lacy patches of crude embroidery stains that remained until the next wave erased them and the process started over. Keeping the coast in sight, they sailed due south for seventy-two hours. The fourth day he put the tiller over on a starboard reach and the horizon melted away thirty minutes later. Blankets were crudely rigged to provide a makeshift shade from a blazing sun that quickly put blisters on any exposed skin. Regardless of how much water they sipped, thirst was a constant companion. Relief could only be found by taking a small amount of water, holding it in the mouth and letting it slowly trickle down the throat until it was gone. Their swollen lips were so badly chapped they cracked and bled at the slightest movement making it almost impossible to eat. Caldwell was sinking into a desperate, black mood. Brooding and mumbling constantly while cutting his eyes toward the Mexicans. Jacobs was holding his own despite a horrid appearance. His salt encrusted hair stood out in complete disarray. With skin the color of fresh cooked lobster and eyes nearly swollen shut he looked like a demon. James watched him as a coy thought drifted through his mind. A pitchfork and horns, along with a black cape, would set him in good stead for a costume ball. Maria and the two Spanish men were making the best of it. She seemed undaunted by the trials and hardship. The Mexicans were seasick and dehydrating rapidly in the sweltering heat. Lewis was a hardened veteran of sea life and seemed the strongest of the lot. James pondered his uncertain future while the fishing boat wallowed and fought her way through the heavy swells. He'd lost his ship and a number of able seamen and stood in direct disobedience of orders. He was wide of the mark, and entertaining thoughts of coming out alive seemed to be splitting the hair uncommonly fine. His career was ruined and if by some miracle he found a way to return to England he was as good as dead. He was in the middle of a southern ocean, and for the most part—lost, with no means of navigation, looking for a sheltered island somewhere south of his present position. He laughed out loud. Griswall was right. The hangman's noose was a faster way to die and probably far less painful.

Days passed in endless progression and despite a valiant attempt to keep a proper log he soon lost track of time. The sun blazed down on them with complete disregard to their suffering. Three barrels of brackish water remained along with a few pounds of dried meats. Eating salt-cured ham fueled their desire to drink more water, and there was precious little left. Growing too weak to man the tiller, James jerry-rigged a set of lines to hold it in place for a short time while he dozed. It was rarely touched after that. Griswall was delirious and too weak to take anything more than a sip of water. Concern for his welfare soon gave way to apathy. He died some hours—or days later; no one knew the exact time of his death. His body was wrapped in a blanket and placed forward with a few ham bones and stale water. He knew they would have to survive on his flesh—it would have to be done quickly, before the body putrefied. That evening he gathered them around and broached the subject.

"We must eat the flesh of our brother. He has died so that we might live to see another day. I believe we are close to our destination, the island, and our salvation *cannot* be far away." He whispered in a raspy voice that could barely be heard. He sat; head drooping, overcome with fatigue. Hours later he awoke to see the setting sun peeking through a sickly band of mottled haze far in the distance. A stark realization struck him like a scepter. For the first time in his life he knew death was imminent, and for some unknown reason, he welcomed it.

A hand lifted his head. He perceived something being forced past his swollen lips; something warm and faintly moist. A voice, coming from far away, spoke to him insistently, urgently, saying, "Take this—swallow it quickly. It will bring strength."

He tried valiantly to summon the courage to part his lips but failed. His mouth was too dry to speak, much less eat. He felt a finger push something into his mouth again and he immediately coughed, retching up the foreign object. A trickle of water passed over his face, dribbling into the corners of his mouth, moistening a thick swollen tongue. A thin, wavering groan wailed from deep within his chest. Another sip of water brought him back from a dreamy world he fought to stay in. Barely able to open his eyes, he gazed through red slits to see a shadowy figure hovering over him. The angel of death was with him; drifting just above his body, waiting to hear the last sweet breath of life depart before whisking him away. He thrashed about, trying desperately to fight off the black devil hovering just out of reach, but to no avail; it remained, gripping him tighter and tighter, until he collapsed, trembling in the waist of the boat. The mysterious hand lifted his head again and forced another piece down his throat. This time, with the help of water, he swallowed without really tasting anything. A few more slivers of the slimly substance were fed to him before sleep overcame him.

Hours later he awoke to the strange sense of strength returning to his limbs. He sat up, weakly grasping the railing beside him. Looking about he saw four retched forms draped over the gunwales and across the stern sheets. He tried to speak but a garbled incoherent babble greeted his ears. Maria crawled to him and lifted a trembling hand to touch his leg.

After numerous attempts he finally cried, "What of the others? Are they sleeping? I see only four. Someone *must* see to the tiller or we'll drift off course!"

"The others have died. There are only…four."

He looked about him and saw the mutilated remains of a human arm swaying to the motion of the boat dripping black, sticky fluid from its fingertips.

"Did we? Have I?"

"Yes. We have no choice. It is the strength you feel inside. Put it from your mind."

Jacobs and Lewis were nothing more than skin stretched over bones. He could count every rib on their bodies. For a fleeting moment, he thought they were dead before seeing a tiny movement from Lewis. Casting his eyes to the heavens he caught sight of the canvas sail flapping, unattended, in the morning breeze and turned around slowly to see if the rudder was missing. Lines limply held the handle as it swayed idly back and forth. Crawling aft, over the last seat, he cast off the lines and then gripped the tiller, watching the canvas fill as the boat healed over. Leaning to starboard he checked the trim and let his gaze drift to the far horizon. Endless water stretched as far as the eye could see. A faint dot in the sky caught his attention. Blinking to clear his vision; he looked intently at the object again and recognized the outline of a sea gull soaring in the distance. He decided to watch the gull and follow it for the remainder of the day. As the sun dropped below the horizon in a blaze of golden glory he made a mental note of his heading. Later that night he verified it by the position of the stars. They were heading almost due southwest.

The next day he held the same course gauging his position by the rising sun. Just as the first hint of twilight descended over them and the air began to cool for the evening he caught sight of a dark purple form on the edge of the world. It wavered and shimmered in the distance before disappearing into the gathering darkness.

The last of the water was drunk the following morning. Griswall's remains were tied in a blanket and rolled over the side; his flesh bubbled and oozed a fetid odor that could no longer be tolerated. Unable to look at one another, they dined silently on one of the Spanish men, cutting thin strips of flesh from a thigh and swallowing it whole. Sitting quietly along the rails of the boat they seemed to be set apart from the world around them. James shuffled aft and took the tiller, resigning himself to suffer through another day of unbearable heat and thirst.

The dark purple outline grew more distinct with each passing hour and by noon he could make out hazy cliffs with jagged points of timber on the skyline. Overjoyed, he steered toward the island in hopes of finding fresh water and food. Hours passed as the island grew more distinct ahead of them. Midday was approaching and the haze lifted just enough to see a rocky shore line jutting out into the breakwater. It looked familiar, but his feverish mind couldn't put the pieces together. He was lightheaded from lack of water and the island seemed to float delicately on a molten pool of quick silver that shimmered and changed shape constantly.

Movement along, and above, the tops of the far off tree line caught his attention. Some of the dead trees were moving! The barren trunks were shining brightly in the morning light as they passed in stately procession toward the open water. He frowned, trying to make sense of the strange sight far in the distance. Leaning forward, he lifted a shaking hand to shade his eyes from the glare and saw another thin tree trunk suddenly emerge from the edge of the lagoon…the bow of a ship appeared!

Fear gripped his heart as cold chills coursed over his feverish body. A wrenching sob caught in his throat as he clenched his fists, shaking them above his head, "Nnnnnooooooooo!" he screamed at the top of his lungs and then collapsed, pounding his fists on the rough deck boards.

Tears blurred his vision when he looked up again and saw the main courses fly and fill with air.

It was the *Rose*.

CHAPTER TWELVE

A warm gentle breeze moved over the water of a quiet secluded lagoon, stirring up tiny wavelets that could be heard lapping peacefully against the distant shore. The exquisite whispering palm leaves and faint murmur of song birds brought a sense of complete contentment, far beyond anything he could imagine. It was paradise. The sand, as soft as the down of a new born chick, caressed each ache with a mother's loving touch. Soft beams of sunlight broke through a scattering of clouds to dance over a landscape engulfed with butterflies and honey bees, flitting amongst countless flowers, each in full bloom. A subtle fragrance assailed the nostrils with sweet delight while, here and there, a refreshing hint of musty earth, just after a spring rain, gave an invigorating feeling of being one with creation. An electrifying energy, often felt before a thunderstorm, coursed through his body surrounding him in a halo of warmth that could only come from the hand of God. He had passed from life so gently—so quietly; completely unaware it had happened. A ship waited in the harbor to take him to glory; beckoning him with rays of golden sunlight gleaming from polished brass and rigging. The indistinct image of a beautiful woman appeared to hover just out of reach.

"Mother, is it you? Oh, Gawd, how I've longed to see your lovely face after all these years!" He cried, summoning what strength remained in a feeble attempt to rise; reaching out with trembling hands to embrace the face floating above him.

"Is father near? Pray tell…have him move closer…for I cannot see him." he begged as tears spilled down leathery cheeks and over parched lips.

"It is Maria, you remember: from the Spanish prison where you were held captive."

"You mean to tell me I haven't died and gone to my reward? Look about! The birds, the beautiful palms, and this heavenly bed I lay on, so warm and peaceful. Is this not paradise?" he sniffed, disconsolately.

"My dear captain, you are quite alive. Although there were times, times indeed, that I would not have placed a shilling on it." It was Beale who spoke. "It was the rarest stroke of luck, a pure happenstance, that the watch, just after ascending, mind you, glanced about the horizon, as is his usual custom, and beheld the craft...and what remained of the crew. We were quite busy making sail...for jolly England, having given you up for lost. We waited an additional fortnight, you understand, and by the Gods, there you were, in damned deplorable shape. We hauled our wind, put the jolly boat over, and brought you aboard." Beale seemed anxious to tell the story and continued before James could interrupt.

"You've been quite delirious for the better part of three days and able to take only a broth of fish soup and a few sips of water every half hour. Today marks the first day you've spoken in what seems a rational tongue. With complete rest, and solid nourishment, I believe I may pronounce you perfectly recovered within the month. Your body has been tested to the extreme, and it will be some time before we can say, with confidence, that you health has not been affected by the ordeal. We thought you were dead. It was a ghastly sight!"

He patiently listened to the recitation with knitted brow while Beale administered cold compresses to his forehead. "Well, if I'm not dead, for Gawd's sake, prop me up. I've a notion to have a look 'round!"

"Forgive my boldness, but I *must* caution you against the least activity! Nature must mend the tissues sufficiently, and exercise brought on too swiftly can only do you harm," he said sternly. "The blood is weak in the extreme, and the heart greatly taxed, along with the entire body. Complete rest will be the only cure, and sufficient sleep."

"The hell you say! Prop me up...and be damned quick about it! He wheezed, struggling to sit up.

Maria and the surgeon exchanged worried glances but reluctantly lifted him, as gently as possible, to a sitting position while placing a rolled blanket behind his shoulders.

He sighed and then promptly fainted, sleeping for the remainder of the morning.

A few days turned into a week before he felt strong enough to sit for any length of time. Fatigue plagued every move, sapping his energy, leaving him trembling and exhausted. The surviving members of the harrowing voyage, to his great astonishment, seemed little worse for their suffering and had recovered rapidly. The sparse rations of shipboard life, no doubt, contributed to their stamina and as soon as they had taken sufficient liquid, and rested for several days, returned to limited active duty.

Maria took over the responsibilities of nursing him back to health and noticed that he seemed sullen and withdrawn. She sought out the surgeon to express her concerns late one day saying,

"The captain is troubled...he is much too quiet and stares into the distance. The conversation...it is broken, and he cannot concentrate on what I tell to him. There is no joy in the soul, no spark of life in the eye. Is there not something we can do to restore the love of life within him?"

Beale couldn't help noticing how Maria wrung her hands nervously while talking to him. He smiled inwardly; knowing, all too well, the budding signs of deep affection. "Damned if she isn't in love with him!" he thought to himself while making every effort to remain professional and keep his emotions in check.

"I wonder when all this happened," he thought; trying to concentrate on the conversation. "I'm sure Ms. Bidwell will have something to say about it when we drop anchor at Hampshire!" He'd lost track of what Maria had said but it didn't matter...he knew what plagued the good captain, and despite all his medical training, realized that there wasn't much to be done in the way of a cure. Diseases of the mind proved mystical, even to the most learned physicians of the time. It was a subject not well understood. Usually the patient recovered spontaneously or descended to the black pits of despair and eventual insanity. There was no known cure for "the blue funk" that possessed patients in otherwise good health.

"Are you listening...Mr. Beale? Mr. Beale?"

"Yes, yes. I quite understand what you're saying...just lost in thought for a moment," he said gruffly, while placing a forefinger to his chin. "I shall have a word with him at the first opportunity. After he's taken the noon meal...would be the proper time...while he's digesting. Food seems to calm the nerves to a great extent...just after a meal, you know, the body concentrates its efforts on digestion, causing a state of lethargy in the mind. I'll have a word with him then. Fetch me upon the hour after he's taken nourishment."

A light breeze, with a hint of impending rain, brought on a chorus of tree frogs with a din of chirping so loud it drowned out the thunder of distant surf hammering away on windward shores less than a mile from where they sat. Beale, contentedly propped against a large piece of driftwood, sat beside Howlette watching a horde of insects flitting about. He carefully studied him from the corner of his eye while picking at a tooth, trying to dislodge a stubborn bit of crabmeat with a stem of grass. Beale was troubled, unsure just how to broach the subject and had decided to wait and see if he would save him the trouble. The better part of half an hour passed in silence and finally, his patience growing thin said, "My dear captain, a thousand pardons. You may think me the boldest of scoundrels for what I'm about to say, but you *must* inform me of your misery. Pray tell, are you feeling well? As your physician it is my responsibility to see after your good health. The welfare of the crew and the ship depend upon you, and we shall have to make sail eventually, for better of worse. Do I make myself clear?"

The appeal seemed to pass without the slightest hint that it had been heard. He sat, unmoving, as though Beale didn't exist; lost somewhere deep inside himself. Beale opened his mouth and was just about to carry on when he was brought up short.

Howlette cleared his throat and spoke so softly that he had to lean over to hear what was said. "Stephen…(in times of great distress he addressed the surgeon by his first name) Stephen, my good friend. Where do I begin? It has all gone horribly wrong, and I cannot, for the life of me, justify my actions. I stand in direct disobedience of orders plainly stated and clearly understood. Greed and vanity have overpowered my judgment, and I shall be held accountable for the lives lost in what can only be called 'folly.' I have no argument to substantiate any of it. I shall be flogged 'round the fleet, and hanged.

Maria stood, a short distance away, tending a steaming pot. He looked in her direction and then back to the surgeon. Beale followed his lead and glanced around, waiting for the remainder of his confession. "Go on…" he insisted, with a nod of his head.

"Stephen…I'm entertaining thoughts of mutiny, of asking the crew to stay on the island or appointing Kingston acting commander and releasing the ship in his custody. I need not tell you that it pains me grievously to the heart for what I've just said. I'm an officer and a gentleman. I have sworn allegiance to the king and pledged my life to uphold the articles of war. My career is over. I face the most difficult decision of my life. I have one of two choices: sail to England and die, or stay here and live. I simply don't know if I have the courage to live with my conscience if I choose to stay behind. I stand helpless before you, Stephen, struggling with a decision I cannot resolve in a clear-cut manner."

He stopped speaking for several minutes, lowered his head, and then continued. "I believe I shall release the crew. They were only following orders and will be held blameless should a court-marshal be convened; as for myself...I will make the best of it and stay on the island," he said, dismissing the subject with a wave of his hand. He waited for a reply. There was no answer, so he went on.

"If you would be so kind as to convey my apologies to Molly I should greatly appreciate it. I fear I haven't the courage to write a letter of explanation to her...a coward has little to say in his defense."

Beale was struck to the heart. Howlette was right. There *was* no clear-cut answer. If he insisted they return to England it would be a death sentence for his life-long friend; on the other hand, if he suggested that he should stay behind, he would live in exile, alone for the remainder of his life. He sat against the twisted driftwood log trying to decide the lesser of two evils. Stephen Beale, learned surgeon and honors graduate of Medical College, was at a complete loss for words. How does one diagnose and treat anguish? Medicine would not heal this wound...only words would suffice. His mind reeling, he desperately searched for something to say but silence overpowered him. He gazed out over the secluded lagoon knowing, full well, that he could offer no comfort to ease the pain of his dear friend. Grief and anguish would run its course and the mind would come to a justifiable conclusion he could live with. Nothing more could be done.

"James, I wish I..."

"Stephen, there's the problem of Maria." he interrupted, speaking now barely above a whisper. "The crew is considerably at odds at having a female aboard ship...bad luck, you know, and I fear she'll come in harm's way before the voyage is over. Several hundred men and one female can only lead to trouble. Do you suppose there's a way to return her to the village?"

Beale was on the verge of offering a suggestion when he cautioned him, "Have a care Stephen...she's bringing a bowl of soup in our direction!"

She placed the steaming container in front of the captain then sat down between them, crossed her legs, then smoothed her dress.

"Captain, I have overheard some of the conversation that you say in private. I think I know what is the trouble. You think life is at the end and there is no future. I think it is the French ship that causes the problem. Yes? No? Your future lies in the harbor along with the ship that you tried to take. Am I not right, eh?"

Maria was greeted with blank stares on both sides. Howlette slowly leaned forward, raised an eyebrow and tilted his head in her direction. A smile of reassurance softened her face.

"You forget that I have lived a long time among many friends, and my parents are much revered by the peons. I know the way to take the ship that causes you the trouble in the heart. It can be done with what you call ease. I have only one request…that you keep your promise and take me to the new country called England. I have no future here. I have only a small trunk of belongings that will take little room to stow…it is all I have in the world. For this I will tell you…how you say…the simple way, to take the ship and return the joy to your heart."

Beale looked at him and saw the same anxious expression etched on his face that was, no doubt, on his too. Maria beamed a confident smile and waited. Stephen was the first to speak.

"Taking command of a French Man-of-War with several hundred men is not an easy task. What ridiculous notion makes you think it can be done easily? I can think of nothing *simple* that would succeed. The ship is closely guarded and anchored deep in the harbor under the protection of the garrison cannons."

"But you have overlooked several of the simple things," she interrupted; it takes much time to make the gunpowder and the cannon ball. The ship's crews are sleeping in the village. It is much too hot for sleeping on the ship, eh? There is only the small guard watching the peons loading supplies. Most of them are bored and tired. They pay little attention to what they are doing. Your ship, the *Rose*, is gone, and they think they are safe, eh? If you will sail to the North; I know a small harbor where I can be put ashore. Within a few days, on a fast horse, I can return to the village and have a little talk with many peons. When the ship, she is loaded, I will instruct them to overpower the guards late in the evening, wait for a signal, bring the crew, make the sail, and leave quietly after the workers have rowed back to shore. The ship is yours…full of supplies…and we are gone. Eh…what do you say?"

Howlette was completely taken aback. If what she said was true, it could be done without a shot being fired. It was late August; there was a real possibility that most of the crew was ashore waiting for orders. The deck watch could very well consist of less than a dozen men, just enough to oversee the laborers and inventory the supplies as they came aboard. There was only one problem…they may have waited too long. Several months had passed while they were in prison and he couldn't recall just how long it had taken to reach the *Rose*.

"Maria, do you think they've sailed? Have we waited too long?" it was James speaking. "Spring and summer have passed, and before long the fall months will be upon us. Surely they have been re-supplied and have sailed."

"There is only one way. I will have to return to the village. While I'm away you must sail the *Rose* back to the little harbor and wait until I can send someone to inform you of what has happened. It is the only way. If all is well, and the ship is there, I will make the plans with the villagers, and we will set the date. While it is dark you will see the light and send a crew over to make the sail. I will be on the ship should you entertain the thoughts of leaving me *again*. We will come back here and divide the supplies. The island we are on is seldom used, only by occasional fishing boats. It is a long way from the coast, and will be safe for as long as you choose to stay." She glanced casually at each of them and then said, "I will leave now and let you decide what the fate has in store for you."

She was about to stand but he reached out and placed a hand on her arm. His knee overset the bowl of steaming broth, spilling the contents on the sand, but it was of little interest to him now. His attention was riveted on her as he cried passionately, "This is not the time for idle jest! Don't think, for one minute, that you can tempt me into making an ass of myself again."

"What do you have to lose? Is it not worth the try…to see what you call the situation is? There can be no harm in having the look. If the ship is gone…then the decision will be made, and the case will be closed. On the other hand, you will wonder for the rest of your life whether I was right…or wrong," she said, smiling brazenly, challenging him, with a fiery glint in her eye.

He remembered that same look just after she'd been discovered in the fishing boat during the storm and realized, for the second time in a few short weeks, that her spirit would never break, regardless of what hardship stood in her way. She would rise above it and he vowed, then and there, to be at her side if it cost him his life. Admiration filled him so completely it was difficult to speak. He gave Beale a questioning look but his mind was already made up.

"Mr. Beale, would you be so kind as to summon the officers and midshipmen? I would most appreciate, and enjoy, the evening meal, and a bit of light conversation with them. By Gawd, Stephen, I do believe my appetite is on the mend! Have the men dredge up the best offerings of this beautiful island, and we'll enjoy a delightful repast. And have the ship's purser break out a barrel of our finest rum, if there's any left," he said, with a chuckle.

It was the first time the surgeon had seen him smile in weeks. He would remember this day for many years and warmly recall how a few words from a lovely Spanish maiden had restored hope to a lost soul…and all in a matter of minutes. He stood, shook his head, and smiled; realizing he'd just witnessed a miracle as he strode down the sandy beach in search of the purser and first lieutenant.

The small island cove and surrounding coral reefs abounded with countless varieties of shellfish while the late summer days brought forth an abundance of tropical fruit. The *Rose* had been at anchor for the better part of forty five days and the crewmen had become well adapted to finding the best fruit and fish with little effort. Racks hung with fillets over fires that continuously burned day and night. The lower decks were slowly filling with fruit packed carefully away along side barrels of dried, smoked fish. The aroma wafting throughout the gun room and upper decks would fairly set a mouth to watering. The fruit would spoil rapidly in the stuffy holds of the *Rose* but the crewmen were allowed to eat their fill three times a day and most everything would be consumed long before they sailed for England.

The sun cast lengthy rays of burnished copper spears through a scattering of peaceful pink clouds on its way to the other side of the world. Howlette sat discontentedly watching the colors subtlety change as the golden orb settled quietly toward the dark waters. A fretful nervous energy caused him to squirm about and drum his fingers on a log as his mind raced with the possibilities of what the future held in store. Regardless of what Maria said he still faced the possibility of death for disobeying orders and it hung over him like a dark evil specter drying up the joy he'd felt just hours ago. Even if the mission was successful, would it be enough to sway the judgment of the Admiralty? He sat watching the men prepare the evening meal and pondered his bleak future while Maria's words echoed in his mind. He would have to set the matter to rest once and for all. He would either remain on the island or sail back to England with the French first rate in tow in hopes of saving a voyage he'd botched from the very beginning.

His attention was drawn to a small group of officers and midshipmen making their way up the sandy beach and took the opportunity to appraise them carefully, trying in his mind to understand what their reaction would be when he broached the subject of making another attempt at capturing the ship. The surgeon led the way and was the first to speak.

"Gentlemen, the good captain has graciously invited us to dine with him this evening," motioning them to take a seat.

After they had settled in the sand comfortably and the rum passed around, the captain raised a silent toast to the king and tossed back the entire contents of the beaker. "Gentlemen, I've been presented a proposal from Maria." He paused, looking around him, delicately touching the corner of his mouth with a fine handkerchief before replacing it on the driftwood log at his side. "'Tis a mission that could well be the beginning of the end for the vile bunch of renegades that have caused so much discontent and hardship amongst the entire crew."

Mr. Garrett wasn't so sure. "Nah, pocky bitch like as that, she be a wantin' ta bring us down. It'll be the rest o' the British Fleet comin' ta save us afore it's over!"

The others exchanged glances. It took little imagination to guess that something was afoot. There was quiet. It didn't sound like something that could be done easily and for all they knew would be the start of a great battle involving the rest of the Fleet—but anything that offered a break from the monotony of sitting around a smoky fire day and night would be welcome.

"We, together with a few of our Spanish friends, may have won the opportunity to cast a lance into the very underbelly of the enemy. We are going to join with them in an attempt to restore our former glory. Maria has proposed a clever plan whereby we enlist the aid of the peons in recapturing the ship…by deception. She has offered to ride back to the village and convince a number of workers to overpower the watch. She believes most of the crew have taken leave of the ship and are sleeping ashore until ordered to sail. I believe she may be right."

A restless muttering rippled through the men crowded around but he continued before anyone had the chance to voice an opinion. "Our objective will be to secure the ship, once the workers have detained the watch, and bring aboard enough able seamen to sail her out to clear water where she will rejoin with the *Rose*. I intend to return to our present position, re-supply the *Rose*, sell off the remainder of the stores to the villagers, and return to England in triumph. I shall ask for volunteers to board the ship—and might I add that you will certainly share in whatever spoils of war Providence brings."

Significant looks were exchanged. This was far more to the point than they had expected.

"Volunteers may approach the first lieutenant after dinner. God save the king!"

The conversation among the men was subdued and at times an awkward silence engulfed them until someone found the courage to engage the person next to him with a bit of idle chitchat. Garrett and Purcell had drifted off into the shadows and were intently discussing the situation.

"I say we be in fer another thumping at ta hands of them Frenchies, be my way o' thinking'." Garrett commented. "We be 'bout ta lose another round o' good men fer nothing."

Purcell frowned, scratching at an imaginary itch, then declared.

"I know what ye are a thinking' bullyboy, but I'm half a mind ta believe ta Cap'n's on a right smart tack. It could just be them Frenchies would never suspect their friends ta turn on em' hell...how many times we been billeted ashore fer months while ta ship was in ta yards fer overhaul...ye ever think o' that! 'n all ta time we's a thinking' we's safe...snug as a bilge rat on friendly shores. Ta same thing coulda happened ta us were the circumstances a tad different.'

"Ye got yer mind clouded a'thinkin' 'bout all the gold that's on one o' them ships. What are ye a'gon' ta say when we's discover thar's nothin' but powder and shot aboard, and them Spicks have gone and taken the coin with 'em? Ye damned stupid idget...ta frigate's all snugged up tight on her anchor chain, jus' a'waitin' fer some more fools ta make the same mistake twice. It be a wonder she didn't open up with a broadside ta first time t' Cap'n tried ta take 'er," Garrett stated with conviction, tossing the remains of a crab leg into the night.

Purcell pondered the statement at length and was on the verge of comment when Garrett offered up another idea.

"Did ye ever give any thought ta the fact that ta gold jes' might be on the frigate? Tell me so 'n' ye can have me extra ration from the grog monkey when it comes 'round. Them scoundrels jes might do it...'n' be a'laughin' our stupid arses clean out ta sea." He chuckled at his joke, waiting for Purcell to best him with an off-color comment.

"Ye can say what ye will, bullyboy, but my money's on ta cap'n,'n' I'm a'thinkin' I'll volunteer—jes' ta have some fun. Ye be a'forgetin' how ta cap'n explained what's ta happen. Hell, boy, all's we got ta do is wait fer ta signal, row over, and take charge. Couldn't be easier fer an extra share o' ta spoils, eh?"

Garrett scowled. "It ain't gonna come ta no good. This here voyage been plagued from ta start 'n' it 'Pears ta be a'goin' sour agin. I'm not sa' sure we all be a'dancin' from a yard arm a week after we's drop anchor at Chatham. Ta damned Lords 'll take a dim view o' what we's been up to. Might as well a mutinied fer all the good it's done us."

He took another swill of rum and belched loudly to add emphases to his statement.

"'Pears we's a'bein' ordered 'round by a woman, fer Christ's sake! 'N fifteen years o' sea behind me, in't *never* seen the likes o' it. We's a'goin' straight ta hell in a regulation handbasket 'n' the devil's a'holdin' ta door wide open fer us!"

The following morning found James in his cabin aboard the *Rose*. Maria and the surgeon, along with First Lieutenant Purcell were gathered around a small table discussing plans for sailing back across the bay to a small inlet that Maria said she could recognize.

"I see you've gathered an impressive group of volunteers by the looks of this list," he noted with satisfaction.

"It appears there are more than a few who agree with me...ah...Maria that we might be able to recover our self respect. Having thought it over for the night, are we overlooking anything?" He glanced over the group quickly. "If not, time is of the utmost importance, and I suggest we sail in two days, provided everything is in order."

Looking over the table at Maria he said, "It appears the entire mission is in your hands, at least for the present. I understand it will take two or three days to arrive, by horseback, at the village?"

She nodded.

"Then we shall wait for eight days. If we have not received instructions by that time we will return here and decide our future."

Beale was silent, reserved, offering nothing to the conversation. Purcell drummed the table with his fingers, clearly uneasy. Noticing his discomfort, James offered the floor to him saying, "You seem at odds over something, Mr. Purcell, and I shall hear what's troubling you."

Purcell glanced up from studying his hand and sniffed, "What are we ta be a down' 'bout ta frigate, sar? She be mighty close ta that Man-o'-war with er' broadside pointed, a right smart towards us, sar."

He smiled, and said casually. "I've a mind to pour her full of grape and thirty-two pounders. You seem to have forgot, Mr. Purcell...the charges have been pulled. Before you weigh anchor instruct the men to load the cannon, and as you snub up on the chain, when the anchor just clears—fire a round into the frigate. Need I remind you there are fifty cannon per side? I should think that would be enough to reduce her to ruin before they could load a single shot in defense; wouldn't you agree? At that range a thirty-two-pound ball would go through two or three feet of solid oak without a moment's hesitation. I fancy it just might clear the other side if aimed properly. Of course, several shots cleverly placed at the water line would put things in proper order."

Purcell nodded in agreement while rubbing his chin. "Beggin' yer pardon, sar…but it'll take a right long while ta bring up powder 'n' shot from the holds, 'n' load fifty cannon. 'N' without powder, boys, 'n' a proper gun crew, it could take hours afore 'tis done proper."

"You'll have all night to make the arrangements, Mr. Purcell. You will weigh anchor with the earliest land breeze. I shall assign two extra gun crews to man the side properly. As the ship comes to bear you'll fire as many cannon as possible. If the guns can't be rolled out in time I order you to open the gun ports and fire through them if need be. I want the frigate reduced to splinters. Is that clearly understood?" he rumbled, pointing a finger in his direction.

"Yes, sar! 'twill wake the garrison, 'n' we stand a good chance o' takin' some damage from 'em, but with any luck we jes' might be out o' range afore they's get us sighted in."

"I realize we may be making plans for nothing. The ship may well have sailed long ago, but if Providence smiles upon our efforts and we succeed in our goal, I fully intend to cause as much havoc as humanly possible before the ship clears the harbor. I can still recall that black-hearted French devil running steel through a helpless man, and I should like nothing better than to see the look on his face when he discovers his ship is gone!"

He looked intently at the faces around the table. "We sail in two days!"

The *Rose* bounded joyously through heavy rollers. Clouds of spray cascaded over her bows covering the decks with white foam that ran in torrents through the scuppers. She seemed glad to be released from her confines and eager to run before the wind. Timbers creaked and groaned; unaccustomed to the strain placed upon them as the crew cracked on more sail. In less than a week they would sight the mainland and search for the small inlet where Maria would put ashore. Howlette voiced his concern about her welfare and how she intended to find transportation.

She gave him a relaxed smile and said, "With my father's permission, I have traveled the costal roads for many years with my friends. There was nothing else to do, and we traveled far, often taking meals and sleeping at many of the farmers' homes along the way. I know them by heart, and they will be only too glad to rid the land of enemies. I will have no trouble borrowing the horse."

Daily shipboard life quickly returned. The crew knew they were sailing for England. It would be the better part of a year before they sighted the Channel and the Straits of Dover and despite the perils they faced upon returning seemed happy to be at the end of the voyage. The island of Formentera had provided a rich bounty of food and a chance to rest and re-fit the ship. Maria said the inlet would be near Cullera where the Cabriel River met the sea. She would ride north to the village of Sueca and enlist the aid of many men and return to Gandia. If the ship was there a messenger would return to Cullera and sail with the *Rose* south along the coast to Gandia. There they would wait. Under the cover of darkness the *Rose* would sail within sight of the harbor and watch for the signal to board. Maria, in the mean time, would inform the workers and by the time the *Rose* arrived everything would be in place.

The Mediterranean Sea was usually calm in the late autumn and the winds rarely turned fowl. The *Rose* sailed easily along with only an occasional fuss with lines and trim—the wind being two points abaft the beam. James spent much of the time in his cabin recuperating. Still weak and easily exhausted from the slightest exercise; he was months away from full recovery. The surgeon thought it remarkable that his mind seemed fully recovered.

Seventy-two hours after the first sea gulls were seen the watch sighted land fine off the bow; the sun just clearing the horizon through a scattering of purple overcast and thin clouds racing with the wind. Twelve hours later details began to form and take shape as the *Rose* neared the mainland. Maria constantly scanned the distant coast line for hours trying to recognize a familiar landmark and finally decided they were too far north. With the first hint of twilight he ordered the sail shortened. They would coast along on their present heading and turn south early the next morning. The evening passed quietly. The gun decks were somber with little of the usual bantering heard around the mess tables. Purcell was optimistic and in high spirits. Mr. Ruben, as was his usual routine after the meal, carefully chose a book from his sea chest and quietly left the group. Purcell followed him on deck and watched as he climbed up the shrouds disappearing through the lubbers hole on the main mast. A few minutes later he followed and eased down beside him. Ruben cast a measured glance in his direction before taking up the volume balanced on his knee.

"A fine evening I'm a thinking'," Purcell said, at a loss for words.

"Indeed it is. One rarely has the opportunity to enjoy such peace and tranquility."

"Ye seem ta be a right educated man…don't seem proper fer no able seaman."

"I've had an extensive education, and have studied abroad for many years."

Purcell frowned, pondering the mystery of why such a man would choose the hardships of sea life. "Ye be a pressed man?"

"No. I'm here of my own free will…a sabbatical, if you will." Ruben closed the book and looked out over the lengthening twilight; a painful thought creased his face with deep lines.

"Yer running away from somethin' ain't ye?"

"I quite sure it's none of your concern, and I resent your feeble attempt at prizing out information that's of no interest to you in the least."

Purcell took the hint and started to leave, saying, "I's jes' tryin' to make polite conversation, but I sees ye not be interested in ta likes o' me, an' I be taken my leave o' ye, sar." Ruben placed a hand on his arm.

"Forgive me, sir. I have shown you little consideration in the matter. Please accept my humble apologies. I mean you no disrespect."

"Maybe 'nother time, sar."

"Perhaps."

Dawn came quickly, greeting them with bright white clouds and deep blue sky. The ship was brought over with the wind four points large on a southwest course. Just before the second watch was brought up, Maria hailed the quarterdeck, pointing off the starboard side, smiling. The wheel was put over; the wind one point abaft the beam, and the *Rose* crept closer to the shore. An hour later the unmistakable outline of the inlet opened to reveal the lower reaches of a large river. The lead was hauled out while they carefully entered the sheltered cove surrounded by dense undergrowth. Maria went below, changed clothes, borrowing trousers and a light jacket from the purser's stores. A few minutes later she emerged on deck with a canvas duffle stuffed with food as the boat was swung over the side. James waited on deck by the rail, watching her every move. She was about to step over the side and down the rope ladder when he grasped her arm. "Maria, I...be careful. It would pain me greatly, should you come to harm."

"You worry too much!" she laughed heartily. "The farm is just over the cliff on the flat land. I have been there many times, and I will be most upset if they do not remember me! I will return before the eight days if the ship has gone. Will you still take me to the England land?"

Howlette smiled and nodded, "Yes. I will see that you have safe passage. You've saved my life. How could I refuse?"

Their eyes met...and then she was gone. He watched the boat until it disappeared from sight, turned and went to his cabin closing the door behind him. Crossing the tiny room, he collapsed behind the desk.

It was a waiting game now.

CHAPTER THIRTEEN

A cold drizzle brought an end to a gray cloudy day. A chilly northwest breeze sent most of the off duty watch below to gather the remaining warmth offered from the gun deck. Distant breaks in the clouds foretold a miserable time of it for the night watch coming up in an hour. Day seven was drawing to a close when the lookout spotted a boat pulling away from the banks of the distant river. Word was sent below for the captain and minutes later he was on deck anxiously scanning the outlying shore in the evening twilight. A half hour later a boat bumped along side and a greasy Mexican hauled himself up the ladder dressed in rags that threatened to fall off the poor devil at a moments notice. Disheveled, matted locks of raven black hair framed a deeply tanned face.

"I have been sent to inform you that the Senorita, she had decided to stay in the village and make the plan for you."

"Pray tell, what is the name of the Senorita you're talking of?" he interrupted.

"Her name is Maria. Why should you ask?"

"Just a precaution, nothing more."

"The senorita has told us of a bold plan against the Frenchmen in the harbor. We think it is the good one, señor. I think will be done, how you say, eeeasily. There are only a few of the sailors on board, and…"

"You mean to tell me that the ship is still anchored? And what of the frigate?" he was thunderstruck by the news, and somewhat beleaguered by it.

"They are still there, señor. It takes the long time to make the powder and ball, although we are almost finished," he stammered.

"You must make the sail at once, señor, or we will be too late for the plan! Maria, she will be on the ship waiting for you. She has been in the village now for several of the days making the plans with the peons that load the powder, and they are willing to do as she says, but you *must* sail at once or we will not arrive in time! I have rode hard for two days! You must go *now*!"

Howlette drummed his fingers on the tariff rail digesting the information. Glancing in the direction of Beale he said, "It will be impossible to sail out of this inlet in the night. We have no choice but to wait until dawn. Inform the bosun, and I shall see him on the quarterdeck, if you please."

Minutes later the bosun appeared and after a smart salute they were seen in close conversation. It was decided to sail at first light, as soon as the lead could be thrown with some assurance of accuracy. A deal of treacherous shoals stood in the way before they could reach the open sea. And he would have no part in grounding the ship for the sake of ten or twelve hours gained by leaving now.

First light found the entire crew on deck cracking on canvas and taking up slack in the sheets for better trim. The *Rose* swung on her chain and snubbed just as the anchor cleared the bottom; the capstan clacking away as the dogs found their paws and held until the next turn was made. The land breeze was picking up nicely and within the hour they could make out the gentle rollers of open water. Howlette ordered the mains loosed and as the helm was put over the *Rose* found her head and responded. It would take three days following the coast to reach the harbor where they would wait on the horizon for the signal light. The weather co-operated with a steady breeze that called for little adjustments in trim. The watch had little to do except prepare for battle. Charges were pulled and the cannons swabbed. New powder was rammed home followed by freshly chipped ball. They would be prepared, should the need arise, to defend their prize.

A hazy outline of cliffs signaled the entrance of the infamous harbor that brought back so many memories along with images of Maria. Staring through the telescope he could just make out the entrance in the distance. The game was about to begin again.

February, a notorious month for bad weather, made its entrance with modest fanfare on the heels of a rousing blizzard that had paralyzed London for the better part of five days. It seemed a lifetime since autumn breathed its last. Shuffling amongst ledger sheets scattered over a small table in a private room just off the main hallway across from the vault, Morris, with a look of intense concentration, scribbled yet another column of figures and sat about, adding them a second time. Now three thousand pounds poorer for his efforts, he carefully finished the addition, tossed the quill in its well, leaned back with a sigh, drumming his fingers on the arm of the chair. With any luck—and a second mortgage against his holdings, should see him through to November…the last payment to Miss Bidwell's account. She had been true to her word—disappearing, for the most part, since their conversation at the hospital some three months past. The bank president, a close friend, had mentioned—strictly off the cuff, that she made a habit of checking her accounts monthly and had recently asked for a large draft. He thought it somewhat strange of her to withdraw such an amount without naming a custodian, but shrugged it off as the whim of womanhood. Besides, he would eventually know where the money was deposited when the draft returned for payment.

Morris said nothing after querying the man. He had a vague idea of what she was up to. And he wouldn't be a bit surprised to hear the funds were leaving the country. She had opened a vain and was bleeding him dry. A cold, empty feeling passed through him, a familiar one, he knew it very well, and he should have paid attention long ago but it was too late…the damage had been done and there was no turning back. Shifting to a more comfortable position, be tried to fetch a scheme to mind that would remove her permanently, but failed. Somehow he had the vague feeling that Harry might be part of the problem. He and Molly seemed to be close friends. Turning, he looked about the airless room; a triangle of peeling paint, wedged against a section of ancient oak molding, captured his attention. "Hell," he thought. "The damned letter she'd waved under his nose was probably right here in the vault!"

A spasm of coughing overtook his concentration, and left him trembling. Tired and disgusted, he arranged the scattered papers into better order, replaced them in a tattered folder, shoved the entire affair back in the black cavity of his personal drawer and slammed the lid shut, locking it with practiced experience.

A cane leaning at a precarious angle against the table clattered to the floor as his foot connected with the table leg. "Damn!" he growled, shaking a clenched fist—it was just out of reach. He tried, repeatedly, to coax it closer with his foot, but after several attempts, exasperation got the better of him and he called for assistance. A pale, anemic fellow, rail thin, with spectacles and sleeve garters arrived. With nervous, darting eyes, he followed a finger pointing at the floor, retrieved the object, and handed it to Morris.

"Thank you. I could very well have fetched the retched thing myself, but as you can see, I've been considerably indisposed with the fevers. If you will be so kind as to assist me for the briefest moment, I shall be on my way."

Details of the coast were coming into view, as a deep-rooted hatred of the audacious French scoundrel reared its ugly head. In his heart he vowed that once back in the harbor there would be no effort spared, no nerve he would not strain to bring the beggar to justice. He harbored no illusions. And so he smiled at the task before him. It required a staggering amount of willpower to stave off an impetuous need to charge headlong into them with guns blazing, but common sense ruled the day as he stood on the quarterdeck gripping the rail, knuckles turning white with strain, trembling in anticipation. A cloudless sky hung overhead as the cold front passed high above, shifting the wind around to a more northerly direction, causing them to change course away from their prey.

Morning found the *Rose* coming up over the horizon in the lap of a smoldering sun to take a final bearing that was duly marked on the log. They would return at sundown and wait for the feeble signal light. As the ship fell off and disappeared over the horizon Howlette ordered a brisk cannon drill for an hour, followed by the usual holystoning of the decks. As best as he could tell, it was Sunday and the rest of the day was devoted to make and mend, allowing the crew to repair their clothes, and pass the remainder of the day at leisure.

The ship tacked an hour before dusk and under reefed main sails crept back on station as night overtook them. A sea anchor was dropped overboard while the breeze steadily plied the limp sheets forward and back in a rhythmic slap that matched tempo with the gentle waves lapping the sides of the hull. Every eye was straining, trying to be the first to glimpse a signal from the man-of-war. Just as darkness wrapped them in a velvety blackness, a weak, yellowish pinpoint of light, glimmered at the waters edge far in the distance then winked out. It was almost impossible to see. It was the bosun who spoke,

"Damn me, Cap'n, but I could swear I jes' saw a wink o' light. Me eyes are a'playn' tricks, I do believe."

"Where away?"

The newly appointed bosun replied, "Pardon me, sar, if I jes' might direct ye a little."

A rough hand on his shoulder directed him to stand in front of the bosun. "Jes stand right here in front o' me and wait fer a spell...maybe she'll 'Pear again. Jes' wait."

"We're much too far away, man. We'll have to sail in a deal closer than we are at the present to make out any such light..."

He never finished the sentence. The tiny speck of light appeared again, winking on and off three times...he could hardly believe his eyes.

" By Jove, did you see that? Was it the signal?"

I do believe it be yon signal, Cap'n, sar. 'Tis ta same one I jes' seen a spell back," the bosun replied in a fevered pitch.

He spun around and ordered the boarding party to form up at the ladder in preparation to go over the side. Within minutes they pushed off their craft from the hull of the *Rose*, bent to the sweeps, then, hoisting sail, headed back to the harbor intent upon reaching it as the shadow of darkness fell. And Howlett, huddled in the stern sheets, sat silent, his black brows knitted, lips pursed, malevolence smoldering so overwhelmingly he could hardly contain himself. It was a long soundless journey over gentle waves that slapped against the boat as they plied the calm waters of the inner harbor. An hour later found them along side the man-of-war. A hushed call soon produced a rope ladder that crashed against the side of the ship from far above, followed by a wavering voice.

"It is Maria...be quick! We have little time before the sun rises. The ship is ours! I have waited. Where have you been? The peons grow anxious to be gone, and I have had the bad time trying to keep them on the ship!" she cried with great emotion.

Within the hour all the boarding party was safely gathered in the waist of the man-of-war. All appeared to be quiet and the only light to be seen was on the quarterdeck just abaft the compass. The rest of the lights were extinguished, and caused him some discontent until he realized it had been done on purpose. A lantern could only invite disaster in the hands of someone below decks wanting to start a fire.

"We came as fast as we could. Where are the prisoners being kept?" he asked in whispered tones to Maria.

"They are most secure in the captain's quarters in the back of the ship where they can cause no harm. All is quiet with them. They are tied and gagged and cannot make the noise. We have the ship; she is ours. What do you want us to do?"

"Instruct them to help bring up powder and shot to the gun crews...On second thought…have a round of grape shot brought up as well."

He turned swiftly to the bosun and hurriedly said in muffled tones, "Make a quick check of all the cannon, and load them…including the stern chasers. We will make short shrift of the frigate when it's light enough to safely fire a broadside in her.

There was little time lost in sending the peons down to the powder room and within an hour the starboard cannon were loaded and ready to be ran out at first light. Over a dozen would be loaded with grape shot and fired into the frigate before hoisting anchor. Howlett made a quick inventory of the stores in the hold and was astounded at the sight of barrel upon barrel of powder stacked in neat rows and tied securely with large hemp ropes. The huge hold of the man-of-war echoed with each footfall as he went about with a small lantern checking first one thing and then another. He was astonished at the food stores, casks of fresh Spanish beef, mutton, salt pork and hundreds of oaken casks of fresh water. He realized they had come none too early—from the looks of everything the ship was prepared to sail any day. By all rights she should have sailed already—except for the final loading of powder and shot, everything was in its proper place.

He hurriedly climbed the ladder to the gun deck and sought out the bosun. They double checked the cannons.

"Very good…very good. See that the remainder are loaded just so…snug up each and every line on the gun tackle. I shall want them ready to be run out at a moment's notice, when I give the order. Do I make myself perfectly clear on the matter?"

"Oh, yes, sar. I'll have 'em snugged up real tight in 'ha blocks with 'er noses next ta th' port 'oles, Cap'n, sar. Ye can count on it!" he exclaimed in the weak lantern light. "One good heave and them cannon'll be poppin' their black noses right proper like. Jes' give me th' word!"

"As you were…I've pressing business on the quarterdeck. Pass the word if you should need me…Carry on."

He ascended the remaining ladder to the ward room and then into the Captains quarters to make a quick check on the prisoners. An evil-looking Mexican, with skin the color of mahogany, stood guard in one corner of the elegantly furnished room, brandishing a large shotgun, picking at a tooth with a black finger. By the looks of the prisoners huddled together in the semi-dark corner of the room, they had been lucky to come away with their lives. Tattered and bruised; some with blood soaked bandages that had now dried to a dark chocolate brown.

"I can see you have the situation under control."

"Si," the Mexican said through a mouth of rotted teeth.

James could tell by the way the man had answered, that he understood nothing of what was said to him. A grim smile passed quickly across his face. He left him to finish the task of cleaning his teeth.

A few quick strides—he was at the door leading to the waist of the ship. Dousing the lantern, he threw open the door and as quickly closed it behind him. Maria was on the quarterdeck and called down to him.

"What is to be done? I have all the peons at work bringing up the powder from below."

"What a splendid job you've done…and in such a short time; there is nothing more you can do. If you would be so kind as to go to the wardroom…that's the cabin just below the captain's quarters, and wait for me there. I shall be there just as soon as we clear the harbor and are safely out in open water. Please go now to the safety of the wardroom."

Morning twilight was stealing away the night. Dim outlines of masts and tackle lent an eerie, surreal atmosphere, as swirling fog blanketed everything with shimmering drops of dew. Outlines of men scurried about, arranging each sheet and coiling it in its proper place, could be seen about the waist of the ship. A grim smile broke through an otherwise stony countenance as he strode about the ship, double checking each tackle and stay. The ghostly silhouette of the frigate emerged from the swirling fog like an evil specter, taunting him. The land breeze could just be felt on the face as dawn broke on this infamous day.

He stopped one of the men, saying, "Pass the word for the bosun, and have him report to me at once if you please."

The man nodded and disappeared into the fog. Several minutes passed before he emerged from the companionway door and hurried to his side.

"Ye sent fer me, sar?"

"Yes, my good man. I've a notion to back the sails as soon as it's prudent. Snub the ship to the anchor as quietly as you can. I've a notion to swing her on the anchor chain before we leave."

"But, sar! Do ye realize ye'll a be pointin' her right smartly toward the shore?"

"I'm completely aware of it…You have your orders…as soon as the light clears a bit more, be ready on my command. Do you understand?"

"Yes, sar…on yer command!"

"Time is of the essence...are the remaining cannon loaded and tight in the blocks...both broadsides?"

"Yes, sar...all hundred 'n' ten of 'em, sar."

"Good. Have the gun crews standing by on the starboard side with slow match at the ready. We'll have a go at yon frigate first off. Is that clear? Let there be no mistakes! Instruct the crews to aim for the water line after a round of grape shot across the decks. Man the stern chasers next, should there be any relief coming from shore. After the starboard broadside, have the crews man the larboard cannon. Don't bother trying to reload the starboard cannons. Is that clear?"

"Yes, sar! Are ye a plannin' ta wage war here in the harbor?" said the puzzled bosun.

"That's my intention. Now off with you; there's not a moment to lose!"

A burnt orange sun peeked over the tree studded hillside as Howlette climbed the quarterdeck ladder and surveyed the quiet harbor. Nothing seemed out of place as the sleepy town awoke and started another day of toil. He observed a hoy shoving off from the pier and watched it pull toward another ship in the harbor. Several boats were being loaded on shore. The land breeze was picking up. It was time to put his plan to action. He signaled the bosun to begin taking in the slack on the anchor chain. The steady clack of the capstan began, and slowly, the ship creped forward, while several crewmen busied themselves backing the sails. As the man-of-war turned on her anchor chain, he went below to the gun deck.

A heavy silence permeated the close quarters as he personally sighted down the length of a starboard cannon; when satisfied, he lowered the slow match to the touch hole. A huge thirty-two-pound shot was hurled across the short distance and into the hull of the frigate less than a hundred yards away. Seconds later another cannon unleashed a round of grape shot, as the silence of the sleepy lagoon was broken by earth shattering explosions that echoed throughout the hillsides. Timbers and rigging crashed down to the decks of the frigate amid the screams of wounded and dying men. The surprise was absolute and complete. He ran back to the quarterdeck to survey the damage. Huge splinters of oak were flying everywhere as the frigate suffered under the attack. Another shot—and the mizzen mast went by the board. Spouts of water leaped high in the air as round after round sought out her water line. Within minutes she was listing heavily. He dashed down the ladder and hailed the bosun.

"Have your men aim the long guns at maximum elevation. I've a mind to pepper the garrison with a few rounds, if they'll fly that far. Aim the stern chasers at anything that appears to be pulling off shore to assist the frigate. A few shots at the villa just below the fort would give me great pleasure!"

Captain Rondeau was just sitting down to his morning tea when he heard the first explosion. Leaping to his feet, upsetting the table, he dashed to the window over looking the harbor to see a huge cloud of smoke drifting down the harbor entrance. Complete astonishment drained the blood from him as another explosion shattered the silence of early morning. He watched mesmerized, confused and bewildered at the sight before him.

"What the deuce?" he exclaimed. Turning to summon his aide; he was in the process of gathering his coat and tricorn when the first round shattered the corner of the guest room to his right. Dust, masonry and timbers crashed down; the concussion sent him flying to the floor in a heap. Crawling over the debris, he struggled back to the window to see his ship club hauled around her anchor. The larboard side was swinging slowly towards the fort...the frigate's mizzen mast was down. Several more rounds landed too close for comfort and he ducked behind the wall for safety. Dust clouds blocked out further observation. Crawling on hands and knees to the back door he scurried out into the patio.

"Sacre Bleu! What is happening?" he screamed, balling his fists in rage. The frigate was listing badly...she would sink where she lay. Round after round pummeled the villa. He lost count of how many cannon balls landed just below the fort...the range was too great for an effective shot. Boats pulling away from the pier were quickly turned back by the six pounders. He watched, completely helpless as the main sails were loosed and his beloved ship found her heading, turned and slowly gained speed for the harbor entrance, sailing away in a cloud of smoke...

The gun deck was a maze of smoke and sweating bodies. The cannon were left where they lay as the scant boarding crew ran up the ladder to the waist of the ship and on up the ratlines to help trim the sail to draw all the land breeze they could get. The man-of-war was picking up speed slowly and seemed to be drawing water nicely. The ballast appeared to be properly placed, but she was a little heavy in the bows. James paced the quarterdeck like a caged lion; hands clasp behind his back, stopping only occasionally to appraise the scene slowly disappearing behind them. A grim, defiant smile etched his features as the helm was brought over and they stood out for the channel and open waters ahead. The rollers were coming from across the larboard side—he could see the *Rose* wearing around and cracking on more sail. Kingston was a good man...he would shadow them on her windward side—making her less vulnerable to a weather gauge attack.

It was the purest stroke of luck...not a shot had been fired at them. The frigate was down; only her masts were showing above the water, and would be no threat to them. The rest of the ships were still at anchor in the harbor, their crews still mustering on shore and rowing out. But it would be too late to form an affective chase. The ship was secure; he went below to check on Maria.

"Maria?" he said with a gentle knock at the wardroom door.

"Please come in," was the muffled reply

He entered and gently closed the door behind him, strode across the room and collapsed in a leather chair. "It's done...we sail back to our island with the *Rose*, transfer enough food stores and take on fresh water for the voyage back to jolly old England within the month. I couldn't have done it without you. I owe you a dept I can never repay. You've saved my life. If only the Admiralty will show leniency toward us I may yet come away unscathed."

"It is the chance we have to take. You must not dwell on what may happen in the future. You must live only for today; tomorrow is the dream, and yesterday is only in the memory."

The voyage back to the island was uneventful. Light winds kept the need to trim and tack the ship to a minimum and the *Rose* was always on the weather gauge. The bosun kept a steady lookout on her, and when she went about on another tack; he ordered the man-of-war to the same heading. In this manner they sailed on to the tiny island retreat and made land fall ten days later. They had a tricky time of it; getting the huge man-of-war through the coral shoals and shallow waters of the inlet, but she eventually dropped anchor in the lagoon along side the *Rose*. Preparations for the transfer of stores started the following morning and a water party was sent inland for fresh water to fill all the remaining casks in the two ships. Howlette ordered the stores of the man-of-war removed to the last barrel to better take inventory...a task that took several days to ferry ashore. Evening was drawing to a close some three days later as the last of the barrels were off loaded. He assembled the crew that evening around a roaring fire to offer his congratulations.

"Men, we have done the impossible: captured a first rate, one-hundred-ten-gun French man-of-war without so much as a pistol shot being fired, sunk a frigate without the loss of a single soul, and sailed away with a full load of stores in the process. I would be remiss to say that we owe a dept of thanks to our esteemed Maria, and I should like to take a moment to extend personal salutations of gratitude." He doffed his hat and presented an elegant leg; bowing with a sweep of his plumed hat.

She blushed, and hid her face behind her hands.

"I should think the peons deserve something for their efforts. Bring out the freshest of the beef and whatever else you may find, Purser, and we shall have a feast before I send them on their merry way home. Oh...and by the by, Purser...a gold coin from the French captain's private stores should be in order...wouldn't you say?"

The evening went well. Everyone was in a jovial mood and the festivities went well into the wee hours of the morning. He asked the peons to stay on a few days longer to speed the transfer of stores to the *Rose* and to help in the filling of the remaining water casks.

The following day James was on the beach observing the workers and occasionally casting an eye toward the man-of-war. Something wasn't right...the ballast of the ship was too heavy, and she seemed to lay with her bow down. He decided to check the bilge before the better part of the stores were re-loaded and have a look at the placement of the ballast stones. The ship would sail much better if the bows were slightly higher and moving the stones was the only way to trim the ship. He, along with the bosun and Mr. Beale, went out to have a closer look. Rowing around the hull convinced him the ballast needed to be re-adjusted, so they pulled alongside and boarded the ship. Descending into the hold, they opened a large hatch cover leading into the bilge and were greeted with an overpowering stench of rancid sea water and scurrying mice as a light was shone through the opening. They entered carefully, and with the lantern held high overhead, took stock of the situation. Casting forward, he found everything as it should be. The majority of the weight seemed to be in its proper place. He thought this rather strange and after climbing back up into the hold, stopped for a moment to mull over what he'd just seen.

"Gentlemen, I've a notion to remove some of the ballast. She sits too heavy in the water. Removing some of it will allow her to sail closer to the wind and give a knot or two more speed...don't you agree?"

"Aye, Cap'n, ye be right 'bout that. But if I may be so bold as ta say...she's trimmed right smart. I be a'meanin' I don't see too much stone in 'er. 'Er bottom is foul with weed is all."

The next day a man was sent over the side to see how much sea weed was on the hull only to find her copper plated below the water line. Another mystery; if the ship was empty, the copper plate should have been several feet above the water. What would cause her to list towards the bow? They made another tour of the hold looking for an answer...nothing. The bosun was forward when he called out for the captain and Beale. The bosun was on his knees looking intently at the flooring of the hold, eyeing it with great interest.

"Have a look, Cap'n, sar. Don't this here deck seem ta be right smart new lookin' ta ye?"

They bent down and held the lantern high while they inspected the decking the bosun was pointing at. Running his hand over the boards the bosun declared, "Seems ta me, Cap'n, sar, these here boards 'pear ta be 'bout new!"

"Fetch something to pry one up, and we'll have a look, if you please, bosun."

Minutes later the bosun returned with a wood chisel and mallet from the carpenter's stores and set about worrying a plank loose. It took the better part of fifteen minutes to work it free, but one last tug, a grunt from the bosun, and the task was accomplished. A light was immediately held close to the opening which revealed a false floor. They looked at each other in bewilderment. Without saying a word, the bosun tore another plank loose...still nothing. Another plank, and then another—until suddenly the glint of gold bars shown brightly in the feeble lantern light. They spent the next hour prying up a line of planks some forty feet long. Drenched in sweat they sat, cross legged, in the humid hold of the man-of-war; in stunned silence looking at each other.

They were sitting on a fortune of gold!

CHAPTER FOURTEEN

In the glory of dawn, crisp and clear after an evening storm, with a refreshing, briny tang in the air from a salt incrusted shore line just south of the island, a curious scene was unfolding on the beach. A make shift tent made of old canvas was erected for the purpose of addressing the crew. After a long, and at times, heated debate in the hold of the man-of-war between the bosun, Beale and himself, over what should be done with the gold, they were eventually faced with one conclusion—sharing the bounty according to Admiralty laws. The gold they were sitting upon amounted in the tens of thousands of pounds British Sterling. The fact of the matter was simply this: There was entirely too much gold to keep hidden from the rest of the crew—if they found out, and they surely would, a mutiny would ensue, bringing with it, more difficulty than they wanted to face. It was decided to muster the entire crew, much to the chagrin of the bosun who was in favor of replacing the deck planks as if nothing had happened, and enlighten them.

And so, in the bright glow of morn, Captain James Howlette, enthroned upon an empty water cask, set about the business of making himself safe amongst the crew and officers by addressing them thusly.

"I've the pleasure—and the duty—to inform the crew of the *Rose* and all who sail within her that a recent discovery was made just this past evening, that I'm sure will delight the hearts of every man jack of you. Take a moment to notice that yon man-of-war appears to sit low in the water—even though all stores have been removed."

He indicated with a wave of his hand.

"After a careful tour of the empty hold, our bosun observed what appeared to be new decking, and after prizing one of the boards loose, discovered a false deck lined with gold."

Stunned silence hung over the gathering as he continued with his narrative.

"After considerable thought on the matter, I've come to a number of possible conclusions. The gold is evenly distributed, allowing the cargo to be stacked above it—although she sits too heavy in the bows, making for a neat arrangement in the holds. Another thought that seems to enter my mind, all too frequently, is the fact that the gold was never delivered onto Spanish soil *before* the powder was loaded. The only other alternative being; the filthy French pirate, without the decency, and without honor, intended to sail away, post haste, fully loaded, gold and all! I still have a deal of thought to put my affairs to rights on this issue, but we must realize the fact that we are at war and can ill afford to return the gold to its rightful owners."

"Cap'n sar," someone spoke from the gathered crowd in a plaintive voice. "Cap'n, sar, jes' how much gold thar be in the Frenchie?"

"Gentlemen...I cannot count, with any accuracy, the amount we have before us. Suffice it to say," he said with a sweep of his hand, "It is enough to make each and every one of you a rich man, and I shall be bold enough to say, that should you invest it wisely, your days at sea will be put behind you. We will commence on the morrow to off load the gold and divide it between the two ships, therefore avoiding disaster; should we meet with storms and lose one the remainder will survive."

There were a few shouts of joy, but the greater part of the crew talked quietly amongst themselves. This came as a shock to him, for he fully expected a riot to break out with men trampling each other in their haste to board the man-of-war and tear up the decking to have at the gold.

"If I may have your attention for the briefest of moments," he said as he stood, dusting off his trousers.

"The purser will take charge in offloading the gold bullion...each and every bar will be duly counted—the serial number carefully noted for the Admiralty. As you may recollect—some months past we disobeyed orders by attempting to board yon ship. We must stand accountable for those actions. I am of the opinion that the Admiralty will grant clemency considering the spoils of war, that, with any luck, we shall bring home to England. I've no doubt that we have, in our possession, enough gold to influence the economy of Britain! Fate has indeed, smiled upon us!"

And without further ado, he stepped away from the tent saying, "Carry on, men."

A rousing cheer met his ears as the crew acknowledged him. The following days turned into the better part of a week before the gold was offloaded and counted according to his instructions and divided between the two ships. The copper plating of the man-of-war rose several feet above the water line after she was emptied of her burden, and after the decking was replaced and re-loaded, sat much better in the water. The *Rose* was able to carry about a third of the horde—but no more…it was simply too heavy and threatened to overset her balance and seaworthiness. The percentage he would get as commanding officer would be sufficient to put him up in style for the remainder of his life—his days at sea would come to an end—if he so desired. Although he faced the fact of proposing to Molly the moment he set foot in Chatham—his future seemed bright enough, if he survived the inquiry board.

With the last of the decking replaced and caulked thoroughly, the man-of-war was, at last, pronounced seaworthy. Much toil and sweat had passed during the last weeks before they sailed away—each member of the crew anxious to be underway back to their homeland. The last of the fresh water was laboriously swayed up the side of the *Rose* and sent into the hold to be tied in place. The peons would wait on the island with a gold coin in their pockets, Spanish fishermen would pick them up in a few days. The island had offered its finest fare to them, as the last days of summer drew to a close. Fresh tropical fruit along with a stack of coconuts that resembled oblong cannon balls were tucked away in a far corner of the hold beside a multitude of mangoes giving off a mouth watering aroma that permeated the ship from stem to stern.

The offing was uneventful. The *Rose* swung around her anchor and hoisted a smattering of topsails to give her steerageway while the man-of-war awaited her turn, manned by a prize crew to sail her out. A light, tropical land breeze wafted through the palms offering up a last, sighing farewell. The man-of-war had less difficulty making the passage through the coral shoals now that she was sitting higher in the water. The *Rose* wore around, waiting for the French ship to make for open water, and within the hour they were underway with the *Rose* leading on the weather gauge. The French ship seemed to have a life of her own now that her burden was lighter and surprised him by sailing a point closer to the wind than he'd expected. She was well built and now that the ballast had been shifted further aft, responded to her stays with little effort.

Fourteen days later, while sailing easily on a starboard tack, the *Rose* hoisted a signal flag and the lookout quickly hailed the deck. Pointing away he yelled,

" Deck ahoy! ta *Rose* be sendin' a signal. Ship sighted. Await orders!"

Within minutes he was on deck and snapping out a telescope; aimed it at the *Rose* saying, "Mast...where away?"

"Don't know, sar...can't rightly see a thing from here. Has ta be starboard o' the *Rose*."

"Bosun...send the *Rose* a signal asking where away, if you please."

Minutes later the *Rose* responded by raising her flags.

"French Frigate two points off the starboard bow...hummm," he muttered under his breath. "She must be just over the horizon. Bosun...signal the *Rose* to hoist the French flag. I've a notion to have a bit of fun. Beat to quarters, if you please, and hoist a French flag up the main mast."

"But, sar, what if we be hulled and all 'da gold goes ta th' bottom. Won't be a'doin' us much good down thar, sar!"

"Bosun—need I remind you of your orders *again*? I believe we will have a closer look. I've a plan about me to take the ship without firing a shot! Hoist the flag and put her over on a larboard tack...we'll have a go at her."

The man-of-war fell off as the helm was put over while the French flag was hoisted briskly up the main mast. The sails quickly filled and minutes later the *Rose* followed suit. An hour later the hull of the frigate was visible. James ordered a signal to the frigate to heave to and prepare to be boarded. The *Rose* lowered her topsails and took a reef in the main sails bringing her speed down to just enough for steerageway. The man-of-war closed in on the frigate at a rapid clip and soon hauled her wind within two hundred yards of her. The *Rose* was abaft the frigate on her weather gauge to the starboard side. The French captain had a glass up and was inspecting the man-of-war closely for the slightest sign of trouble, but soon recognized her as a flag ship and snapped to attention and fired a salute. Howlette was smiling like a child in a sand box—this would be much easier than he thought. He turned and swiftly left the quarterdeck for the captain's quarters where he quickly stripped and put on the French captain's accoutrements and returned to the quarterdeck. The *Rose* was ideally positioned—just off her starboard side. He ordered the bosun to fire a warning shot across her bows while the French flag was quickly brought down to be replaced with a British one. At the same time the gun ports were lowered and the cannon were run out smartly.

An officer was seen, in a heated debate, with a wildly gesturing figure on the quarterdeck, both occasionally pointing towards the man-of-war as if trying to settle some vague point of view. The French captain, quiet bewildered, ordered his colors struck, signaling surrender. The figure suddenly struck the French officer sending him to the deck just as Howlette was pulling off in the captain's gig for the frigate. The *Rose* had slowly pulled closer and was lying off a hundred yards away awaiting orders; her gun ports bristling with cannon. Twenty minutes later he was along side making his way up a rope ladder to the waist of the ship. Two French crewmen helped him aboard the ship and after a smart salute ushered him to the quarterdeck ladder. Seconds later James confronted them, and the sight before him came as a great shock to his senses; for there stood the very man that had condemned him to death some few months ago—indeed, it was Captain Rondeau whom had slaughtered his crew member in cold blood. Anger and outrage consumed Howlette leaving him trembling with cold fury deep in the pit of his stomach.

"So we meet again! This time I believe the pleasure is all mine!" he growled. "I've a little surprise awaiting you at the yard arm that I'm sure you'll enjoy…but only for the briefest of moments." Turning, he signaled his men to place the man before him in irons, saying, "Fetch a length of rope for our dear captain and run it through a block on that yard arm there, and be quick about it!"

"Mon Dieu! Sir, you have no right to what you are about to do. What of zee proper trial? You would do such a thing as this without zee trial? Have mercy!" he pleaded.

"I shall accord you the same courtesies you've so kindly extended to me. Surely you've not forgotten the matter of running cold steel through a defenseless crewman aboard that very ship!" he shouted while pointing towards the man-of-war. "It gives me great pleasure to extend a measure of respect toward you that has been long overdue!" he hissed through clenched teeth. And with that said he promptly slapped the Frenchman across the face sending him to the deck in a shower of blood. "Oh, and by the by, I should be remiss not to thank you for all the powder and supplies, not to mention the gold you so cleverly secreted away in the hold. Very clever indeed, sir; we were hard pressed to discover your little cache, but my bosun is a learned man of the sea, and new planking in the hold raised a question in his mind. I shall see that he is rewarded in good measure for his efforts, and now, on with the task at hand," he said, eyeing the rope as it was reeved through the eye of a block and pulled taut while a noose was fashioned at one end.

"You've shown no mercy towards me, and as an officer and gentleman, I shall show no mercy towards you. If you will be so kind as to step to the waist of the ship we shall get on with the business at hand."

The French officer regained his footing and threw back his shoulders in arrogance. "You, sir, are zee swine, and you shall not see me whimper in zee face of death! Do what you will with me, and let us have an end to it!"

He was led down the quarterdeck ladder and minutes later the noose was placed around his neck. Howlette signaled with a downward thrust of his arm and the man was quickly jerked off the deck, arms flailing and legs kicking at the air beneath him in a dance of death. He took the opportunity to address the rest of the crew that had assembled on the decks to watch.

"Gentlemen…you are now pressed into service for the British Navy, and as such, are under my direct command. Anyone who entertains the thought of mutiny shall meet the same fate as the man you see at the yard arm. I expect good behavior, and should you perform well, you will be paid in good time when we make port at Chatham in a few months. I shall assign additional members to the *Rose,* and any of you that would like to volunteer will be most welcome to do so. You will find that I am a fair man. Proper temperament and a will to follow orders are most prized by me, and the prospect of advancement in the British Naval Service is not difficult. You will be treated with respect by members of my crew if you follow orders. Should you prove difficult to work with, the cat will be your reward…do I make myself clear?"

The crewmen spoke amongst themselves, discussing their prospects as newly appointed subjects of the Crown.

"Bosun…assign your men!" he ordered curtly and promptly left the man to his business.

Captain Rondeau was taken down from the yard arm and sewn in a scrap of old canvas with a cannon ball at his feet and dumped over the side with little fanfare. The decks were put in order. New crew members were transferred to the *Rose,* while an acting lieutenant from the *Rose* boarded the newly captured French frigate to take command. And within the span of two hours they were making sail for England with their new prize in tow.

James sat in the captain's cabin discussing his good fortune with Maria. "Fate, at times, can indeed be strange—I would never have thought of meeting Captain Rondeau again…much less in the span of a year. I suppose he was in the process of making all due haste back to France to inform his superiors of the tragic loss of his battleship...ha...and we stumbled upon him quite by accident! Another frigate must have come in shortly after we departed. It's a small wonder we didn't encounter it while sailing away...but on the other hand, we sailed down the coast to the island for re-fitting, so we must have gone in opposite directions."

He paused to look in the direction of Maria, quietly listening to him prattle on about his good luck.

"Was it difficult...the taking of the ship, I mean?" he asked while staring down at the glass of sherry in his hand—from the private stores of the captain's cabin.

"It was not, how you say...difficult. The ship was empty of the crew except for the man with the pen and paper...how you say, the purser and a few of the men to supervise the loading of the powder. It was over in minutes. The ones that decided to fight were quickly taken care of and placed in the room below before they could make the sound to warn the shore," she said, while looking out the stern windows of the cabin. "It took several of the days to make the plans with the workers. Each day I would order a few more men and boats to take the powder out to the ship—then one day the ship, she was ours! They will speak of this in the village for many years to come. The children will be told how the workers captured a huge ship with nothing more than knives and a few hatchets."

He glanced up while Maria was speaking. Their eyes met, and for a brief moment, they exchanged a glance before he interrupted her saying, "Maria, my dear Maria...how can I thank you for all you've done for me in such a short time? Do you realize you've saved my career, and quite possibly my life? All these things and so much more...nursing me back to health after the ordeal in the fishing boat...riding to the village, and capturing the ship. And all you want is to set foot on the shores of England?"

"My mother spoke often of England when I was a child, and now I have the chance to see for myself!" she said, a bright smile on her face. "I have brought with me all that I own. It is not much, just some clothes and a few of the papers that were dear to my mother, that is all. Soon I will see the England she spoke of so often...you will show me how to conduct myself so that I will not get lost?"

"Of course, my dear; after the settlement of what we have in tow, I shall put you up in the finest hotel that England has to offer. Wait until you taste the fare offered up in the restaurants. It will be much different than what you've had in the village, but I'm sure you'll like it—given time. There's the matter of some pressing debts I shall have to settle. I've a small acreage—Briarwood Estates that is sorely in debt as we speak, but with the prize money I'll gain from the sale of the man-of-war and the frigate, not to mention my share of the gold we're carrying; will be enough to put us up for the remainder of our lives."

He suddenly realized that he had unknowing included Maria in his future plans and let the sentence drop. Clearing his throat he continued after a small sip of sherry.

"Maria, there's a matter that needs be discussed before we make the channel and the cliffs of Dover. The image of you in the fishing boat, after you were discovered beneath the casks has never been far from my mind. You've a temperament about you that I find quite appealing, and for the life of me, I quite admire it. I should tell you that I've a lady waiting for me in England that I've known for several years…it is a long-standing relationship, and I fear she may think she's in love with me." He continued on quickly. "I've found that I share similar thoughts with you. There's a fire within you that I quite enjoy, a spark of courage and independence that is rare in women of your age. You seem…well…enough of this." He hesitated. "It would give me great pleasure if you would allow me to get to know you better…pray tell, have I made an ass of myself?" he ended fervently.

"You have not the courage when it comes to women!" she said with a gay laugh, taunting him with a shake of her finger.

"This woman you speak of in England…does she know that you do not love her in the same manner?"

"I honestly can't answer. I've put her up at the estate for several years, and we've spoken of marriage on rare occasions, but try as I might, I can find no love for her in my heart…nothing, and lately I've thought of little except you. Would you give me the pleasure of showing you the sights of my homeland?"

"I think I would enjoy that very much," she said softly while reaching over to touch his hand.

The days passed rapidly while the three ships sailed for their home port. The French crewman proved to be delightful to work with, the only barrier was their lack of English and having to show them some of the finer points of sailing. They were eager to learn and gave a full measure of toil about the ship, asking for little in return. Their mess mates accepted them on face value and it wasn't long before they could be heard repeating jaunty English sentences, to the gaiety of their messmates. The northeast trade winds were picked up just to the east of France and the ships put over for the long run up the coast line for the British Isles. Only weeks away from docking at Chatham, the routine became light and gay. The ships were ordered to be put in proper shape, and from dawn to dusk one could hear mop buckets clattering in the early morn, while brass cannons were polished to a gleaming golden yellow. Lines and sheets were coiled in proper fashion and the decks were caulked with oakum. The smell of fresh tar wafted over the waist of the ships and through the rigging as chafed lines received a new coat of tar and sizing. Days turned into a fortnight before the lookout sighted the distant cliffs of Dover, and within hours the crew lined the decks to see the white brilliance for themselves. They were closing in on the channel by nightfall with the huge, white cliffs of limestone guiding them along with numerous other small vessels that hailed the ships with cheers and waving hats. Two days later they dropped anchor in the outer harbor of Chatham while Howlette and Maria made themselves presentable for the welcoming party lining the shores. Orders to enter and dock would follow just as soon as he had met with the Admiralty later that day. In the mean time, a rousing salute was fired in honor of the king—and Lord Cambridge.

It was a little after two o'clock in the afternoon before the captain's gig pulled away from the French man-of-war and briskly made way for the docks a quarter mile away. The boat crew put their backs into the task and pulled away with a will, and within the hour the bow bumped alongside the wharf as a line was heaved into waiting hands to be tied off. James hoisted himself out and stood with trembling legs for a few minutes before offering a hand to Maria. He held her close while she became accustomed to the stable footing of the shore.

"It will take a few days to gain your balance after being on board ship for so long, Maria; be patient and walk with a care…you'll be fine." He cautioned her.

"The land, it moves under my feet! How can this be?"

"It's the constant motion of the ship as it rides over each wave…one must adapt to it. The motion carries over to the shore after leaving the decks of the ship. Be patient…it will pass quickly," he said above the cheers and shouts of the gathering crowd.

A packet of sealed papers were passed to him from the helmsman as he and Maria made their way up the dock and onto the pebbled shore. The gig pulled away and returned to the man-of-war to await orders. Maria carried a small oiled leather pouch tucked under her arm for safe keeping. A post chase was waiting for them at the dock and within the span of fifteen minutes they were whisked off down the cobble-stone streets toward London.

The carriage ground to a clattering halt in front of the wrought iron fencing of the Headquarters building. James stepped out and offered a hand to Maria as she gathered up her skirts along with the leather pouch. She took his arm as they ascended the marble steps where they were greeted with a smart salute from the Marine guards standing on either side of the huge oak doors. Minutes later they were inside. Maria stopped for a moment to admire the rich detail of the hallway lined with oil portraits of generations of Admirals. Tapestries of intricate detail draped the corridors and Persian rugs adorned the floors at every turn. Maria, overwhelmed by the splendor of it all, gripped his arm in excitement as she muttered,

"Is all of this London…is it all of this fashion? There are more treasures here than in all of the village where I come from!"

"Rest assured, my dear, you will see many sights before the month is out—providing I'm not jailed for treason—and I shall be more than happy to show them to you in due time. But first things first, I must present my report to his Lordship. I need not tell you that it will not be a pleasant meeting. Please remain in the ante room until these matters are settled. I expect it will be a rather bad showing on my part, and I can only hope the treasures we bring with us will sway the judgment of my actions. There's the matter of the pressed crewman…more able hands to fight—but on the other hand—I must account for the lost lives while disobeying orders. It will be most unpleasant, and I should be counted lucky if I walk away with my life….Ah, here we are at his Lordship's office," he stammered.

"Captain James Howlette, commanding officer of the *Rose* to see his Honorable Lordship. I believe my lord is most anxious to meet with me. Would you be so kind as to make the announcement?"

The young lieutenant stood while offering a smart salute—which Howlette acknowledged—and strode down the short hallway, knocking three times on the door. He returned minutes later, and with a wave of his hand, ushered him to the door saying, "The Admiral will see you right away if you please, sir."

He gathered what remained of his courage, and with a weak smile towards Maria, offered her a chair, saying, rather meekly, "If you know an appropriate prayer, I believe you should offer it up. I shall return as soon as I can. Rest assured...this could take the better part of an hour—or less...depending on the outcome of these proceedings."

He gave her a quick pat on the hand and gathered himself, tucking the packet under his arm, and after knocking on the door, disappeared behind it.

Entering the room, he stepped to the huge Mahogany desk where Lord Cambridge sat in stately composure and offered his best salute saying in clipped tones,

"Captain James Howlette of His Majesty's ship, the *Rose,* reporting as ordered, sir...If I may be so bold as to..."

"No! Captain...you've been quite bold already! I have it on good authority that you have blatantly disobeyed the orders of Admiral Morris that stated no force of arms unless absolutely necessary! What do you have to say for yourself?...I'm listening!" he bellowed. "And it had better be damned good, or I've a mind to have you disrated and flogged 'round the fleet. My Gawd, have you no respect for your superiors? Have you gone mad? The audacity of your actions is quite beyond belief.

"Have a seat, Captain. I fear this will be a rather long meeting. I shall have a full accounting of you actions, so I suggest you get right to it," he bellowed, indicating the chair directly in front of the desk with a bony finger.

Howlette turned to stare at the empty chair for a moment, unsure of just what to say or do next. Clearing his throat, he stepped to the side and seated himself while laying the packet on the corner of the desk. Straightening the collar of his shirt that had just this minute became intolerable he gathered what courage remained in him and spoke.

"My lord...if I may take a brief moment to touch upon the actions I've undertaken over the past year," he stammered. "While on patrol in the southern oceans we spotted a French man-of-war escorted by two frigates...quite odd I thought, for two frigates to give escort for the entire voyage. We followed them, while remaining out of sight until the following morning, and then dead reckoning our course for the remainder of the day, trying to match her speed. We were hampered in our efforts by a hurricane, and lost several days steerageway, and upon weathering the storm, discovered one of the frigates to be missing—probably lost at sea." He was gathering momentum, and forged ahead with the details. "It was suggested, by the surgeon, that the man-of-war was transporting gold to the Spanish, accounting for the armed escort. It was decided, after said ships were anchored, that a boarding party should be sent to investigate."

"If I may interrupt, Captain...what was the purpose of this so called investigation? Could it have been greed? Could it have been a desire to plunder the ship? This is not going well, Captain!"

"If you allow me to explain, my lord, you will be most pleased at what I have to say in the matter."

"Well...get on with it. My patience grows thin."

"We were led into a clever trap," he said quietly, and then continued. "Completely overpowered, we were forced to surrender. Several of the boarding crew were taken prisoner, including me."

He took the opportunity to avoid the description of the bloody outcome and the loss of the majority of the boarding crew.

"We spent four months in a Spanish prison. Our only salvation was from a beautiful young Spanish girl whom I befriended. Eventually she orchestrated our escape, whereupon we managed to secure a fishing boat and leave the mainland and sail to a rendezvous point where the *Rose* lay in wait. I have returned with the young lady. But to continue...after a hideous time of it in the fishing boat, and a narrow escape from the clutches of death, we cast off in the *Rose*, and with the help of Maria, returned to the harbor and secured the man-of-war, laying waste to the remaining frigate. We then returned to the rendezvous island, and in the process of offloading the stores...and by the way, my lord, I have the pleasure of saying we've returned with a substantial cargo of powder and ball...noticed that the man-of-war sat uncommonly low in the water. Upon careful investigation, my newly appointed bosun noticed what appeared to be new decking in the hold. We prized up a board..." Here he took a moment to rummage through the packet and produced several sheets of parchment, which he quickly handed over to Cambridge and continued. "Take a moment, my lord, to examine these tally sheets."

Cambridge shuffled through the first two pages, his eyebrows raised as he scanned them carefully. "What have we here, Captain? A numerical accounting?"

"Yes, my lord. Each number relates to an ingot of pure gold!"

"What?" Cambridge dropped the papers to the desk in total amazement.

"There are well over ten pages! My Gawd!"

"Indeed, my lord. There, before you, is a full accounting of gold worth well over one million pounds British Sterling, and a ship, fully loaded with powder and cannon ball. We succeeded in capturing another French frigate by deception on the return voyage, along with a full crew, which I immediately pressed into service for the Crown. I need not mention, sir, that the man-of-war is a flag ship of one hundred and ten guns...captured with the help of the Spanish, without so much as firing a single shot!"

James decided that this was a fine place to end his narration. The room became deathly quiet while Cambridge pondered the issue.

"You mentioned a young girl. I believe her name was Maria. Perchance, did you mention a last name?"

"Sir! I seem to have been remiss in the matter!" He said in utter dismay. "I've not had the opportunity to ask her…but she awaits me in the anteroom just outside."

"Be so kind as to bid her enter. I should like a word with her if you please."

"Of course, sir, I'll fetch her at once." And with that he promptly rose and went to the door to summon her. Minutes later they were both seated in front of Lord Cambridge. The seconds ticked by while he appraised her carefully and then said, "Do you have a last name, my dear?"

"Si, señor. My name is Maria Morales."

"Morales, you say…May I inquire as to your age?" he said, leaning over and placing his hands upon the desk.

"Si…I am the twenty-three years old."

"And your village lies on the Gandia harbor?" he questioned with great interest.

Howlette was more than a little puzzled at the conversation taking place before him. Cambridge seemed to be most interested in the young lady seated in front of him and so he thought it prudent not to interfere.

"May I be so bold as to ask who your mother might be, and is she still alive?"

"Of course, señor, she is Lucinda and I have left her in the best of health…but that was many of the months ago…and anything could have happened. I believe father is well, also, " she stated with conviction. "I would be most happy to show you some of the papers I have brought over the ocean with me…they are the most prized possessions. "I have taken the liberty to bring them with me. My mother, she does not know about this, and would be most upset with me when she finds out that they are missing…but you see, I do not know who my father is. My mother, she married my father when I was a small child. She was very poor and was forced to marry to have a place to live."

"You don't say. May I have a look at the papers?"

"Of course; please be careful with them, señor. That is all I have in the world, and I would be most sad if they were spoiled in any way."

Cambridge picked up the leather pouch and carefully opened it. Pulling out the contents he cautiously examined each page with keen interest. Placing each sheet of parchment face down on the desk, he continued to read carefully. The stillness of the room weighed upon them, broken only by a shuffling sound as each sheet of parchment was placed on the desk, a sound, not unlike that of falling leaves blown by an autumn breeze. Time seemed to stand still as Maria and Howlette watched bewildered, while Cambridge scanned the contents a second time.

"And you say your mother's married name was Morales?" he asked a second time.

"No, señor, it is my mother's maiden name. She never took the name of the man she married. She always say to me…be proud of your name, Maria, for it is my blood that courses through your veins, and not that of the man I live with. It was the marriage of, how you say, convenience."

"Did your mother ever mention another man in her life, possibly a British officer that called upon her?"

"I recall many times that she would talk of another in her life, but my father would get most angry if he heard her say such a thing; he forbid it."

Howlette's eyes darted, first to Maria, and then to Cambridge, completely taken aback by the conversation.

Cambridge was silent for a considerable length of time. He pursed his lips and covered his mouth with a bony hand. A look of anguish clouded his countenance. He leaned back in his chair and stared at the ceiling for a length of time before he continued, saying with great emotion,

"Captain Howette, I see no need to proceed with the matter any further. I have before me a manifest, the contents of which are indeed astounding. A French first rate of well over one hundred cannon, another captured frigate with a full load of cargo and crew, a king's ransom in gold bullion…and enough powder and ball to supply the entire fleet for the better part of a year. I cannot recall a time in my career when so much wealth has entered our waters."

He hesitated for several moments, and with great difficulty, continued, "With the sale of the ships and cargo, and if these manifests I have before me are correct, the entire economy of Britain will feel the effects of what you've brought to us this day!"

James was about to express his humble gratitude when he was brought up short by a wave of Cambridge's hand.

"I'm not finished. If you please, I have another statement to make."

His eyes returned to Maria and a look of genuine grief crossed his features for the briefest moment. Great passion caused his voice to crack. He paused for a second time and then continued.

"If I may be so bold as to say, Maria Morales, that I knew your mother long ago. For you see," he stopped to rub an eye and clear his throat. "For you see, my dear, from the papers I have here before me, there is not the shadow of doubt in my mind that you are my daughter!"

CHAPTER FIFTEEN

"You simply *must* try the Madeira, Stephen." James stated as he held a wine glass to his nose sampling the bouquet, then taking a sip.

"And by all means, help yourself to the toasted cheese. I do believe there is none finer in the entire world!" He was in a cheerful mood and continued on as though the surgeon wasn't there.

"This business of selling off the ships and cargo has fairly set my head to spinning. And I'm so easily called away; one hardly knows where one is supposed to be next! Do you know, Stephen, have you the vaguest idea of the sum of money we stand to gain? I've half a mind to resign my commission. Of course there's the matter of Briarwood, which I fully intend to settle before the month is out. Oh, yes, there's an account I must establish at the bank before the final settlement is made. I'm afraid I've procrastinated in the worst way in regards to that. Don't let me forget, Stephen; I must take care of that on the morrow. My, my, there's so much to do and so little time!"

Stephen Beale cast a measured glance in his direction while fingering a wine glass. "If I may be so bold as to suggest you think on the matter of resigning your commission. It seems to me retirement is the better option. You'll still be a commissioned officer on half pay, not that you need it, mind you, but none the less, there's always the chance you may want to return to active duty some time in the future, and once you've resigned, well, there's little chance of ever seeing the bridge of a ship except from the dock."

He selected a generous portion of cheese from the serving tray and moved it to his plate. Cutting a thin wedge, he examined it closely then popped it in his mouth.

"Indeed. I must agree with you. It is aged to perfection and toasted to a turn. My compliments to the chef!"

After the meeting with Lord Cambridge, Howlette took the liberty of making arrangements at a posh hotel in London for he and Maria until after the sale was finalized. They toured several of the finer establishments until his name appeared in the London Times recanting the story and granting him a hero's welcome. Lately he'd returned to his habit of eating at some of the more private restaurants in hopes of avoiding the crowd. He was hailed at almost every turn; complete strangers went out of their way to greet him and offer congratulations. Maria chose to stay at the hotel while he went about the business of establishing credit and opening an account to receive the funds of the sale. Lord Cambridge had commanded much of Maria's time reacquainting himself with her and recounting all the years that had passed much too quickly. The president of the bank agreed to personally fill out all the necessary forms, smiling profusely while signing his name with a flourish, authorizing an open line of credit to one of the richest men in Great Britain. He was beginning to enjoy the power and prestige of wealth. It was something he was becoming quite fond of.

A month had passed in a whirlwind of meetings and luncheons, leaving him breathless and a little bewildered. The pressing issue of debt against Briarwood overshadowed his festive mood. He had every intention of posting a letter to Molly, but the opportunity seemed just out of reach. The bank president assured him that the outstanding debt could be overlooked for a few more weeks until his financial house was put to order. He often wondered why Molly had not taken the opportunity to pay a visit. Surely the news had reached the estate by now.

The shores of the Irish Sea were so relaxing at this time of the year. Molly drew the rattan hat closer to her forehead as she left the sidewalk café in downtown Liverpool for a stroll along the beach. Just over three weeks had passed and already she was dreading the trip back to London. The dank air and fog was so depressing to the spirit—nothing like the sunny beaches of northern England. She promised herself she would tour the southern reaches of Cardigan Bay before she returned by way of Bristol. There she would spend several more weeks lounging on the beach before returning to Briarwood to finish packing her belongings before leaving Britain for northern France, a short voyage across the channel to Calais and then on to

Bordeaux and the wine country. Two payments remained and Morris's debt would be satisfied. It was a tidy sum of money—enough to put her up in grand style for a number of years. But she must return and retrieve the letter from the safe deposit box and make an appointment at the House of Parliament before she left for the last time.

The post chaste swayed gently, keeping time with the sound of the horses' hooves as they sped down the familiar road to Briarwood. A road he remembered well…he had traveled it countless times. Begging leave from Lord Cambridge and the affairs at hand, he had left Maria in London with her father in hopes of finding out why Molly had not called or sent word to him. Six weeks after dropping anchor and not a single word from her was making him wonder if she had taken ill or if her health was failing. He had posted a short note to her in hopes of putting his mind to rest, but there had been no reply. A personal visit seemed the proper thing to do but a pall of dread overshadowed him. He must find a way to end the relationship. He was in love with Maria. Looking back over the months, he realized he'd been in love with her from the very start—he just didn't know it. As soon as the business at hand was over, he made a vow to himself he would ask her to marry him.

The carriage lurched around the last corner and made a turn onto the lane leading up to the estate. It looked well kept and serene. The creditors must have been kept at bay from the looks of the groomed hedges and trimmed lawn. A smile softened his features—it was just as he remembered. The carriage halted at the cobble stone path that led to the front porch. The driver held the door as he descended and strolled to the door, knocked and waited for an answer. Minutes later Mary opened the door.

"How good it is ta see you, m'lord. Please come in!" she beamed while taking his hat and coat.

"Perchance is Molly about the house? I've posted a letter and have not received a reply. I've been rather indisposed of late and have just this minute found the time to pay my respects. Is she well?" he asked with a note of concern in his voice.

"She has been on holiday now fer," she said, putting a finger to her cheek, "If memory serves me, fer twelve weeks. Yes I do believe this be th' third month now."

"On holiday! You don't say! Perchance, do you recall where she might have gone?"

"Oh, yes, m'lord, 'twas to Liverpool and th' sunny beaches for th' remainder of th' summer. I'm sorry ta say I forgot just when she'll be returnin', though."

He was completely taken aback by the remark, and for several minutes stood without saying a word, with a frown on his face, until Mary broke the silence.

"Sar, ye be more 'n welcome ta stay th' summer until she returns."

"Thank you, Mary, but I do believe I shall return to London. I've pressing matters to attend to, and I'm afraid I cannot stay a moment longer," he said reaching for his hat and coat. "Do you recall...never mind, Mary. If she should return, here is an address where she can contact me. Would you be so kind as to inform her?"

"At once, m'lord. I recall receivin' a letter by post from ye a time back. It's still on the mantle. Would ye like it back, bein' as she's not here to send a reply?"

"I suppose so. On second thought, just drop it into the fireplace tonight. It was of little importance, only a note asking about her welfare. Thank you and good day."

He turned to leave, but stopped and said. "Mary, are the creditors being paid? I've noticed the estate is well kept; the hedge and lawn seem to have been recently clipped."

"Yes, m'lord...I believe all is well."

"Thank you. I'm afraid I must be off. I'm so easily called away these days. My apologies, I'm sure you understand." He turned on a heel closing the door behind him.

The ride back to London didn't seem quite as boring, his mind being occupied with the mystery of where the funds were coming from to keep the debt satisfied. Molly had no talent with needle and thread...therefore she couldn't be employed as a seamstress. The monthly stipend from his officer's pay was little more than enough to put food on the table, yet it seemed the bills were paid...

The post chase stopped at Admiralty headquarters and a guard ushered him through the massive double doors. Minutes passed until he was greeted by Harry Cromwell and escorted down the hall to Admiral Morris's office. Harry knocked and opened the door. Howlette stepped through as Harry closed it behind him.

"Well, well if it isn't our good Captain Howlette! Please have a seat."

A fit of coughing seized him and it was several minutes before he could continue. "Please excuse me. I've had the fevers some months past and have not made a complete recovery. I'm quite short of breath and suffering from rather painful spasms of the chest that leave me weak in the extreme." He paused to catch a deep breath before continuing. "You seem to have made quite a name for yourself. I suppose you'll be leaving the king's service."

"I should like to think the matter over before I give my final opinion. I believe it would be a mistake to resign my commission without mulling it over carefully. It's simply much too early to make an intelligent decision."

Morris was smoldering with rage, but contained himself. "I should think a man of your wealth would have no need of the king's service. What purpose would be served by your staying on?"

"I should beg pardon, sir, but I shall withhold my decision until a later date."

"Very well then, let us discuss the business at hand. I understand you were taken prisoner for a short time after the foiled attempt at capturing the man-of-war?"

"Yes, indeed. It was by the grace of God that I survived."

"You should count your blessings, Captain, that Lord Cambridge has shown mercy upon you and pardoned your little indiscretion. Bringing back the Lord's very own daughter, my, what a stroke of luck!" His chuckle ended in another fit of coughing. "*Two* ships full of powder and ball, fully loaded with stores, and a hold full of gold. I've been informed your accounting will surpass a million pounds sterling, if not a trifle more, before all is said and done. Not bad for a year's work!" he said with a sneer. "I suppose I should be grateful. I believe I'll be entitled to a small percentage as your commanding officer. Count your blessings, *indeed*!" he reflected, "If I were in the lord's position it would have been a very different outcome! Disobeying orders is a capital crime and can only be satisfied by death! You've succeeded in making the French ambassador hunt me down like a rabid dog! It has not been pleasant for me, to say the very least. Stranding the entire French crew on Spanish soil was quite an accomplishment. And you say you didn't know about the gold?"

"It was the better part of a month. I noticed one day that the ship sat too low in the water after the stores were offloaded, and my bosun discovered a false deck leading to the gold. We were able to secure the ship during the last days, just before she was to sail. The payment had not been made; therefore, the gold remained in the hold, and by the grace of God, we were able to secure the entire lot for the Crown."

"Dare I say again, Captain, that it was the purest stroke of luck. You've walked away with a king's ransom and the lord's daughter. It's almost beyond belief! Well enough of this; you're above reproach, and I can do nothing to right the matter. I shall await your partition for retirement post haste, and I shall be only too happy to sign it!" he said, with a sniff, shuffling a stack of stray papers into better order.

"If that is all, sir, then I shall bid you a good day."

"Yes, yes…good day indeed, that's all for now, but I warn you, Captain, do not overstep your boundaries while you are still under the king's commission! I'm still your commanding officer, and as such, I can make things very difficult for you in the days ahead. Do you understand?"

"Yes, sir, I shall consider the matter of my retirement further, and should I decide on that course, will submit the proper forms within a fortnight."

He rose from the chair, offered a salute and left the office, closing the door behind him. Harry was sitting at his desk as he passed by.

"I should think Admiral Morris would have been in a better mood. His disposition appears barely tolerable."

"I can only say, Captain, that the French ambassador has made an appearance daily since you've returned. The man is in a foul humor over the capture, and I can't say as I blame him! You've struck a severe blow to the French economy, a staggering blow! You could have very well altered the outcome of the war by your actions!"

The last official form was pushed across the elegant cherry desk of the bank president's office for James to sign and the transfer would be complete. A voucher from the British Admiralty lay atop a stack of official paperwork amounting to one and one half million pounds sterling to be paid to his Majesty's Captain James Howlette. It was the culmination of weeks of waiting on the Admiralty to decide the fair market value for the remaining frigate and her stores. The gold had been duly counted and compared to the manifest submitted by the ship's purser and under armed guard, hauled off to the vaults of parliament. He had received word that Molly had returned during the past week, but he decided to remain in London—at least for the time being. The debt against Briarwood was in the final stages of settlement and the last of the paperwork would be taken care of in the coming week. An ad in the newspaper for creditors to come forth with claims against the estate produced none. Apparently all the bills had been paid in full. He knew he would have to make one last trip to Briarwood and speak to Molly. He would get to the bottom of this mystery and summon up the courage to break off the relationship with her at the same time, but first he had to honor a formal request to appear before the house of parliament to be granted a knighthood.

The summer days were growing noticeably shorter. The lazy beginnings of fall were coming at last to the rolling hills of Briarwood. Geese would be forming up for the long migration to the southern shores of France within the month. Molly paid little notice. She was too busy packing and making the last preparations for the voyage to Calais. Mary had informed her that James had stopped to pay a visit, but that was of little importance to her at the moment. She intended to be away before the week was out. Her only obligation now was a short detour to the House of Parliament to drop off the letter tucked safely away in her valise and to visit with the high court judges before she slipped quietly out of sight. As she adjusted the leather straps on the last of her suitcases, she heard Mary knock softly at the door to her bedroom.

"Good afternoon, Mary; you're just in time to help me with the last of these straps. I'm afraid I've packed my bags with far too many things. I'm having the devil of a time securing them. Would you be so kind and help hold them shut while I adjust these frightful buckles?"

"Of course, m'lady, th' post has just now arrived, and I've a letter addressed ta ya. If ya would like to read it in private, I should be most happy ta return later."

"Let's have a go at these straps first; I'm sure the letter can wait a few minutes," she said, mopping the sweat from her brow and taking a deep breath. "My, I never realized just how difficult it was to pack a few belongings!"

They struggled with the three remaining suitcases, and fifteen minutes later were putting the final touches on the last one and the gardener recruited to help take them down stairs to the foyer where they would be loaded into the carriage in preparation for an early departure tomorrow morning. The last set of suitcases was being removed from the bedroom as Molly sat down at the vanity and picked up the letter. She noticed the return address was from Admiralty Headquarters—probably another summons from Cambridge—broke open the seal and began to read:

Dearest Molly—

I've taken the liberty to post an urgent letter to you. Prepare yourself, my dear for I've not much time. Lord Admiral Cambridge is dead...He apparently died in his sleep. I've just heard the news, and have, just this minute, returned from his office. Captain Howlette is consoling Maria. She appears to be completely beside herself. Admiral Morris has been appointed to the vacant office, and is now Lord Admiral John Morris. I have been issued sealed orders and am to report for duty within the hour to the bark, Anna. I was not informed of her destination—only to report to the captain with my orders and commission. She sails with the morning tide.

I can only tell you that I shall make every effort to contact you at a later date, my love. I have no other alternative. I fear that Lord Morris suspicions that I'm involved in the plot against him. Until we meet again, I remain...

Your most humble and adoring servant,

Harry Cromwell

The letter was posted three days ago—Harry was gone. There would be no way to contact him now; his ship had sailed two—possibly three days ago. Feelings of outrage and vulnerability crushed her. This was something she could not have predicted. Who would have thought Cambridge would die before she'd put her final plan into action. She sat, motionless, in the lonely bedroom. She would make Morris pay dearly for what he'd done to Harry. She stood, with an air of resolve about her, and went down stairs. The driver was loading the last of the suitcases when she arrived, and within minutes they were on the road to London.

"Miss Bidwell to see you, m'lord," the new aide said as he opened the door to the office now occupied by Morris.

She entered and stood just inside the room as the door was closed quietly behind her. He seemed preoccupied with a sheaf of paperwork, and for a brief moment, appeared not to notice her. She strolled to the desk and cleared her throat to get his attention.

"This is an outrage! You bastard! What have you done with Harry! I demand a full explanation this minute!" she hissed in a smoldering tone. Where have you sent him, and when will he return? If you think you'll get away with this for one minute, you're mistaken!"

"Dear me!" he said in mock dismay. "Your beloved Harry has been sent on a confidential mission known only to me, and that's the way it shall remain: confidential! These are times of war, and the functions of this office will remain out of reach to the general public, including friends and lovers. Do I make myself perfectly clear on the matter?"

"Tell me where he is! You'll remember a certain letter I have in my possession?"

"Yes, I remember. How could I forget? It seems your dear James has caused as much uproar for me as your damned letter! The gall of him! Causing so much trouble! The French ambassador threatens to turn over incriminating documents daily. What could the harm be in one more letter?"

"Very well, then, I shall turn over the letter to higher authorities unless you tell me where he is this minute!"

"How quickly you forget, my dear, we made a bargain. I've upheld my half in good faith. Your accounts verify it. I've just made the last payment. I believe you owe me the letter now!" He howled, slamming his fist on the desk, "To hell with your Harry! He's as much a part of this as you are, and I'll have an end to this blackmail now, once and for all!" He took a deep breath that ended in a fit of coughing, leaving him in a cold sweat.

"Tell me where he is—or I shall demand another five thousand quid for the letter!"

"Fine. Another five thousand it will be! Don't you understand? You've ruined me! It makes no difference how much money you demand. Unless I have the evidence you hold in your hand, all the authority in the world does me little good," he said with a wave of his hand. "All these fine appointments I've worked a lifetime to attain, and now both the French ambassador and you can take it away in a heartbeat. It's my turn for vengeance! I've nothing left. My career is at an end. You'll not relinquish the letter, and I shall not tell you where your dear Harry is. It's a checkmate!" he said, mopping the sweat from his thin features, then continued on. "I've the five thousand quid here in the desk. It's only a portion of the settlement from the sale of the ships that Captain Howlette brought back."

He reached inside a drawer and retrieved a stack of pound notes and laid them on top of the desk. "There...now the letter if you please."

"Not before you tell me where Harry is. Then you'll get the letter!"

"Then it's over. I've nothing more to say! The French ambassador is demanding much more of me than a mere five thousand quid! Get out of my sight!" he roared.

Molly was devastated. She realized instantly that the letter she held meant nothing to Morris. It was the ambassador that held the trump card. She stared at Morris. He returned her gaze with calm resolve. It was over. Her power to force him into action was at an end. She turned, and without another word, left the office.

Morris returned the money to the drawer, closing it softly, and sat quietly, listening to her footsteps fade down the long hallway. He chuckled to himself as he opened a drawer in front of him and withdrew a shiny revolver from its velvet case. Caressing the pearl inlayed handle, he admired the ruthless quality of the cold steel in his hand.

The carriage driver was assisting her into the seat when the afternoon silence was shattered by a pistol shot.

CHAPTER SIXTEEN

It was not until the fifteenth of September that he and Maria moved into the stately halls of Briarwood. The settlement of Lord Cambridge's estate came to a tidy sum of money; which she inherited, upon the shoulders of some little trouble in the proving of her blood line. Upon reading through his personal papers, much to everyone's amazement, he had mentioned his joy at finding a long lost heir, Maria Morales, in a diary. The judge charged with executing the estate was left with one conclusion which was hastily brought before the jury and passed unanimously in favor of her. They each set about the task of re-arranging the décor and making plans for an elaborate wedding in November. Carpenters and stonemasons were heard throughout the building hammering and chipping from first light till dusk making renovations and taking up tiles from the floor. Briarwood was slowly taking on the personality of two new residents. James had asked for her hand in early autumn and she had accepted his proposal of marriage. The two seemed a perfect match. With the settlement now complete and the funds transferred to a trust, there remained little to do except enjoy the last days of autumn and bask in the glow of keen affection shared by two young lovers. The ship's crew had been paid off and Stephen Beale, along with the bosun and ships officers, taken their share of the profit. James honored his promise to Stephen and made him a wealthy man. He was in the process of finding a cottage on the outskirts of London, after retiring his commission, to settle down to a life of leisure and a small private medical practice.

It was much colder now. The sun had not made much more than a brief appearance in the past several days. It was much different than the weather the *Anna* had seen in the days since they had put Chatham behind and far over the horizon. During that time the skies had been a beautiful blue and the wind out of the north, at a steady ten knots that pushed the bark along at a healthy sixty leagues in the past twelve hours. The seas came in long lazy rollers and only on occasion, when the *Anna's* bow struck headlong into a wave did the spray cross her decks.

But all that was in the past and Harry Cromwell didn't need a look at the ship's barometer to know that it was falling. The sky was a dark, muddy gray and the seas had began to reflect that color while the waves tightened into short chops which the bark regularly butted into, causing an almost constant spray across her decks soaking the watch and all the gear. The wind had made around to the southwest and was building steadily, and Harry knew it would continue to do so until it turned into a full gale. He paused at the main mast and frowned at topsails that needed to be reefed, and thought they should have been taken in an hour ago, but the damned captain was wont to make all possible speed at risk of dismasting the entire ship. He shook his head and made for the aft cabin door and a chance to get out of the weather, but a word with the helmsman was in order, so he ascended the quarterdeck ladder and presented himself as best as he could under the circumstances.

"Have a care with the wheel if you please. Keep a sharp eye on topsails and weather leach. Drop off a point and I'll have the bosun trim her off the wind a bit. If we don't, she'll go by the board before the night's out, and then we'll be in a pretty fix, I'm thinking."

"Aye, sar!" shouted the helmsman as he leaned into the wheel and dropped off two spokes. "A point off the wind she is, sar!"

"I'll be in my cabin. Send for me if the need arises. We've a fresh gale on our hands and I'm betting the topsails will be down within the hour whether we reef them or they're carried away." With that said he descended the ladder mumbling to himself, "West Indies packet be damned! At this rate we'll be wrecked long before we reach our destination."

He had given his packet of orders and commission to the captain and had not heard another word from him. It was really none of his business, but it must have been grave if the captain had not taken a moment to inform him of the contents upon arriving aboard, as was the usual custom. Surely Admiral Morris had given instructions to the contrary or he would have known exactly what was in the sealed envelope. The retched bastard…trying to clean house before he was caught…sending him off at a moments notice and not informing him of a destination, and only a short note to Molly. An empty feeling engulfed him as he thought about the possibility of never seeing her again, and wondering if the hastily scribbled note had even survived the post. What was she doing now? Was she safe? Had Morris drummed up some scheme to do away with her? So many questions ran through his mind leaving him in a state of total exhaustion. His nerves were as thin as a chaffed rope, and nothing he could do about it except make the best of the situation he found himself in. He promised he would post a letter to her at every possible occasion in hopes of locating her somewhere, somehow.

It was indeed another hour before the topsails were taken in, much to his surprise. The yards were lowered to the deck and securely lashed in preparation to ride out the storm. Under close-reefed fore and main staysails, the *Anna* plunged through the night and into the next day. The seas had built to over twenty feet and towered over the bark's bow with white caps of spume on their crests before rolling down on the little ship. The *Anna* came down the black walls of water and then up the following side until it seemed they would be hurled completely free and cast into space. Then the huge wall of water would slide beneath the ship, which sank with a sickening feeling to be started all over again. Each flash of lightening froze the scene as though it were a painting while the roar of the wind joined in chorus with an almost constant crashing roll of thunder. Every breath was both equal parts of water and air mixed into one. The gale was weathered and the ship would enter the southern Gulf Stream within a fortnight. Little did Harry know that the *Anna* was just starting a voyage that would cover the better part of two thousand miles.

Molly sat quietly at a corner café gazing at the waterfront traffic in the port of Calais. It would be a number of days before a coach bound for Bordeaux would arrive and there was simply nothing to do except wile away the long afternoons sipping coffee and watching the pedestrians stroll by. The thought of losing Harry was almost more than she could stand. The joy in her life was gone and a deep depression had settled upon her. She realized, several days ago, that she had failed to leave a forwarding address at Briarwood, but it didn't matter; there was absolutely no way to reach Harry by post. She didn't even know what ship he'd sailed on—where it was bound—or when it would return. A long voyage could take the better part of two years or longer depending upon the nature of the cargo. Sometimes a ship would ferry cargo between two ports and be gone much longer.

It was a bright, sunny day and the small harbor town was bustling with people going about their daily activities. She knew nothing of the French language and that made her feel more alone than she'd been in her entire life. The sudden realization dawned on her that she'd not notified the bank of her permanent address, caused her to put her cup down and make a hasty note as a reminder. There would come a time when she would need additional funds, but then again it didn't really matter—she had more than enough money to last out the year. She would take care of the matter in due time.

A wry, fleeting smile passed across her lips. Now that she was financially secure—something she had longed for all her adult life—she found little comfort in it. The man she loved more than life itself was gone forever. There would be no one to share it, and no one to grow old with. She closed her eyes and tried to bring an image of Harry to mind, but failed. Fate sometimes played cruel tricks and she was now its victim. Who would have known Cambridge would die suddenly? She had no idea that Morris was next in line for his office. She recalled the faithful afternoon, and the pistol shot that ended his life and sealed her doom. The letter she had so closely guarded was useless, along with all the other papers in the folder tucked away in his study. No doubt his belongings had been gone through and the traitor discovered—much to the chagrin of the Admiralty. There was little anyone could do now but access the damage he'd done and try to formulate a plan to circumvent future attacks. She made a mental note to herself to send a forwarding address to Briarwood and also one to the bank of London when she finally settled into a permanent house in Bordeaux. By her estimate it would be several months before that happened. It was of little importance to her at the moment—a short voyage at sea often took twelve to eighteen months. Even if Harry posted a letter to her at his next port of call it could easily take the majority of a year or two to reach her depending on how fast the post forwarded the mail. A year or two! The thought raced through her mind again and again. There was every possibility that she would never know where Harry was until, by some slim chance, she received a letter from him.

Harry was not surprised to learn that many of the crew from the *Rose* were shipped aboard the *Anna*. Even after the sale and settlement of the two ships, many of the sailors were busy making a new life with the crew aboard the *Anna*. It didn't take long to gamble, drink and whore away their share of the prize. Most, if not all the crew, had been paid a small fortune by anyone's standards, but most of the men were content to spend everything they had down to the last shilling and sign on with the next outbound ship that was anchored in the bay. Every captain was only too eager to sign on able-bodied seamen whenever the chance presented itself. With the war continuing at a frantic pace, the press gangs had turned up little in the way of manpower. The country side had been stripped of just about every available man, including most of the young boys. And so the crew of the *Anna* was settling into place as the mess numbers were called out. Harry found himself in a cramped little alcove with nothing but canvas curtains for privacy. It was nothing like the quarters he'd become accustomed to at Admiralty Headquarters, but this was shipboard life and along with weevils in the biscuit and a tot of rum each day; it could be worse. He'd shipped aboard as first mate to the captain and, on occasion, would enjoy the privilege of dining with him. Some of the scuttlebutt he'd heard from the other officers told him they were headed south to exotic lands, but the exact destination had not been revealed. He knew they were in the Gulf Stream from the steady trade winds and choppy seas. Violent weather often plagued those unfortunate enough to sail at this time of year. The last gale was still fresh in his memory and there was little doubt that they would encounter several more before the voyage ended.

Weeks of steady sailing before the wind brought them further south while the tarred oakum caulking in the deck planks softened more with each passing day. It was not until some ten weeks had passed when the lookout shouted, "Deck ahoy!"

The captain returned with "Deck aye."

"Sail fine off the starboard bow, sar. 'Pears ta be a fourth rate by the set o' her sail. Makin' up ta us on a starboard tack."

He turned to the midshipman at his side and said, "Beat to quarters if you please and tell the bosun to break out the British Ensign while we're at it. I shall have no mistake about our identity. And while you're at it, pass the word along that I shall expect a much better showing than the last time we cleared for action. It was most unsatisfactory: twelve minutes. I could have done as well with a bunch of milk maids!"

The midshipman hurried off and seconds later drums signaled the larbowlines to the gun deck along with the duty watch. The thud of water buckets and rumble of cannons could be heard throughout the ship as the guns were rolled out. Slow matches were lit as the bosun called out, "Gun deck secure, sar!"

The captain casually looked down at his pocket watch and closed the cover with a disgusted look on his face. "I make it up to be ten minutes, bosun!

I should think eight minutes to be our best time, and I shall settle for nothing less. I can see we're not in shape for a proper fight! Lookout, aye…have you a better range?"

"She's luffing, sar…falling off on a larboard tack to intercept our heading, sar."

"Very well then; we have the weather gauge. Have your best top men at the ready, bosun, and on my signal we shall rake her with our starboard broadside as we come 'round. Have the men on the yards and ready to bring her up into the wind. We'll ware ship and give her a taste of our larboard guns before putting over on our original course. By that time I shall expect the starboard guns to be reloaded and rolled out for a third broadside, should there be need for it. Is that clearly understood?"

"Yes, sar!"

The *Anna* continued on her course while the ensign was run smartly up the main mast. The deck was deathly quiet. The only sound that could be heard was the crash of waves across the bow and the water running out through the scuppers. A bark like the *Anna* was not equipped to put up a proper fight. If the other ship happened to be a frigate she would make short work of her. They had only two choices…stand and fight for it or strike their colors. The next hour would decide their fate.

The silence was shattered with a call from the lookout, "Deck ahoy! Sar, I believe she's the *Kristen* from Portsmith!"

"Are you quite sure? We can have no mistake about it."

"I'm sure o' it, sar; I sailed on 'er back in '85 it were. I'd recognize that set o' sail anywheres, sar. She's ta fourth rate, *Kristen*! Bound fer home she is, sar."

"Very well then," he said while reaching for a telescope held out by the midshipman. Snapping it open he brought it to his eye and carefully scanned the horizon until the ship was in view.

"Stand to quarters until we're absolutely sure, bosun. Prepare to fire a ranging shot from the bow chasers on my command. We'll put one across her bows. Wait, she's hauling her wind! Lookout, can you make her out?"

"She's sure 'nough the *Kristen*, sar…and she's makin' signal…heave too."

"Bosun! take a reef in the main and foresails. We'll coast up on her from our starboard side in case she plans to trick us. Fire as you bear on my command!"

The *Anna* coasted down on the approaching ship and it was no surprise to see the other ship flying a British ensign. In times of war it was a common practice to try and deceive an enemy by flying the same colors as their foe. The distance narrowed while the two ships appraised one another. Minutes later the lookout called down, "She's makin' ta put a gig over ta side sar!"

"You don't say. Haul our wind, bosun. We'll drift down on her with our starboard broadside just in case."

The *Anna* dropped her headway as the sails were backed and allowed to drift within fifty yards of the approaching ship. The captain was on deck with glass raised, appraising them while a speaking trumpet was readied for him. Minutes later he hailed them saying, "What ship?"

The captain replied, "His majesty's bark, *Anna*, from Chatham. And you, sir?"

"His majesty's fourth rate, *Kristen*, bound for Portsmith with dispatches. Have you a packet that I might deliver?"

"I shall inform the crew. Have you seen any French shipping?"

"No, sir, and thank God for it! We're ill equipped to handle a fight. I'm under orders to make all due haste to Portsmith with official dispatches from Jamaica. Might I come aboard for a short visit and a glass of your finest sherry? We've been at sea for some four months, and I'm embarrassed to say my supply of spirits have dwindled to nothing more than a tot of rum!"

"By all means, sir, and welcome to you. Bosun…stand down from quarters and have the sideboys prepare to receive the captain."

He turned to address the *Kristen* again saying, "We are also bound for Jamaica. Quite a coincidence if I may say so. Have you weathered any storms along the way?"

Harry was stunned. He couldn't help overhearing the conversation and for the first time realized they were sailing halfway around the world! He hurried down the ladder to his sleeping quarters and hastily searched for quill and paper. Sitting on his cot he opened a bottle of ink and after inspecting the nib, dipped it into the ink. A frown crossed his face—what should he say? What could he write in the short time span allotted to him? Suddenly he remembered a letter he'd started some weeks ago and frantically searched through an assortment of papers until he produced it. He hurriedly brought forth the sheet and began to copy it down…yes…in a moment he'd decided to send the same letter if he had the chance, no matter how short the time was, he'd have a rough draft to copy each and every time. He carefully noted each word and copied it with diligence making sure there were no mistakes. Reading through the text one last time, he carefully sealed it and melted wax over the fold while fixing his Admiralty stamp on it. He held it to his lips for a moment and then hurried back up the ladder and onto the waist of the ship where he placed it into the oiled skin packet being readied for transport to the *Kristen*. He made a mental note of the time…they'd been at sea for how long? Was it three…four months? And he'd just heard the *Kristen* say they'd been at sea for four months. That meant another four months would pass before he could send another letter to Molly. And if, by some chance, she received his letter it would be another three or four months before the *Kristen* docked at Portsmith…eight months! And Portsmith was several miles from London, and Briarwood several hours ride from there. My God…that was almost a year! If he posted another letter from Jamaica, it would be over a year between postings!

Was she still alive? Could Morris have hatched up some scheme to have her disposed of? There were so many questions racing through his mind. Within the hour the packet would be safely on its way back to England, but what were the chances of the letter arriving? The captain of the *Kristen* was returning on deck just as he was securing the buckles of the packet and wrapping it in oilskin. There were precious few letters in it, but none more so than the letter addressed to Miss Molly Bidwell of Briarwood estates.

Within the hour the two ships parted company as the *Anna* cracked on all the sail she could carry. Harry watched the other ship dwindle to a tiny speck on the horizon and then disappear from sight. He went below and straight to his quarters where he collapsed on his cot. It had been an unexpected day, to say the least. He could only hope the letter would eventually be delivered. Even under the best of circumstances it would be at least a year before he would know if Molly had survived the evil clutches of Admiral Morris.

Stephen Beale, former ship's surgeon, recently retired from His Majesty's Navy, raised a glass of wine in toast to his captain and life long friend James Howlette.

"May you have a long and happy life together, and be blessed with many healthy children. God's richest blessings to you!"

James and Maria raised their glasses along with the guests crowded around the banquet table to the sounds of, "Here,.here!"

Maria Morales-Howlette was a radiant picture of beauty in her flowing wedding gown of sequins and white lace. He touched her glass with his and took a sip of the sherry, then bent down to place a kiss lightly on her cheek before addressing the crowd of guests.

"Thank you all very much for joining with us on this glorious day! We, Maria and I, look forward to celebrating our new life together here at Briarwood. Come, good friends one and all, share the bounty of our table!"

It was an elaborate wedding. They had chosen to be united in marriage at the gazebo overlooking the reflecting pond just behind the mansion. The last of the roses were picked and arranged in huge sprays of color and placed along side the cobble stone path leading up to the steps. Swans and a few wild geese slowly swam at the banks of the pond lending a romantic air to the festivities. Garlands of fresh ivy were hung over the archway leading into the gazebo where Stephen stood as best man, and Mary as the maid of honor. James had place a wedding ring of sapphire on Maria's finger as a token of his undying love.

The brisk autumn afternoon forced the guests to retire to the banquet room of the mansion for the reception. A huge three tier wedding cake adorned a table piled high with gifts for the newlyweds. And after the cake had been cut and served with wine poured in every glass the orchestra struck up a lively waltz for the couples to enjoy far into the evening.

The sun was an hour away from setting when the last guests began saying their goodbyes. The day had passed in a whirlwind of laughter and good cheer while he watched Maria being carried off by the ladies to the drawing room, there to discuss those things known only to women, while he and the gentlemen stayed behind to enjoy cigars and a glass of the finest rum money could buy. There remained behind only those military officers of flag rank accompanied by their aides, and as Admiral Moreland rose with a stretch and sigh, he casually raised an eyebrow to James and said, "I need not remind you of the gravity of the war. I have it on good authority that you are contemplating the thought of resigning your commission."

"Yes, I have given it some...."

"Hear me out on this. The Crown needs good officers with astute minds and the ability to make intelligent decisions in the field. Now, I know the capture of the French ship was, in large part, the doings of your lovely bride, but the original thought came from you, am I not correct in the matter?"

"Well...yes, I suppose you're..."

"Exactly! You were the one to take the risk and make the initial move to put a plan of sorts into action. Precisely the kind of far-sighted officers the Crown is so desperately looking for! Do you get my drift, Captain?"

"I believe I do, sir, but I'm now a married man, and as such, have certain responsibilities to hearth and home. I've given little thought to returning to active duty."

"I have it on good authority that the *Anna* is in route to Jamaica under the guise of delivering an official packet to the Ambassador. Her real mission: to lay at rest the rumor concerning a horde of powder that is ill guarded, and easy for the taking, should the need arise. I should be most relieved to hear that you would consider taking command of a frigate now being commissioned in the dock yards. I believe she should be ready within a short while, possibly a month. She's now being fitted with sail, and as soon as a crew can be put aboard and she's passed her sea trials, well, the command is yours."

"I'm greatly honored, sir. I shall indeed give it some considerable thought, but I must, in all candor, tell you, I have little need for the king's service. I'm sure you understand. I have a new life here now and feel I should remain close to my bride. She would be devastated if I should to return to the sea.

A blistering sun scorched the decks of the *Anna* as they sailed closer to the equator. A brilliant, crystalline sky spread over the horizon as far as the eye could see. The bark rode the lazy rollers with ease, while the wind and weather seemed to settle down and nestle the ship under a protective veil of balmy breezes. The first sighting of sea gulls two days ago along with copious tendrils of sea weed drifting lazily past the bow of the ship foretold landfall, and several of the crew had taken to the rigging each day trying to be the first to sight land. For Harry it had been a long cruise. Wondering each night if Molly would ever know where he was, and wondering whether or not she was safe. His life had turned to drudgery and loneliness. He seldom spoke with the other officers, and they in turn had chosen to ignore him. Each night he would take down the tattered letter he'd drafted so long ago and re-read it as if trying to mentally reunite himself with her. Lying on his lonely cot, he turned to face the after hatchway that was left open to bring fresh air to the lower decks. Staring up through the swaying hatch he caught sight of the moon…that same moonlight was shining over his beloved Molly—so close, yet so far away! Clutching the worn letter to his chest he whispered through trembling lips….

"I shall pull down the sky
From on high above…."

CHAPTER SEVENTEEN

It was mid November and the last traces of fall were now a memory. And in their place came the cold, crisp air of autumn. The stately elm trees that were lost to the brilliant green pines now stood out in stark contrast with bright splashes of red and yellow. Tall brown stalks of grape vines, newly pruned, stood in the vineyards like rows of solders upon a battle field. The first hint of wood smoke carried on the breeze was a comfort to her. Winter would not be far away. It was the time of year the she loved best. She sat idly, outside her town house on the outskirts of Bordeaux, and looked out over rows of barren flower beds. Come spring, she vowed to tackle those beds, just as her mother had done when she was a child, and bring new life to them.

Four months had passed since she had settled into her new surroundings attempting to start a new life. Thoughts of Harry haunted her almost every day. She had missed him before, but not in the way she missed him now. Their relationship had grown from fond affection into love. And then it had all gone wrong. The death of Cambridge set events into motion that she'd never anticipated. The short tenure of Admiral Morris—long enough to send her beloved Harry to God knows where, and then his suicide had dashed her well laid plans completely. She often lay awake at night trying desperately to think of a way to communicate with him, but to no avail. She had underestimated Morris. He was far more shrewd than she thought. Ironically, James had set the stage, quite by accident, for Harry to be sent away. From the newspapers she'd read, recounting the heroic adventures of Sir James Howlette, she'd pieced together the reason why the French Ambassador had pressured Morris. Evidentially it was his actions that had prodded Morris to take his

SOUTH WIND HOME

life, and not her feeble demands for money. Obviously the Ambassador had been outraged over the capture of not one, but two French line of battle ships loaded with powder and a horde of gold. No doubt the French economy suffered a severe blow and the Ambassador assumed it was Morris's fault! It was over now—the blackmailing, the scheming, the greed—it had now come down to this: a life of loneliness and heartache. The very thing she cherished most was forever lost to her, and she was powerless to do anything about it.

February first—a special day for Harry; it was his birthday. He lay below decks watching the lantern sway to the motion of the ship. Word had it that landfall would be within the next four weeks. They would round the outer banks of the Grand Bahama islands, with Florida on the starboard side, but too distant to see. The weather was balmy with a westerly breeze blowing them toward the island town of Freeport. Cuba would be large off the bow in a month—maybe less. They intended to sail around the northwestern tip of the island and then on to Jamaica. The captain had informed the crew that they would dock in the harbor of Kingston. An attempt that might stand them in harms way. It was a notorious port rumored to be secured by the French. The outer banks were a maze of coral reefs and without a harbor master to guide them in; it would be a fair trick of seamanship to drop anchor in the harbor without damage to the ship.

Harry lay with his hands behind his head pondering the lazy roll of the lantern as it moved in slow arcs. It was now the better part of a year—seven months to be exact—since the cruise had begun and even under the best of circumstances, it would be another year before he returned to London and his beloved Molly. He wondered if the hasty letter he'd posted had arrived. Would it find her well? He drew a deep breath and let it out slowly. He was exhausted—the meager joy found in life aboard the *Anna* was little comfort to him. Each day was drudgery, a mindless monotony broken down into four-hour watches. The stale air of the lower decks was almost beyond endurance. Even the sporadic breaths of air coming down through the open hatch was of little comfort, barely enough to cool the sweat beading on his forehead. The temperature was a comfortable seventy degrees on deck, but the gun room and after cabins was sweltering. He longed to eat something that didn't come out of a barrel. The last of the livestock had been slaughtered along with a scant dozen chickens. The holding pens had long since been cleaned and scrubbed down and the last of the eggs had vanished with the hens. They were down to salt pork and brisket. The ships biscuit wasn't even fit for a plum duff. Weevils had eaten their fill and the remains were riddled with holes as a testament to their work. Several casks of sour kraut were all the vegetables they had and the rank odor permeated the lower decks day and night. If it wasn't for the tot of rum and small beer doled out daily it would be unbearable.

There was talk of taking on supplies at Freeport, but the captain had not spoken of it. Some tropical fruit would sit things to rights, he thought, along with some fresh pork carefully roasted over a pit of glowing coals and coconut milk to wash it down with. He swallowed hard, and quickly tossed the idea out of his mind. It would be better not to think of such things until they actually happened.

The *Anna* crept slowly along the coral reefs of the outer banks just south and east of the port of Montego Bay on the island of Jamaica. Sailing into the westerly breeze off the starboard bow in combination with the strong Gulf Stream had caused them to constantly tack the ship in order to make their offing. They would drop anchor offshore to take on wood and fresh water before sailing on to their destination. A man was stationed in the bow casting the lead and calling off the readings every few minutes. With seven fathoms of freeboard and coral shoals lacing the approach, it would take the rest of the day before the anchor dropped. Hands were standing by at the braces ready to adjust sail at a moment's notice. The only way out of the coral reefs was to await the flood tide and then carefully weave their way back out.

Harry was leaning against the weather side caprail trying to steady a telescope that was trained on the harbor approach when he caught sight of a ship healed over with her topmasts down.

"Mr. Weatherby, my respects to the captain, and please inform him that we have sighted a ship, and would he like to come on deck and have a look?"

"Aye, sir," said the midshipman as he scurried away down the quarterdeck ladder in summon the captain.

Minutes later he ascended the ladder and stepped to the weather rail with a telescope under his arm and spoke to Harry. "What have we here, Lieutenant? A ship on her beam ends?"

"It would appear they are scraping her bottom, sir. Her top masts are down, and it would appear she's beached. I would think she's being cleaned and refitted."

"Yes, indeed, let's have a look."

Captain Ashley raised his telescope and adjusted it for a clearer view of the harbor and the ship in question. "I would guess she's a Frenchie from the looks of her, but it's a little too far to be sure. We'll ware ship and set a course for Kingston at once, Lieutenant. I don't fancy a closer look; with any luck she's not spotted us." He steadied the telescope on a brace for a better view. "It's Kingston we're bound for anyway, and the sooner the better. We'll forgo the wood and water for another time. Bring her about and let us claw out of sight for the time being. We'll wait for the ebb tide and then it's back to blue water."

"Sir, if I may be so bold as to ask, well, sir, what are our orders?"

"Of course, of course. I suppose the first officer has a right to know about our mission. Step down to my cabin and we'll have a chat over a glass of Madeira. Bosun, bring us about and kedge the ship if you feel it's necessary. I know we're on the flood tide. Just make the best of it and put her out of sight. We'll hoist canvas on the next tide and be done with this."

With that said, Captain Ashley descended the ladder, followed by Harry, and minutes later they were seating themselves in the cramped quarters of the cabin.

"A glass of wine with you, Lieutenant Cromwell?"

"Thank you sir; I would be in your debt."

"I have a few bottles of an excellent Madeira left. What a pity…they'll soon be gone. Of course there's always a chance we might uncover some exceptional spirits in the port of Kingston. One can always hope!" He chuckled while carefully pouring the precious liquid into a glass and then handing it over to Harry.

He reached for the proffered glass and took a sip. The captain was right; the burgundy liquid had a velvet quality about it that seemed to melt on the palate with a warm, full-bodied delightful aroma. Harry swirled it around his mouth for a few seconds, savoring the bouquet before swallowing it.

"About our orders, the captain continued while pouring a second glass for himself. "It seems we are to land a detachment of Marines on the beach of Kingston and reconnoiter the island for a cache of powder that appears to be loosely guarded. I've heard there's a rather large quantity, something in the vicinity of a hundred barrels somewhere on the island. We've been ordered to wait off shore until the powder has been secured, and then ferry it off the island: nothing more. I'm none too excited about it…coral reefs surround the island, and we'll be at the mercy of the tide no matter where we drop anchor. I like it not one bit, but orders are orders, and we shall make every attempt to see them carried out."

"If I may enquire, sir, I've not had the pleasure of having my packet read to me since we've sailed. I would most appreciate it if you would take a moment to inform me of its contents."

"I suppose there's no harm in it. We've less than three days before we enter Kingston harbor, and I can see no point in keeping them from you. Understand this. I was ordered, under the strictest terms, not to inform you until you were handed over to the British Ambassador in Jamaica. You see, Lieutenant, your orders state that you are to be the special envoy to the ambassador until further notice. It would appear that you are to be stationed in Jamaica until the end of this conflict. You understand, that could be several years. It's up to the Admiralty to decide when you'll be released."

Harry was thunderstruck. Morris had made sure he was no longer a threat. He had been effectively and swiftly removed. And as long as Morris was in office he had little chance of ever returning. He would never see Molly again.

A brilliant blue sky greeted another dawn in the tropics. Huge billowing clouds of snow white mist rolled lazily across the horizon, obscuring the sun for long minutes only to reappear with blinding radiance. The *Anna* sailed along on a broad reach as she approached the coral shoals off the outer reefs of the harbor, bright pink and white mounds of coral shown through the crystal clear waters of the sleepy harbor town of Kingston. With close reefed sail she entered the treacherous labyrinth of coral and rode the tide in with great care. All hands were on deck, including the off duty watch, leaning over the sides of the ship. It would be easy to shoal up on a reef and every eye was alert to the slightest danger. The lead was cast repeatedly from the bow, but it would be the side boys that would save the ship by spotting hidden coral heads below the surface waiting to rend a fatal wound. The coast line could just be seen in the distance several leagues away. It would be some time before they reached the sheltered cove of the inner harbor. Harry was trying to ignore the growing discomfort in his stomach, and turned to take in the view from astern. Something caught his eye…he could just make out the distant shapes of topgallant sails on the horizon. Quickly snapping the telescope open, he turned and steadied the lens on the distant object. His suspicions were confirmed in a heartbeat. He watched the ship alter course and make for the harbor. There was little doubt that it was French, and they had spotted them. He quickly hailed the bosun, "Ware ship, helmsman! Bring her aback at once. Bosun, hands to trim sail! Look lively, men!"

The captain was on deck in minutes. "What the devil do you think you're doing, Cromwell?"

"Have a look, Captain. We have company. With the tide against us we seem to have ourselves in a pretty mess. By my estimation they'll be upon us with in two or three hours, and unless we make it to open water they'll blow us to pieces, and there's not a thing we can do about it!"

The captain searched the horizon for a few seconds. "Quite right; we can take no chances. Bosun! Haul out the gig and make ready to ship the kedge anchor. With the tide against us there's only one way to escape. Hands to the capstan!"

The captain's gig was lowered over the side, and the anchor swayed aboard. The crew bent to their oars with a will as the ship turned in her stays, the sails slatting and banging against the yards. Minutes later the anchor was tossed out of the gig some two hundred yards ahead of the ship.

"Hands to the capstan. Heave away! Hands to lower the stream anchor as soon as the gig returns. Look lively, lads: there's not a minute to lose!" Captain Ashley was peering anxiously at the approaching ship and trying to gauge the distance separating them.

"With any luck, Lieutenant, we'll just make open water ahead of them. Beat to quarters if you please, and have the men standing by with that stream anchor!"

The cable was rising from the water as the men hauled around the capstan. A steady click-clack could be heard as the ship was hauled forward against the oncoming tide. The stream anchor was lowered into the waiting boat, and the men heaved at the oars as soon as it was settled into the waist of the boat. The only way out of the coral reefs was to haul the *Anna* out by sheer manpower.

"Deck ahoy!" A lookout stationed on the main top yard called out.

"Deck aye!" the captain returned.

"She's the *Soldat*, sar...the *Compagnon de le Soldat!*"

"Damn!" the captain growled. "It's a French seventy-four. They've been laying for us!"

Suddenly Harry realized that it was a clever trap set by Morris! The French had been notified of the *Anna*'s destination and the *Soldat* had been patiently waiting for her to show up. They had thrown up the top gallant masts and righted her as soon as they had spotted the *Anna*. And now they intended to sink her while she was trapped in the coral shoals, powerless to return fire! The cold hand of fear gripped him as the realization came fully into focus.

Morris was leaving no stone unturned. This was the day Harry would die or be taken captive!

"Anchors atrip, sar!" The call from the bow startled him into action.

"Look lively, lads; splice on the stream anchor cable and haul away!"

The captain's gig was coming back to take another anchor out to kedge in another two hundred yards of cable. The *Soldat* was making up for the final tack before gaining the entrance of the coral reefs. With the light breeze and another hour she would be presenting her broadside to the *Anna*. It would be close—but there was the slimmest chance that they would gain open water before the *Soldat*. The gig had dropped the anchor overboard and was making for the *Anna* again. A half dozen more trips and they would be able to hoist the jib and fore sails bringing her into the wind.

The bows of the *Soldat* could be plainly seen from the quarterdeck. Suddenly, smoke erupted from her bowchasers followed by a spout of water just off the larboard side. A ranging shot. Another half hour and they would come under fire from her broadside.

The captain shouted from the quarterdeck, "Larboard gun crew! Stand by to starboard, and on my command, fire as you bear! We'll have steerage way within the hour. I shall put the helm down and present our starboard guns. We have only one chance to defend ourselves, and I damn well intend to go down with guns blazing! Is that perfectly clear? Load and run out as fast as you can gentlemen; our lives depend upon it!"

The French seventy-four was closing with amazing speed. With the weather gauge and all plain sail set and foam coursing over her bows she was approaching at a reckless pace. Suddenly she hauled her wind and swung to starboard presenting her guns to the *Anna*. Seconds later the side of the *Soldat* disappeared in a cloud of smoke as she loosed her entire broadside at the *Anna*. Shot could be heard whistling through the rigging and slamming into the side of the ship, splinters flying in all directions. The sheet holding the fore topmast staysail parted and the *Anna* started to fall off, completely out of control; the helmsman threw the wheel over but the steerageway was off her. Cannon fire was sporadic as the men of the *Soldat* reloaded and fired while the ship heeled over on a larboard tack in relentless pursuit. Another twenty minutes and they would be close enough to board. The decks were stained with dark pools of blood and screams of agony as men were carried below decks to be attended by the surgeon. One of the starboard cannon was upset and parts of the weather rail were completely torn away. A section of the lower mizzen mast was blown almost in half. It looked as if it might topple at a moments notice. The bosun and several of the crew were hurrying forward to splice another line to the staysail in a feeble attempt to gain control of the ship, while others gave their attention to the mizzen mast. Another round from the bow chasers of the *Soldat* was directed at the captain's gig in an attempt to sink it, but it fell wide of the mark.

The *Anna* was powerless. Her bows were pointed directly towards the *Soldat* and they were still several hundred yards from making it clear of the coral. The French seventy-four was wearing about on a larboard tack in preparation to send another broadside into her. Harry was ascending the quarterdeck ladder when the *Soldat* unleashed her larboard cannon. A shot whistled across the quarterdeck just above his head taking the binnacle box and killing the helmsman instantly. Hot blood blinded him momentarily and he slipped on the ladder rung and fell headlong into the waist of the ship bruising his knee. A round of grape shot howled through the air and Harry felt a searing pain in his side and looked down to see blood soaking through a ragged hole in his shirt and coat. He tried to stand, but the pain was too intense. Gathering what strength he could muster, he pulled himself slowly towards the mizzen mast and collapsed against it. He was bleeding profusely. He sat there and quietly watched his blood form a tiny rivulet that trickled slowly across the deck boards beneath him. Looking up and across the expanse that separated the two ships he was suddenly aware that the fore mast was down on the *Soldat*. How could that be? They had not fired a single shot at her. He watched, in a trance, as the main top gallant mast swayed and toppled forward dragging the gear with it. Someone far away shouted. "She's hard aground!, Shoaled up on the coral, sar!"

The *Anna* was beginning to respond to her helm as the new sheet was bent to the fore mast top stay sail. Captain Ashley was at the helm trying desperately to throw the helm over and present her starboard battery at the *Soldat*. The *Anna* was slowly responding and swung about. A crewman raced to the helm and relieved the captain, while he descended the ladder and ran to the nearest cannon.

"On my order cut loose the stream anchor, and fire as you bear, lads!" the captain screamed. "Hoist the main topsails as soon as the anchor is free!"

The *Anna* came about and slowly gained steerageway as the first cannon went off. With little more than a hundred yards separating the two war ships it was almost impossible to miss, and when the smoke cleared the breastworks of the *Soldat* was missing. Masts and rigging were a tangled wreck and she was listing badly to larboard. Another cannon went off—then another, and still another as the *Anna* emptied her round shot into the French seventy-four. Splinters were flying everywhere and the screams of dying men could be heard over the roar of cannon. In an instant the tide of battle had turned. The stream anchor cable parted from the blow of an axe and the *Anna* leaped forward through the narrow coral reef and entered the slow rollers of open water. They had escaped to fight another day.

It was two hours before the time she would normally have risen had she been at Briarwood. The trip across the channel had been long and tiring. She felt the hand of the servant gently shake her awake. A lonely candle stood silently on a night stand by the bed. A flickering flame guttered in the light breeze that wafted through an open window.

She swung her feet out of the bed and onto the smooth wooden floor and sat there for a moment, rubbing the sleep from her eyes and taking stock of what had to be done today. "Thank you," she muttered and the servant disappeared as quietly as she'd come, leaving her alone with the hollow echo of retreating footsteps.

She looked around the lonely room as far as the yellow light of the candle would allow, and let out a low moan. Forcing herself to stand, she went to the dresser, tossed off the robe and sat down to comb her hair. Within the hour she would be on her way back to London and one last visit to Briarwood. Fond memories coursed through her mind in a flood, leaving her breathless, with thoughts of Harry and the time he'd held her in his arms while they watched through the window overlooking Morris's office. It had been so very long ago, but yet she remembered it as if it had only happened yesterday.

The coach and four arrived early and within the hour she was bound away for the Bank of London. She had grown tired of her life in France and vowed to find a cozy little cottage somewhere close to Briarwood. She found it amusing when she thought about it—she never realized just how much she would miss those stately halls but now that she was gone, it was never far from her mind. If anyone had so much as insinuated that she would want to return to London she would have laughed at them—but it was true. A twinge of anxiety stirred in her chest at the thought of what she was about to do, but nevertheless, her mind was made up. Without Harry there was no need to spend the rest of her life in a country whose language she didn't speak, much less understand. Her homeland was England and she intended to spend her remaining days living a life of leisure.

The coach rolled to a stop in front of the Bank and the driver assisted her down with a hand while she brushed the dust from her skirt. She adjusted the small valise and tucked it under her arm, entered the bank and strolled to the teller window. "I would appreciate it if you would inform the president that Miss Bidwell is here to see him; he's expecting me."

A moment later an elderly gentleman approached her saying, "How very nice it is to see you again, Miss Bidwell. Please come into my office. A cup of tea perhaps?"

"Thank you, but I shall not be staying long. I've just this minute stopped by to secure additional funds. I've decided to make an offer on a small cottage on the outskirts of London. I find the confines of France not to my liking: the language, you know; can't speak a single word. And I should like to make a stop at the post to see if perhaps there's any mail. It's been the better part of a year.

"Good day, sir," she said to the gentleman standing in front of the window at the post office. I'm Miss Molly Bidwell. I must confess I've left no forwarding address. I've been out of the country for some time…on business, you see. I was wondering if perhaps there might be something for me."

The clerk raised an eyebrow and smiled. "A Miss Bidwell, you say? I shall have a look. One moment, please."

Minutes later he returned and handed her a letter saying, "This seems to be the only parcel for you at the moment. Sorry, there is nothing else with the name of Bidwell."

Molly took it with trembling hands and started to break the seal and read, but changed her mind and hurried from the building. She found herself sitting on a stone bench under a spreading chestnut tree staring down at the letter in her lap—almost too afraid to open it. It had the official Admiralty seal on it—it could be a final note from Morris. Gathering her courage she took a deep breath, broke open the letter and read:

My Dearest Molly;

I have but the briefest moment to write. I'm aboard the bark Anna. I shall post another letter at the earliest convenience, but I fear it will be several months before you shall hear from me. My heart is in your hand. I miss you terribly and long to hold you. I shall stop at nothing to be at your side, for all I need is a south wind home.

GERALD LEWELLEN

A sob caught in her throat as she turned the page:

I shall pull down the sky,
From on high above.
And a beautiful dress of blue,
I'll make for you, my love.

A thousand snowflakes, I'll find,
To sprinkle in your hair.
From a piece of every rainbow,
A ring, I'll make, for you to wear.

With strands of glistening dewdrops,
A necklace I shall weave.
And a warm coat too,
From Autumn colored leaves.

I'll harvest the warm sunshine,
Tied in bundles just for thee.
To prove to one and all,
Just how much you mean to me.

But...what gift shall I send,
On wing of snow-white dove?
It's the greatest gift of all—
'Tis my undying love!

Printed in the United States
55712LVS00005B/124-306